THE GREAT FAKE BOOK

BOOKS BY VANCE BOURJAILY

The End of My Life
The Hound of Earth
The Violated
Confessions of a Spent Youth
The Unnatural Enemy
The Man Who Knew Kennedy
Brill among the Ruins
Country Matters
Now Playing at Canterbury
A Game Men Play
The Great Fake Book

Vance Bourjaily

THE GREAT FAKE BOOK

A Novel

WEIDENFELD & NICOLSON

NEW YORK

Published by Weidenfeld & Nicolson, New York
A division of Wheatland Corporation
10 East 53rd Street
New York, NY 10022

A signed first edition of this book has been privately printed by The Franklin Library.

Grateful acknowledgment is made for the following:

From "The Waste Land" in COLLECTED POEMS 1909–1962 by T. S. Eliot, copyright 1936 by Harcourt Brace Jovanovich, Inc.; copyright © 1963, 1964 by T. S. Eliot. Reprinted by permission of the publisher.

I'M GONNA SIT RIGHT DOWN AND WRITE MYSELF A LETTER, Music by Fred E. Ahlert, Lyric by Joe Young. Copyright © 1935. Renewed 1963 Fred Ahlert Music Corporation, Warock Corporation, Pencilmark Music. Used by permission. All rights reserved.

I'M GONNA SIT RIGHT DOWN AND WRITE MYSELF A LETTER by Joe Young & Fred Ahlert. © 1935 Chappell & Co., Inc. © Renewed 1963 RYTVOC, Inc. and Fred Ahlert Music Corp. International copyright secured. All rights reserved. Used by permission.

JA DA by Bob Carleton. Revised lyric and arrangement by Nan Wynn and Ken Lane. © 1918, 1939, Renewed 1946, 1967 LEO FEIST, INC. Rights assigned to CBS Catalogue Partnership. All rights controlled and administered by CBS Feist Catalog, Inc. All rights reserved. International copyright secured. Used by permission.

BLUE MOON by Richard Rodgers and Lorenz Hart. © 1934, renewed 1962 Metro-Goldwyn-Mayer Inc. Rights assigned to CBS Catalogue Partnership. All rights controlled and administered by CBS Robbins Catalog, Inc. All rights reserved. International copyright secured. Used by permission.

THE JAPANESE SANDMAN by Raymond B. Egan and Richard A. Whiting. © 1920 (Renewed) Warner Bros. Inc. All rights reserved. Used by permission.

PRISONER OF LOVE by Leo Robin, Clarence Gaskill and Russ Columbo. © 1931 Edwin H. Morris & Company, a Division of MPL Communications, Inc. © Renewed 1959 Edwin H. Morris & Company, a Division of MPL Communications, Inc. International copyright secured. All rights reserved. Used by permission.

I WISH I COULD SHIMMY LIKE MY SISTER KATE. Words and Music by A.J. Piron. © Copyright 1919, 1922 by MCA MUSIC, A Division of MCA INC. Copyright renewed and assigned to MCA MUSIC, a Division of MCA INC., and JERRY VOGEL MUSIC, New York, New York for U.S.A. Used by permission. All rights reserved.

GEORGIA ON MY MIND by Hoagy Carmichael and Stuart Gorrell. Copyright 1930 by Peer International Corporation. Copyright renewed. All rights reserved. Used by permission.

Library of Congress Cataloging-in-Publication Data

Bourjaily, Vance Nye.
The great fake book.

I. Title.
PS3503.077G7   1986   813'.54   86-10998
ISBN 1-55584-003-5

Manufactured in the United States of America by
Maple-Vail Book Manufacturing Group
Designed by Irving Perkins Associates

10 9 8 7 6 5 4 3 2 1

This One's for Robin

THE GREAT FAKE BOOK

1608 Argo St., Apt. 16
Washington, D.C., 20518
December 29, 1979

Mr. John McRae Johnson
Last Deadline Ranch
Capsicum, Colorado 81666

Dear Mr. Johnson:
About a minute ago I finished writing you a six-page letter. It's an inquiry about my father, Mike Mizzourin. He was a reporter who worked for you on the New York World-Telegram *in the late 1940s, when you were executive editor. I wonder if you remember him?*

He was killed in an auto wreck, I don't know where, in 1950. I would have been less than a year old. I haven't any recollection of him, and no idea what sort of man he was.

The person who was nice enough to give me your address was reluctant, thinking you might not want to be intruded on. I agreed I'd start by sending you this brief note, asking permission to send on the longer letter. May I?
Sincerely,
Charles Mizzourin

Last Deadline Ranch
Capsicum, Colorado
January 2, 1980

Dear Mr. Mizzourin:
Please! Your little note has upset my husband so terribly! Someone very malicious must have given you our address. Please, there mustn't be any more correspondence, and especially not your "longer" letter. Thank you so much for being considerate.
Most Sincerely and Gratefully,
Christine Johnson

1

Last Deadline Ranch
Capsicum, Colorado
1/3/80

Dear Mizzourin:

You will disregard my wife's reply to your recent, restrained note, which upset neither me nor the pome-fruit chariot (id est, applecart). I don't know precisely what Mrs. Johnson said. She claims not to remember the language used—likely enough!—but let us not indulge her frantic, female fussfeathering.

I do not deem it improper that you send along your letter of introduction and inquiry, though I will not, sight unseen, undertake to answer all, or indeed any, of the points you may see fit to raise. I am, however, quite willing to consider them, and am curious to learn more about yourself. I do recall your father well enough.

I note that you live in Washington. Are you in government? You may not be aware that, after I left the World-Telly, *I joined the Eisenhower administration as a member of Ike's White House press team, under Jim Hagerty. With the tragic election of the young roué Kennedy (I had forebodings of his fate and worked hard for the election of his opponent, the vastly misunderstood Dick Nixon, a personal friend), I chose to leave government for the new challenge of a journalism school deanship in this state, from which I retired last year, as perhaps you know.*

Since you are familiar with my name, I may be coupling what engineers call a "redundant information-retrieval system" with what you have already learned. Who was it, may I ask, who gave out my address? It is not that it matters greatly, but I am working at my memoirs, journalistic, political and educational. In what is curiously called retirement, I work from caw of crow to calling of coyote. I dilly not, sir, neither do I dally, and must be on my guard against insidious intrusion, although, as indicated, I'm inclined toward interest in your inquiry and invite you to inveigle me.

Yours very truly,
John McRae Johnson

1608 Argo St., Apt. 16
January 8, 1980

Dear Mr. Johnson:
Thank you, sir. Enclosed is the letter I wrote to you on December 29. I'd seen your name on the masthead of a 1948 issue of the World-Telegram *that same day. My father's name and those of his associates were never mentioned when I was growing up. I was a small boy during the Eisenhower administration. So there was no way in which I could have known about you, or I might have*

written long ago. I am in government, but about as low down in it as you can get. I work in the office of a Congressman, doing research and sometimes writing briefing papers, when I'm not being sent out to buy whiskey or show some constituent the monuments. The question of who gave out your address is answered immediately, below. Thank you for letting me mail the enclosure. I hope it's okay now with Mrs. Johnson.

Sincerely,
Charlie Mizzourin

ENCLOSURE, WRITTEN DECEMBER 29, 1979

Dear Mr. Johnson:
This afternoon, in the microfilm room of the Library of Congress, I met your former assistant, Suesue Landau. We had both put in calls for film records of the New York World-Telegram.

Mrs. (Miss?) Landau had wanted to find a photograph of herself holding up a copy of the New York Daily News with the headline "DEWEY BEATS TRUMAN," which appeared in your paper of 1948. She wanted offprints made of it to send to some friends. She asked why I was interested in the paper, and I explained that I was looking for stories with the byline of a certain reporter, my father, Mike Mizzourin. He left my mother while I was still in the crib and was dead and gone by my first birthday. I don't even know if I ever saw him. Mother flatly will not talk about it. I'll be thirty next year and know as little about my father as if I'd been adopted and my natural parentage kept secret.

I used to assume he'd been some kind of monster. As kids will, I let it scare me. I thought maybe I had monster blood. I honored my mother's sense of injury and shared it.

One day, three years ago in New York, I was waiting in line for an unemployment check. The man behind me heard my name called out. He grabbed my shoulder, spun me around, and said:

"You kin to Mike? Let me see you, yeah, you gotta be."

He was a stocky, good-looking, middle-aged black man with two fingers missing from the hand that was holding me. I said yes, I was Mike Mizzourin's son. The man hugged me and lifted me right off my feet. His name is Scholay Gopeters.

"Mike was the prince among us," he said. Actually, he shouted it. "I was best man at his wedding."

After he set me down, we picked up our checks and walked outside together. Mr. Gopeters is a musician. He had to rush to an audition. We had only about half a minute to talk.

"You didn't know Mike was a reporter?"

He was a little stunned at that. I was stunned, too. He didn't seem to be talking about a monster. He couldn't think which paper, but knew it was one that was gone. He said the accident was a long story.

I asked, "Did you keep in touch at all with my mother?"

He shook his head. "We called her 'Stick.' No disrespect. She was just so thin. We'd say, 'That Mike's a snare and a delusion, Stick. Give him a rim-shot. Go on. Hit him a paradiddle.' We had some fun. I'd send her warm regards, but I don't guess she wants them."

Scholay Gopeters gave me a number to call, so that we could get together, and I tried that evening. But he'd got the job that he auditioned for, I was told. He was already on the band bus, on the way to Boston, and I haven't been able to find him since.

Sunday mornings, here in Washington, I began the search of past New York papers for the late 1940s. The Herald Tribune, *the* Sun, PM, *the* Mirror, *and the* World-Telegram. *They're all here, the great dead papers, on little frames of film. I'd been through a couple of years of front pages and local news pages of the* Herald Tribune *and* PM, *and had just begun on the* World-Telegram, *when I met Suesue Landau today.*

She is, excluding my mother and stepfather, the second person I've ever met who knew my father at all. She remembers him, but I can't tell how well or how kindly, for she doesn't really want to talk about him except in hints and generalities.

"Of course, I knew all the boys on city side," she said. "But not Mike particularly. They were a bunch of dolls, but Mike was short. You're taller, and I love your ruddy complexion. Sure it's not pancake?" She touched my cheek with a fingertip and then pointed it at a page on the film machine. She was indicating your name, smiling. "He was Mike's boss."

She did say my father was considered a good reporter. She found one of his stories with a byline: "By MIKE MIZZOURIN." It made the hair on my arms prickle to see his name in print, written evidence that he really had existed, held a job, done his work.

We went to a bar to have a drink at noon. Suesue ordered something called an ABC, which turned out to be Amaretto, bitters and Calvados. There Mrs. Landau said one revealing thing, in her warm, husky voice:

"Mike was a wild man, dear, and needed lots of discipline. That made him Johnny Mac's baby, didn't it?"

"John McRae Johnson, you mean?"

"Did I say Johnny Mac?" She blushed about it. "I think I'll give you his address." She got an address book out of her purse, and wrote the name of your

ranch on a napkin. "Will you write a little note first, dear, to get his permission before you try corresponding?"

"Sure," I said.

After that I took her home by cab. She said a lot of affectionate things about you, but that I wasn't to mention her in the first note. She seems in fine health, tall with nice, round arms, but not heavy. She has light hair and very large, dark eyes, which dominate her face and make her exceptionally attractive. She told me she was forty-seven, but she looks much younger.

"I hope you'll find out what you want to know, Charlie," she said, and that's what I'd like, good or bad.

My father's parents are both dead. They weren't encouraged to visit when I was young. I have just one photograph of myself at three, sitting on my grandmother Mizzourin's lap, with my granddad standing behind us. She's wearing a jacket and a contrasting skirt, a traveling outfit I think. He's in the uniform of a Navy CPO. They look to be in their fifties. She is slight with a strong, pleasant face. He is short, erect and burly, but his face is in shadow and I can't make out the expression on it.

About the photo, mother once said, "I'm sorry I kept it for you," and that's all she would say. I know it was hard for her to give it to me. I was fourteen then. I bought a Christmas card to send my grandparents, but mother denied she knew their address.

Any pictures she had of Mike Mizzourin were by then long since destroyed, so that, except for Suesue Landau saying he was short, I don't know what he looked like.

Last fall, just before I came down here, I thought I'd had a break. I was living in New York, doing maintenance work in a big apartment building in exchange for a place to live, and odd carpenter jobs for income. I was also saving up money to go back to graduate school second semester. A letter from a lawyer in Des Moines, Iowa, changed the direction of my life, from trying to learn everything about nineteenth century Russian history to trying to learn something about my father.

I was one of twenty-eight people who got copies of the lawyer's letter. We were the heirs named in the will of a great uncle. I was a minor heir ($212, which I'll be happy to get, if the will is ever probated). Two of the major heirs ($4,240 each), Edward "Ned" Mizzourin and Peter Mizzourin, were asked to confirm that their brother Michael was deceased.

I'd never so much as known that I had two uncles. Their addresses were in the lawyer's letter, and I wrote them both.

Uncle Peter, the younger, is an engineer who works overseas for Petrolat, the big oil company. The letter I wrote to him was opened and replied to by a

Petrolat legal department worker, about a week after the American hostages were taken in Iran. My uncle is not one of the hostages, but the letter seems to say that he's in jail someplace else in the Moslem world.

"Peter Mizzourin is under temporary detention in an Arabic-speaking country," is the way they put it. "We are working carefully toward his early release."

I'd written the older uncle, Ned, twice but gotten no reply. He lives in a town called Calder Plain, in southwest Iowa. It's a town of 30,000 people where, I now suppose, my father must have grown up. I called there, as well as writing, but the woman who answered the phone hung up before I finished explaining who I was. I also called the lawyer in Des Moines to tell him about my response from the oil company. The lawyer said he was finding Petrolat difficult, too, and Uncle Ned much more so.

I stayed around Washington asking questions, including some at the State Department, where the answers were practically interchangeable with the ones at Petrolat. It was then that I got my present job. I'm good at research, and have a background in economics and statistics as well as history. The Congressman I work for knows Uncle Ned. When the farmers demonstrated, Ned drove a tractor from Iowa to Washington. He was briefly famous because he insisted on using the Interstates, though the road gear on his tractor wouldn't move him along at the forty-mile-an-hour minimum speed. He defended himself against hundreds of dollars in traffic fines spread out over fourteen hundred miles and made some headlines. He's also been a Republican committeeman, my Congressman says.

That's the story up to now. Can you take time to write me about Mike Mizzourin? I'd like to know what kind of man he really was. I'd like to know, if you remember, who his friends were. (Maybe you and he were friends?) If he was wild, I'd like to know some of the wild things he did. I'd like to know if he really was a good reporter. I'd like just to know what he looked like. Is there someone you can think of here in the Northeast who knew him, with whom I could talk?

More than anything else, I wonder about the way he died, at pretty much the same age I'm at now. Once I overheard my mother say about it to my stepfather: "Just another traffic accident." She said it in such a bitter, unforgiving voice that it became an echo in my head that won't die away.

Sincerely,
Charlie Mizzourin

"Mmmm. Huh. Hello?"

"Hello. Is Charles Mizzourin there?"

"Yes. Yes, ma'am, speaking. Can you hold while I turn on the light and find my glasses?"

"Oh, dear. Is it so late? Oh, I'm so sorry. Shall I hang up?"

"No, it's . . . there. Got'm. Well, it does seem to be two A.M."

"Oh, I will hang up. Yes. It's only eleven here. I do forget about the difference. But your voice, it's like your father's!"

"Ma'am? Who is this, please?"

"It is. The voice, I mean."

"Who's calling?"

"Didn't I say? My husband's gone to mail the letter. John."

"Is it Mrs. Johnson?"

"Christie Johnson. You did send that letter to my husband?"

"I had his permission, Mrs. Johnson. I'm sorry if it's still against your wishes."

"I knew he'd got your letter. He was secretive and smug. But broody, too, the way he gets. I think he went to mail an answer to you now. He'll tell me tomorrow, won't he? Working and working on it. After he torments me, Mr. Mizzourin? Do you mind if I call you Charles?"

"Charlie, if you like. Did you know my father?"

"Charles, tell me something quickly. I don't dare have a long phone call even at night rates, it's much cheaper after eleven, but I'm sorry I woke you up. I have my own line. His is for business."

"Shall I call you back?"

"But then I have to pay my own bills."

"What's the number?"

"Oh no, I'm sorry. No. John's car. In the yard already. See, he's just pulled in, and turning out the lights. Charles, who gave you our address?"

"It's no secret, Mrs. Johnson. As I wrote your husband, it was a woman who used to work for the newspaper called Suesue Landau."

"Oh, guhgod. Guhgod. Suesue beast. I might have known, guh . . ."

"Are you all right?"

"Guhgod, that animal."

"Are you all right?"

"Oh yes. Yes."

"Sure?"

"I'm all right. I think John just mailed an answer to your letter."

"That's good news."

"Is it? Oh, I hope so. I do hope so. Dearest Charles. Goodbye."

Box 203
Capsicum, Colorado
1/12/80

Dear Mizzourin:

To this extent will I follow your lead: letters other than brief notes shall be double-spaced, with normal margins. Henceforth, for easier annotation, use one side only of each sheet of paper. For your further guidance, I enclose a copy of the World-Telegram Style Book, as revised under my supervision.

And now let us understand one another. I don't know how extensively we are going to correspond, but without a proper understanding between us, my part will end with my signature to this. All will depend on your reply. I did not achieve mutual understanding at the onset of my relationship with your father. Quite the contrary (as I am prepared presently to divulge, should you elect to do your part). In fact, with regard to your father's and my first encounter, only the then-prevalent sentimental attitude toward war veterans, and foolish guilt I shared with others who, chained to our desks, spent the war informing the public, prevented my discharging him instantly.

Thus you have another unexpected legacy, my mistrust, and probation pending of another kind. Yet, may I add, I hope you'll earn it, not just for the paragraphs of reminiscence I will write, some of them perhaps transposable to my memoirs, but more simply because I feel I might like to know you.

In your letter, you maunder on at some length about yourself, while omitting much information that would tell me what manner of young man demands my time and my attention. If you would have them, sir, please answer, truthfully and completely, this tridecemoquiry (i.e., set of thirteen questions):

1. For which Congressman do you work? What are his state and party? Is he a member of the conservative, moderate, liberal or radical branch of that party (yes, there are radical Republicans, like that deplorable young man from California, Pete McSomething (McNothing!), who raised his puny fist 'gainst Kissinger and Nixon. Surely it is not Mcjudas for whom you work?

2. Having succeeded in getting (Mrs.) Suesue Landau drunk and into a cab, did you then (a) enter her premises on reaching them? (b) Even if you did not, please describe what passed between you in the cab, in addition to her saying "affectionate things" about me. Nota bene—make that, multabene: please address all future correspondence to Box 203, as above. I will not have my mail interfered with or pried into.

3. Assuming the propriety of your answers to 2 (a) and (b), would you be willing to see Mrs. Landau again? (She married Landau, an airline passenger service representative, in 1950, but stayed with him only five weeks.) I should like to know more of her present circumstances, employment, associates and

*manner of life. I should prefer it if this meeting could take place at a nonalco-
holic time and place, and perhaps even with a third party present, with whom
you could compare impressions of the accuracy of the information gained. By
yourself, I fear you are vulnerable to her prevarications. Her age, for example,
is forty-nine, not forty-seven. She was not my "assistant" but merely a secretary.*

*4. While I find unremarkable if uncondonable the presence in a welfare line of
a zoot-suited, unemployed performer of caterwaul, I do not comprehend why
you yourself were there. Can you defend it? Please describe yourself as to facial
hair, hair length, manner of dress, etc., both then and now. Also please describe
your physical appearance in general (you wish to know what your father looked
like, I to know what you look like.)*

*5. I knew your mother, both from visits to our newsroom and from social occa-
sions. She was, as of course you know, a beautiful and much-sought-after young
fashion and photographic model, a bit girlish and notoriously underweight, but
nevertheless a celebrity of sorts. Proprietary as the common man is about his
celebrities, it does not excuse the negro Gopeters referring to her by nickname.
You may be certain it was fuzziness or mendacity on his part to claim to have
been your father's best man. Since you are barred from discussing this with your
mother, I hope you will take it on my authority. As to her differences with
your father, understand that I knew the situation. She was entirely in the right.
On her side were education, motherhood, sensibility, morality and breeding. If
this be unpalatable, let the grapes of future correspondence remain untrod. Remember me to her, if you will.*

*6. Yes, your father was "a good reporter." I assure you, he would not have
worked for me a single day had such not been the case. However, the account I
may send you of our first meeting may also diminish this charitable view of his
professional attainments. It may also provide you with an example of his writing style less impersonal than were his (adequate) news stories. Do you wish
to have my account of our first meeting and the document I refer to?*

*7. The supposition that your uncle Peter's arrest is somehow related to the
national disgrace brought on by Peanut Carter's weak handling of our policy
toward Iran I find icthyoliferous—i.e., smells fishy. You will find that in general when an American is jailed in a Moslem land, with a responsible government, the cause is sexual immorality or drugs. Does your uncle use drugs, or
endorse promiscuity? Do you yourself? If you truly believe politics to be involved, perhaps you should insist on it to people at a higher level in the State
Department. Under pressure from them and your employer, Petrolat might be
compelled to full disclosure.*

8. As to your farming uncle, hip hooray! Has it occurred to you that he may be a semiliterate man who does not reply to your letters because he is hardly able to? Had you at any time considered this possibility? I dislike arrogance and pomposity, especially in the young, and feel those words may well describe your view of this honest farmer. See him on his tractor, a giant, green-and-white John Deere, I fancy, grinding toward Washington. Disdaining the paltry signs decreeing minimum and maximum, he moves at the speed that grows our food. See him at his Republican meetings, listened to with reverence for his common sense. But see him, Charles! In him you may meet the sort of man Michael Mizzourin might have been, had war not torn him out from tillage of the earth.

9. Are you married, or engaged to be?

10. With what church are you affiliated, and how often do you attend?

11. Discuss your use of alcohol, your diet, your patterns of exercise, and other methods of conditioning and health.

12. In regard to education, you speak of Russian history, economics and statistics. What level have you reached in these disciplines? What use mean you to make of them?

13. During your late adolescence and young manhood, your country was at war in Vietnam. Were you (a) an honorable participant? (b) a xanthroventric skulker 'neath the almaternal kirtle—i.e., yellow-bellied college hideout? Or (c) pure slime, one of the despicable protesters whom I will not honor with droll coinage.

Here I shall break off, having thrown the gauntlet to you. Can you pick it up? Shall we joust, to mutual advantage and enjoyment, or will you withdraw? Incidentally, I would appreciate your enclosing, each time you write, the customary self-addressed, stamped envelope. Also, please remit $3 for the Style Book, *a significant bargain in these inflated days.*

Sincerely,
JMJ

"Congressman Esterzee's office."

"Darlene, it's Charlie."

" 'lo dreampie."

"Did Deke get a copy of my letter from a guy named Johnson?"

"He's been roaring at it in his office."

"Is he free to talk a minute?"

"He's got his door open and his shoes off. I can see his big argyle feet on the desk. Deke, it's Charlie on line two."

"Hey, bo. You out there usin' drugs and endorsin' promiscuity?"

"In my spare time. It's just a hobby. Listen, I finished putting all the grain embargo stuff through the computer. The damage is about three times what Agriculture said.''

''My farmers gonna be real pleased to hear it.''

''I've got an appointment here at the economic section. They're going to show me where I'm wrong, unless you need me there for something else.''

''No. Go on in and listen to them lie. And I want you to start asking some questions. Want you to ask around in Agriculture, how come so many little grain elevators goin' bankrupt? Wonder if the big grain companies are to blame for the little ones failing?''

''Okay, I'll start asking.''

''Speakin' of questions, what's the answer to number two, here in the letter from Johnson? You enter that Suesue's premises pretty good, did you?''

''Isn't that a nutty letter?''

''Some makes sense. But I love the part about them listening to Ned Mizzourin with reverence.''

''Think I should answer the damn thing?''

''You got something against jousting?''

''Wouldn't know what to use for a lance.''

''How about the damn truth?''

''Like, just for starters, you're the most radical Democrat in Congress?''

''I didn't say the *god*damn truth, bo. Give him stuff he can swallow, just a little bit hot. Not pure pepper. Anyhow, I'm a populist 'cording to the newspapers.''

''What's your reasoning?''

''Man's fishing you like a bass. Provoking you on purpose. Now, you've got to show yourself, make a big, noisy splash, but not get hooked. So's he knows there's a good fish there, but he hasn't got him yet. Now, what you wanta see is his good bait, anecdotes, the document he hints at, right?''

''What's he want from me?''

''I dunno. Maybe he just wants you to stop pronging this Suesue Landau.''

''Come on. She's a nice, middle-aged drinking lady.''

''Well, your John McRae Johnson's mighty damn possessive about her.''

''You know, I'm inclined to make friends with that lady, if I can. If she'd open up a little about what my father was like, on the job; maybe give me the names of some of his friends. I might not need Johnson."

"It's him that's got a document, bo."

"I think I'm going to ignore that, Deke."

"Interestin' idea. Might work."

"I wasn't talking about it as a tactic."

"Hey, don't be a dumb little pissant, Charlie."

"Oh? Right, I'll try not to be one of those, Deke."

"What time's your appointment?"

"Ten minutes ago."

"I'll let you go. But Charlie?"

"Yes?"

"Cut down on that arrogance till you get just a little bit older, okay?"

"Yes. Yes, I will."

"The pomposity, too?"

"I'll try hard."

"Hello?"

"It's Christie Johnson calling, Charles."

"Hello, Mrs. Johnson."

"Are you going to be stiff with me?"

"I hope not, Mrs. Johnson."

"What time is it there?"

"Only eleven-fifteen."

"John's been watching the mailbox for two weeks for your answer."

"Did you read the letter I'm supposed to answer?"

"He's here, you see. He wanted me to call. You remember how we spoke before? So late at night. Are you still angry about that? I'm so sorry, and I know you need your sleep, working so hard."

"Mrs. Johnson, I was never angry about that. Your husband asked me questions I just don't choose to answer."

"He does have things to tell you. He wants to write to you. You may not be pleased but you'll be . . . enlightened."

"Will I? There's some document, too, isn't there?"

"He did know your father. He did, Charles."

"Look, Mrs. Johnson. All right. I'll answer. Mr. Johnson may not be pleased, either, but he'll be enlightened."

"I saw you when you were a baby, Charles."

(SHUT UP, CHRISTINE. GOD'S SAKE.)

"We never had children of our own . . ."

(CHRISTINE, STOP IT.)

"I can hear your husband, Mrs. Johnson. Am I causing trouble?"

"He worries about you in Washington. And I do. Overworked . . ."

(NONE OF HIS DAMN BUSINESS, YOU, SHUT UP.)

"I'll write to him tomorrow. Shall I hang up?"

"Don't be stiff with me. John has already written about his first meeting with your father. It's ready . . ."

(GOD'S SAKE, I SAID.)

"Goodbye, Mrs. Johnson."

"Not yet. Please? *John! John, no.*"

"I think I understand. I'll keep talking."

(CHRISTINE, GIVE ME THE PHONE. GIVE IT.)

"Ow, John, John . . ."

"Hello, Mizzourin. You seem to be making my wife a bit hysterical."

"Sir?"

"Do I have to hold this instrument up to her face, so you can hear the whimpers?" (CHRISTINE!)

"Sir, this is awful."

"Now I suppose she's turned you against me, and you won't reply at all, is that it? Well, she didn't want us to write, did she? Interfering, stupid."

"You're quite wrong. I just told Mrs. Johnson I'm willing to answer you. I'll do it tomorrow, as soon as I get home from work."

"You have five days to get your letter to me. Is that clear? Good night."

"Hi, hi, hi. It's Suesue speaking, and I'm sorry I'm not at the telephone right now. I'm having a nice evening and hope you are too. Do leave your name and number, though. If you need to get through this evening, you'll get a call. Otherwise, it'll be fun to talk to you in the morning, after ten o'clock, when I'll have lots of time. Your turn on the tape, when you hear the beep."

Beebeep.

"Suesue, hi. This is Charlie Mizzourin, and you certainly don't need to call tonight. John McRae Johnson and I are corresponding. I'm writing my second letter to him just now. He says he wants me to see you again and to write to him about you. Well, I do want to see you, but I won't necessarily write to him about it. I'll call in the morning. Hope we can get together soon. It's up to you how much I tell Johnson."

1608 Argo Street, Apt. 16
Washington, D.C. 20518
January 26, 1980

Mr. John McRae Johnson
Box 203, Capsicum, Colorado

Dear Mr. Johnson:
1. I do not work for Congressman Pete McCloskey. I do admire his independence very much. I work for Congressman David Esterzee from the Eighth Congressional District in southwest Iowa. He describes himself as a populist. Perhaps I should explain that I looked him up on my first trip to Washington. I hoped he could help find out about my Uncle Pete, since Pete (and, of course, Ned) are from the district Congressman Esterzee represents. He couldn't help, but he hired me.
2. I wasn't asked in when we arrived at Mrs. Landau's. I didn't expect to be and can't say whether I would have accepted. Probably not in the sense of your implication. In terms of finding her good company, I liked her. I hope she liked me.
3. I left a message for Mrs. Landau just now, saying that I'd enjoy seeing her, and telling her that you were interested in knowing more about her life these days.
4. Scholay Gopeters was not zoot-suited, if I understand what that means. He was dressed in a conservative, three-piece suit. He did wear a wide, blue, flowing necktie. This, he told me, was similar to part of the uniform worn by the band for which he was about to audition. I was on welfare because the university in New York, where I was a graduate teaching assistant in history, stopped meeting its payroll. I was in the grad student uniform of the time—short beard, medium-length hair, jeans, sweater, granny glasses and a knit shirt. These days I shave, my work requires a tie and jacket, and I wore tortoise shells until an ecological lady lobbyist shrieked at me. Now the rims are black. As for general appearance, I've asked Darlene, the receptionist in our office, to write you a separate account of it. She agreed, provided that I'm never to see a copy, and I believe it's already in the mail. It seemed like fun that way. I hope you enjoy it.
5. Coming to my mother, perhaps we reach bargaining ground. You imply that I must find your total support of her acceptable. All right. So long as that

doesn't mean I'm bound to adopt it. If you stop to think about it, she never gave me any kind of shot at understanding or supporting either side of what went on between her and my father. If I learn about him, I learn about her, too. She's always been half-mysterious to me. I love her, she loves me, and we fight like hell. When she remarried, it was to quite a nice, breezy, stockbroker named Scott Helmreich, whom she'd known since girlhood, the kind of man she was raised to marry. She'd broken an engagement to Scott when she married my father. Scott waited. When they married, Scott wanted to adopt me, but though I was only seven, I didn't want to be Charlie Helmreich. That was the time for mother to have made her case against my father, wasn't it? As long as she held back, I held back.

She's still beautiful and still underweight, though no longer celebrated. Strangers do notice her and think she must be someone. She hasn't lost her presence, but she doesn't look girlish anymore, either. She looks dramatic, and generally wears black or white. On rainy days, when I was a kid, I used to study her portfolios of magazine and fashion photos, taken before she married Mike. Tucked into one was a story from an old Life *magazine, about Katharine Hepburn's sisters. Mother could have been one of the Hepburn sisters in looks, but at the time I was too young to consider what that meant. Didn't it mean that her aristocratic, north Italian heritage was pretty well layered over by Scarsdale and Bennington?*

"Education, motherhood, breeding, moral sensibility," are the qualities you list in taking her side. Well, the education was adequate, but she doesn't do anything with it now except read book club selections and make Scott take her to an art gallery opening or an opera or a concert now and then. She and Scott raised two quite nice daughters. As to her motherhood before she remarried, I was very young, of course. There were a lot of men. And babysitters.

I'll quote you a little speech I listened to her make one day. I was about six and got called in to be shown off to some fashion guy she knew. I used to listen hard when she talked about the past, as you can imagine, but I never learned much.

"Crouch-Hilyer decided to go into maternity clothes when they heard I was pregnant. They really did. They'd been thinking about it anyway, and I was the whole campaign. Every month. The queen of Parents' Magazine. *They had Yollie Rogenmetz and Charles Bouleme on staff, designing . . ." (That's how I remember the names, anyway.)*

"Livia, really? Just for you?"

"Every stitch I wore for nine months was custom-made. But you know, some of the photographers made me pad the stomachs in those dresses, even in the fifth and sixth months?"

"Pad them?"

"I just didn't look pregnant."

"Livia!"

I felt like I must have been the fetus of the invisible man. As I got older, she did seem to want to mother me more.

As to breeding, the Scaligers were some family all right. She says she can go back to Bartolomeo Della Scala, who was boss of Verona in Romeo and Juliet's time, and I'm willing to be charmed now by her wanting to insist that we've got Capulet in us. There was a time when I was stuffy enough to want to show her it was unhistorical, and another when I told her Juliet was dumb, but I'll admit it's all a lot more elegant than Mizzourin.

Deke says the Mizzourins are Bohemian, from Czechoslovakia, so I figure that if mother's forebear was Juliet, then about that time Dad's was probably Yonder Poor Man, being pointed out to his page by by Good King Wenceslaus.

No, Mr. Johnson. I do not see that all of this has anything to do with anybody's worth, or "moral sensibility." I'll stay skeptical until given something to think about.

Maybe I'll try remembering you to mother, as you ask. It'll make her spit like a cat, like any other reference to my father.

6. I will be very grateful for your account of your first meeting with my father. I am, quite frankly, excited at the prospect of having a copy of the document you refer to. I enclose $4, $3 for the Style Book, *and $1 for Xeroxing and postage.*

7. I have no more information about Uncle Pete's arrest, but a sad little thing happened just today. A note he wrote to me before he disappeared got here from the Petrolat office after a long delay. They had opened and read it, as a matter of fact. Uncle Pete wrote it to me the same day the Des Moines lawyer's first letter about the inheritance reached him.

"I'm glad you're still around in this world," it says. "I still miss Mike sometimes, after all these years. We were close when we were kids. Mom favored Mike. She was librarian in town (as well as ran the farm) and Mike read books. He and Ned were always fighting. Ned had a temper. I tried to be a brother to both, but sometimes you couldn't. Ned was biggest, and Mike tried to protect me. When Ned dodged the draft in the Second World War by putting in for a farmer's exemption, Mike got really pissed. I'm sorry you and I didn't get to know each other after Mike was killed in the wreck, but your mom didn't want it. I only met the lady once, as a matter of fact, at the wedding. She was lovely-looking.

"I'm glad you want to know about our part of the family. I hope you can talk to Ned, get on his good side. He's got one. He'll do anything in the world

for you if he likes you, so you should try to get off to a good start with him. As for me, when I get my next home leave, let's get together someplace for a beer and a good talk, okay?"

As you suggested, I tried talking to the State Department again, this time to a woman in the Middle East section. She's supposed to be an expert on Iran, and I couldn't persuade her to refer me to someone else.

"The best thing you can do is write a personal appeal to the Ayatollah Khomeini," she said. "I'll give you an address."

"But my uncle isn't in Iran," I said. "He's not one of the hostages."

"Poor man," she said. "Actually they're quite well treated."

"We don't know where he is. Petrolat probably knows, and Congressman Esterzee hopes you'll join us in pressing the company to talk to us."

"We must keep the pressure on," she said. "Public opinion! It's really our very best chance. In your letter, you must appeal to the Ayatollah on religious grounds."

I left wondering how much this Iranian expert really knows about Persian tradition. On religious grounds, Khomeini's kind of Islam courts public opinion by throwing acid in his sister's face if she's suspected of

"Hello?"

"Hey, bo. What you doin'?"

"Writing to Johnson, Deke."

"Gonna get done in time to drink a bourbon and watch the Hoyas play Virginia basketball?"

"My God, you've got tickets?"

"Fella forced 'em on me in the corridor after we recessed."

"Vote for his bill, whatever it is."

"I had to hold back his arm and stuff a twenty in his pocket to pay. It's that corn-sweetener lobbyist."

"I'll pour some on my cereal in the morning."

"You tell Johnson about seein' the State Department lady?"

"I'm just getting done with it."

"Carry on, bo."

inchastity.
8. My farmer uncle, Ned, is a graduate of Iowa State University, and therefore quite possibly literate. My boss, Deke Esterzee, knows him slightly as a political enemy. Ned Mizzourin was a heavy financial backer of Deke's opponent in the last election. Mike, Ned and Pete Mizzourin's grandfather—my great-grandfather—was a Republican henchman who held various state-level jobs.

Their father farmed until the depression, but then rejoined the navy where he'd served in World War I. The depression hit the family hard, but over the last thirty years Ned has rebuilt the family farm into a prosperous operation, with over a thousand acres owned and leased (Deke estimates).

Uncle Ned is said to have a volcanic temper. His chief amusement is bar fighting. He was considered a troublemaker until he killed a man, some years ago, in one of his fights. The man was armed, and feared locally. Uncle Ned was unarmed, and the episode made him some sort of hero, though he's quite feared, too.

When I talked to the lawyer in Des Moines last time, I mentioned the possibility of visiting Ned and was advised against it.

"You wouldn't be welcome, as one of the minor heirs to your great-uncle's estate. Edward Mizzourin resents there being anyone in the will other than his brother and himself."

"As soon as it's settled, I'll go see him."

"All I can say is, when you do, see him before sunset. He's quite abusive once he begins, well . . ."

"Drinking?"

Frankly Mr. Johnson, I mean to see Calder Plain, Iowa, as soon as I can manage it. And I certainly mean to seek out Uncle Ned.

9. I am not presently married or engaged.

10. I think the Mizzourins were Lutheran, but know nothing about it. Mother was raised Catholic, and sometimes talks about taking it up again. Scott, my stepfather, is a nominal Christian Scientist. I haven't much personal inclination towards religion, but am awed by its enormous impact on history.

11. I drink socially, as you know from my first letter. I've never smoked tobacco, and found that marijuana gives me a severe sore throat. I like to eat well, when there's time and I can afford it. I'm generally too busy or too broke. I'm thin and don't gain weight. Like most people my age, I went through my health-food days, but it doesn't seem to have done me any permanent harm.

In school I thought I was a hockey player, which turned out to be dumb when I got to college, because I have poor eyesight. After that I thought maybe I was a speed skater. Then I met some real speed skaters. Finally, I found my sport in cycling, at which I'm pretty good. I have a touring bike on which I ride back and forth to work and get around the city. I sometimes ride it in one-hundred-mile touring events. I also have a racing bike and compete in amateur races. I do pretty well. But on lunch hours, Hon. Esterzee often cajoles me into working out in the gym, playing basketball one-on-one. He's huge, used to coach the game, and stomps me every time.

12. This is the resumé I use with job applications:

Charles D. Mizzourin
Born March 14, 1950. New York City. Single.
Primary education: Scarsdale, N.Y., public schools.

1964–68,	Washburn Preparatory School, Horton, New Hampshire. (Scroll, '68. Latin Club, '67, '68. Hockey, JV, '65, '66; Varsity, '67, '68.)
1968,	Fall, Campaign staff, Shep Sheplund, Democratic-Farmer-Labor candidate for Congress, 4th District, Wisconsin. (Driver, short advance work.) Defeated.
1969–70,	Alternate Contractors. (Construction; carpenter and electrician.) Also, travel abroad in 1970, summer.
1970,	Fall. Entered University of Wisconsin. Worked as a volunteer in Rep. Sheplund's second congressional campaign, in which he was successful.
1972.	McGovern For President, Midwest Regional H.Q. (Coordination, research and writing.)
1973,	January. Reentered Univ. of Wisconsin as second-semester sophomore. Major, History. Minor, Economics.
1975,	June. B.A., University of Wisconsin, with Honors in History.
1975,	Peace Corps. Ghana. (Teaching English and Coaching).
1976,	Staff of Rep. Shep Sheplund, research and writing. Mr. Sheplund was defeated in the fall general election.
1977,	Entered graduate school in January, at C.U.N.Y., M.A. History, 1978. Special area, 19th Century Russia. Accepted as a Ph.D. candidate. Proposed dissertation topic: a comparison of the economic consequences of freeing the serfs in Russia with those of emancipation of the slaves in the United States. These studies were suspended in 1978, and I am now on leave.
1979	Staff of Rep. David Esterzee. Research, writing and coordination, to present.

Languages: Russian (reading knowledge). French (reading and conversation).
Career goals: Foreign trade, Public Service, Foreign service.
Clubs: Amateur Bicycle League of America, Long Island Wheelman's Association.

13 (a), (b) and (c). To answer those questions, we go back again to 1968. I was just out of prep school, eighteen years old, and trying to figure out for myself what was going on in the world. I put on contact lenses and enlisted in the marines. A couple of weeks later, at the second physical, the Marine Corps threw me out. I still didn't understand what was happening or how I really felt about it.

I hitchhiked to Chicago, because according to the newspapers, that was where the action was going to be, at the Democratic National Convention. If I had any politics at all, I probably thought myself a Republican, but I wanted to see. I got my head busted in Chicago, and met some people who were a little older, people already in college, who changed my thinking completely.

I lived the next fall and winter at Big Frostbite Commune, in the Minnesota woods, where I became a fair carpenter, a self-taught electrician, a high-production dishwasher, and helped grow a mountain of vegetables in the spring— peas, snow-peas, spinach and five kinds of lettuce. In late spring I left the commune, went to Minneapolis, and joined Alternate Contractors (we did remodeling). On my vacation, I went to the Woodstock Music Festival and subsequently to Spain and France, cycling and staying at hostels. After which, see resumé. Those were pretty interesting years!

Now for the slime. In May 1971, along with the majority of the student body, I helped close my university down after the Kent State shootings. I became a sort of political ski bum, working in various campaigns and causes. It wasn't until I reentered school that I began to be passionate about learning whatever they had to teach. After that, I suppose I'd have fought to keep the university open, but it wasn't necessary any longer.

Candid questions, candid answers. I hope you will now respond as promised.
                                        Sincerely,
                                        Charlie Mizzourin

"Hello?"

"Is that my finger-lickin' chicken?"

"Hello, Darlene."

"Whompsie, did you get an answer from your friend Mr. Johnson?"

"I just found it in the mailbox."

"I got one, too. To my li'l physical description of you."

"That right? What's he say?"

"He sent me his *Style Book*, and a bill for three dollars."

"Going to pay?"

"What's your letter say?"

"I'm about to pour myself a drink and sit down with it."

"Be sure it's not a letter bomb. You'll get vodka on your podka."

"Night, Darlene."
"Night, light."

Box 203
Capsicum, Colorado
2/1/80

Dear Mizzourin:

First: have no fear that I will, even under threat of torture, release to you a copy of the description of yourself offered by your associate, Darlene Rhodes. Yet no fire is hot enough to cauterize from memory a letter which begins:

"Him have gorgeous boo-boo browns . . ."

Next: you are either an undertone-deaf, semantic simpleton, or insolent beyond belief. I must persuade myself it is the former. Otherwise, the implication of your closing line is that you question that I am a man of my word. I would advise you not to make such an allegation lightly. I command Hiberniation! Do I make myself clear, young man? Scotch it.

Now: shall I condone the conspicuous contrivance with which you seek to answer my artless queries? I am onto you, sir. As you intended, I found much of the information outlined disturbing to disgusting, though mitigated at the end by the note of contrition, the hint at maturation. Very well. Simply by accepting, I stand belabored but unpiqued, for all your vigorous thrusting. Acknowledge me the senior swordsman. Lunge as you will, this one small point will stand for my ability to parry and riposte them all: take now the negro Gopeters' mode of dress. I have firm evidence of his zoot taste in haberdashery, evidence which you, of all judges would be most hesitant to disallow. Ah, but shall I reveal it? In good time! (Perhaps.)

By the way: it matters little, but may have been unwise of you to mention to Suesue that I had any but a passing interest in her present circumstances. For, slight though that interest is, knowledge of it may yet breed dissembling in its object. Let reflection reflect: think twice.

Finally: thank you for the $4, for which this will serve as your receipt. I am glad to think you mean to meet my expenses, and will keep note of them. Now I shall delay no further your reading of the enclosures, the first about my meeting with your father, the second a product of that meeting. Read on.

JMJ

J. M. Johnson/DRAFT MEMOIRS/Breaking in a New Man

I was out of town when Mike Mizzourin was hired. By the time I interviewed him, he was in his second week on the newspaper. City

Desk said he was a tough, young reporter, still learning, so that he worked low on the Newspaper Guild scale. I said that sounded fine. City Desk also said that Mizzourin had been fired by one of our competitors after a few months work. Allegedly, it was "overstaffing." Actually, it was because Mizzourin had posted this jibe on their news room bulletin board:

> Modern man retains something of his youthful gaiety and nimble mental habits far into adult life. The great male anthropoids, like editors, lose the playful friendliness of youth. In the end, the massive skull houses a small, savage and often morose brain.
> —Loren Eiseley; rev. M. Mizz.

City Desk thought that funny. I agreed, but asked for the paragraph, wrote "Team player?" on it, and put it in the new man's file. After a time I had the quote located, and learned that Mizzourin's revision had been to substitute the phrase "like editors" for the original author's "by contrast."

When time permitted, I asked City Desk for a look at some of the new reporter's copy, and was sent two takes, just completed, on the retirement of an old gentleman who'd worked in Special Collections at the New York Public Library.

There was nothing in particular wrong with the piece, but it occurred to me that a little harder digging by the interviewer might have produced more anecdotal gold. I also thought the new man had better learn immediately where authority was vested. I sent for him.

He came into my office smiling, in shirt sleeves, short, dark-haired, chesty, slim in the waist and stout in the legs. His complexion was dark and slightly flushed. He had noticeably white teeth, a hawk nose, and intense, brown eyes. I believe the paternal background to have been Czech. He had a fast, come-and-go grin that helped give a strong impression of restless energy, waiting to be directed.

My first feeling on meeting him was genuinely one of warmth. Indeed, most people on meeting Mizzourin found him likable, often, I fear, to their eventual regret. I felt the energy above all, and felt challenged to channel it.

"This story doesn't do much, Mizzourin," I said. I did not ask him to sit down. "Here's a man who's handled a Gutenberg Bible, helped catalogue J. P. Morgan's rare book collection, known the great scholars, writers, theater people. Worked with them."

He nodded. These matters were listed in his story.

"Did he have nothing to say about any of that? Thefts? Security? Vandals? Quotes from famous names?"

"He's just an assistant, but he might have," Mizzourin said. "Sorry. Poor old boy'd been out to his testimonial luncheon. They'd got him smashed. He kept going to sleep on me."

"Well, well," I said. "And in your many years as a journalist, you've never heard of following up?"

"I phoned over there this morning. He had even less to say. Life's last big hangover, I guess."

He flashed the come-and-go grin. The going of it nettled me, and I said: "I want an adequate story, Mizzourin. I want anecdotes. I want color. I'm sending a photographer. I want three more takes."

"You're not kidding?"

"I don't have time to kid. I'm running a newspaper."

He picked up his two sheets, shrugged and said: "It's a dull story, Mr. Johnson."

I could hardly believe he was giving me the cue for the oldest squelch in the editorial profession, but of course he was still learning. "There are no dull stories." It came out automatically. "Only dull reporters."

"Terrific, sir!" The grin came and stayed through the rest of this. "There are no dull landscapes, only dull painters. Have I got it? Hey, there are no dull stores, only dull shoppers? No? Three more takes?" He was almost out of the office. I allowed it to appear as though I were not listening to these foolish attempts at what was called, in those days, a snappy comeback. He paused at the door and said: "Got it. There is no dull hair, only dull barbers."

I ignored it, of course. But often I have wished, not because of that nonsensical episode so much as because of what happened later, that I had said, calmly: *Never mind the story, Mizzourin. Clear your desk and drop by Friday for your dull paycheck.*

But I didn't say it. I think I felt that he wouldn't have cared, and I confess that I wanted to make him care.

Later the five takes came in. It was perfectly subversive stuff, of course. I suppose he thought he'd made what was called a shaggy-dog story out of it. Mizzourin had got the old bore started telling anecdotes, all right, and I read about the assistant librarian's several failures to meet J. P. Morgan; about how Florenz Ziegfeld once wanted to have follies girls photographed gathered around the folio Shakespeare—our assistant librarian, temporarily in charge, thought it improper; and finally, how the assistant's doubts as to the authenticity of the Gutenberg Bible were not shared by his superior, who turned out to be right all along.

I disciplined Mike Mizzourin in kind. I ran that story word-for-word as he had written it, and gave him his first *World-Telly* byline on it. Naturally, it caused laughter in the City Room at his expense. I was able to acknowledge several smiles of tribute directed at me as I passed through next morning.

But I'm slightly ahead of myself. When I went out the evening after the interview, the City Room was almost deserted, Copy Desk closed down, City Desk with a skeleton crew, a man at the wire-service ticker, all this in the half-dark. I realized I had worked late.

There was the sound of a single typewriter, and a pool of light at a single desk: Mizzourin's.

I stopped by and said: "Work to finish?" City Desk was not always careful about letting people collect unnecessary overtime.

The new reporter had been deep in concentration. He looked up, startled, and spoke soberly: "Something of my own, Mr. Johnson."

"On our time?"

"No. On your typewriter, though. You object?"

"Of course not."

"Your copy paper?"

"Really," I said. "I suppose you're writing something you fancy you might sell? The newspaper's entitled to first refusal, you know."

"This couldn't be printed," he said, smiled, turned the smile off. "It's quite personal, anyway. I'm just reacting to something I saw today."

"Are you saying that you like to write?" Reporters notoriously do not.

"Second best," he said.

"What's first?"

"Music. Jazz."

I was curious, and concealed my distaste. "And why can't your— your personal meditation be printed?"

"I was shown a manuscript at the library today. Something they're considering buying for a lot of money. It's very secret. The girl who showed it to us would lose her job if anyone found out."

"Us?"

"Burke. The photographer you sent. He photographed some pages for me."

Again I concealed my feelings, though any private use of our film, flash and darkroom materials was against regulations and repugnant.

"May I know what manuscript?"

He paused. Then he said: "Off the record? Not that it's front-page stuff."

"Off the record."

He indicated the page in his typewriter, looked at me and said: "Tomorrow morning."

In the morning there was an envelope marked "Personal" on my desk, and I felt I'd won Mizzourin's trust.

CM—Of the carbon copy your father left for me, I enclose a photocopy, which is not, I'm afraid, altogether legible. The carbon itself is more than thirty years old by now, and the newsprint, cut sheets of which we used for copy paper, browns, fades and fuzzes through the years. I think you can get the gist. The first three lines, in caps, are the titles of obsolete songs.

Mrs. Johnson is knocking at my studio door, and I know what mincing mumble she will mouth: "Hurry, dear, if you want to catch the mailman." Deusnospickleus. (God preserve us.)—JMJ

"Deke Esterzee's office. Darlene speaking."

"It's Charlie."

"Angelcookie. I thought you were right here in the office."

"Tell Deke I've gone to the Congressional. Is he still on the floor?"

"No, he's back at his desk with the door open. Opening and closing his drawers."

"I have something to read. It's faded and blurred. I'm getting help from a document guy."

"Document guy or document person, sugarpet?"

" 'Bye, Darlene."

"Mmmmbye, wait. He wants to talk to you."

"Okay."

"Hey, bo."

"Hey."

"Looking over the new Johnson stuff you left me. What's this thing your daddy wrote, anyway?"

"I can't read it. That's why I'm here. What Johnson sent isn't even a Xerox. He did it on a home copier."

"Have to send him a dime for a Xerox."

"I've got a friend here who's taken it into the computer room. Thinks he can get the machine to read it and give us a printout."

"Ol' pal sitting there in Colorado chucklin', isn't he?"

"Is he still trying to get a fishhook into me, or just being cheap?"

"Well, I'd have to say he seems fond of his little jokes. But he does want you to spy on this Suesue girl."

"I guess that's what he wants."

"Oh. Yeah, yeah. Let's see what else we got here. Ummm. Say, can you put a little more weight on those allegations in the future?"

"I'll try."

"And, um, keep that insolence over here this side of belief?"

"Okay."

"Now, when you lunge, you won't try any of those what they used to call snappy comebacks, will you?"

"No."

"Nor write no shaggy-dog letters? I mean, these things kin get carried in a man's genes."

"I'll be careful."

"Hey. Bring me a copy of your daddy's piece. What the hell manuscript did he see, anyway?"

"If I find out, you'll be the next to know. Deke, my guy's coming. He's nodding. Looks like we've got it."

M. Mizzourin/**SONGS (6/13/48)**

MY EVALINE
BY THE WATERMELON VINE
THE CUBANOLA GLIDE

In 1922, T. S. Eliot published his great, sad, misty poem, *The Wasteland.* I was born that year, but I don't think Mr. Eliot got the news. In the 27th Infantry Division, I had two friends who made me read poetry; one of them taught me to call the poet Tough Shit Eliot.

That friend was a Communist; the other was a fag. They hated one another.

The fag, who was much the nicer, was killed by Jap artillery one day on Okinawa, while talking over a field telephone. I don't think it was a line-of-duty call. It was a quiet, sad, misty morning, with the smell of blasted sugarcane in the air, and I think Much the Nicer was zapped during one of the long talks he liked to have with his friend, the clerk at Company B.

When the Communist and I heard, we were in a captured bunker, with our rifles disassembled, cleaning them. A thin guy named Donnelly followed his thin nose into the bunker and said Alan Daye was dead. The Communist swallowed a grin and then gave us a little lecture about the shrapnel used in Jap shells. It was made from scrap iron, he told us, which Japan got by buying salvage rights to the capitalist elevated railroad on Sixth Avenue in New York City. This was when what he called the El was torn down in the 1930s.

I put my M-1 back together and moved to the narrow opening in the sandbags to leave the bunker for a foxhole, where I could sit by myself in the preferable mud. The Communist was building a pretty nifty joke in his Bronx accent: ". . . ya know, the 42nd Street/Sixt' Avenue station, right? Maybe he gets a little piece from dat stop, right?" Bad News Donnelly was laughing at the accent, exaggerated for the occasion. "Know why. Dat's where duh fairies always get off duh train . . . Mike?" He noticed that I was on my way out. "Hey, come back, dumbass. There's shooting out dere . . ."

Out dere I could see that the sandbags around the bunker had Japanese writing on them, and my own small mind made its own nifty connection. It was a song of the twenties:

There's a Japanese sandman . . .

Then, if it was a crooner, he would sing, parenthetically:

(Oooh-ooo-oooh . . .)

In 1901 a songwriter called Mae Anwerda Sloan published "My Evaline." My mother was born that year on a farm in southwest Iowa, but I doubt that Miss or Mrs. Sloan got the news. Mother was not a crooner. She liked to sing alto, and could play a little on the piano, so perhaps she played and sang "My Evaline." And now and then, mostly under my breath and to myself, but more then than now, I recite bits of *The Wasteland*.

April is the cruelest month
Oooh-ooo-oooh . . .

I saw the first draft of *The Wasteland* today, at the New York Public Library. It's their secret bibliographic atom bomb. It doesn't start at all with April.

The discarded opening has an altered line of Miss or Mrs. Sloane's hit song in it, crossed out, and then a couplet from a George M. Cohan song substituted. And crossed out. So were lines from two other songs—"By the Watermelon Vine," by Thomas S. (Stearns?) Allen, 1904 (Mr. Eliot would have been fourteen the year that one was written), and "The Cubanola Glide," lyrics by Vincent Bryan, 1909.

Tough Shit was persuaded to cross out more than half of the 1000 lines from his first draft of *The Wasteland,* 567 altogether. I don't know who counted them, but there's a note.

The persuader was Ezra Pound, for whom we had no name in the 27th Infantry Division. We just thought of him—Alan, the Communist and I—as a sad, mad, misty old traitor who had broadcast propaganda for Mussolini. Tokyo Rose, Berlin Sally and Rome Ezra. He's in St. Elizabeth's cloudcuckooland now, in Washington, D.C., refighting lost battles, *oooh-ooo-oooh.*

Some of the lines Tough Shit discarded were quotes from long gone lyrics. Maybe Pound was right.

"Listen Buster," old Ez from Idaho may have told the Harvard kid. "You don't hit immortality with bullets from 'My Evaline' and 'By the Watermelon Vine'."

"What can we say, Evaun? Shall we agree?

"Hear these lines they kept:

>   "What shall we do tomorrow . . .
>   . . . What shall we ever do?"

The music for "The Cubanola Glide" was by Harry van Selzer. I don't know where we'd go to hear it. The Doctor's disappeared. But if there's someone still around to hum the tune, then don't cry, Evaun darlin', we could fake it, you and me.

1680 Argo Street, Apt. 16
Washington, D.C. 20518

Dear Mr. Johnson:
Just as simply and sincerely as I can, I want to thank you. It's as if I'd just heard my father's voice for the first time. Do you know who Evaun was? Or the Doctor, who might have known that tune?

Charlie Mizzourin

". . . first three minutes, please."
(CLANG, CLANG, CLANG, CLANG, CLANG, DING, CLINK)
"Hello?"
"Charles, it's Christine Johnson, calling from Durango."
"Give me the number. I'll call back."
"Oh, no. We can't. John is waiting in his car. He thinks I'm calling the maid."
"For a dollar and forty cents?"
"He can't see me, Charles. I just want you to know that he showed me your last note. About hearing your father's voice. I cried."
"I'm sorry."
"Happy tears, for you."
"Thank you."
"But John didn't take it very well. He, he wanted you to be upset, I think. Disappointed. It sounds strange, I know, but it's as if he wanted you to choose him over your father."
"Yes. That's pretty strange."
"What did he send you? Something Mike wrote?"
"Yes."
"Something about the newspaper?"
"It's hard to describe. Did you know someone named Evaun?"
"What?"
"Evaun?"
"Charles, please. Send me a copy, too."
"Sure. Or someone called the Doctor?"
"They called a doctor? Oh, I don't understand. Please, General Delivery in Durango? And I'll pick it up, but make it say 'Please Hold.' "
"The Doctor was someone . . . oh, all right, Mrs. Johnson. I'll send it."
"Goodbye, Charles, goodbye."

File on my father. Notes:

Send readout to Christie, Gen'l Del, Durango.

Is she as cagy as Johnson, in her own way? Bogus scatterbrain? Or: the brain scatters, but she permits it, because she has track and control of the fragments.

Back to Johnson's letter: what does he mean by "firm evidence"?

Scholay's zoot suit? (Turns out to have been a style worn by blacks in the east, chicanos in the west, during the second war.)

Other documents by Mike Mizzourin? Who were Evaun and the Doctor?

> *Box 203*
> *Capsicum, Colo.*
> *2/16/80*

Dear Mizzourin:

In future please type all correspondence.

Your ludicrous longhand lacrimosity in response to the dubious document which I dispatched meseems a maudlin misappraisal. One does not speak ill of the dead, and particularly not to a precariously surviving son, but I had hoped for clear perception from you of how the dead man spoke ill of himself.

My so-far defeated purpose, to which I dedicate myself anew, was to enable you to conclude that your late father, Michael Mizzourin, was a sociopath.

I repeat: the pages sent are not the only evidence I have, yet why are they not sufficient? Perhaps analyse du texte *will bring us to agreement.*

1. Relished besmirching leading poet with obscene nickname.

2. Made derogatory reference to unfortunate class of sick persons in use of slang word "fag," yet

3. In referring to political degenerate, avoided words like "red" and "commie," even capitalizing "communist."

4. Showed rudeness and insensitivity in leaving bunker while red comrade was offering manly comfort with humorous remarks, however crudely chosen.

5. Invited pity by exposing self to enemy fire needlessly. Dereliction here of soldier's first responsibility, to survive or die fighting.

6. Mimicry of Bronx accent in poor taste under circumstances.

7. Slighting reference to his mother.

8. Showed sympathy for traitor-poet.

As to the creatures named in his conclusion, very likely they can be lumped with the answer to one of your particular, early inquiries, as to "who his friends were." You know now: homosexuals, political deviates and negro would-be swells.

Following that, in your letter #2 (I trust you are keeping copies) you wrote to me: "Perhaps you and he were friends?" I did attempt to befriend your father, insofar as the difference between our positions allowed it. It must be evident now that he was not the sort in whom I could feel confidence or toward whom sustain warmth. Charles, I am a stubborn and resourceful man. I mean to win you to a realistic view of your parent.

Meantime, I await with unusual patience your decision as to whether you are willing to write to me concerning Suesue Landau.

Yrs.,
JMJ

"Hi?"

"Charlie Mizzourin calling. Is that Suesue?"

"Yes, darling, and I've found you in the book and tried to return your call. You're never home."

"My boss went out of town. A lot of late work at the office."

"So Johny Mac is writing to you?"

"Yes. And keeps urging me to see you."

(Laughter) "That's our Johnny Mac."

"He's an editor who wants a story, I guess."

"Let's give it to him. Anyway, let's get together."

"Shall we have a drink this evening."

"Do you like the Willard Bar?"

"Sure."

"We'll make it dutch, all right?"

"I did invite you."

"Let's do, anyway."

"See you this evening."

"Morning."

"Candycane. Late night at the Willard? Now, right shoe goes on right foot . . ."

"I was halfway out the door, Darlene, when the phone rang. With both shoes on."

"Deke wants you here to call him on the WATS at nine sharp."

"That's eight in Iowa. He's already called in from there today?"

"He didn't go out to the district to take middle-aged heat to fancy bars."

"Deke Esterzee here. What can I do for you?"

"It's nine o'clock."

"Hey. That sounds like a precariously surviving son."

"I've got some cost-of-living stuff worked up."

"I'm going to put Stuart on to tape it. And whatever you're getting on grain elevators. I got a prayer breakfast in twenty minutes. You hear the President's speech?"

"No. Bob did. I can put him on. I went to a Kennedy rally."

"Big crowd?"

"He's not drawing."

"Say anything new? How could he? Hostages the only thing they · wanta hear. Ayatollah's gonna nail down the nomination for his friend Jemmy, and then help someone else nail Jemmy in the general. Lil ol' Republicans'll beat us with anybody, startin' with Orphan Annie."

"I hope she's not running."

"Her Daddy is. War-movie bucks. Get Bob on the legal research."

"Grain elevators?"

"Seed companies. Grain shippers. Illegal interlocks. Okay?"

"Deke, Bush beat Reagan there in the Iowa caucuses, didn't he?"

"Yeah, but Ronzo's gonna get the nomination."

"You sound sure."

"Why do you think I'm goin' to a prayer breakfast?"

Washington
Feb. 23, 1980

Dear Mr. Johnson:

We do read differently. I hope it won't continue to irritate you when I say I liked my father pretty well from the fragment you sent. We're on different sides of the street. You were responsible for the way he did his work, and he seems to have been a handful sometimes, but I do recall your saying you considered him "a good reporter."

Let's set this aside for now; I've seen Mrs. Landau again. I thought it right to offer to send her copies of this and future letters. She laughed and said, "Never mind, darling. Be my guest."

Feb. 22, at 6 p.m., we met at the Willard Bar, where she's obviously a regular. There was a table reserved, and the waiter, an older man, said:

"Good evening, Suesue. What'll it be?"

"Shoot me, Kenneth," she said. "This is Charlie."

"Same for you, sir?"

"What's it mean?"

"A Bloody Mary, followed by a bullshot, followed by a bloodshot."

"That should do it," I said. "Okay. Shoot me, too."

Suesue was wearing a very becoming dress. I asked and she told me the shade is called "winter white." Her hair color has changed, to a sort of bronze. Her jewelry was conspicuous, but attractive since it seemed in character for a large, handsome, generous woman. She attracted her share of looks and waved at a number of people she knew or recognized. One man, a former Senator (Otis Hibben of Michigan), who now directs the dairy lobby, Suesue told me, got up from the table he was sitting at, came over, and was introduced.

"Charlie's the absolutely key man," Suesue said, the way people do around here. "In the office of that wonderful young Representative from Idaho, Dick Esterhouse."

"Say, does Dick like cheese?" The ex-Senator asked. He's big and portly, and quite magnetic in a jowly, locker-room kind of way.

"Pretty much a meat and potatoes man, Senator," I said.

When he left, Suesue laughed and said, "Did I even come close on your boss's name? Not that Otis will remember from this drink to the next." I corrected the name for her. She asked me to write it down, which I did, and she tucked the card away in a wallet full of others.

Now that you and I are corresponding, Suesue's a little less reticent about my father. I gathered she was sending messages to you in some of the things she said (not exact quotes, but close):

"A lot of women on the paper had eyes for Mike, darling, but not me. I was a one-man girl, right from the start. And a very young one, too."

She told me she was still sixteen when she went to work for you in 1948, but said she was well-developed and knew how to dress to look twenty. "Didn't lie to anyone about my age. I just smiled and wiggled a little bit, except when I had to write it down. Then I had to fib. Darling, I could have had any man on the newspaper. I had my chances elsewhere, too. Men always liked me, I'm a man's woman. That's like a lady's man. Not a letch. Someone who thinks it's fun to be nice."

Later on, she was telling me that my father wasn't one of the heavy drinkers, not an abstainer by any means, though, and great fun at a bar or party. Then she said: "He could raise hell cold sober. One time Johnny Mac dictated this memo to me, saying the general assignment guys were overusing cars belonging to the paper. You know, cars were still tough to find then, because of the retooling after the war. So Johnny Mac thought they ought to use more subways and buses, and other 'alternate forms of transportation,' though he said watch the taxi bills, too. He was right, but you know what your father did? Well, the copy boys were dropping off these memos at everybody's desk, and as soon as Mike read his, he jumped up and ran out of the building. He stopped a kid on a tricycle, gave the kid's mom a dollar, and told them to wait. Then he leaves the trike by the elevator, comes in, borrows a hat, writes PRESS on a piece of white paper, sticks it in the hatband, goes out, and rides back in on the trike, wearing the hat, all around the city room and right past Mr. Johnson's door. All the guys were laughing and clapping."

She said you ran "fiercely" out of the office, and that my father picked up the tricycle and ran away with it, sort of waving it over his head.

"Johnny Mac would have fired him," she said. "But pretty soon, Johnny Mac was laughing, too, the way he did, and shaking his head. But maybe he should have fired Mike."

When I asked her why she said that, she shook her head and said, "It's not my story to tell, Charlie, even if I did know all about it. Which I honestly don't. There were things nobody told, not to me anyway."

After that, we stood up to leave. As Kenneth the waiter was helping Suesue with her coat, which seems to be vicuna, we heard grunts and gasps and a small squeal or two. We looked over. Senator Hibben and the dark-haired younger man with whom he'd been drinking were having a scuffle. The squeal came from a good-looking redhead who'd been sitting between them. Though Hibben's much larger, the younger man managed to wrestle the ex-Senator back into his chair and slap his face, though not very hard.

Suesue said, "Stavros!" quite sharply.

Hibben roared up, and the younger man backpedaled our way calling out Suesue's name, though he didn't seem to be taking things too seriously. Stavros got our table between himself and Hibben. The ex-Senator stopped, very flushed and breathing hard. Suesue had her hand up, close to her chest.

"All ready for a little assault charge, Greek boy?" he said. "I can't have more than two hundred witnesses."

Stavros was smiling. He said, "Deeplomat immune, Otis."

"There's no damn diplomatic immunity on IOUs," Hibben said, and I saw he had some crumpled paper in his hand. Suesue took it from him.

"What is all this?" she asked. "Shame on you, Otis."

"He's a deadbeat fart," Hibben said.

"No. You fart," Stavros said, but he kept smiling.

"Both of you. Sit down," Suesue said, and damned if they didn't. The redhead had got into her coat by then and was watching more or less amused. Suesue sat, too, sifting through the four or five IOUs, and then said, "All right, now." With that, she got a checkbook out of her purse, wrote a check (I have no idea for how much), handed it to Hibben, and gave Stavros the wads of paper.

Stavros said, "Suesue, I weel—"

*"No," she said. "You won't. I don't want your IOUs. If you feel like
paying me back, let me know. If not, goodbye, darling."*

She got up. Stavros rose and bowed, and we left.

*All she said was, "Boys will be boys," so I can't explain or analyze it for
you, except to say that I admired the way she took charge.*

*Suesue invited me to have lunch with her at her home next week, when
Deke gets back from his district visit, and I'll have more time. I'll learn more
then about how she lives and, since she genuinely seems to have no objection,
feel free to write you my impressions. As to the story which Suesue says isn't
hers to tell, I assume it's yours, at least in part. I hope the time when you're
willing to write it will come soon. Meanwhile, may I ask three particular
questions?*

*It's silly to harp on it, but how do we manage to disagree so about Scholay
Gopeters' clothing? Maybe the next is the same question: When you say "not
the only evidence I have" (that my father was a sociopath), do you mean you
have other personal things he wrote? (I can sympathize with you about the
tricycle episode, yet it seems fairly harmless—were there more serious things?)
In case there are other documents, I enclose a twenty-dollar bill to pay for
commercial Xeroxing and to reimburse postage, gasoline for trips to town, and
any other expenses.*

*My third question: Evaun, of course, is not my mother's name. Do you
know who Evaun was? My regards to Mrs. Johnson.*

Sincerely,
Charlie Mizzourin

Capsicum, Colo.
Feb. 29, 1980

Dear Charlie:

*Well, well, you must think me a humorless curmudgeon indeed if you accept
Suesue's childlike version of my response to your father's tricycle tantrum, a
half-forgotten episode now brought back clearly to mind. I did not, you'll be
pleased to learn, run out "fiercely" or in anger. I strolled to my office door, and
stood there relaxed, watching the young man clown about in his exuberant
way—yes, he could be quite engaging—and when he rode past me, I remarked,
"Be sure to send in your gas bills for that, Mizzourin." It's possible that
Suesue, behind me at her little desk inside the office, failed to hear my timely
quip, but others did, out in the City Room. And back to work they went,
tension relieved. Frankly, I felt your father's horseplay nicely underscored my*

point about vehicle use, and I shall get a nice paragraph for my memoirs out of the anecdote.

But I was roostrapedestrian in that shop, believe it: cock-of-the-walk.

Now then, let me in all other regards commend your first report. I should like, if I may, to have a few more details about former Senator Hibben, whom I vaguely remember from my own Washington days. What would you guess to be his approximate age? And was his attitude toward Suesue when initially introduced—gallant or respectful?

As to the ensuing skirmish, let us apply Occam's razor, that is, the explanation requiring the fewest assumptions. It would appear that a young blackguard was trying to cheat an older gentleman, who had perhaps been kind to him. It would appear that Suesue, in assuming the blackguard's indebtedness, quick-wittedly placed the cad in a socially disadvantageous position, perhaps making him look bad to the comely tête-rouge (although she may have been an accomplice). Interesting, certainly; perhaps you will learn more about the episode.

Suesue continues, as I'm sure you are perfectly aware, to lie to you about her age. She was certainly of age (eighteen in New York State, at that time) when she came to work for the World-Telly. Ah, vanity! As to her being both a "one-man girl" and a "man's woman," this may be true. To resolve this apparent paradox will be an interesting intellectual pastime in our correspondence, through your observations and my reflections.

She seems more affluent that I had imagined. Your estimate of the home she lives in, its furnishings and appurtenances (fresh flowers? luxurious food?) may show it to be more modest than her dress and regularity of attendance at the Willard Bar, which I know to be expensive, might indicate. Vanity again perhaps: une façade?

I too hope we will in time reach the stage of serious intimacy at which I may write for you that story which, as Suesue says, is neither known to her nor hers to tell if it were. I do not promise this, yet to write of being unburdened of that story is no mere metaphor. And now you will perhaps see something of the beginnings of it in what I enclose, perhaps rashly.

Here is an autobiographical episode of your father's authorship. It is set three years earlier in time than the last fragment I sent. Your father spent a lot of time after hours at the shop, working up this kind of thing. He was typing and, I think, revising, from old legal pads he'd kept in longhand, interleafing the finished pages in what he called his "fake book." You will learn what that term means from what follows. Yes, I have that book he made.

You will also catch, quite incidentally, a brief glimpse of Gopeters demonstrating that I am correct about the silly, as you say, point we've been disputing.

Not at all incidentally, you will have once more to judge, my dear young man, what sort of human being Mike Mizzourin was, and again by words of his, not mine.

Two of your three questions answered: on zootness, of other evidence. And now the third: why not, for now, take Evaun to be one of those imaginary nymphs whom poets address, as Shakespeare Sylvia or Dowson Cynara?

So that you will not find it burdensome to take Suesue, some time following your luncheon there, to a decent watering hole (as we used to call bars), I am returning $10 in change from the $20 you sent me.

> Faithfully yours,
> John McRae Johnson

File on my father: Notes.

This typewriter. Scarred, it was white once. Olympia. Portable. It's more like an organ by now than a machine, I've had it so long. How many history papers, letters, draft reports? A lobe of my brain.

I've just read quickly through the pages Johnson sent. In a moment I'll get into bed with a glass of the cognac I bought to celebrate these pages coming, and read them through again slowly. There are more, of course. Johnson means to use them, a few at a time I suppose.

I can almost invent Mike Mizzourin now. He's saying: *Johnson's starting to get nice now, Charlie. Make sure your ass is padlocked to your vertebrae.*
Yes, sir.
Sir? What's wrong with Dad?
Hoped you'd say that.

Dad?
What?
We don't say "negro" these days. The word is "black."
No shit?
Did you really call bars "watering holes"?
Grow up.

Dad, if I owe you anything . . .
Pay it to Johnson.
. . . it's to get the rest of what you wrote. Maybe it's myself I owe. How would you have got it? With a ski mask and a toy pistol, staged a stickup?
Sure, Charlie. Take a rubber dagger, too, to scare Christine, and a T-bone steak for Johnson's dog.
Are the other pages out in Colorado, like these I have?
No, they're like Il Penseroso.

All about youth and music . . .
What else is there, baby bird? . . . youth ago, and long time music.

M. *Mizzourin/*BEGIN THE BEGUINE/*12/29/45*

Today, on my bittersweet way out of the army discharge center in Faraday, North Carolina, I stole that goofy-looking horn. There it lies, coyly shining at me from the other double bed in Room 300G, the Grand Commerce Hotel.

A group of nine of us new-hatched sweet veteran bitter birds were scratch-and-pecking out of step, toward the main gates of Faraday, carrying duffel bags and green musettes. We passed a fine, pink-panted, first lieutenant bird, peered at him, twittering, and jointly failed to raise our wings, save for a curly-crested, tall T-3 named Lon, who hollered " 'Tenshup," dropped his gear, and rose into a salute so strong he could have bruised his forehead with it. We applauded. The lieutenant hurried on. We started past a double-deckered wooden barracks building with an open door. Me, Mike, I always look in open doors.

And inside this one was a room where I could see a tuba on its side, looking quite drunk. And there were music stands, and then a row of snare drums on the seats of chairs, flutes, clarinets, garrison caps, and full-dress jackets hanging on the chair backs. I slowed down, fell back from the group that I was pecking with, stuck my head in the door, and there was no one in the room.

There were a lot more instruments, saxes, bones and piccolos. High boys. Glockenspiels? I set my duffel down and slid in fast, wanting to clip a trumpet.

When I got in, I could hear talking and pissing in the other room. I grabbed the first hand-sized brass instrument with valves I saw, and got back out again. It seemed to me that this thing I had, stuffed part-way down the bosom of my Eisenweasel jacket, might just be comical and oversized. I didn't quite dare look.

There was a handsome trash can just outside the door, its cover off, and crumpled in the trash, a big, brown, empty paper sack. Lifted that sacksucker, hunched over it, and glancing away and whistling now to show how unconcerned I was, bagged my fat horn. Picked up my duffel, swung it high, showing the folks my young exuberance, and double-peckered up to catch my flock.

In charge, but not much, was a buck sergeant. His name is Fetlock, an agreeable, plump, buck sergeant, and to him the best of Fetlock luck

and pots of beer. He'd dreamt aloud of beer all morning as we processed through.

"Mike. Mike, my boy. What's in the paper sack?" he asked, when I
caught up.

"Budweiser," I said. "You want a can?"

"Don't we wish?" said Sergeant Fetlock.

What I wished when I looked at the good, pink, sweating sergeant,
who'd had mortar teams at Guam and Leyte and been wounded twice,
was that my eye didn't keep rending him to bloody chicken parts. We
nine freed bipeds, like zing-thousand more, were being let out early
'cause we'd met the weasel.

I kept chickens as a kid, and two or three times had them killed, but
never dreamed I'd be one. Gnaw, comes the weasel, chewing into the
coop, and then his mad little twitchy nose pokes in, and his whirly
cartoon eyes, and he snickers and gets his tiny hard-on for the killing—
the same teensy hard-on as the admirals and generals get, and probably
the presidents and kings as well, worshiping the weasel god. "Charge,
men." Then the cute rascal kills or, nutsy and indifferent, just half-kills
every fuckin' chicken he can catch, and may or may not trouble to eat
one before he realizes that the yardarm's up there buggering the sun
again—time, time to slurry over to the weasel club to slarf some bourbon or some vod, some sake, cognac, schnapps, or say, an ounce or
two of pissy, half-warm Scotch.

And what's left behind, in the caves and on the beaches? Piles of half-
animate blood and shit and feathers.

That will do for the bitter. I suppose the sweet's remembering the
extra shot of morph your friend the medic gave you when he found
you hurting in the pile, little Balfour, popping himself a shot for company, and to keep from crying. That, and the long dream of love some
people seemed to think was out here for us, past the gates of Faraday.

M. Mizzourin/LOVELY TO LOOK AT

When we got to the entrance of the army camp and could see town
out beyond it, I moved to the middle of our sloppo little tachmo, where
the sentries paid no tenshup to my ridgeback paper sack.

The sentries were two privates with no ribbons on their bright dress
khakis, so they hadn't been cooped up for long.

"You never had it so good," my buddies serenaded them, and "Ah,
my ass doth bleed for you." Me, Mike, I kept quiet. In the still of the

night, even with the weasel caught and caged, their downy balls would
drear regret it, but I didn't want to point that out. I'm twenty-three.
I've been Sam's flightless cage bird for four years. I had no burning in
my dodo heart to hassle the draftees.

The sentries. They could have asked to see our papers, check our
gear. We knew they wouldn't do it, though. My sack and I were clear.

We nine came to a stop beyond the gate. Unskilled at freedom, we
took our first, shy look around. And every store that fans out from the
gate is a civilian clothing store, the merchants in their doorways
beckoning like whores in sailortown. No one in our group knew any
of the other eight before we processed out today, but now we turned
toward one another and stood close.

"Anyone want to find a tavern?" Sergeant Fetlock asked. A couple
of guys said sure. The curly-haired salutatorian said hey now, seriously, men, we'd ought to all come with him to the Baptist Church
and there give thanks for safe deliverance. Fetlock, milder than I could
have been, said well, he thought he'd just give thanks his own way,
Lonnie. A negro corporal of engineers with fingers missing said byebye, new clothes for him, but not the threads they sold here by the
gate, the shapes weren't drape, the pleats weren't reet.

Buck Sergeant Fetlock looked at me: "Well? Tavern, Mike?"

I smiled, and wanting nothing more than seeing what I might have
hidden in my paper bag, said: "No. But thank you, Sergeant."

"Did you get the mouthpiece?" Fetlock said.

Good question, good my sergeant. I don't have much blush left in
me. I did a graceless Susie-Q to say farewell and took off down an
alley, horn in hand. The sack was getting pretty nubbly. I held it tight,
the duffel in my other hand, the musette riding on my shoulder like a
canvas chimpanzee.

In my four years, this final day had offered the one chance I got for
any decent looting. Rapine and pillage opportunities hadn't been too
great, either. So I stopped in the alley, sat on the duffel, away from
pries and eyes, got out the instrument to have a happy little gloat.

It sorely puzzled me. Still does. It's too long and too plumpet to be
a nice trumpet, its tubes are too straight and it's got that really big and
silly-looking mouth.

I looked down its bell, there in the alley, and pushed its valves in and
out. It sort of simpered back at me. I tried grimacing at it. Sneering.
Shook my head and frowned. Finally, I felt myself smile and I said to

the horn, "You goof," and put it back in the sack, whereat it tucked itself under my arm, like some kind of ugly, trusting pet.

And Sergeant Fetlock was quite right, of course. I haven't got the mouthpiece.

M. *Mizzourin*/BE CAREFUL, IT'S MY HEART

Maybe if they'd had a band waiting for me and Fetlock and Lon the Baptist and the disfingered, slim brown corporal of engineers, waiting at the end of the four-year, thirty-thousand–mile, round bumpy trip, waiting when we finally slouched off the heatless bus from Nashville, after the overheated train from Oregon, after the wallowing slow troop ship from Japan, maybe, if, smiling and standing straight, the army band had just been waiting there, to start in playing welcome-home-guys as we stood with souls so dead, dry-eyed, ever to ourselves saying, "This is our own, our native land," maybe I would have left the man his horn.

Now, as it is, it's mean fun to think of him with that homeless mouthpiece, coming back in from a break, thinking to start rehearsing up again, getting the music ready for some sweetheart officer function; bet they're right now pulling on their pink pants, gonna have a stink dance, and hey?

"Hey! Babyration." I don't think I actually called out loud to my imagined dehorned blower from my duffel in the alley, but perhaps I did. "Hey, now, I got you a good idea for the officers' entertainment, 'kay? How 'bout you drop your khakis, bend over, and ram that pretty mouthpiece halfway up and squeeze? And have your friend the tuba player blow some real fine high notes through, while you open your mouth to let 'em out like bursts of joyous song?"

Oh, clean and smooth, this Michael mind of mine, exactly like a trap that's been left underwater for four years, sprung, rusted out and silted over.

"C'mon horn," I said, there in the alley. I guess this part I did say right out loud. "Let's find us a hotel, and spend some of this mustardy out pay." And I strolled along, singing the well-known joyous song, "Mustardy ouch, custardy couch, piss and douche and over the river." Maybe it was the weasel sprung my trap, but I'd got a little snip of toenail off him, here under my arm. So that made the horn more than a pet. It was my date now, my affianced, my too long, too fat, straighttubed, comical and only big-mouthed girl. I smoothed her brown-paper party hat, in case the millinery police were out and looking.

The alley opens onto the town square. On your left, coming off the cobblestones, is Merrill's Music Mart, on the right, Bobby's Booze Bargains. It being after five, Merrill's, where a mouthpiece might be got, was closed. Bobby's was open, though. When I came out with a bourbon bargain, I saw this hotel, the Grand Commerce, red brick, plate glass, and hello, Edward VII, diagonally across the square.

As I was staring at it, a nasty little dream came true. An insinuating voice behind me said, "Looking for a hotel, buddy?" It was my wish turned dark-side up, a dear MP. They usually come in couples, which is sweet, and are Military Poleese, but this was a splendid, solitary, Sergeant Military Polouse. He wasn't there to make a pinch, though.

"Relaxed hotel? Everything your heart desires?"

"Everything I can't afford," I said.

"Try that one over there," he said, icky-friendly. "Do yourself a favor."

I nodded, in preference to extending the conversation, still pretty uneasy.

"You tell Pete, on the desk, Gatch sent you." He flicked his fingers to his cap, winked, remarked curiously that he would see me later, and went cophopping off.

So I said "Gatch" to Pete the Desk, who turned out to be of the purest strain of Southern shithead: "Wait till I'm damn good and ready, soldier, all right now, you pay me in advance, let's see some cash." When I had a receipt and a room key, I got Pete to admit that he was a Real Ace. He was pretty modest about it. I had to ask three times, the last time pretty firmly, before he'd agree to accept the title.

Maybe if I hadn't recommended myself by naming Gatch, Pete would have treated me more civilianly.

M. Mizzourin/**BOULEVARD OF BROKEN DREAMS**

Later, same room, same date, here laid I down my horn, here had the orgasmic pleasure of taking off my army boots. It felt so good I threw them out the window. I drank. I wrote. I went to sleep, and I was eating pearls with Pearl and emeralds with Emily when hunger woke me. I put on sneakers and went down.

There in the lobby, the Real Ace was gone, and the hotel restaurant was closed.

There was a thin, wrinkled, big-toothed and bright-eyed, natty old gent at the desk. A nameplate introduced him—COSMO SELKIRK— and our conversation went like this:

"Place to eat open someplace, sir?"

"San'ich all night. Crossup squayah, leavup cahthouse. Tansy's dinup." His accent is too marvelous to spell, and I won't try hard—old New England, loose teeth and a Carolina overlay. " 'F another discharge fella comes in, wants a room to share, should I book him in with you?"

"No, please don't," I said.

"Save you four bucks." He meant it kindly. "If you don't mind doubling up."

"I've been doubled up too long," I said, not mentioning troopled and squadroopled.

He chuckle-upped and said: "Wanta give me a dollup?"

"What for?"

"Case you git lucky out there." He held out another key. "This 'uns for the lobby door, outside. I stay back there." He pointed to a little room opening off beside the mailboxes in the back wall. "You come back lucky, might not feel you want to ring and wake me up to let you go up to your single room. Back steps for morning."

My turn to chuckle.

"Here," he said. "Take the key and keep it, don't say a word and never mind the dollup."

"Thanks," I said and took the key, and damned if the good old guy didn't try saluting. "Hey," I said, returning it. "You've got pretty good form there."

"Remember the Maine, and to Hell with Spain," Cosmo Selkirk said. "Have a drink."

I thanked him. We were alone in the lobby. I took a pull off his jug of Crab Orchard and asked if he'd fought in that one.

"Born Valentine's Day, '74," he said. "Was on the farm in New Hampshire when the spicks blew up the Maine. That were February of '98, and we didn't even hear about it till spring thaw. McKinley, though, he had a yellow streak. Put off declaring war till April, and that we didn't hear about till May. My Uncle Tod who lost his arm at Appomattox started drilling us, me and my younger brother, after chores. And Fatha said as soon as we got done haying we could go enlist. Come July, and Brother Billy met his Wilma at a picnic on the Fourth and changed his mind, so off I started, riding down to Portsmouth on the gray . . . you wanta hear this stuff?"

"Damn right," I said. "I love it." We each took another drink, and he told me, laughing at himself, that by the time he rode into Portsmouth, the war'd been over for a week. Came the First World War, and he was turned down for being overage.

I had a pocket full of service ribbons; I sorted out the one that goes with the good conduct medal and awarded it to him. He accepted, after a little argument, with more solemnity than the paltry thing deserves, letting me pin it on his brown alpaca cardigan, just above where the old, gristly heart bangs away.

When I got back from eating and checking the taverns (I couldn't find Fetlock), Cosmo Selkirk was asleep in the little room opening off behind the reception desk. He looked frail, sleeping with his clothes on except for shoes and socks, and I was glad he'd given me the key so I didn't have to wake him.

I'm ready for sleep now in 300G. What am I supposed to do for you, horn? Fluff up a pillow?

"The Boulevard of Broken Dreams" is a wonderful, mawkish song in which walk my favorite couple, Gigolo and Gigolette.

M. Mizzourin/THE BEST THINGS IN LIFE ARE FREE (12/30/45)

Standing behind the counter at Merrill's Music Mart when I walked in this morning with my no-name horn back in its sack again was an amazing young clerk, the only human male I've ever seen who could be called china-doll pretty. One of those antique china dolls.

His hair is ash blond, and he wears it in the first duckass haircut I've seen, outside of pictures in the Tokyo edition of *The Stars and Stripes*. He has great lavender eyes, brows darker than his hair, and a mouth in which the coral pigment is so bright, and the cleft in the upper lip so distinctly outlined, I thought for a moment he had lipstick on. His skin is tawny-pale, almost transparent. You feel as if you can almost see the X-ray shadows of his cheekbones. He's not a very big kid. He's probably seventeen. It was so spooky when the thought came that he might be drafted soon that I was very close to blurting out, *Goddamn, don't ever let them take you,* but I didn't say it.

Instead, took little bighorn out of the bag, put her on the counter, keeping a light hand behind the bell, and said, just like it happened all the time: "Say, I lost my mouthpiece."

"Well, I don't wonder," said the clerk. "You always keep yo' horn in a paper sack?"

"Sure," I said in a kind of *doesn't everybody?* voice.

"You'd oughta keep it in a case."

"You got a case?"

He shook his head. "I'm not even sure we got a mouthpiece for that," he said. "What is it, anyhow?"

He isn't exactly delicate-looking, just a touch unearthly. And won't they just find earth enough for this one in the chicken yard, if they get him there? It's a hateful vision, that boy in green fatigues, with horse-hung, regular army noncoms leering at him, training him, a vision that's still stuck right in the middle of my head, between the eyes.

I said: "Mind seeing if you've got one?"

"Case?"

"Mouthpiece."

"Mouthpiece for what? I mean, well what in the world is that?"

I looked away casually and muttered a word of which he was meant to hear only the final syllable: "Mmmduckasshorn."

"Why sure," he said. "I just never did see one afore." He smiled and fetched. "Well, here, we got cornet, trumpet and euphonium. Got sousaphone, well, for the high school band? We got us a ready high school band."

His effusive voice was pretty phony. I watched him mess around in a deep drawer that opened out of the back of the counter. I leaned over so that I could see into it. It looked like the place where mouthpieces go to die.

There were some new ones in boxes, but it was mostly old, tarnished pieces, and nicked, and scarred; silver and chrome and nickel and bronze, the washes and plating worn away to what base metal I don't know.

"Trade-ins," my sideblond burnboy said. "Well now, kin I find one, I kin git you a dollar off if you got a trade-in, too."

"Well, now, I swear to God, I just don't got one." It made him laugh, and he started trying various of the secondhand mouthpieces to see if one of them would go into the tube at the playing end of my horn. The cornet ones were tapered wrong, and the trumpet ones would just go in a little way.

"Just put it in a little way," said a smirky voice behind me, and I looked back to see a big, pale, flaccid, blue-jowled man around forty in a green-checked jacket, who had come out the storeroom at the back of the store and up behind me. He was wearing steel-rimmed glasses.

"E. B. Binkie Jones," he went on, speaking to the clerk, raising his voice to falsetto on *Binkie*. "Can I just put it in a little way? It won't hurt much, I promise." Then the green-checked, flaccid man went into an office off the sales floor, laughing, and closed the door.

My sideboy squeezed his mouth up tight and was trembling hard enough to make the flesh of his cheeks shake. The great, luminous, deep-set lavender eyes teared up.

I said: "E.B.? The boss, huh? Shit, man, it doesn't matter."

E. B. Jones turned loose his tightly-held-together mouth just long enough to say, "I'll kill him." Then he pulled the big showcase drawer all the way out, heaved it onto the counter in front of me, and ran. He went, obviously, to the washroom, in which dark sanctum, I could tell from the briny smell of food and stomach acids when he got back, he'd had to throw up.

By the time E. B. Jones resurged, purged of the urge to regurge, I'd sorted through some few of those mouthpieces and found one that by God merged. Stamped into the metal is the formula BACH 10½ C FL, which didn't mean a thing to me, but it slipped into my looted beauty like the last piece for a jigsaw puzzler. When I saw E.B. coming back, brighter and tighter-lipped than ever, it occurred to me to take this fitting mouthpiece out again and lay it aside, in with some others.

"You. You find anything?" he asked.

"Not yet."

"I sure am sorry."

"Sokay, E.B. Forget it."

"He makes me th'ow up purt near every day," the young clerk said. The accent had lost class. It was pure hillbilly now, and I liked it better.

"Maybe one in that pile there will fit," I said.

"Purt near every day, talkin' or grabbin' at me." Odd. It hadn't occurred to me to suppose E.B. really effeminate before he said that, so much as young and Southern. Now I began to wonder. Meanwhile, he was picking up mouthpieces from the little pile I'd made, trying them, sorting through. "Sometimes, what he likes to do is knock, just with his knuckles light on the washroom door whilst I'm apissin, and he'll knock and just stand out there breathing till I just can't help but puke and then he laughs . . . hey, look. Hey, lookie here." Suddenly he was smiling. "Hey, sojer, look."

He had it, BACH 10½ C FL, snug into the horn.

I grinned back and said swell, marvo, goodney, and how much?

E.B. looked over at the office door, gave it a vicious, corkscrew finger, and handed me the mouthpiece. I shrugged, smiled, put it in my pocket, and I swear it was still sliding down to the bottom when the office door opened. I looked over at steel glasses and green checks rippling toward me.

Why do I remember his clothing in such detail? I can't say. The pants were brown and baggy, the shoes brown and dull, and he wore a yellow sport shirt with a white Peter Pan collar, spread and spaced around outside the collar of the jacket. His face looked ripply now, as if I could see black, close-shaved beard undulating, trying to grow back out through the pallid flesh.

He held my eyes for a good long beat before he said: "Well. Getting what you crave, soldier?"

"You haven't got it."

He came over to look. "Hey, boy. Flugelhorn? You need a mouthpiece, do you?" He reached.

Flugelhorn?

I didn't like it being him who told me what I'd stole. I said, "No, nothing," and I moved the horn away. I didn't want him pawing at it.

He didn't. Instead he changed the direction of grab and circled the young clerk's wrist. E.B. snatched his arm away, blowtorched.

Greenbeard churgled and said, in his soft, suggestive voice: "Where did you get that flugel, soldier?"

"Pawn shop," I said. "And I'm no damn soldier, anymore."

"What pawn shop was that?"

"The one your mother runs to Friday nights," I said. "To sell her ass for muscatel." It was my fear reaction. It's about all you learn in the army: when you're scared, hit. He was reaching again for the instrument, and I said, "Leave it the hell alone."

His voice got really soft, which was really scary. "I kin get you a mouthpiece," he said, and it sounded about the same to me as it would have if he'd whispered: *I kin call us a policeman.* "High school band director's got one extra, gottit from me, I know he did, so you come back now in the morning, hear me?"

Yes, I heard, me and my flooted lugelhorn. There were no sirens in the streets, but we wanted to run away together. Still want. Can't. Even though we've got an okay mouthpiece now—on which I've huffled hard and cannot get a piffle out of yet. Oh, little horn of Faraday, I want to leave here now. Want to go and look for New Year's Eve, dear, anyplace but Carolina.

So why don't we pack up and go?

Because when ripply flaxxied back into his awful orifice, the translucent, coral-lipped kid with amazing eyes, who had given me a fresh-stole mouthpiece for my fresh-stole horn, grabbed my hand. E. B. Binkie Jones did that, he grabbed it tight in both of his and asked me urgently: "What's your *name?*" It was a goddamn plea.

"Mike," I said. "Mike Mizzourin," and couldn't get my right hand loose unless I'd fought him for it with my left.

"You gotta come back tomorrow, Mike," he said. "That's what he wants."

"Why?"

"He's got some reason. Listen, if you don't, he'll know I give you that mouthpiece for yore duckasshorn."

"Let me pay for it," I said to E.B. "Tell him you found it after he went back into his wretched office." E.B. just clung. "It's a flugelhorn," I cried. He clung tighter. "All right," I said, and got my hand back. "I'll be here."

M. *Mizzourin*/FASCINATING RHYTHM (12/31/45)

But then this morning, in my letterbox, there was a note on the back of a blank sales slip from Merrill's Music Mart: "Can't get you mouthpiece till after dinner. Come 4:30."

Gave me a lot of time to buy a Parker 51 pen, a couple of legal pads, and do this writing. I bought shoes, too, moccasins, and ran into Fetlock at the shoestore. So finally we had our beer together. He was tactful, didn't ask about the horn. I walked him to his train. Our first and, I would guess, our only beer, bye Sarge.

When I went in to the music store, about an hour ago, E. B. Jones was exactly where I'd left him yesterday, standing behind his counter, staring over it at me.

He tried for a smile, but I could hear him sigh a little as I greeted, waved, winked and went, horn in sack, the first mouthpiece now left behind at the hotel, into the office where the green-checked man was waiting. Only today his jacket was a different shade—kelly green, maybe?—with blacker green in flecks instead of checks. Today's shirt was unbelievable. Orange and sort of hairy with bone buttons. His cheeks were still loose, the shaved area still dark and undulant, the glasses' rims black today and somehow wet-looking, like reboiled coffee.

"Hey, come in," he said. "You brung it." It seemed to make him happy.

His office is small, with one little window about head-level that opens into the same alley that I traveled yesterday. Green was sitting behind a desk of golden oak and had a chair set out in front for me. He said: "Yes, yes. You brung it. Give it here a minute?"

I stood there staring at his orange animal of a shirt, shook my head *no*. He reached into one of the desk drawers and took out a little box.

"Looky here." He passed the box back and forth from one hand to the other, flipped off the lid and let roll out on the desktop a silvery mouthpiece like the one I'd left back at the hotel, but much, much shinier. He picked it up and pointed it at me, and his voice seemed hardly there. "Now looky, if you got yourself already one of these, gonna be one that you and little Binkie found, found yestiddy, that right, all right, b'lieve there was one, 10½ C, I'm halfway sure, this here's a 7, you gotta sales slip there?" Slurpy the Urp man spoke it, just like that, and just like this: "Got you a sales slip, sure you do, from that ol' pawn shop where you bought the flugel you was saying, sure you do." He kept rolling his new mouthpiece back and forth from hand to hand across the gold desktop. "Now they's a pawnshop here in town, but just the one, and he don't b'lieve he sold no flugel, didn't yestiddy, nor ever in his life." There came a nutty shift into pathos. "Hey, boy, been try'n to buy me flugelhorn, this war, and things so hard to get, these metal things they make'm into shell fire, bang, bang, it's all gone like you should know, look here: now I got this one part, and you the other."

"My part's not for sale." I said it sharply, trying to cut the mood. "How much for yours?" Time for the stickup, anyway. He could hold that mouthpiece on me, now he knew what way I'd got my horn, and I'd pay any price he named. Then he surprised me:

"Gotta different idea, wouldya trade, wouldya trade it though, wouldya listen, wouldya want . . . ?" Bastard was practically singing as he reached behind himself down to a shelf, swung a case onto the desktop, opened it. Lovely and shining, nestling there in blue-green felt, there was a perfect little horn, the petite and darling, kid and shimmering sister of my fat and tarnished flame. "This sure a nice cornet by Olds, the finest line they is, and best they make, look here, she got the trigger, got the slide, the quick round change to A . . . now wouldya try it, wouldya want it . . . ?"

Oh yes, I wanted. Its valve caps are mother of pearl. More than a trumpet, more than a countess or a Packard car, I wanted. "No," I said.

Greenbeard's smile went wise. He put the cornet to his lips, he looked away, toward his little window, and played a short, meditative phrase of blues, paused, and added another, twice as long, slow and soft with quick hard edges. Then he repeated the pair with hard and soft reversed, added a new phrase, medium speed and pretty, and collected it all in a logical cascade of double time. But then. Then the bastard retarded his resolution to a last linger, and oh, oh God, it was coming out so sad and gold, like a gauzy girl in sunglow putting flowers on a soldier's grave, and I wanted him never, never to stop playing.

Yes, I yearned for an instrument with sounds like those, and Greenflecker smiled his flastid smile, and slightly moved the burnished cornet toward me. I sat down then, but hugged big silly tighter.

Green took off his blacks and showed me dark, hurt, naked eyes. I guess he knew he had me moving.

"Hey," he crooned. "Hey, now, know anythin' at all 'bout that psychology?" It could have been the starting of a vocal to what he'd been playing.

"Huh?"

"Psychology thought maybe, you been to college, sure."

"Psychology thought maybe junior college just before the war," I said.

"Long time and let me tell you wish I had and look: I bet you thought I shouldn't say that thing I said to little Binky yestiddy? You thinking that?"

"Your business. Jones did mention he might like to kill you, though."

Greenbard smiled. "Sensitive, ain't he?"

I kept my smile to myself.

"Now that's a little country boy, E. Binkie Jones, from way back up the hill. Picks country guitar pretty good, and sing those country high sweet songs. Got him a girl now, that surprise you?"

"Why should it?"

"Well, seems like sometimes he's about half girl hisself, you didn't notice?"

I stood up again. I thought about squeezing out between the sandbags and looking for a foxhole, where I could be by myself.

"Now wait right there, horn. You studying up that junior psychology in college, might you could set me straight. Might be you'll tell I'm doin' wrong, but listen first. When E.B. was a little fella, his bad, biggest brother Marvin, see, these boys my nevviews?" He stood the little cornet on its bell, caressed its pearly valves, revolved it slowly so it threw off light. "My sister's boys, now don't you see, an' fatha died? Big Marvin's kinda bad, now see, he'd come home drunk, they's poor, lived in a little hutch out there, so then the boys slep' in the same bed, an', well, Marvin'd get in there, well, and drunk, just like I said, with E.B. now, and turn him over."

"What?"

"Turn him over, put it to him, and here's just the thing I think, now maybe you can hep me. E.B., he's just that shy. I've gotta push on him like a stalled car to get him to go over there and play a little for the public, sing a little, there at Rhombo's. You been to Rhombo's? Now Binkie's gettin' straight, an' gonna be all right, an' I'm his uncle, here's the thing I'm hoping now: You say E.B. oughta pretend all that with Marvin never happened? Ain't it psychology that E.B.'s gotta say, hell yass, that happened to me, face it and forget it, and cuss out ol' drunk Marvin that's in jail now, anyway, and E.B. just go about his guitar-picking business? That's why I bring it up, see, say I'm right?"

"No," I said. "You're wrong. The way you do it makes him puke."

"It does?"

"I think you'd better leave the kid alone."

"That's right?"

"It's damn right," I said.

He stroked his chin. He halfway nodded. Then he smiled a new, beard-shadowed, pale green smile, hangdog and winning, laid the cornet in its case where it kept burning at me, and said: "Need a Fake Book, doncha? Say, tell me your name now, willie please?"

"Willie Please," I said.

"Come on now, and sit down?"

"Mike," I told him, and sat.

He nodded and winked, as if *Mike* was the name he expected and perfectly all right with him, too. He got up and went past me to the office door, opened it as if to make sure no one was listening, closed and locked it. "Fake Book?" he whispered. "Got one to go with yo' horn?"

I didn't have the slowest motion what he meant, and I'm sure it showed. Everything I feel shows on my idiot face, but the green slick man pretended to ignore it. "Bet you don't, horn. Been in the army all this time, maybe lost it, kinda forgot it, but you'll sure remember how goddamn illegal it is, won't you?" While he did this verse he was unlocking a drawer in his desk, he was getting out a fat book, 8½ by 11, with a brown, light-cardboard cover in a spiral binding. He flicked, and it slid toward me, stopping just under my nose. "Touch it? You can go to jail."

I didn't touch it. I read the title: *VOLUME ONE of over 1000 songs . . . for professional musicians and is not intended for sale to the general public.* "If you say so," I muttered, wanting to open it.

LIMITED EDITION—PROFESSIONAL USE ONLY—PRICE $50.00

I touched it. I opened it to page 63. There were the choruses of three songs on the single page: "A Little Bit of Heaven," "Pretty Baby" and "Prisoner of Love." The melody for each was written on one staff of treble clef, with the words of the lyric below it: *"Alone from night to night you'll find me/ Too weak to break the chains that bind me . . ."* Up above the staff, in abbreviation, were the names of the chords—Fm7, B♭7, E♭, C9—placed over the note of melody where the harmony would make each change.

"Now if you know you chords," the man was crooning, "you kin fake 'bout any song you'd ever want to play from just this one book here, just like you had the whole dang score. Here's four-five lines of music and those chords. Make you arrangement for entire orchestra, just build it up. Why ever' little band they is has gotta have their Fake Books, else they'd have to buy that sheet music, pay those royalties, now you know that. . . ."

I might never have heard of the Fake Book, but I'd heard of the copyright law, and I understood Greenboo's dramatics. Still it was nothing like fear (I turned to page 176, where I saw "Cherry," "Chicago," "China Boy"), nothing like fear that made my pores pump cool and the body hairs stand up. It was pure thrill, as if he'd handed me a working book of magic spells. These are the songs, shallow, silly or sentimental, every one, but utterly profound in the depth to which they can stir memory, revive hope, promise beauty. And they are the songs, still more important for a nut like me, of jazz—the canon of jazz, like Homer to Greek tragedy, or the nut who wrote the chronicles for Shakespeare's history plays.

"Mike, Mike, name me a song," the madman said.

" 'Ja-Da'."

"Turn to 190." He said this in a tone so close to reverence that if he'd added "Let us pray," I might have hit my knees.

Page 190, yes. "I Would Do Anything For You" on top, and "Jazz Me Blues" below, with "Ja-Da" in the middle.

"Ja-Da." Oh, didn't that green-flecked shit play "Ja-Da" on his low-cut Olds cornet? It is not right to play "Ja-Da" fast, nor did he. It is played as if it were a ballad, in such a way that the nonsense words *("Ja-da, ja-da, jing, jing, jing . . .")* sounding in your head become the poignant echoes of lost meaning, and you feel the loss. If "Oh, Didn't He Ramble" is taps for the funeral of a negro jazz musician, maybe "Ja-Da" would be taps for the funeral of a white one, but the green and flaccid bastid didn't give me time to think of anything like that.

"You name a song now," he said urgently. "You name one."

" 'Ghost of a Chance.' "

"You turn to 21 now, Mike. You turn there."

But he was playing that sweet, strange song before I found the page, vaporizing it into a tumble of rending sounds, like perfect paper tearing perfectly as he came out of the release, and he had barely finished before the cased cornet was in one of my hands, the Fake Book in the old paper sack in the other, the flugelhorn in Greenland, and me, Mike, on my way out of the office, the door to which I heard him close and lock behind me.

I stared at E. B. Jones, still standing behind his counter. I was too dazed by the music to think who he was at first. E.B. was staring at what I carried in my right hand, looking a little dazed himself.

"He didn't ever," E.B. said.

"He what?"

"That there. It's his cornet you got."

I nodded.

"I heard the playin'. God almigh, he give you his cornet."

"I guess. We swapped . . ."

"Swapped you? God almigh, he must. He must'uv wanted. That some kinda horn of yourn."

I started coming to then, and said, "He might quit riding you."

"Riding?"

"E.B., he's your uncle."

"Yessuh?"

"He told me about your brother."

"My come again?"

"Your brother Marvin, who's in jail."

"God almigh."

"You've got a brother?"

"Got just one sister's all, my twin. Hey, he's been—"

"You don't come from a little hutch, way back up the hill?"

"Lived here in Faraday, my whole dang life."

"You don't play the guitar and sing?"

"He's been telling you his lies."

"At a place called Rhombo's?"

"He sure can mix'm. Yessuh, I do play at Rhombo's. Nossuh, I don't sing at all. Play with a trio, and my sister sings. We twins."

"Country, high sweet songs."

"Suh?" He shook his head. "Nossuh. We try to swing."

I shook my head. "E.B.?"

"Suh?"

"You know anythin' at all 'bout that psychology?"

That ended it, pretty much, though he did tell me that Rhombo's is just down the street, they'd be playing New Year's Eve tonight, crazy place, maybe a l'il bit rough, but why didn't I come, maybe ten o'clock? Git me free drinks, he said, and hey, bring horn, that cornet there. Come on, sit in, they'd sure be free drinks then.

I said thanks, I wasn't hurting for money.

"But you bring it, no one care. Gonna be fun."

I smiled. "See you later." I said, backing away.

"You gonna sit in with us?"

I waved, glad to know of someplace to go. I faded out the door, like the ghost of a chance, like ja-da, like a prisoner of love. I turned toward the hotel, but as I went by the entrance to my familiar alley, onto which Green's window opened, music stopped me, music pulled me; up alley, under window, it was "Georgia on My Mind." Nobody had to tell me it was being played on flugelhorn. Nobody had to tell me who was playing it, trombone mellow in the trumpet range. Bye, Fluge. All's fair. The lover she deserved had won her from me.

"Georgia, Georgia, the thought of you . . ." There was no blare to it, no bite, yet the notes were all complete and clean, just an old sweet song, round on the ends and high in the middle, and as I listened I thought it was the soldier, after all, who held pale flowers, and that he'd search forever for the lost, wild grave of the gauzy, sunglow girl.

Another chorus started, ineffable. It was as if the notes were thoughts, and the player polishing to clarity each one, sliding them through the smooth, dark tunnels of the flugelhorn, out the little office window, into the evening air. I opened my cornet case, took the little beauty out, put in her short, sweet mouthpiece, closed the case. Set it on its side on the cobblestones, against the stucco wall, under the small high window, and sat down on it. I opened the Fake Book to the index, found my number in the dusk, turned to page 182, and raised the horn.

"Georgia, Georgia . . ."

Pressed the mouthpiece to my lips.

". . . the whole day through . . ."

And then, pushing down one valve, now two, now three at random, whispered into the cornet one small puff of breath for each of the green man's notes as they floated out above my head, pretending I could play.

"Deke Esterzee's office. Darlene speaking."

"It's Charlie. I'm going to come a little late."

"Oh, doodlemuffin. I can hold back, too."

"Jesus, I do leave myself open for stuff like that, don't I?"

"Yes, dear."

"I want to finish some reading."

" 'kay. You got messages. Suesue confirms. Lunch next Tuesday, twelve-thirty."

"I'll put it on the calendar."

"Can you wait that long?"

"I'll try, Darlene."

"She says call her if you like. What would you like to call her?"

"Dear friend and gentle soul. Anything else?"

"Lots. Here's one Deke dictated on the WATS about an hour ago."

"What happened to the tape machine?"

"The A-reel set screw came loose and fell into the ancillary Tebbett drive. Darling."

"Read it, please."

"Minute. Okay. 'Charlie. Greetings from Calder Prairie, yore dad's hometown, where a Democrat's 'bout as welcome as hog cholera. Foundation in Des Moines is organizin' uh big fuckin' conf'rence here . . .' Am I getting the accent right?"

"Beautiful."

"He didn't really say 'fuckin'.' I put that in for verisimilitude."

"A little less verisimilitude would be okay."

" '. . . conference here they're gonna call "America's Future." ' They got me on a panel talkin' about land use and regional planning. That's just two weeks from now, so I'll be with you soon, and then out here again, but you know who's going to plan regional with me? Uncle Ned Mizzourin, bo.' "

"Wow."

"Who said you could interrupt? 'Hadda fella drive me past yore family farm early this mornin'. Frost on the ground, and snowbirds hoppin'. Patches of white in the corn stubble. Guess Ned don't believe in fall plowing, or maybe he was runnin' his pigs in the stocks this winter. Nice big white wood house, on the edge of town now, that used to be out in the country. I took a picture for you.' "

"Isn't he a lovely man, Darlene?"

"Deke Esterzee? Charles, grow up."

"Read the rest."

" 'Heard yore granma was librarian in town when yore Dad was growin' up. Took a picture of the library. Fella who tol' me is the county chairman didn't come to Calder Plain till after the war. Even so, heard tales about the wild Mizzourin boys, but not Pete so much. Ned and Mike. Pete's the baby and the sweet one. Says the whole town's real worried with the way Pete's come up missin'. County Chair don't like yore Uncle Ned much. Thought I might pay a call myself on yore behalf, but I'll be seeing Ned out here in just two weeks. We've seen each other through the years at different meetings, but we're just eyeball acquainted, so far.

" 'Here's what I want now. Spose you'll piss and moan and make all kinds of excuses. Still, I want you to come out here bout three days before the meetin' and advance it for me . . .' "

"Lovely, Darlene. Consider yourself hugged."

"Funny, I don't feel a thing. Shall I read the rest, or are you too dizzy?"

"Let's have it."

"Want you to see a man named Chester Brinnegar. Investigator. Did some good work for one of the crime committees. See can he stay loose till I get back, might have some agribusiness crime for him to work on for my subcommittee. Had another elevator fail west of here, just yesterday. Something called triticale's involved. New kinda grain. Want you to find out all you can about it.

" 'Right? Now. You see that corn-sweetener lobbyist, Darlene's got his phone. See can he get us tickets for North Carolina State-Hoyas, Friday week. Be sure he lets you pay, and stay loose in the hips and tight in the butt, and I'll be there fore game time.' Got a pencil?"

"Sure."

"614-3561. Corn sweetener."

"Thanks, Darlene."

"I called Brinnegar for you. He stopped by. He'll be back at eleven."

"Is he working on something else?"

"Available."

"Anything more I ought to know about him?"

"He's got class-seven clearance, a semistrangulated hernia and a little brown mustache."

"That'll do."

"His wife is overweight and his daughter's anorectic."

"Glad I asked."

"I'll have a file ready, if you ever get here."

"Thanks. Any more messages?"

"A little number with a British accent, named Roxanne Talley. You're supposed to phone."

"What's it about?"

"She said social, passion pup. Hands across the sea?"

"I've never heard of her."

"Hulloo?"

"This is Charles Mizzourin, calling Roxanne Talley."

"Oh yes."

"Is that Miss Talley?"

"I should think."

"I have a message here to call you. About a social matter?"

"Whoever is it again, please?"

"Charles Mizzourin."

"Oh. Oh yes. Of course. Terribly sorry. I thought it was quite a different chap. Now, then. We're to meet at lunch, at Suesue's, did you know?"

"No. I guess I didn't."

"Don't sound so bloody enthusiastic."

"Sorry."

"If it's a tête-à-tête with her you want, I can quite simply bow out, you know."

"Of course not. I look forward to meeting you."

"That's a bit better. Now, I thought you'd like to know . . . are you quite sure you weren't dreaming of seeing Suesue alone?"

"Frankly, there's a private talk I hope to have with her some time. She knows about it. It can wait until she's ready."

"I see."

"When she's ready, I'm sure she'll let me know."

"Meanwhile, you've no private objection to meeting me, is that it?"

"Sorry. Was I offensive?"

"Oh, not at all. Not in the least. How could you be? Shall I say why I wanted you to ring up, Mr. Mizzourin?"

"Yes, please."

"Unless there's some pressing private matter you'd rather attend to."

"I said I was sorry."

"I thought you might bloody well like to know that Tuesday's Sue-sue's birthday."

"Thanks. Thanks. I'm glad you told me."

"You're ever so welcome then, aren't you? Goodbye."

CLICK

"Goodbye, lady."

Calendar

FRIDAY, MARCH 5.	BANK. SERVICE BIKE. PACK. RENT CAR. TO MORGANS-TOWN.
SATURDAY, MARCH 6.	WEST VIRGINIA WHEELMAN'S DOUBLE CENTURY. START 10 A.M. NORTH LOOP. M'TOWN TO PARKERSBURG.
SUNDAY, MARCH 7.	SOUTH LOOP. P'BURG BACK TO M'TOWN. DRIVE BACK. RETURN CAR.
MONDAY, MARCH 8.	A.M. LIBRARY. LUNCH: CHESTER BRINNEGAR. P.M. WRITE TRITICALE REPORT.
TUESDAY, MARCH 9.	DEKE GETS BACK. LUNCH: SUESUE.

" 'lo?"

"Deke."

"Hey. Is that you, Charlie?"

"Thought I better call in. Welcome back."

"Good to be off the damn airplanes. Hey, you get the basketball tickets?"

"Safe in my desk."

"Knew you could. Hey. Tell me where you are. I'll call back in a little."

"Someone with you?"

"Man from Justice, telling about bankruptcy law. They gonna help us draft something. Maybe. Your Brinnegar boy waitin' with Darlene for next, but listen, we got things to talk about, you and me. Where you callin' from ?"

"Deke, it's lunch hour."

"I know that. My stomach knows that. What we don't know is where the hell you're calling from."

"Well. I'm at Suesue's."

"Suesue's?"

"Yes, Deke. Darlene could have told you."

"Heyhey."

"We're just about to have lunch."

"Lunchlunch."

"Yes, damm it."

"Need to talk to you 'bout Calder Plain, bo."

"What?"

"When you come in. 'F'm still here. Meantime, leave that number with Darlene, just in case."

"I'll make excuses here, if you want me back."

"No. I don't know which ten things I'm going to try to do next, anyway. You enjoy your lunch. I'm gonna switch you. Hey, Darlene. Pick up. It's Charlie."

"Okay. Hey, Charlie."

"Hey, Darlene."

"Listen. Deke's come back pretty upset. Things got rough out in the district."

"All right. I'll cut it short over here."

"No. He'll be gone. He doesn't know it yet, because I've been holding calls. But CBS wants him for a news taping."

"The grain elevator hearings?"

"No. They know he's just back from a trip home. They want to know about farm belt support for Carter's handling of the hostage crisis."

"Is Deke ready for the taping?"

"Bob's done a position memo. Joannie put some phrases in."

"Deke will take it with him, mislay it, and be himself, like he always does. Should I go to the studio?"

"No. Back here, and hold his hand when it's over. He dictated a long memo for you about the trip. I'll have it typed by the time you get back."

"Okay."

From: Deke
To: Charlie
Halfway confidential. I don't want people here getting twittery about this stuff, so let's leave Bob, Joannie, and the rest out of it for now.

Here's what happened. You know Stuart who runs our district office. Stuart meets my plane in Des Moines, four in the afternoon. Says somebody called in to tell him I'd be on a later flight, but he checked the airline and knew different. Had a fella with him called Tobert, from the Prairie States Foundation. We have a drink at the airport bar. Tobert tells me his foundation's putting on the big conference I told you about, called "America's Future." They got governors, senators, a couple of cabinet guys; they got state and country-wide TV, big newspaper coverage. They've picked Calder Plain for it, in my district, because of its size, Midwest location, mix of agriculture, education and light industry. And they can use the junior college campus, because of spring break—auditorium, eating facilities, guest houses, meeting rooms, hookups. Will I be on a panel on land use, planning, controls, that stuff? Probably. We could have talked it over better if some operator in California hadn't kept paging Tobert to the telephone and then cutting him off.

Stuart drives me down to Walkerville where I used to live a peaceful life, coaching and teaching social studies, when Bobby Kennedy got shot and I decided politics had got to be my game. Had dinner there with constituent friends. Okay? These friends are going to see me later where I'll be having open house in my motel room, the Galway Inn. Don't expect a big crush, but Stuart's talked with several said they want to see me. Nobody comes. Not one. Stuart goes to the lobby, comes back with the local paper. Mystery explained. Right on page one, it says: Esterzee's switched to the Holiday Inn. Stuart gets out a copy of the release he sent to the paper from his briefcase. Release says open house at the Galway. Who changed it?

Who told the motel desk, saying it was me, to hold my calls? Good thing I got that straightened out, of course, because I finally do get a nice call at 2 A.M.

"How can you walk around with your head stuck up your ass, Deke?"

Hung up before I could explain how I do it.

Morning, Stuart goes to the newspaper. They told him it was my office changed the place for last night's meeting, calling from Des Moines. Thing is, I don't have an office in Des Moines.

While Stuart's there. I'm on a radio call-in show. Opened up talking farm credit crisis, bankruptcy, grain elevators. Then a little bit about Iran, and asked for calls. Later they told me the switchboard was totally lit up before the program started, people holding and waiting.

First question:

"Mr. Congressman, don't you think we gotta stop this dirty sex education in the schools? Do you support my right to sue the school board?" Said anybody's got a right to go to court, next question.

Next was how come I enjoyed abortions so much? Then gun control, how would I like to have some maniac shoot me and not be armed myself? Then a guy asking me if I favored Fidel Castro—I couldn't figure out for which office.

So nobody's worried about losing his farm, right? Or wants to hear the latest on the hostages, right? Wrong. All those calls were planned to tie up the lines for anyone that really wanted to talk with me. All out-of-town calls, too. Operator couldn't say where they came from.

Afternoon, Stuart and I are able to guess where the calls came from. Been announced I'd be at Joe Leffert's Cafe, Joe'd put out free coffee, two to four. Got there and found the place knee deep in pamphlets on single-issue shit. Joe said a guy dropped them off and spread them around, saying they came from me. "Your Right to Bear Arms." "Your Children's Right to Pray." "A Woman's Right to Be Female." All printed up by something called the New Freedom Publishing Group, address, Calder Plain, Iowa.

Things go a little better next day in Saranola, except the Sunrise Optimist Club, where I had that prayer breakfast—they'd been phoned and told they'd need to get a different speaker. Luckily, they checked with Stuart and knew I was coming for sure, but they did get nervous. So did I.

Felt kind of nervous too in the next town, Islington, where right on Church Street a fellow jumped out of a big, black car at me, shouting and swinging fists, and of course you can't blame him for it, seeing as I want to murder unborn babies and not even let the poor little fuckers have guns to defend themselves with. That's when I'm not busy making young girls go into the army and sit down in the john with leering, rapist soldiers.

Darlene says I have to tell you that this angry fellow explained the above while I had him caught in a bear hug. Then he bit me on the shoulder. He's a well-known, semiharmless local nut, but I got tooth marks, and the big, black car went tearing off soon as they let him off the leash.

Damn story made the news. Next day in Welford, the county sheriff meets me and wants to know if I'd like a deputy to babywalk me up and down the street. There's been a phone threat. This one they could trace. Came from a pay phone in Calder Plain. Well, nobody showed up with a bomb, but someone did start the electric bells ringing in the high school when I was trying to talk to the assembly there. Drowned me out, and hell, the kids thought it was a signal for the next class anyway, so they left. And naturally, when I had my evening meeting, making a dedication speech for the volunteer fire company's new engine, somebody set fire to an abandoned barn out in the country. There I was, standing on the hood of the new engine—they about drove it out from under me and took half the audience riding away.

Next day I send Stuart down to Calder Plain, to see what he can find out.

Things have changed in this country, Charlie, since your Dad got out of the army. Darlene says I should get to the point, but I've been waiting to say this to you—it's the kind of stuff I start thinking about on an airplane, when the fat lady in the next seat goes to sleep, and the stewardess leaves off two Bloody Mary's. Your Dad would be a man of sixty now. I wonder how he would have liked what's happened? I was a boy then. Things were a little rapid after the war, but people surely meant to slow them down. They were confident under Truman and then Ike, and they were getting things together. They figured other folks were rational, good-hearted, sometimes mean or weak, but mostly okay. What I'd have to say is, starting with Lee Oswald blowing away Jack Kennedy, this country started to go irrational, and life's got evil. Or maybe it started back with Hiroshima and took a while to catch up. Creeping preposterousness. Instead of good, old original sin, which could get baptized away, we got into existential guilt, which you can't even get psychoanalyzed away unless you're rich, and probably not then, either. From a country that would elect Truman and Ike, to one that went for a bright, religious nut like Carter, and is going to get itself a dumb, movie-actor nut next; well, you're the historian. Are we in a tailspin here? Is there a pilot in the plane?

New Freedom Publishing Group, Stuart found out, is a busy little bunch. The new free publisher himself's a guy named Blair, got canned from being junior college dean for the things he tried to make his teachers teach. He's got a steel building on the highway outside Calder Plain, ten employees, printing presses, a phone bank, and a bunch of new group groupies. They raise money around the country, do mailings for cash flow, but to start out, Blair had to have a backer, and he did: your Uncle Ned put up, Stuart heard this, twenty grand.

Publisher Blair's also got a sister, name of Sister. Sister Blair is state vice-president of Right to Life, registered lobbyist against ERA, and used to be an evangelist. Say she can shout pretty good. Say she may be fixing to run against me in the fall.

Another thing Stuart heard about your uncle: four years back he resigned as Republican district committeeman. This spring, he's got the job back again. Now, Calder Plain's a Republican town, but it's been moderate, good old Bob Ray boys like John Lucas, who ran against me last time. Now John never called me anything worse than a red communist traitor, and I have never called him worse than a heartless skunk lackey of the plutocrats, so we're pretty good friends. Day before I got to Calder Plain, I called up John to ask him what was happening.

He didn't sound too comfortable, but he did mention that he doubted he was going to run again. He was one that mentioned there was a woman making politician noises, Sister Blair.

That night Stuart and I drove into Calder Plain late, and guess what? Our reservations at the motel were canceled, and it was all filled up with a convention of the Western Iowa Gun Idiots Association. They showed me the written notice to cancel my reservations, too, and it surely looked like it was written on my office stationery. You had to look pretty close to see it was a Xerox of the letterhead, with the message below blanked out so they could write in "Please cancel," and it damn near took a magnifying glass to read the signature, which was Minnie Mouse.

That's why I was staying with the county chairman when I drove out to your family's farm next morning. It was quiet and innocent there early in the morning, and it got me all calmed down, so I felt maybe I was seeing just a bunch of bum-luck coincidence after all. Then we got back to the county chairman's house, and while I was talking to you in Washington, Stuart was trying to get through to tell me all the air's been let out from the tires of the car we were driving. Made us a little late for our next appointment, which was Meet the Young Democrats at the junior college. They were all back in class by the time I could get there. There'd have been an indoor picnic at the Elks next, if the three-bean and potato salads hadn't got themselves dressed with turpentine.

Here's the final thing: remember Tobert, from the Prairie States Foundation? I called him late that awful day and asked him to tell me really why they picked Calder Plain for their big meeting on the American future. He started in with "small midwestern city" again, and I said, "Come on," and he said, well, there was a year's planning went into this conference. They had a profile of the kind of place they wanted, and sent it around to the different chambers of commerce for bids. It was your uncle made Calder Plain high bidder, getting the campus for them rent free. Nothing wrong with that. It'll be nice and picturesque for television, kind of slender, old brick buildings with white wood trim. You think it's where your father went one time?

But here's what else they did: chose all the local people for the different panels, moderators, chairs. Well, Sister Blair's chair of the Future of Women panel, and Publisher Blair Future of Communications, Ned's on my panel, and on and on and on. Nestor Holcomb, he's a right-wing evangelist, that's the keynote speaker. What I'm saying is, this turns out to be the kick-off of the fall campaign, and the other guys win the toss with a two-headed coin. Here it is, early April, not even primary season yet; well, of course, a Congressman starts running for reelection the minute he sees his opponent on TV making the concession. But you don't expect to be in the high middle of it eight months before election day.

So Tobert says: "Do you want to change your mind about appearing, Deke?" He knew all along I was getting sandbagged.

"Hell, no," I said. "I'll be there early and stay late."

Charlie, I'm mad. I'm hellbent to get back there for the shouting match, if that's what it's going to be, and there's a few on our side, and I'm sure of my topic. Federal land control's got to come. Look at this. The credit crisis, and the farm auctions. Speculators, developers, damn fool farmers themselves, helping inflate land prices to where a man that's got to have more land to farm, because of high overhead on big machinery that can't stand idle, is paying $2,500 an acre. You can't make taxes and interest on a $2,500 acre with rates where they are. Cost it out. We've got to start saying this: Prime farm land's a natural resource to be protected by federal law, and when I say it, I can guarantee the shouting's going to start. We've got a big speech to write. We've got heavy briefing to do.

So I need you right here in Washington now, not Iowa. As far as advancing for the conference, turns out that's what the other boys have been working on at least six months. Stuart's moving the whole district staff into Calder Plain right now to organize, talk to the press, call our people in to the meetings, check the rooms, check out the other panelists, and try to catch up. People there know Stuart and Stuart knows the ropes. You're too good a pro not to see that this would be just the wrong time for me to send you away.

"Studio Twelve."

"Congressman Esterzee, please. Charles Mizzourin in his office calling."

"Will you hold?"

"Sure."

" 'Lo, Charlie."

"Good God, Deke."

"You mad, bo?"

"Everything in the memo makes me want to get out there for you."

"I'm truly sorry, bo."

"Deke. I'm glad you want me here to work on the speech and the briefing. And of course Stuart's people have to do the advancing. But when we're ready, I want to go to that conference with you."

"Knew you'd say that. And I'm still sorry."

"Why the hell not?"

"Kind of a conflict of interest, wouldn't you say?"

"You don't want me on staff? Give me a week's leave. I'll pay my own way out."

"I know how you feel. You're my best starting player, and I tell you you're benched for the big game. Charlie, I know you'd handle yourself fine. It's Ned that worries me."

"I want to meet Ned, too."

"This how you want to meet him? Backing the other side in a brawl?"

"I'll take the chance."

"You're being reckless, Charlie."

"If I'm not worried about hurting my own cause, what harm can I do yours?"

"We got two different kinds of business with your uncle. Yours is family and friendly. Mine, well. I'm not going out there looking for a fight . . ."

"But you don't want to hold back if it comes."

"I don't want to be stopping and thinking about you."

"Damnedest conflict of interest I ever heard of. You going to be safe, Deke?"

"Yeah, bo. I plan to."

"I hate to see you go this way. Stuart's not young, and you'll have to take Joannie, so there'll be a woman."

"County Chair's got sons played tight end and nose guard for Iowa State."

"Screw it. All right, Deke."

"Thank you, Charlie. You'll get to Calder Plain for us soon enough."

"All right. Let's move on."

"Gonna be a long campaign."

"I said, let's move on."

"Okay, well. You read your new stuff yet, from Johnson?"

"Figured I'd save it till we got this over."

"How was your lunch?"

"Some things happened."

"Like what?"

"I've got to sort it out. One good thing, I got a terrific new apartment."

"Hey, how come?"

"Tell you later. It's quite a place."

"When you moving?"

"Tonight if I want."

"You got stuff to do there at the office?"

"Plenty."

"Report to Johnson?"

"For one."

"Hang on. I'll come by when I'm done here and pick you up. We'll get dinner and I'll help you move. Just clothes, isn't it?"

"Clothes, stereo and my two bikes. I've got a rack for them. Give me a call when you're ready to leave, and I'll be down on the street waiting."

"Deusnospickleus, Charlie."

"God preserve us, Deke."

Notes for Report to Johnson on Lunch with Suesue:

1. *The gray Continental, I.* Parked opposite when I rode up on bike. Late model, midsize limo. Appeared empty. Thought there might be other lunch guests already inside. No other guests inside. Later learned two male occupants: the driver, probably in front; Otis Hibben (dairy lobby, ex-Senator) in back. Both apparently ducked out of sight when they saw me pedaling around the corner, with my bicycle pannier sprouting yellow roses.

2. *House and furnishings.* House four stories tall. Reddish-brown stucco front. Row house. Larger than I remember noticing the time I first dropped Suesue there. Wasn't noticing that day. What the hell am I noticing for now?

   Five steps up, street to stoop. Wrought-iron picket fence and rails, pickets suitable for bike-chaining. Vietnamese maid answered door, Suesue on stairs behind her.

   "Darling. Right on time."

   "Happy birthday, Suesue."

   First floor: corridor, stairs up on left. Enclosed basement steps underneath them. Cloak room on right, opulent half-bath (doublesink, marble, beveled mirror, stall with oak door).

   Past all this: corridor ends at double-doors, opening into dining room. Didn't go in. Could see oval, walnut table, silver candlesticks, twelve (re-pro. Fr. antique) chairs. Beyond dining room, I was told, are kitchen and small suite for maid.

This is a rich person's house.

Suesue, wearing blue, explained, accepting yellow roses and peck on cheek: she bought the place cheap years ago, before the neighborhood was revived and got classy again. She said it took a long time to finish the restoration and remodeling.

I said: "I have a pretty good idea how long. I helped remodel big old houses in St. Paul and Minneapols for a year or two."

"Darling, you didn't!"

"Getting the woodwork right is what takes the time, isn't it? Other stuff, like wiring and plumbing, you can just rip out and replace."

What I didn't say: what's been done on Suesue's house generally costs about twice what you buy the house for.

If I were estimating? If it was as run-down as she says, mid-seventies prices, $60,000 to $70,000 worth, including decorating and furnishings. But Alternate Contractors never did one this lavish.

Stairs up have oak steps and risers, gold-carpeted, white and gold painted bannister, gold tassels on the newels.

3. *Suesue is wealthy?* Yes.

First floor all one long room, more French antique repros., room so large there are various seating groups strung through it. Put me in mind of the lobby of an elegant little European hotel. We sat first at the street end, by voluminous drapes, and the maid served Pernod and hors d'oeuvres from a little bar-pantry, halfway back in the room where the stairs come up. Lunch (later) was at the garden end of the room, where the drapes were open, and we did overlook a little garden, but there's nothing out there to see this time of year except some dwarf trees. Suesue projects a Japanese garden ("But won't someone buy me a Japanese gardener? Charles, do you do landscaping, too?") Next flight up, she sleeps, dresses, and has guest rooms. She told me. I didn't go up.

"I've hit my thumb with enough hammers to turn it every color there is, but never green," I said.

"Are you a wonderful cabinetmaker?"

"No," I said. "I haven't the patience. I do know a guy—"

"But maybe I could use you," Suesue said. It was then the doorbell rang, and she said, "Oh, here's Roxie," and got up to go to the stairs and partway down.

"May I make a quick phone call?" I asked.

4. *The gray Continental, II.* I was on the phone, first with Deke, then Darlene. As I hung up, I heard a brisk, British voice say:

"Whom do we know that's driven in a large gray auto?"

Suesue came past me, pulling aside a drape, and looked out at the street.

"Never mind," she said. "It's leaving." But she kept watching, and said back over her shoulder: "Charlie, this is Roxanne."

Looking directly at me, backlit from the rear windows so that I didn't really see her face, was a young woman.

5. *Snakebite for Charlie.* I walked toward her, and she toward me, and all I really registered were huge, dark-blue eyes.

As we met, she said, and by now the voice was making me shiver: "Is your name really Charlie, like our prince?"

"Yes."

"Are you a prince?"

I held out my right hand, and she grabbed it with both of hers, looked at me and sucked in her breath sharply, and I was gone. Tingling. Breathless.

"I wish I were," I said.

Dammit. All we did then was look at one another, while she kept hold of my hand, some kind of deep, dumb look into the eyes. I guess I mean dumb-speechless, as much as dumb-dopy. We were still standing that way when I heard Suesue say: "Looks like it only went around the block, dears. It's back now, and to hell with it. Let's have lunch."

6. *The new apartment.* It was Vietnamese food, on white china, and it was probably very good. I don't remember. Roxanne Talley and I kept catching one another's eyes, and staring.

Suesue was amused, chatted along about this and that, and I was paying so little attention I don't seem to have realized that she was offering me an apartment.

"I've some other houses, Charlie," she was saying. "Including side-by-side twin houses in Georgetown Made into floor-throughs. Roxie and her roommate live in one. The vacancy is in the other."

"They're quite lovely flats," Roxanne said. "I knew the chap that's just moved out of yours."

"Mine?"

"Idiot man," she said. "Haven't you just told Suesue you'd take it?"

"I can't afford a flat in Georgetown."

"Haven't you just heard Suesue say the rent's the same as what you're paying in the rooms you have now?"

"I don't need a deposit," Suesue said. "No rent until the first, but you will help take care of things when you have time? Would you like more wine?"

"He would not," Roxie said, covering my glass with her hand. Slender hand. Then she took it away, in case I did want some. "Charles, you sot. It'll be four hundred a month. Unless you prefer not to live next door to me?"

"Come along," Suesue said. "Let's show it to him, Roxie, come with us?"

They exchanged a glance. Then Roxie shook her head. "I must work," she said.

"Shall we drop you?"

"I'll wait and finish my coffee, if I may, and then take my own cab."

"Yes." Suesue nodded, considered, and nodded again.

"Quite independently of you both."

Suesue smiled and said to me, "We'll need a big cab to get your bike in the trunk."

Roxie had signaled for an intermission, a little relief from the soap opera in pantomime we'd had going all through lunch. For the first time I was able to look at something besides her eyes.

Tanned face. Short, yellow-brown hair, curly. Not very tall. Looks taller because she stands very straight. Wiry. May not weigh much over a hundred. Nice teeth, small hands and feet. Small waist. Proud bosom. Wearing a dress that a fashion-model's son recognizes as high-fashion-simple (one of those things with a sailor-suit collar). A mobile face. Exquisite ears. You want to take one in your mouth.

7. *The gray Continental, III.* It wasn't in sight when Suesue and I hailed the cab, and I certainly wasn't aware if it followed us to the apartment building on Q Street. What a place.

The twin houses are brownstones, each narrower than Suesue's house, each a story taller. My apartment is on the third floor of the eastern house. I don't know which floor Roxie and her roommate have in the western one.

I now will have, if this isn't some nutty dream: a living room, with nice, mostly leather furniture. A little study with desk, Eames chair, studio couch. A big bedroom at the rear. Twin three-quarter-size beds. A big kitchen, with a dining area divided off by a mahogany counter, a gas stove, new refrigerator, microwave, disposal, dishwasher. A maple table in the dining part that seats six. Rugs, not carpeting (Chinese). Some paneling, also mahogany, in the living room and study, and bow windows overlooking Q Street. My god, Deke doesn't have as nice a place, and he pays seven-fifty.

I said, "Suesue, I love it, but you can't let it go for four hundred."

"A union carpenter's eighteen dollars an hour, Charlie. Electricians get twice that much. Anytime you fix a leaky faucet or relight a hot-water heater, it'll save me fifty dollars."

"You have to let me set aside a couple of weekends a month for maintenance then."

"Any way you want to do it, but why don't we just let people call?"

"Are there other buildings, besides your house and these two?"

"Oh, but I just want to use you here, dear. There'll be enough, don't worry."

Sure, lady. If there's a catch, I don't guess I want to know about it.

The gray Continental was smack in front of the house when we came out on the stoop. The steps to the street are quite wide. Standing on the bottom one, glaring up at us, flushed very red and sweating in the frosty air, was ex-Senator Hibben, the dairy lobby man. Behind him, standing by the car, was a uniformed chauffeur.

"Goddammit, Suesue," he yelled.

"Otis."

"Why didn't you return my phone calls?"

"I'm doing business, Otis. This is my new tenant."

He came up one step closer, and the chauffeur moved a little toward us, too.

"You promised you'd let me know when that apartment came up."

"I want a man in the apartment, Otis. You're drunk."

"How the hell do you know I haven't got a man?" He came on up to our level now, puffing. "Answer me, how the hell?" He raised a hand. "Answer me."

I stepped in front of Suesue then and said, "Hello, Senator." He caught me across the throat with a beefy forearm, and my damn glasses flew off.

I couldn't see anything much but blurs, then, but I felt Hibben trying to push past me. I ducked my head and grabbed him under the arms and wrestled him aside. He smelled awful.

"Where's Angeline?" He was yelling, or that's what it sounded like.

I heard Suesue yelling back: "Is that the trouble, Otis? You nasty, drunken old sonofabitch . . ." She was in a real fury at him, and trying to push past me to take a whack at him. I think the chauffeur was halfway up the steps by then, and I heard Suesue, in a very different voice, calm and sharp.

"Police car, boys."

Suesue backed off. I let go. Hibben turned toward the street. Suesue handed me my glasses. A prowl car had cruised to a stop beside the limousine, and there was a cop looking out the lowered window at us.

Everything stopped. Suesue smiled and waved at the cop. "It's all right," she called. Then to me: "It's all right, Charlie." She took Hibben's arm and said very pleasantly, "Come along, Otis. Let's go for a drive. Come on."

And left me standing there with the apartment keys in my hand.

How much of this do I tell John McRae Johnson?

"Hulloo?"

"Roxie? This is Charlie Mizzourin calling."

"Angela here. I'm Roxanne's roommate. Whom shall I say?"

"Charlie Mizzourin. Roxanne and I just met today. Is she there?"

"You're not the first to confuse our voices, you know. Hold on, please."

"Good evening, Charlie."

"I'm glad I had your number. I thought you might want to know about the gray Continental."

"Oh, yes. Did it reappear?"

"It was a drunk, following Suesue, I guess. A dairy lobby man named Hibben?"

"Monterrey Jack?"

"That what he's called?"

"So very many names. Yogurt Otis is another. Senator . . . What, Angie? . . . Oh, shut up. Sorry, Charlie. She knew another name. We know of him, you see. Rather notorious."

"What was the other name?"

"It's quite improper. Where are you now?"

"I wonder. He might have mentioned Angela."

"Not likely. Where are you then?"

"At the office, waiting for my Congressman. Practically no one else in the building."

"Shall I nip over with a tot of gin?"

"I wish you could."

"You've work to occupy you?"

"Something to read. A report to write, but I probably won't start tonight. What else do you know about Hibben?"

"Not much. Oh, I know he's quite good-sized, isn't he?"

"He's huge."

"Right, then. There was a cartoon showing him as an enormous bull 'For Contented Cows.' Just a moment . . ." (Pause) "Hulloo, Charlie? Angela's just told me that she does know Hibben, and she's seen you, too."

"Me?"

"Not long ago, at the Willard Bar. She was with Hibben and a diplomatic chap. You were with Suesue."

"Is Angela redheaded?"

"Ginger do you mean? Yes."

"Is Suesue in business or something with Hibben?"

"Now what do you mean, 'or something'?"

"Involved. In a personal way?"

"Charles that's a very rude question. I should think there's no involvement of any kind whatsoever."

"Sorry."

"You're forgiven. Shall you be coming to your new flat tonight?"

"I think so. Deke's got his car. He's offered to help me move my clothes and stuff.''

"Would you care to drop in for that gin, then? Pardon again . . ."
(Pause) "Will you be here by nine, do you think?"

"I'm afraid not. It's already eight."

"Because Angie's just reminded me, we're to take supper with a chum
who's being married . . . Angie, do shut up . . . so we shan't be here
after nine."

"I wish you were going to be."

"I, too, Charlie. Soon then. It's just next door. Of course, you know
that. The fourth floor. What is it you're to read now? Political bosh?"

"Maybe I'll tell you sometime. The other line's flashing. I suppose
it's Deke."

"Cheer-o, then."

"Thanks. Goodnight."

"Congressman Esterzee's . . ."

"Okay, bo. I'm still at CBS. We're done taping the interview, gotta
play it back and edit."

"How'd it go?"

"I'll see in a minute. Felt good. Getting hungry?"

"Half-starved."

"I'll be forty minutes. Then I'm gonna buy you a lobster, give you
an idea what your Uncle Ned looks like."

"Good. I'll eat his claws. Deke?"

"Something on your mind?"

"You know anything about ex-Senator Hibben?"

"A lot of people eat his lunches. Say he's an old fart-hound, but he
probably knows where the good bones are buried."

"He's got these dairy nicknames. Yogurt Otis."

"Butterfatso."

"Do you know of one a proper English girl wouldn't want to repeat?"

"You got a proper English girl?"

"Met one. She'll be living next door."

"There's some calls him Whippin' Cream. Only, it's Whip *and* Cream.
That help you any?"

"I hope not."

"What's the news from Carolina?"

"I'm just looking through, about to read. 'And the Angels Sing.'
'Am I Blue?' 'Almost Like Being in Love.' You know those songs?"

"Last one's a show tune. 'What a day this has been/ Dumdumdum

mood I'm in . . .' Get me out of this dumb mood and into a vodka
tonic, will you?"

"Hurry over."

"You'll have time to read your pappy, bo. Make a copy for me."

Last Deadline Ranch

Charlie, my boy: you have a friend or, as she might prefer, an auntie in Chris-
tine. It is at her insistence that I hurry along these pages of anacreontica (a
word, sir, not a coinage). I do not, you will be relieved to know, permit Chris-
tine to peruse these passages passed on from me to thee, and yet, to parry her
proboscothrusts, I do impart particulars in precis. For myself, I read along just
ahead of you as time permits, ordering those things which may not be clear.

Thou shalt not edit, sayeth Christine. As well forbid the owl to hunt by
night, the wolf to groom its cub, the hippopotamus to bathe, say I. There are
no pencils but blue pencils, and with them was I born to attack the infelicitous
word, the infidel phrase, the infiltrating disorder of event, the infinity of the
erroneous and the erratic, the purple and the puny, the turgid and the tawdry.
If you like it not, you like me not.

In spite of which—for do not e.g.'s of all of the above abound in the ff.?—
my hand has been lightness itself in dealing with this ms. Remember that your
father was working from a running account he'd kept from day to day, and
sometimes hour to hour, as these events occurred. The account was in longhand
on legal pads. He was typing it up, presumably editing himself, at a much later
date. Since your purpose is to know the man, and mine to have you do so, I
have let his work stand. In this installment, he gathers wool to weave a fine
noose with which to hang himself. I have prefaced it with 1) a copy of the cover
of the "Fake Book." You should understand that there've been other Fake
Books since, reprinting newer music, but this was the original one, or in your
father's words, the "great" one, 2) the first page of its index, with a holograph
notation by your father. We have been told (by a hypnotic voice, from
what distant past?) how a musician could use this to "fake" any song as if he
were reading from completely scored music.

Read on. Mizzourin's New Year's Eve of 1945–1946 begins. We hum
along with him from "And the Angels Sing" through "Smoke Gets in Your
Eyes," from pondering poetaster to prancing popinjay, condoning (can we really?)
his severe case of cryptoycleptomania, i.e., a passion for bestowing titles of
obscure relevance. Read on. I am pleased to feel confident, even as I seal this
up, that your essay, "A Landau Luncheon, or Suesue's Sumptuous Salad,"
will cross it in the mail.

Your Devoted Dutch Uncle, John

VOLUME ONE

(REVISED)

OF OVER

1 0 0 0 SONGS

This collection of popular music has been compiled
to furnish a compact library of the most requested songs
for professional musicians and is not intended for sale
to the general public.

THIS IS THE INDEX TO THE GREAT FAKE BOOK, BOOK OF
THE GREAT FAKE LIFE WITHOUT WHICH REAL LIFE WOULD
BE UNBEARABLE.

M. *Mizzourin/*AND THE ANGELS SING(12/31/45)

. . . *the Great Fake Book, book of the great fake life without which real life would be unbearable.*

Come on, sucker. What's it supposed to mean?

It comes out of a meditation provoked by my fine old desk clerk friend, Cosmo Selkirk. I was coming through the lobby excited, carrying my acquisitions from the magic music store. Except for Cosmo behind the desk, there was no one around but the MP sergeant, Gatch, the one who directed me to this hotel. Gatch appeared to be reading a newspaper. He waved big at me and started to get up, a haberdasher's dream of elegant accessories—spit-polished paratrooper boots, extra-wide belt in matching leather, white whistle-cord, and a garrison cap with the fashionable hundred-mission crush. I waved back small, eyes away, and hurried by.

At the desk, Cosmo grinned and beckoned. "Been out shoppin', Mike?"

"I just stole the crown jewels," I whispered, showing him my cased cornet and hundred-mission paper bag.

"Come on." He led me through the door behind the desk, into the little room he sleeps in. He sat on the cot, took the cornet out of the case, and said it was a wonder.

"But here's the thing," I said, and showed him the Book.

"What is it, Mike?"

"All the songs I grew up with. Danced to. Fell in and out of love to, eight or ten times an evening." Derivative, superficial tunes and mindless lyrics, that's the stuff. Nobody ever fell in love to real music or real poetry; they demand too much attention.

Sitting on his cot, Cosmo took the Fake Book and placed it on his lap, hand on the cover, shook his head and said: "There was a song like that."

"What, Cosmo?"

"I had songs like that."

"Everybody does when they're young, I guess."

"One special. It wouldn't be in here. These'll be newer songs."

"What's it called?"

" 'My Sweetheart's the Man in the Moon.' " Still he didn't open the Book. "New Year's Eve tonight, Mike. Seen sevenny-one of 'um."

"Yes."

"The best and the worst was forty-seven years ago, when I was twenty-five."

"When 1899 changed to 1900?"

"Ninety-nine to double-ought." He was a rising young assistant manager of the McHester Square Hotel in Boston and had charge of the ball that night. There was a pretty young girl there with her family, whom he'd met not long before: Grace Brookes. "And I'd dance every dance I could with Grace, and git the band to play it. Then I'd ask her, like she was just a little girl, 'Who's your sweetheart, Grace?' In time so's she could sing it back."

" 'My Sweetheart's the Man in the Moon.' " I took the Book from him gently and looked through the Ms in the index. There are thirty songs starting with the word "My" in the Great Fake Book, but Cosmo's isn't one of them.

"No, it isn't here," I said. "How does it go?"

"I can't remember, and I can't forget."

"What happened with Grace Brookes?"

He shook his head. There was a kid stabbed in the hotel billiard-room shortly after midnight that night, an Irish gang matter. The victim died in Cosmo's arms, and it was dawn before everything could be cleaned up and straightened out. He remembers waiting outside for the horse ambulance, and can still see it "coming through the fall of snow, drawed by a team of dapple grays that looked like falling snow theirselves, with gas lamps in the blowing snow behind, Mike boy . . ."

I felt as if I could remember that myself.

Because he'd known the boy slightly, Cosmo was fired. He'd have called on Grace, otherwise. He'd started to feel a little bit serious, but he was out of a job. Best job he ever had. Sweetest little girl.

"That man-in-the-moon song," Cosmo said. "For a time I didn't want to hear it played. But later, anytime I got to drinking, then I'd ask for it. Six or seven years went by, they didn't know it any more."

I'd opened a pint and we drank from it. "Wish I could hear it one more time," the old man said.

I guess there was a tear, and that is what I mean: "without which real life would be unbearable." It was a real tear, but for a song, not for real sorrow—it only felt that way. Tell me it's not a blessing that the facile emotion brought on by half-memory of a fleeting tune can let a man off from confronting what he cannot stand to think about.

So I look through the index of the Great Fake Book, and my songs are there, songs that bring greeting-card sadness, tinsel joy, jellybean satisfaction, crocodile regret. How could we live without them?

For some reason all this got me thinking of my brothers, without one of whom I can live just fine. Big Ned Baby, the only family left at home in Iowa. If I ever do see Ned, and I suppose I will sometime, we'll hug once, tie each other up, break dirty, and come out fighting, as we always have. And I'll get myself creamed, as I always do, because he'll always be bigger and have that natural good punch, and I have a natural hard head and won't quit.

I heard just once from Big Ned Baby during the whole damn war, while we were island-hopping in the Solomons. We were worn down thin as onion skin—Christ, I'd actually forgotten this. Ned sent a power-of-attorney he wanted me to sign, so he'd be free to borrow working capital against the farm. There was even a mushy little note with it. Sure, Ned can be charming when it suits him. Three years after I'd gone away: "Dear Brother Mike . . ."

I dear-brothered him good. I signed the damn document, only because Pete already had, and wrote my own mushy note: "Dear Edward Mizzourin, Jr.: I trust this will enable you to pursue your important endeavors, so essential to the national effort. It's good to have people like you behind us. Sincerely yours, Michael Mizzourin, Pfc., A.U.S."

Suppose I shouldn't have. Suppose I wouldn't have, if Mom'd been home, and where in the hell is the old lady, anyway? I mean I know she's running a U.S. information library in Paraguay, but where in hell is Paraguay? This war's been one big, jolly, rascal spreader-out of your dopey family—Dad in Hawaii, a CPO forever, Pete in Alaska with the Seabees still. I will get a place in New York, I think, where Pete can stay with me when he gets out knock, knock.

Knock fucking knock?

Killjoy was here.

*M. Mizzourin/***AM I BLUE?**
>At the door
>Was a whore
>With a sergeant, wanting d'argent,
>Nothing more.

At the head of his troop, like a true leader, was Gatch, the Military Pleasema'am.

"Hey, buddy," he said, twirling the garrison cap around his finger, dazzling me with the brilliance of his hair and teeth. "You should have stayed in last night."

"Hi, handsome." Milady was standing a couple of steps back in the corridor. She looked blond and tubercular in the dim light. "Wanta have a party?'

("Your hospital room or mine?" I didn't say it.)

The harlot's pimpernel smiled and oiled his vocal valves. "Don't mistake my uniform. Consider me the bellboy from room service." Gatch, the hotel hawker, director of traffic to the Grand Commerce for petit mal, a little sexilepsy, Gatch is the Real Ace, after all.

"Wrong room, Ace," I said. "I didn't order any."

"Don't get it wrong." He laid a hand on my arm, nodding back toward his merchandise. "I only put the baggage in the room. The baggage handles the tipping later on. You don't owe me anything but thanks."

"How about no thanks?" I said, and pushed the hand away. Gently, of course.

"Asshole."

The whore said: "Don't waste my time, Gatch," and he invited her, with his well-known, instinctive courtesy, to shut up. Which prompted me, with my well-known, instinctive gentleness, to explain how I had mistakenly identified someone else as the Real Life Real Ace, which title the fine sergeant was willing to accept without false modesty, due to the caressing action of the door against his shiny paratrooper boot.

They left, and I'd been somewhere that I cared to be, dreaming of New York, meditating on the songs youth owns. I want to play them all, the few that are jazz, and all the rest as well—the ones that bring nostalgia, that idiot addiction to a sweetness that never was. Which can't be altogether true. The color of fool's gold is still golden, and there's a poignance in the evanescent charm of ordinary songs, mirrors of the evanescent beauty of ordinary girls, sincerity of ordinary boys.

Aren't these three things precisely worth the world's forgetting because they stay so little time, all replaceable by the next girl, next boy, next song? Isn't that why youth must always own the music?

And if there really was a charm, a beauty, a sincerity, these qualities of boy and girl do fight to live on, don't they? Won't you kiss me? Can't you trust me?

As for the song, it's as if it, too, has a strange little soul that whispers, more and more faintly to those who loved it once, please sing me, hum me, play me, please, or I will die.

M. Mizzourin/ALMOST LIKE BEING IN LOVE

Reverie time was over. It's hard to focus thoughts, to make a channel that confines the old, meandering, backwatering stream of consciousness. Often it's best to let it go its way and see what floats up. Like this:

I'd picked up the horn for the tenth time and tried to get a sound out of it. According to the GI Bill of Rights, the Veterans' Administration was obliged to buy me music lessons and pay me twenty bucks a week while I learned to be a brass man. It seemed a sorry joke so far, because each time I'd held the cornet to my lips, blowing, puffing up my cheeks, snorting into it, I'd get no more than a kind of echo down the tubes.

And was that Gatch out there, pounding on the door next door? The Real Ace, with his Queen of Hearts—I tossed the horn down in exasperated frustration and made fists. I was about to open my own door and yell, "Quiet, goddammit," ready to back up the request, when a voice from the not-too-distant past floated up, a cockney voice saying, as if it were the most solemn profundity:

"Don't never 'it a bloke you wouldn't want to kill."

Kill Gatch? No, Billy, not tonight. I smiled. *I think I'll take a shower instead.* Billy was our hand-to-hand combat instructor when we retrained in Australia—if bayoneting folks were an Olympic sport, Billy would have been Jesse Owens: "Thrust, withdraw, parry, and swivel your gun-butt into 'is privates." In the shower, I soaped my privates and laughed, remembering what Billy taught me that was better than the butt-stroke: rhyming slang, a code, when it goes fast, like any rebel language.

In place of *wife* you say "trouble and strife."

I put my tit-for-tat on the Cain and Abel means "I put my hat on the table."

Then there was one that explained a great, old word-mystery: Why do we say, "Give him a raspberry," also known as a Bronx cheer? Give up? Well, sir, what rhymes with raspberry tart?

How do you imitate one? Purse lips, thrust tongue, withdraw buzzing—I made one in the shower and Yessirree Billy! That wet and soapy-headed fellow me was in Eureka. Gave himself a stinging butt-stroke for being so slow to catch on and ran, leaving spongy footsteps on the old carpet of the room, grabbed his cornet, shivering with chill and huge anticipation, pursed lips, pressed the horn against them, drilled in the tongue, razzed and withdrew, and out it came—one raggedy, round, distinct note of brass music.

I laid the cornet down in awe, still shivering, and shook my Thomas and Ted, knowing the first principle of art: that it, too, rhymes with raspberry tart.

Went back to the shower, cleaned off, glowing, got dressed, and had me a horrid little stumble and stink from my pint of brown and frisky, took a couple more razzes on the glad I was born, skipped down the trouble and cares to:

The Grand Commerce Cafe.

Where I laughed down a cup of soup and grinned my way through a pork tenderloin sandwich on a great speckled bun. It came with an ice cream dip of lyonnaise potatoes, tenderly browned; a slice of translucent dill pickle, cut the long way; a cup of creamy slaw; brisk leaf of lettuce; round of pink, white-grained tomato; and a gorgeous, thick, white slab of onion. Since Cosmo Selkirk had wished me luck, I ate every bit on the white, oval plate—crumbs, seed, bulk and fiber—all but the waxy, moist, the cellular onion.

My waitress noticed. She bears a little nameplate on the bosom of her greenish-yellow uniform. The nameplate is rose-colored, and the gilt letters proclaim her Hazel. This same nameplate, Lord, rises and falls like prayer with her breathing, and she is young, and delicately overblown, with a burst red tulip for a smile, an upsy sort of daisy nose, and bluebell eyes.

She bloomed at me, picking up the little oval platter on which the isolated onion slab now shone all solitary, absorbing part of the light, while the porcelain surface around it reflected back the rest.

Waitress and goddess, Hazel gazed on this white still life, asked softly, "Who is she?" and slewed her eyes to meet my own.

I caught my breath and bowed my head, hardly daring to feel *this* lucky.

"Come on," she said, closing the tulip to a bud. "You can tell *me*." It wasn't what she said, or even the way she implanted the final word *me*, that made my skin flitter so. It was the way the petals of her free hand brushed the left side of my neck under the brutish and defenseless ear.

"Ne-wah," I said, to open my devotions. "Uh, new, wah, town, mean discharged-charged . . ."

"You sure you're all discharged?" hummed this naughty Hazel nymph. "Hey, what's your name?"

I thought it might be Mike. I tried adoringly to tell her so.

"Wah-Mike," she mimicked me. "You want to have a New Year's date?"

Did I wah? Did I wey? Did I wih, woh, wuh, wen? Ecstatically worshiped me.

" 'bout your room? 'bout mi'nigh'?"

"Hazel. Do you? Don't you? Want to go out, out somewhere, somewhere first? 'bout Rhombo's? Know this guy . . ."

"Workin'," Hazel said. "You write your room number on the . . . *tip.*" Boy, can that Hazel finish a sentence. The way she lipped the final word would have got music out of a ram's horn, and I don't think anyone would have had to hold the ram.

Funny thing, though. Pencil won't write on a fifty-cent piece. I'd intended no greater measure of homage for my three-dollar check, but would not any sinner sacrifice a wholly green for the cultivation of Hazel's garden?

Repenting, and unfurling a bill, I watched her swaying off, turning to look back so that I could see all the flowers of her face bloom at me once again. I wondered if I could buy champagne someplace, or, if not, what else might feed her roots instead. Sunny whiskey? Refreshing rain of gin?

I used her very own ravishing little stub of pencil, that she'd left beside the check, to write "Room 304" across George Washington's brow. Smiling looked I up, and frowning down to cross the number out, for there my Hazel was, four tables off, flittering shit out of a couple of artillery corporals, and back into my head came rhyming slang: her educated stay and lingers were causing visible vibrations on their oh-by-hecks. She was standing right between their tunes and airs, flittering in the short GI-haircut fuzz above the khaki collars, doing both these scuts at once.

So if I was on for 'bout mi'nigh', when might their minute waltzes be on working Hazel's New Year's dance card?

The air went out of my lungs, the tickle out of my groin, and the sparkler out in my head, its steel core dimmed to afterglow. I'd already had a tenderloin between two halves of speckled bun and didn't care to be one—I've been a sukiyaki sandwich, and a kangaroo sandwich, and a pineapple sandwich, and what I want now is just a little piece of heart.

So: I retrieved my Terry and Tuck, thinking she was probably look-

ing for five more like it anyway, put out two quarters, poured me a
nice little touch from my pint, down into the water glass in my suddenly quiet lap, and drank it down. And my drinking song was a sur-
prisingly cheerful chorus of Bach's little B-minor caprice, though I'd
forgot the Latin of it:

> Hear all ye people,
> I shall not dance
> The prepaid poontang polka
> On this joyous night.

This got a new sparkler lit off the heat in the steel of the old, and I rose
up and saw, sitting at the table nearest the door, the slick-haired sergeant, Gatch himself, commanding a cup of coffee.

M. *Mizzourin*/SMOKE GETS IN YOUR EYES

Bearing no chocolate fudge, I tipped him a clatter and clink.
"Hello, shithead," said Gatch.
His obdurate hostility quite thrilled my endless ass, and so I stopped.
"Why, it's the Real Ace," I said.
"I don't think you'd better say that again."
"But why not? It's true. You are the Real Ace, and it's a terrific
privilege to tell you so."
"Fuck off."
"Hazel!" I said. She was going by, and it seemed presumable they'd
be acquainted. "Isn't Gatch a real ace? Aw, look at him blush."
He started to rise up. She looked, scared, over a biggish lady, all
yellow kitty cats on the big black dress, standing over at the cash brass
register. "Gatch!" Hazel said.
"Hazel wants you to sit down, Ace," I clarified politely.
He tried to drill me. I stood at ease. He reached into his pocket, got
out his MP armband and showed it to me, in case I'd forgot, half under
the table. I reached into my pocket and had a ribbon there, Pacific Theater
with three battle stars to show him. So we considered one another's
validators, and he said his was taller.
"I'd recommend a nice, quiet evening, asshole," he said. "I work
real close with the sheriff here."
"Why that's the sweetest story ever told," I said. "I know you'll be
very happy together."
"I can make civilian arrests, jerk. I've been deputized."

"That must have hurt," I said. "But I'll bet you were real brave about it."

And went out, delighted, into and across the lobby, where I cried out to my wise and wrinkled friend: "Cosmo, Cosmo. I am out of the fucking army for the whole, wonderful rest of my life."

For Cosmo kept wishing me luck, and army guys were the unlucky who had to pay unlucky Hazels in the Real Ace world, over there in the dining room behind my back. My sparkler was going strong again. "Would you drink to freedom?"

Cosmo Selkirk said: "You know that Gatch? I saw you talking."

"He was working the upstairs earlier."

"Bother you?"

"Gatch?" I laughed again. "I pushed him out of my room, all but one foot. Now you going to have a drink, or do I have to stand on your foot, too?"

"Just want you to know, I ain't supposed to keep him out of here, but I don't take his kind of money, either. You get him mad at you?"

I shrugged. Cosmo frowned. Then he beckoned me back behind the counter, in through the swinging panel. I kept the bottle low when I handed it to him. The lobby was leaping with loafers and lookers.

He lowered the pint and held it still. He said: "You like to read?"

"It's my main sin," I said. "But I don't plan on committing it tonight."

"Want to give you something, Mike," he said. He slid my bottle onto the shelf under the ledge of the registration desk, went into the little room where he sleeps, and was gone a couple of minutes.

I watched the traffic. It wasn't really paying me much heed. It was flowing toward partyland, upstairs, in fits and starts. There must be service guys in every room by now, and not a man without a bottle in a bag.

Cosmo came out pretty soon with a round, white box of heavy cardboard, muttering that he'd once had a fine top hat that fit in there. He set it on the floor, lifted the lid, and brought out a leather-bound book. It's a glorious thing.

Nothing among the fine editions in the little library Mom tended back home comes close to its luxury. The leather is soft and shimmery, so brown it's almost black. There's an egg-and-dart border, filled with gold, tooled in all around the edge of the front cover and inside that a curious, repeated design of bones and curlicues. In the center is a stylized Roman warrior in profile, with crested helmet in gold and green, the visor up to show his long, imperial nose. On the spine the letters are blurred, for the volume seems far older than its keeper, but one makes out, also in green and gold: SHAKESPEARE'S WORKS★★★ *Titus Andronicus.* The edges of the pages gleam with gold, and the covers are held together with a gilt, slide-and-snap fastener of antique design.

"That's a beautiful thing," I said.

"Here. Open it up. In my time everybody read him, claimed they did anyhow . . ."

He offered me the volume. I checked to make sure my hands were clean.

". . . country people in the winter, city folk and preachers . . ."

Taking the book carefully while he talked, I put it on the counter between us, where it was lustrous in fluorescent light. I undid the fastener, and the top cover sprang up with a whir and a hiss. A black and gray snake jumped straight at me, wiggling, from inside.

I yelled and threw myself backward, out of the way, and Cosmo went off into such hoots and spasms he could hardly talk. Finally he said, "Durn. Oh, durn, Mike."

"God, that's real." I leaned down to pick up the snake from the floor, and it wiggled and buzzed and felt so alive I dropped it again.

" 'Tis, too," Cosmo was still wheezing a little. "Stuffed young timber rattler. You not mad?"

"No," I said, starting to laugh. "Just scared to death, you old scoundrel."

This time when I picked it up, I managed to hang onto his snake and hand it to him. He folded it in thirds, put it back in the false book, and closed the covers. The lining in the box is lilac colored, watered silk. Keeping a hand on it, he looked at me and said: "We was talking about that Gatch."

"You made your point."

"I 'uz gonna give this to you anyhow."

"What?"

"This snake book."

"You can't do that," I said. "It's a work of art. But thanks for a warning I'll never forget."

"It's yourn, Mike-up."

"Thanks," I said. "But no. I can't."

"Had it since the las' time I ever went home to Hampshire," he said.

"In ought-nine, to my fatha's funeral. This was the only thing he had I brought away." Stroked it. "Made by a neighbor called Levi Hand, that was old even when fatha was a boy. Make anything. Here now. I want you to have it."

"Let's drink to that," I said, opening the pint and handing it to him. "But people collect things like this. They pay good money. Probably should be in a museum. Anyhow Cosmo, you enjoy it."

He shook his head. "Never know if I'm gonna laugh or cry myself to death these days. Jokes change. Was young. People had things like this, play on each other. Thing was see how slick yore pitch was, fool your friends . . ."

"You sure did me." It occurred to me to read the spine again. SNAKESPEARE WORKS is what it really says. *Bitus Andpanicus.*

"But now today, people won't take a joke like that. Get mad. Not you, I knew you wouldn't, so you take it, Mike. Please, now. Just promise you'll remember who made it."

"Made by Levi Hand," I said. "Gift of Cosmo Selkirk."

Foolishly solemn, we shook hands, and I moved the book in front of me.

"Got some more junk to give you," Cosmo said. "Here." He lifted the white hatbox onto the counter. "Shame the toppah's gone. You'da looked good." Then, from inside the box, he took out a black silk cummerbund and a black bow tie. "Wanna wear these?"

"Damn right," I said. I was in khaki shirt sleeves, with a stupid military tie which I tore off. "Wrap 'em on."

Cosmo tied the bow tie on me, I buckled into the cummerbund, and we were both chortling like a couple of happy crows.

"And one more thing," he said. "But I hope you never use it." And he pulled out, of all things, a genuine, old-time blackjack of soft brown leather with a walnut handle. "Tie's from my headwaiter days," he said. " 'Jack, I had it managing a flophouse in the big depression. Twenny-five cents per night per bed, in New Orleans. I used 'er once or twice, but be ascared to now."

I put it with the snakespeare, wrapped them both in a sheet of tissue paper that he handed me, waved off my pint when he tried to give it back, and watched him grin.

"You ready for a happy new year, Mike?"

"Ready, sir."

I could see Sergeant Gatch and Miss Snatch watching as I dropped the army tie in the lobby trash can. I had strong flutter and burning to go ask the Sergeant if he liked to read. Didn't think my pitch was slick enough, though, and I had Rhombo's on my mind.

"Hello?"

"Well, hello Lucky Knuckles."

"Scott?"

"Forget you had a stepfather, Charlie?"

"It's been a while since we talked."

"You can always make a call home yourself, you know."

"Sure, Scott."

"Are you in a mood to reason together with your mother-person?"

"Sure."

"She'll be relieved to hear it. I think."

"You placing mother's calls these days?"

"I just thought I'd better tie the white hankie on the old broomstick and wave it over the trench first. We're low on ammo here."

"I won't shoot."

"She wasn't sure."

"I'm sorry she felt that way. Our last conversation was a little loud, but it was mother who got upset. Not me."

"Still working for the pink panther?"

"Keep it up, Scott. It really helps."

"Is that what you and your mater went ten rounds about last time?"

"Mother and I fought because mother and I fight. You ought to know that."

"I did grow up on it, as you say. Or old. That and taking out the garbage."

"Are you okay, Scott?"

"Thank you for asking. Yes. My tennis balls are dead, but I can still bounce 'em on the golf course."

"You always could."

"You could have been Jack or Arnie yourself, if you'd worked. Classy with the mashie . . ."

"You certainly did your best with me. Want to put mother on?"

"Hello, Charles."

"Hi mother. How are you?"

"I'm going to be in Washington in about ten days."

"Good. May I take you to lunch?"

"Thank you, darling. I'd love it."

"I've just moved into this new apartment. Want to stay here?"

"What a surprise."

"Is it? Are we estranged or something?"

"I hope not."

"I've never really had a decent place to put you up before."

"I won't be in Washington overnight this time. But thank you. What are you doing this evening?"

"Well, I've just eaten. First dinner in the new place."

"What did you fix?"

"Soft-shell crabs. But someone else fixed them. A delicatessen."

"What will you do now?"

"I'm going to a basketball game. Georgetown against North Carolina, with Deke. Afterwards I've been invited to stop in at a neighbor's for a drink."

"Are you drinking a lot these days?"

"Not like Scott, if that's what you mean. He sounded far gone."

"Are you seeing any girls?"

"The new neighbor's female."

"Tell me about her."

"I don't really know her yet. She's British."

"Pretty?"

"Yes, she is."

"How old, Charles?"

"I haven't asked."

"From London?"

"Haven't asked that yet, either."

"I set London back on its heels, Charles."

"I'll bet you did, Mother."

"How's the job going?"

"I like it very much, I'm afraid. How's Scott's business?"

"Very uneven. The market's very uneven. After the election . . ."

"Mother, did you ever know my father's brother, Pete?"

"Charles!"

"Sorry. I don't mean it as a red flag. I was going to tell you that he's in jail, somewhere in the Middle East."

"I hope it's not Iran . . ."

"No."

". . . but I have to add that it isn't something I'll discuss."

"Let me try another one. Did you ever see a book, well, a leather box that looked like a book, and a snake jumped out—"

"Stop it, Charles."

"You saw it, didn't you?"

"Stop it, or I'll hang up."

"Made by Levi Hand. I'd like to have it, if it still exists."

"I called to have a pleasant visit. I could shake you."

"All right."

"You're a morbid young man."

"Mother, let me know what day you'll be here. We'll have a hell of a lunch."

"Well. A week from Friday."

"Give me the time and flight number, and I'll meet your plane."

"With a bicycle?"

"I'll rent a car."

"Let us. Scott can put it down as business."

"I'll do the car. Just let me know the time."

"See you a week from Friday, then. Enjoy your basketball."

"Thanks. Take care of that stepfather of mine. He's a sweet man."

"I know. Goodbye, Charles."

"Hullo?"

"Roxie. It's Charlie. I'm back from the game."

"Oh. And did the right side win?"

"Not tonight. But it was a great game."

"Do hurry over. I'm quite in need of company."

"Hulloo?"

"Oh, Roxie."

"Oh, Charles. Did you leave something?"

"Check around under the seat on that green sofa. You might find my heart."

"How sweet."

"The people are still there?"

"Quite settling in, dammit."

"Does Angie often arrive unexpectedly with friends?"

"Not so very opportune, what? But you needn't have fled."

"I was in no shape to sit there making conversation. Shall I come back?"

"If you won't be bored."

"But you do have to be up early?"

"To go to Virginia."

"And the people are staying."

"I can't ask Angela to take her young men elsewhere, can I?"

"Young men."

"They're all young to Angela."

"They're not all strangers to you, are they? The Peruvian . . ."

"Charlie, I'm going to whisper and ring off. Can you hear me?"

"Yes."

"I was feeling so . . . I won't say it. You know quite well how I was feeling . . . I also want you to know, well then. I was *most* put out when Angie arrived."

"She say anything?"

"Bloody winks and knowing glances. No matter. We were a bit disarrayed, weren't we? When shall we see each other?"

"Have supper here with me tomorrow."

"I'd love to. Very soon, but not tomorrow. Can you hold?"

"Sure." (Pause)

"We shall be in Virginia several days, it seems. I'll ring up first thing when we're back."

"No chance at all of seeing you later on tonight?"

"I'm afraid not, the way they're swilling cognac."

"You can't slip off and come here?"

"It wouldn't look."

"If things quiet down, and you're not tired, let me know? No matter how late."

"Ah, Charles."

"Goodnight, Roxie."

"Goodnight, luv." (Kiss)

"Hello?"

(Kiss)

"Roxie!"

"Guess again, fluttercup."

"Darlene."

"Hot l'il midnight phone call, and don't him sound pleased. Deke's here."

"Hey, bo."

"He's on the extention."

"Hi, Deke."

"I dropped off here—"

"He came to bum a drink is what, and got some big, bad news."

"How bad?"

"Bo, we been stalkin'-horsed."

"I always wondered what that meant."

"Remember I was telling you about this Sister Blair?"

"She's the one whose brother is the right-wing publisher?"

"She's the one that's president of this and chairman of that, and wants to dee-fend your right to bear arms but not bare ass. Used to be evangelist. Now politics."

"You heard she might be the Republican against you in the fall."

"That's what they put out. That's the old stalkin'-horse move."

"She's not running?"

"Sister Blair ain't running against Congressman Esterzee in the fall, not at all. Been a registered Democrat all her life, got a statewide following and dreamin' of the Senate race in '82."

"That's good news, isn't it? Or did you want her?"

"Darlene's got a letter for us from her campaign manager, bo. Registered, special delivery, after I left the office. Challenging debates."

"Campaign? . . . Oh no."

"Oh yes. She's running against Congressman Esterzee, but not in the fall. Right now. In the Democrat primary."

"Uh-huh."

"They waited till late afternoon the last day to file her petition."

"How much trouble can she give you, Deke?"

"Lot more than I need. She won't beat me for the nomination, but that's not what your little dapple-gray stalking-horse is for. Just her being in splits the party, left and right. Then she tries to push me on the goddamn single issues, one by one, and each time I can lose some votes, no time can I win one. You hanging up, Darlene? Darlene's hung up on us."

"I heard. We're not going to debate the Sister, are we?"

"Hell, no. Which means she gets to carry the empty chair around."

"Pretty old wheeze."

"It'll work with some." (HEY, DARLENE. GET OFF.) "And just the fact she's a woman . . . hold on, Charlie." (DARLENE, CUT IT OUT.)

"We'll talk tomorrow, Deke."

(QUIT, NOW.) "Charlie, I 'spose it's gonna be John Lucas again. I never thought he'd get this cute." (YOU BIG COW.)

"Sounds like hang-up time. Night, Deke."

File on my father. Notes:

I've caught the writing flu, from Mike Mizzourin, I guess.

Bad virus, kiddo.

Or maybe I'm just too high to sleep.

Hearing your friend Deke get woman-handled mess you up?

It didn't help. After the green-sofa session with Roxanne. God, there's a million things I'd like to talk to you about.

Never find more patient ears than mine and Yorick's, baby bird.

I've been a monk since I got here to Washington. It's like you said about Hazel. What I wanted when I got here was a little piece of heart.

The green sofa, Monk baby.

I walked into Roxanne's apartment tonight after the game, feeling easy and thinking I might banter with her some about Suesue and Otis Hibben. It wasn't on the docket. I'm not even sure we said hello.

She was wearing no shoes, and some unfair rose-colored number that came down to her ankles. It made her face glow and her feet, too.

She grabbed my hand in both of hers, the way she did at Suesue's. There was the same, sharp intake of breath, the intense, scared-but-excited look. She moved me toward her, almost without pressure, stopped me as easily, turned us in what could have been a slow dance step till she was able to press her shoulders back against the door and shut it. We closed together in slow motion, hugging long and hard before we kissed.

Then she said, "Well, Charles," and I said, "Well, Roxanne," and we started to laugh at ourselves.

"Now we shall have a drink," Roxie said, and I agreed that was certainly the thing to do.

"Whiskey." She didn't ask but told me, disappeared into the kitchen and came back with two Scotch and sodas. Mine had ice. Hers didn't.

The green sofa is probably too nice an antique for what happened next. It's early Victorian, I guess. I once restored one like it—French-curved legs with claw feet and a scrolled-wood back that frames the upholstery which is all in one piece. The seat is one piece, too. No cushions, mahogany stain on the wood, and fabric pale, worn down almost to white in places, even elegantly frayed.

"This is the best Scotch I ever drank in my life," I said.

"A gift from Suesue."

"She's done you well in furniture, too."

"Has she?" Roxie's hand slip up my back and stopped on my neck, and then we were wrestling and humping around on that fragile old piece, more like a couple of boys tussling for fun than it was like anything romantic. She stopped us by rolling me the most of the way off, onto the floor, and then locking her fingers in my hair.

"You're an utter beast, you know." Then she kissed me and stood up in a way that made it almost automatic for me to wrap my arms around her knees, stand up, too, raising her off the floor, and spin her onto the green sofa again. Ah, she was light.

God, she smelled good.

"Finish your drink before you ravish me," she said, and it was while we were drinking that the tone changed and got quite sentimental.

"I think of you, you know, all during the day. Over at your Capitol, doing important things."

"Very important," I said. "Like thinking of you, after I get all the pencils sharpened."

The next embrace was slower and fonder, with less laughter. What's the phrase? Slowly, with feeling. When she pushed off, very gently, this time, she said: "I don't say I didn't know we'd feel this way, but I'm not sure I'm altogether ready for it. Are you?"

"I don't mind being slowed down."

Who did you think you were kidding?

Still, it was nice to feel we were taking a little care with one another. Then we'd get monstrously excited all over again. The rosy wrapper was all the way unwrapped and the bra was on the floor when Angela came on with the troops.

And you never did ask about Hibben.

That's getting complicated. I'm all bogged down in the luncheon report to Johnson, what to tell, what to hold back.

Hit him over the head with it. That's what he always did to me.

I'm not going to tell him anything I'm not dead sure of. That Suesue's wealthy, sure. That there's trouble between her and Hibben about money.

But I've learned some things about John McRae Johnson himself that make me feel cautious. There was an Interior subcommittee hearing yesterday that Deke wanted to know about before he leaves for Calder Plain. I was sitting with a *Denver Post* guy I know during a recess, and I asked if he knew of Johnson.

"That's the wreck of a heck of a man," he said. "Big, commanding presence, very able when he's in his right mind. I was in journalism school when he was dean. They had to ease the old boy out after he disappeared with a girlie and half case of Seagrams Seven. He surfaced in a motel room in L.A., insisting that the girlie was his adopted daughter, and they were hiding from the CIA. That was 1978, but he was talking about Lyndon Johnson's CIA ten years earlier. Said he had stuff on the Kennedy assassination that could get him and his daughter killed. They had to dry Dean Johnson out and get him a little psychiatric help to bring him up to date. Gold watch time."

Ain't it wonderful how Mafia and CIA are interchangeable in the public mind? Same kind of people—ruthless, secret and totally dishonest.

I guess I understand now why Christine didn't want me to start corresponding with her husband. There may be some upsetting stuff coming his way, but I don't want to report it before I'm absolutely sure.

I've got to put myself to bed. It's going to be a long and busy day tomorrow getting Deke ready to go meet America's future in Calder Plain, featuring Uncle Ned and his merry men on the other side.

"Hel-lo."

"Hi, Darlene."

"Hello, Charlie. You got him off?"

"The plane was a little late leaving, but he's on his way. Stuart's going to meet him and drive him down to the conference."

"He'll be going in tomorrow with six minutes' sleep."

"He was in high spirits, anyway."

"On the midnight plane to Midnight, Iowa."

"You sound down."

"I am. Down in my bed with a cold, cold lonesome back."

"Sorry."

"It's bare, too."

"I thought you'd want to know he got off, in spite of our little friend who called up."

" 'Wis is Amewicum Airwines, we sorry. Dee fwight Congwussmum Efferfee on been cancel.' "

"They don't quit trying, do they?"

"Be in the office early, will you, Charlie? He may call. Or Stuart. Any time. They'll need stuff."

"See you there at dawn."

"Unless you'd like to bike over and help with my lower-back problem?"

"Now you sound like your old, enticing self."

"Never too old for a chiropractic housecall."

"Pleasant dreams."

"Wimp."

"Charlie Mizzourin here."

"Hey, bo. Bob in the office with you?"

"No. Shall I find him?"

"No."

"Been waiting for your call all day, Deke. You sound beat."

"Make a little sign, will you? DO NOT DISTURB. Put it on the door outside and lock yourself in. Turn the tape on, on your phone."

"That bad?"

"Do it, will you?"

"Okay."

(Pause)

"It's done, Deke."

"Don't interrupt me unless something's not clear. I want that tape to have it, fresh and bloody. Here it goes."

This whole thing is even more of a damn right-wing hoedown and barbee-cue than we thought, with me and about two other guys turning on the spit over the coals. That part I don't mind, except for how the Great Plains Foundation turns out to be part of the shill, but Stuart's got people here and we're making some noise back at them. That part's even fun, but I'm going to skip to after the meeting this morning, which was loud and hot, and after it my schedule says, "Coffee and Press Conference at the Best Western."

That's on the edge of Calder Plain. You can see your family farmhouse from the lobby, and the fields. I stood there a minute looking, thinking well, Charlie's old, sonofabitching uncle's got something to yell about, the way he did at the meeting, after all. Those fields'll go for developing if we don't restrict, and Ned wants the dough. And I walked into the press conference, but there wasn't any press there.

Instead, it was Ned Mizzourin and some other halfway important people. All Republicans, but it never hurts to shake a hand. They want to have some fun with me, I'll play it straight and quick and take off. Which I start to do.

Ned Mizzourin, whom I'd kinda went past with a wink, says: "Wait a minute, Deke. Hey, Congressman."

"You were pretty good in there this morning, Ned," I said. "How's Barbara and the girls?" Yeah, you got twin first cousins, Charlie, two girls. And that's his second wife, Barbara. They say he scared the first to death.

"Sit down, Deke," Ned says. "And have a drink with us. We want to talk to you."

Someone had sent for a couple of pitchers of beer already, eleven A.M., but that wasn't what Ned was buying. He had his bottle in a brown bag. Took a big pull off it and held it out to me. So I looked him in the ugly eye, took a pull like his, and handed it back. Your uncle's a fat-looking guy with a mean, dancy little smile and black eyes, and when you look again what you see is a hell of a pair of shoulders and less gut than you thought. He's got a red face and dark hair, and he's not real big but he manages to look big.

"We got you here to tell us what you're gonna do about Eye-ran."

"Everything a Congressman can do. Which isn't a damn thing."

"I don't mean you personally. Hell, you wouldn't know an ayatollah from a tractor hitch. I mean demee-crats." He says it like it like it smells bad.

This is definitely not the place for me to fight, so I say: "The President's got all kinds of things going that we don't hear about."

"Like burning up a few more helee-copters on the desert?"

I'm not going to miss a chance like that. "You blaming that on Jimmy Carter? Weren't you ever in the army?" I knew the story there, didn't I? "You know how they do things."

"What kind of smartass thing is that to say?" I'd got to him. "I knew you were a stupid prick, but not that goddamn stupid."

So I smiled and said: "If we're going to sit here name-calling, I'm not going to sit here, Ned."

"I'm just as goddamn patriotic as you are. There's Congressmen today trying to get into Eye-ran. You one of them?"

"I would if I thought I could do a lick of good. We all would, and that's why the administration's against it. Man's got to have a particularly, personal reason."

"Like one of your own damn constituents, maybe?" I shoulda seen it coming. Dumb me. "I got a brother over there in jail. You know that?"

"I've been to the State Department three times about Pete. And I've gone with your nephew, Charlie, over to the oil company Pete works for. You're not telling these people Pete's in Iran, are you?"

"Mike's brat, huh? I'll betcha he's a dilly. We know damn well Pete's not a Eye-ran hostage, smartass. He's a mystery hostage. Why don't you take one of those Congress junk trips and find out where?"

"You want me to charge the taxpayers for a fishing trip?"

"Find Pete and get him out. Set an example. You can't raise the money for it, I know who can."

I didn't want Ned saying he'd offered to buy me a trip. I said thanks for the drink, see you this afternoon, and got up to go. "I'll keep pressure on State. Charlie will, too. And on the oil company. If a trip abroad looks feasible, I'll do it like a shot."

"Sure you will. And stay in some ree-sort. Sure you will. I'm talking about going out there where the shit's flying. And I'm telling you who's got the money and gonna do it. Not but one taxpayer, bub. That's all it takes."

I could see it coming. "All right Ned. Make your announcement."

Ned stood up. "Fast, ain't you? The next Congressman from this Eighth Iowa District. That's who's goin' to find his brother. Your Reepublican opponent, Mr. Estersissy. If I don't get whipped in a primary, and you don't."

His boys were clapping, and he smiled and bowed his head at them, and went on: "Might be one of us not going to get opposed in the primary. Might be one of us gonna be traveling abroad on peree-lous business. That'll make pretty good reading back home."

"State will try to stop you, Ned. Airlines won't let you board a plane without the right visas."

"Well, I ain't planning to swim, Congressman. You gonna do something about it?"

"You want us to help in Washington? Sure."

"Sure. You do that. And if you ain't got enough weight in your ass to swing your dick, I'll use my own connection. Congressman." That got a laugh. "I can get to Europe. I can get to Libya. And once I'm there, figure I've got the money to buy my way in anyplace it looks like I oughta go."

"Congratulations," I said, and left. That's it, Charlie. All the news from Calder Plain. Tomorrow's Saturday, right? If I need somebody to cuss, I'll call you at home.

"Hello?"

"Good morning, Charles. Do say you're thrilled to hear my voice."

"Hey, Roxie. How's Virginia?"

"No end of party."

"Are you a bridesmaid, in an organdy dress?"

"More like an organdy bikini, darling. There's an indoor pool."

"I see."

"Mine's black, and quite naughty."

"I'd have to close my eyes."

"I'm absolutely stunning in it, I'll admit."

"Are those pals of Angela's there, too?"

"Just the one who drove us down. Otherwise it's quite a different set. I do wish you were here."

"Is Suesue there?"

"Oh, yes."

"And Senator Hibben?"

"Don't be tiresome, Charles. I did say I wished you were here, didn't I?"

"Give me directions. I'll bike down and take you to lunch."

"Forty miles?"

"I can do it in an hour."

"But then, it's ever so far out in the country. There aren't restaurants. What else shall you do?"

"Go to the office, I guess."

"On a lovely Saturday? Poor Charles. Shall I ask if you may have lunch here?"

"Let's let it go. Deke has a hearing to get started. There's work to do on that. Lists of questions to go over. Mail to read."

"From whom, may I ask?"

"An old gentleman in Colorado, named Johnson. To hell with this, Roxie. Thanks for calling."

"You do miss me?"

"Yes, damn it. I do. Please hurry back."

"In another two days, I should hope. Do keep the evening clear so that we may have that supper. I've the rest of the bottle of Scotch you liked so well."

"Roxie, Suesue pretty much fixed us up, didn't she?"

"Fixed us up?"

"Wanted us to meet?"

"Of course, luv. Such a busybody, but I'm glad. Say you are, too."

"How do you happen to know Suesue?"

"But whom doesn't she know, after all? Get along to your mail, darling. I must ring off now."

"All right, Roxie."

"Ciao." (Kiss)

"Ciao."

"Hello?"

"Hey, bo."

"Welcome back. You at Darlene's?"

"Yeah. Want to come over?"

"No, Charlie does not want to come over, bigfoot."

"Tell him what happened then, willya?"

"Some lawyer dropped by at State today with your Uncle Ned's application for special clearance to Libya."

"Why Libya?"

"Petrolat's main operations center. Pete's company."

"Is Ned going to get the clearance?"

"They're inclined, poppyseed."

"Any special reason."

"He's a hybrid seed corn dealer."

"They gonna send Libya some hybrid rainfall, too, to make it grow. Bo, I want you to see your Eye-ran expert lady over there in State. Straight off Monday morning."

"We going to try to block it?"

"No. We gonna be all for it. You are, anyway. First, tell her what's goin' on. Let her know your uncle's got something more 'n seed corn on his mind."

"Aren't we a little bit concerned for his safety?"

"Not you. Maybe your Congressman, but you think it's a great idea. Tell her how Uncle Ned's dynamic. Forceful. Gonna kick Moslem ass from Libya clear to Afghanistan till he finds Pete. Tough. Rowdy. No conciliation. So please, mum, won't she do everything she can to help out with the passport folks? She should be in an ice-cold sweat by then, so leave the rest to her."

"That's beautiful."

"Darlene's idea."

"Just one of many, dreamo. It should throw the whole State Department into at least a six-week conference."

"Ain't she a pisser? Told Ned we'd cooperate."

"Deke, do you think Ned might find Pete?"

"If I did, I'd do everything I could to help him out. Ned antagonizes people, that's not the way. But I'll tell you where I'll be Monday morning, Charlie, while you're at State, because there's one thing Ned is right about. Pete's my constituent. I hadn't thought about it before. Where I'm going is back over to Petrolat, right here in Washington, put on a Congressman show and find out something for a change."

"Go get 'em, Deke."

"You, too, bo. Night."

"Hello. This is Charlie Mizzourin calling. Is Roxanne there?"

"Honey, this is Suesue."

"Hello. Aren't the girls back?"

"No, darling. I'm so sorry."

"You were in Virginia with them?"

"Oh, yes. A lovely party."

"Who got married?"

"Oh. A lovely girl. It was Barbie Driscoll. The parents insist on keeping the party going. Such hospitable people, and the girls are staying on."

"How long?"

"Just another day or two. I'm here trying to find some clothes they want me to send down."

"Suesue, come next door when you get done. I'll give you a drink and a rent check."

"Oh, thank you, Charlie. I'm afraid I've got to find these damn clothes and then I'm going back down myself. There'll be a suitcase to pack, and I'm supposed to pick up a lot of other stuff for the Driscolls."

"Doesn't Roxie have to work?"

"You like my Roxie, don't you?"

"I think you guessed I would, when you introduced us."

"Scrape the paint off a middle-aged woman, dear, and you'll find a matchmaker every time."

"I do like her. You're quite right."

"I'm going to quote you on it, honey."

"She knows it, Suesue. Tell her I miss her. Is there a number I can call her at?"

"Oh, I'm afraid they're all out to dinner. There's a lovely little French restaurant, just down the road."

"Is there? Suesue, could I call her in the morning?"

"Of course. But, oh damn. I don't have the number. And, of course, the Driscolls are unlisted."

"Of course."

"Charlie?"

"Yes?"

"Oh, well. Goodbye for now. Will you come to lunch again soon?"

"Thank you."

"I'll tell her . . . you want her to hurry back. Have you been hearing from Johnny Mac?"

"Yes, I have."

"I'm so glad I was able to help. Byebye, now."

"Goodbye. Suesue."

LIVIA SCALIGER HELMREICH
March 2, 1980

Dear Charles:

Scott and I will arrive in the forenoon on Friday. He has some business to attend to and must rent a car, so instead of your meeting us at the airport, I will have him drop me off at Le Coq d'Or at 12:30. Please get reservations for us, and meet me there at that time. Lunch will be my treat, please, for it's such an expensive place, and I know you are not earning a great deal of money. I am looking forward to a friendly luncheon with my son, after which Scott and I are going to drive down to Charlottesville to see Lily and Pauline. (Do you remember your old joke about two half-sisters making a whole sister? It used to make them so angry, poor things. They do adore you.) Is there a chance you might be able to drive down with us to see them at college?

Love,
Mother

To: Charlie   March 5, 1980
From: Darlene
Subject: Backfire, or the trouble with irony.
My lousy idea and your lousy sincerity sure did the trick. Your Iranian specialist lady heard your plea to expedite the Ned Mizzourin special clearance, ran to her boss, they ran hand in hand to the passport people, and it's done. Totally. They're giving us exactly what you asked for (who ever heard of such a thing?). They will publicize the humble dirt farmer going on his own to seek his brother, world opinion will be swayed, and the Ayatollah's heart will melt when he learns about how a brother country let an innocent captive go.

Deke said: "Okay, damn it," and went back to Petrolat again. "Pete's our first concern. Ned's on his way. The people who can help Ned are the ones who know what happened in the first place, and I don't see they've got much choice but try giving him a hand, way things are turning out. Something's got to give."

Meanwhile he wants you to call your Uncle Neddums, and tell him how this office cut the red tape into red ribbons. We may as well get credit for it, even if we didn't mean to dive so deep and stay under so long.

"Yeah?"
"This is Charlie Mizzourin calling. Is that Edward Mizzourin?"
"Yeah."
"Hello, Uncle Ned."

"I'll be damned."

"I've written you before, and tried to call."

"I know you did. Wanted to get your money from that will."

"The will? Sir, I'd honestly forgotten the will, though it's what started me writing to you."

"Yeah. Whaddya . . . wait a minute. Wait a minute. Shit." (Laughter)

"I didn't know about you and Pete at all until I got the letter about the will from that lawyer in Des Moines . . ."

"Cocksucker in Des Moines."

"Since then, I've read some about you and Pete, in something my father wrote."

"Yeah? Whatever he said about me, he's a lying prick . . . usetabe . . . little Mikey."

"I want to meet you."

"Yeah, I know. Hey, Charlie?"

"Yes, Uncle?"

"Don't pay too much attention to me. I'm drinking."

"Doesn't matter. I'm glad we're talking."

"Hey, nevview."

"Hey, Uncle."

"You wanta work for me?"

"Sorry?"

"I'm gonna beat the broke-down basketball coach. I'm thinking it'd be nice, be real nice . . . here I've got a nevview knows what's what in Washington. All right, Charlie? See what I mean?"

"It's a little soon for making that kind of plan, isn't it?"

"Hell, I'd like to have you with me on the farm this spring, boy. Help with the campaign, couldn't you? There's a whole lot I don't know. Now, I'm not going to take it bad if you say no, but if you want to quit that job and come on out here, Ill pay for your fare and match your wages. Is that fair?"

"Uncle Ned."

"There's people here knows politics. Sure. They'll help. But someone that's a blood relation. That's different."

"It's sure hard to say no."

"Huh?"

"I can't do it. Thanks anyway."

"Don't that take the rag off the bush?" (Laughter) "What am I beggin' you for?"

"This is a business call, really. I have some good news."

"Yeah? Just a second. Shit." (Pause) "You made me knock my fuckin' glass over."

"Are you all right?"

"Just a goddamn minute." (Pause) "All afternoon, sittin' in a nice warm office with your telephone, huh? I been in frozen pig shit up to my galoshes tops. You got any pig shit on your galoshes? How 'bout Esterzee?"

"Uncle Ned?"

"You two can go to hell."

"I'm calling for Deke. He's got your travel approved."

"Is that right?"

"We've got your visa for you. I'd like to meet you with it. Do you plan to come through Washington?"

"No. Nope. Huh-uh. Whoo-oo . . ." (Laughter) "Hey, your uncle . . . never mind."

"Jesus, are you all right?"

"Never goddamn mind, I said."

"Could I meet you in New York?"

"I'll be flying from Casago. Chisago. You know, Charles? Charles."

"Listen, I'll call back in the morning."

"What the hell for?"

"I'll send your travel documents by overnight mail. Do you have a departure date?"

"What are you, the spy?"

"We'd like to keep track of where you are. If you run into problems, we may be able to help back here."

"Oh sure. You'd just love it. Whoo boy, wouldn't you?"

"You know, Pete Mizzourin's my uncle as well as your brother."

"Do fuckin' tell. Hey, listen to this. You listening? Tell Pigshit Usterson, Estersun, listen. Tell him he can keep all the tracka me he wants. Right in the newspaper. Follow it, right in the *Register*. Every day, in the Big Pink Stink."

"The *Register?*"

"All arranged, sonny. Gonna phone um. Every day. Anywhere in the world I'm at, gonna phone um." (Laughter) "Hello, Pinkos? Ned Mizzourin here. You tell . . . Esther. Esterzee."

"Yes. I will."

"Good old Esther Dick. Read about me every day. Hey, tell him I'll

send special, special dispatches. Whenever I can find . . ." (Laughter)
". . . dirty postcards to write um on."

"I'm going to ring off, Uncle Ned. We'll be glad to hear from you."

"Jesus Christ, what are you, a boy or a girl?"

"Good night."

"I'm gonna leave Thursday."

"All right."

(Laughter) "Charles! What a fruity name. Mike musta had his head . . ."

"You and my father didn't get along, I know."

"He was a little prick, Charles."

"I know about the letter he wrote during the war. He was sorry he'd written it."

"I know that, dumbass. He tried to 'pol, apologize."

"You saw him after the war?"

"Once. Even shook his stinking hand."

"Where, Uncle Ned?"

"Go to hell, nevview."

"Hello?"

"Charlie? You talk to Ned?"

"Yep."

"Not much fun, huh?"

"Nope. What did they say at Petrolat?"

"Everything's backfiring today. I told them they ought to go hand in hand in hand with State, help Ned. They don't like the way State does things. They don't give a damn for world opinion, and they plain hate publicity. It breeds more incidents, and they got a lot of people in the field to protect. The most they said is they'll have their Tripoli office talk to Ned when he gets to Libya, but I get the feeling if they want to use him, it'll be different from the way State wants to use him. Frustrating, ain't it?"

"It's every bit of that."

"Any news from Carolina?"

"Johnson's pleased with my last report. He's sent a bundle."

"The little guy still jimmying that Gatch?"

"Haven't read it yet. I hope not."

"Me too. Worry about him."

"So do I."

Last Deadline Ranch
Capsicum, Colo.
March 5, 1980

My dear boy:
Well done, good and faithful savant. Succinct. Clearly written. (I might caution, though, against overuse of contractions. Didn't *is less emphatic than* did not, can't *less emphatic than* cannot. *Mark me.) As to the substance of your report, I am, of course, delighted that my former secretary is doing so well. When I left Washington, she was merely a receptionist at the Pentagon. Do lead our Horatia Algeria on to speak of how she has built what seems, at least, to be a modest fortune. Human it is to enjoy telling one's tale of success, and human is Suesue, mark me. How did she get started? With whose advice? How well now consolidated, or can you detect overextension in her sinodelphic wafer (i.e.—Chinese fortune cookie)? Perhaps, subtly, you can obtain addresses of her real estate holdings, have a look at them and estimate net worth and probable cash flow from rentals.*

I have, and why should I conceal it from you any longer, unfinished business with this unfinished business woman which, in due time I'll divulge. (Here the contraction is deliberate, preserving a desirable ambiguity which would be lost should the writer commit himself as between I shall *and* I will.*)*

As to former Senator Hibben, Suesue seems to have a powerful friend, whom I calculate, however, to be several years my senior. (Now for a look: Aha! Who's Who *bears me out. He is seventy, an age which makes it seem probable Suesue is more protégé than* pro tem femme. *Mark me.)*

But monitopaso, i.e., watch your step. Are you aware of how powerful this Hibben must be as head of the dairy lobby? The dugs on that great udder squirt not merely into Agriculture but into Defense, for it is an enormous purchaser of milk, butter and cheese, needed for the nutrition of our fighting men; and into HEW, because of the scandalously wasteful school lunch and daycare programs; even unto Foreign Relations, because of the vast quantities of stuff like powdered milk squandered under aid and relief programs. Is it possible that the motion-picture actor Reagan is at long last speaking sensibly about these issues (and even that the martyred Nixon guides the actor's thought)? I reserve judgment on R.R.'s soundness, but listen with care. (No, on careful thought, I do not think Dick's pride would permit his using Ronald as a puppet. What says Washington rumor on this point?)

Sometimes, when I am writing to you and thinking of you, there where the power and the action are, no matter how peripheral your job, I would fain be back in that city. Only the delicacy of Christine's physical health and mental balance keeps me in this isolation. But should my men return to office, and should a call come . . . mark me!

There are seven enclosures. The first has been moved forward from a position later in the manuscript, an editorial decision with which I feel completely at ease.

Aff'ly,
Uncle John

Enc: EAST OF THE SUN, THE MUSIC GOES DOWN AND AROUND, BUT NOT FOR ME, GOOFUS, THE DIPSY DOO-DLE, DOWN HOME RAG, I HAD THE CRAZIEST DREAM.

Mizzourin/EAST OF THE SUN

Rhombo's. In the mornings, the farmers go there to eat eggs and drink a mixture of tomato juice and beer. On certain days I watch, sipping my own, straight, frosty suds, not caring for the pink. The beer does cut the grease, as farmers say. The front room of the tavern faces west onto the square, where the winter sun is bright, though the room itself is somber and the pink-beer-breakfast eaters pensive. I take my own beer to the back room, where the dance floor is. I sit there by myself, in the mild glow from the eastern windows, among the empty tables and tipped-forward chairs, in the party smell persisting over-night. I listen to the murmuring voices from out front, and can tell when it's eleven by the rising sound.

Eleven's coffee, coke and boasting time in Faraday, and when I walk into the front barroom, there are a few bold secretaries with their soft drinks and loud laughter, their junior bosses from the courthouse, legal firms, insurance offices, men from the dealership making boisterous plans for when there'll be new cars to sell again. They will all be rich. The younger ones drink coffee straight. The older lace theirs with bourbon. The room is less shadowy now.

At noon, when the sun is overhead, the room's quite bright but more or less deserted. No one eats lunch at Rhombo's much, but Tim and Rowf, the all-day drinkers, nurse their beers. Old Tammy closes up the courthouse newsstand when lunch hour begins, brings the day's coins to Rhombo's where she counts them, pushing every third aside to pay for schnapps. A crew from city street repair may bring their paper sacks of sandwiches, sit in a booth along the north wall buying pickled eggs, drinking Thunderbird on the rocks. And sometimes soldiers from the fort or discharged guys.

Then there's no real change up front till cocktail hour, if you can call it that. Drinking of shots and beer. Noise happens. Light streams in from the west showing the stamped patterns on the metal wall and ceiling tiles in high relief. Only now and then someone calls out "Martini" or "Manhattan," a small-store manager or side-street dentist mixing with the farmer-labor crowd.

At six there comes the real transformation. Meat rationing makes porterhouse a word like Cadillac, filet mignons rhyme with diamonds, and Tommy Rhombo's brother has a cattle farm up in the way-back hills. The brothers are the butchers for the menu in the tavern, where you order in code. A Catfish Special is a bootleg T-bone, a Catfish Combo is a sirloin strip. If Helen Rhombo doesn't know you, they've just run out of that, until you tell who told you. Then it's "Rare, well-done or medium?" and there'll be a chunk of fried fish on your plate next to the steak. Nice hush puppy, too.

Many in the dinner crowd at Rhombo's are dressed up for it, thin bankers, fat doctors, with their sweet-face, puckerass wives, and other fine folk who live on the hill, along with salesmen from out of town, escorting dental hygienists and ladylike beauticians. No other place in town has Catfish Specials. And there are musclenecks, too, from the tougher, best-paid, draft-dodger unions—teamsters, operating engineers—with their rayon-shiny, beehive consorts.

Nine P.M. in Rhombo's: watch yourself. We've got the ten meanest survivors from each one of those day and evening crowds. They're mostly strung along the dark-oak bar, where stools are bolted down and spittoons are functional. There are young, mule-whipping mountain boys in new straw hats, and hard-ons from the blue-collar crowd, only now their collars are crazy, though it wouldn't do to laugh—floral print, Peter Pan collars, worn outside of cardigans with vestlike leather inserts. There'll be a salesman or two, just now come back, who couldn't get his beautified hygienist to the dotted line, sitting sullen, a little pig-eyed now from booze. There'll be pole climbers and feed handlers, and soldiers always, and a few white-collar boys who think they're hard enough, with their ties loose now.

The men in this crowd can't stand still. They shift from the front-room booths and bar to the back room where the trio plays, some of them ready to fight to love. Others in the ten o'clock crowd just love to fight. That was the time, ten P.M., at which I first saw Rhombo's, last week, last year, on New Year's Eve.

Mizzourin/**THE MUSIC GOES DOWN AND AROUND**

There's no neon sign sticking out over the sidewalk from Rhombo's. On the front window, long and thin above the brick front wall, the name is lettered: RHOMBO'S TAVERN. Arriving there at ten, in black tie, cummerbund, khaki shirt and Eisenweasel, I stopped in the front doorway to look in, and could see the fight card had already started.

I stepped inside, wondering where the trio I'd been told of was. I saw an open double-door, back behind the people, and guessed there was a room there beyond. Meantime, a loose-tie Ted and a fat-arm Freddie were squared off, the other customers laughing and watching, and a long-faced man behind the bar had a little miniature baseball-bat-thing in his hand, but was grinning mournfully and watching like everybody else while the Teddy hit a smart combination, one-two-three, and the Freddy pushed off and wound a haymaker around the Teddy's neck. The action wasn't what I craved.

I stepped back out, went around to the south side parking lot, past the open kitchen door by which stood garbage cans, saw another open door, twenty feet farther on, saw purple light, heard music then: the sound of jazz. There was a neon sign this time, a little modest one: RHOMBO'S ROSELAND.

I looked inside and saw, taking a guitar solo with drums and piano, everyone's pet music clerk, my sideboy, Binkie Jones. The tune was "Laura" and the boy could play.

I watched with pleasure his pink and white face, ashen hair glowing purple in the light, as he played into a microphone. The notes were fast, distinct, percussive. A dark-haired drummer, maybe thirty, was going swish-swish-swish with steel brushes on a snare and a pianist I couldn't see was hitting chords.

Then I looked closer, because the drummer certainly had steel brushes but I could hear sticks working, too, in some funny muffled way. Dark Hair the drum didn't have sticks, no. No.

And then a voice spoke: "Hey, Mike."

Where?

Over my left shoulder, somewhere near the kitchen door, and made me jump like snakespeare had.

"Hey, Mike. You like it?"

Back against the outside well, cut off from view of anyone on the street by the way the kitchen door stood open, was as auld an acquaintance here in Faraday as I'd never brought to mind, the negro T-Corporal with missing left-hand fingers, from my discharge group. He was holding drumsticks, playing on a practice pad he's set up on a packing crate.

I walked over there and said: "Sure I like. Guitar solo. Sounds fine."

"Sounded fine when Charlie Christian played it, too."

"Who?"

"Christian. Never hear him?"

"Haven't heard much at all these last four years."

"The Goodman Quartet."

"Oh yes."

The information man came into the light. He was drape-shaped in chestnut brown, a little lighter than his skin. He has a lean jaw and a round dome, with lovely teeth and short like me. I'd liked his looks before, and now I liked them even better.

Has a mustache started. "Hi," I said, "I'm Mike Mizzourin," holding out my hand.

"Heard our sarge say Mike, but didn't hear the funny half," smiled, and took the hand I offered.

"You got a name?"

"Both halves funny. Scholay Gopeters."

"Gopeters? That's terrific."

"Started out plain Peters. When they watched me playing drums they hollered 'Go.' I was fourteen years old and liked it that way."

Me, Mike, I was seventeen before I ever saw a colored person, and had never exchanged any sort of touch with one before, but whoa, Mike. You never wallowed skin-to-skin in Japanese, and especially one, Chizukuo by name, lady of the night by trade, sweet thang? Colored sweet thang? And in Hawaii, Polynesian mixed with Holstein-fresian, swee cow and oh-what-eyes? Colored swee cow? Say negro if you mean it, Mike, okay? Okay: first time I ever touched a negro. First time I ever touched a hero, too.

All heroes, whole damn race. Paul Robeson first. Bill Robinson—I suffered Shirley Temple gladly just to see him dance. Joe Louis, fighting Schmeling on the radio—the German won the first battle, the American won the war. Marian Anderson. Jesse Owens in Berlin, making Hitler puke all over his shoes. And the bandleaders and musicians:

Lunceford, Ellington, Kirk, Basie, Henderson, Tatum, Hines, Waller, Turner, Holiday and Ivy Anderson. Much as I love Beiderbecke, and would rather play like Berrigan than anyone, I know the king is Louis A. So when I squeezed on Scholay's right brown hand, it was an homage, and I think he knew it.

"Your boy's playing off the right guitar in there. That's how it starts."

"What about the drum?" I asked.

Scholay snorted. "Fee's a drummer, I'm a plumber. Better when he played his bass. Slightly poo-fessional, you got my meaning?" There was a big string bass indeed beside the drum set. Scholay bowed. The trio finished "Laura" with an abrupt stop, restart, blam.

I returned the bow.

"B'lieve I slightly got your meaning, sir," I said. "Imitation guitar, and plumbing on the drums, Mr. Gopeters? You must be here to listen to piano."

"You will hear it, Mr. Mizzourin, any minute now."

"Isn't there any music . . . ?" I didn't know how to say it.

"In Niggertown? There are blues shouters there, and country licks. There is also fried pork, larded greens with vinegar, white whiskey and something unbelievable called cornpone. And disgusting home brew, stronger than the whiskey. I'm a boy from Broadway, Mr. Mizzourin. Cognac, caviar, Lindy's cheesecake and the sound of Mr. Yardbird Parker suit this man. Should be on a bus for there right now."

"You stayed for New Year's Eve?"

"I'm here because some burrheads got me in a crap game, and I'm now an honorary member of the posse looking for the one who brought the dice."

"Hurting for money? I've got extra."

"Thank you, Mike. Between Bell Telephone and Western Union, and an odd job at Jocasta's cornpone castle, crib and cathouses—an establishment you surely ought to see—but . . . oh, now. Listen."

Inside, Erstwhile the drummer had moved to bass and was starting up, bwomp, bwomp, badoomp, badoomp, and Scholay started playing too, quietly, on his practice pad; I could feel as much as hear it. And E. B. Jones picked up the rhythm, chording off the beat of the bass, and then piano started, a long, downward cascade with four odd, loud, harsh chords at the end, and Scholay called the tune before there was a bar of melody.

" 'How High the Moon.' There goes the Doctor." The time doubled, the piano took off. I'm not a big fan of the tune, I couldn't see the player and wasn't sure I liked what he was doing, either. Smashing chords, runs that fooled me. I got lost trying to follow. Then there'd come a few notes of melody, oddly embellished, something like:

Somewhere there's bodleedada-deebo? How dadaahda-ehda-boobay . . .

and where it went from there were snakes and bees on the keyboard and Scholay going crazy goodpecker on the practice pad, and I wished I could bring it all together. I might not like it, but I knew intensity when I heard it. *Brrr-oopahdadoop,* straight chord offbeat, done.

"Christ, Scholay," I said, a little bit excited in spite of myself.

"You don't care for it."

"Chinese poetry."

Scholay was grinning and, weirdly for one who'd made so little sound, sweating handsomely as well. "You'll get it, Little Mike. Got ears."

"Let's go inside."

"Huh?"

"I want to see this guy you call the Doctor. Come on. I'll buy drinks."

He gave me a look like zip-your-fly-stupid, and I felt rightaway branded IDIOT on the forehead, even before he said: "Whose balls these Carolina boys going to grind up first, your pinks or my charcoal grays?"

"Sorry."

"Get outa here, Milktooth Mike," he said. "Go on inside, now, fore some cracker comes along and kicks your ass so hard you'll find a cheek in either pocket."

"You a drummer, Scholay?" I don't know why I kept trying.

"Self-inflicted."

"They could use a drummer in there."

"What are you saying?"

"I know the guitar player. Want me to ask if you can sit in?"

"Hot damn," Scholay Gopeters shook his head. "Little Mike from Mars." He picked up his practice pad. He grinned. He squeezed my shoulder. "What's your plan? Fight 'em? Reason with 'em? Make 'em hear the music till they change their hearts? You want to hear me? Track me in New York."

"That's where I'm going to be next week," I said.

"Just call the union," Scholay said, and left.

Mizzourin/**BUT NOT FOR ME**

There was a lot of yelling from up front in Rhombo's. I went in the back. I stood just inside the back door, and listened to the trio play "Lover" in dance tempo.

Rhombo's Roseland has eighteen tables in it, mostly round ones, some for two and some for four. They're set in two three-quarter circles around a small dance floor, with the front edge of the bandstand, one step up, cutting off the final quarter of the first circle.

There are some bigger, rectangular tables at the rear, and one more up front beside the bandstand, with chairs on the side away from the music and at each end. This table has a card on it that used to say RESERVED but somebody blacked out the first syllable and changed it to PISS ■■SERVED. This table is for the trio between sets.

There were two couples on the dance floor crotchlocking to "Lover," and one other, dressed up, in their thirties, looking like they actually liked to move their feet. About half the tables were in use, and others filling up as people came back from watching whatever the excitement may have been up front. At the musicians' table was a white-headed female wearing a low-cut evening gown, interposing a nude back between me and my view of the trio. The back was made-up, and looked flat in the colored light.

E. B. Jones saw me standing by the door, waved excitedly, and beckoned.

"Mike," he called out, over his chords. "Hey, hey." I smiled and saluted and waited for the tune to end. Then I went around to meet him on the floor as he stepped down, where he grabbed my arms and yelled: "Got you pitcher of beer on the table, or would you want a drink?" He was pushing me that way.

"I'll git it, Binkie." It was a sweet girl's voice with a little bit of hillbilly whine in the accent, like E.B.'s—it was the eyes. The same pair that had been haunting me, big, lavender enigma eyes, set deep and almost slanted under ash-blond hair I'd thought was white. Replica eyes. I looked back at E.B.'s again, almost confused. Twin eyes.

"That there's my sister," E.B. said, with pride. "That's Evaun. Ain't no damn good to anybody."

Evaun Barlow. She is almost seventeen, and married once already, once-divorced, to a soldier who left her his name and nothing more, from whom she hasn't heard since the day he left her in Faraday more than two years ago. When she was almost fifteen.

She slow-smiled me and was on her feet. "Rhymes with fawn, you know, a baby deer? Whatcha gonna have, Mike?"

She's slender and looks taller than she is, but that's the wrong way to start. Like E.B., she is beautiful; like a slim, surprising doll. She has squared-off shoulders, like a boy's, but is rounded other places as a girl should be. She's all firm except her bosom, which seems wiggly for almost-seventeen. Her stomach's flat, and the off-white dress was tight across it so you saw the fabric dip over the naval. She was wearing too much makeup; if her skin was like her brother's, any makeup at all was too much.

She was all girl, but when she moved off to fetch my whiskey, she rippled in her pale dress through the purple light, like some kind of water animal swimming.

I was annoyed that she was there. It was the music makers I wanted to commune with. If I felt it might be okay, too, to meet a female on the festive night, please make it a woman, not the rippling, rounded childbride of the goddamn unknown soldier.

As she went across the dance floor, I heard the woman member of the older couple, waiting for the music to resume, call out: "When you gonna sing one, honey?"

"When I git back, Mizz Terrell," Evaun promised in an awful, molasses-in-the-throat voice, different from the one she'd used to me. Her public voice, I thought; please not her singing voice. Back up on the platform now, E.B. was beckoning to me, bobbing his own pretty head and saying to his comrades: "This here's Mike!"

The pianist stood up to see me better. He looked like an aging, nervous, pygmy hornless goat in black-rimmed specs.

"It's Doctor Wanderbaum!" E.B. cried out, and then, a little less enthusiastically, indicated the bassist, six feet tall, well-built, black-haired, affecting bangs and cowboy boots: "And Johnny Billiard here."

Doctor Wanderbaum and Johnny Billiard. They were the two phoniest names I'd ever heard in my life. In spite of which, as I got up on the stand to shake hands, I felt a small thrill at being with professionals and, for the first time, on a kind of eminence where I mean to belong.

"Happy New Year, Mike," the pianist said with a kind of mocking solemnity. "What do doctors hate?"

God, I didn't know. Illness? Dirt? Hypochondriacs? "Tell me," I said.

"People who call them 'Doc,' " said Doctor Wanderbaum. "Where did you find a cummerbund?"

"A gift," I said.

"Couldn't buy it in this town for fifty dollars. Will you take sixty? Sold to Doctor Wanderbaum for ninety dollars." He shook my hand. "Next the pants?"

"Ha'r ya?" said Johnny Billiard.

" 'Sit Right Down,' " said Dr. Wanderbaum, but he didn't mean me. He was calling a tune, "I'm Gonna Sit Right Down and Write Myself a Letter." I went over to the table.

They started in the usual way, with an introduction you could tell they'd often played before, and then into the melody of the chorus. It wasn't really fast, but they swung it hard—straight, not in the strange manner Scholay liked so well—and I relaxed to it, subvocalizing happily, when an arm came over my shoulder from behind, setting down a double shot of whiskey on the table, closing lightly then across my chest, and there was breath on my neck, and a voice taking the words out of my mouth, changing them, not much over a whisper:

A lot of kisses on the bottom/ I'll be glad I got 'em.

Evaun. The way she did it had the quality of a child telling a joke it knows is dirty but doesn't really understand.

Then she was gone from behind me, on around the table, rippling up onto the platform like a cross between a cheerleader and an otter.

She faced the audience, smiling, arms up and out, switched her tail at her twin brother, wheeled and took his mike away. He played at trying to fight her for it, she hugged the thing and shook her head and he let her win the clowning. She pivoted away to the front of the platform, tapped her foot, waited for the moment, and came in on the last lines of the chorus, hollering:

I'm gonna sit right down and write myself a letter

and the band hollered with her, pointing at E.B., who cringed theatrically.

And make believe it came from you.

At this nonsense, Doctor Wanderbaum at the piano twinkled and laughed, threw his goatish head back, and played, beginning with an unexpected little signal chord, four digressive bars to which he sang:

> *This is a bit too low, E.B.,*
> *Let's kick it on up to the key of G.*

Evaun smiled and tapped, motioning them to get on with it, and
Johnny Billiard teased back with some fancy chord work, E. B. Jones
with little runs, till the instruments were all adjusted together. Then I
could follow the way Doctor Wanderbaum led Evaun into her vocal,
but I found the whole stagy thing bothersome. I was here for musicians, not entertainers. That was the trouble with having a girl around.
She was sweet enough—but enough of sweet. Make music. Good luck,
Mike.

With the Doctor's right hand in the treble sending her through the
phrases, Evaun got her vocal off to a nice, lilting start. She had a pretty
voice, higher than I'd expected and nicely coached. People looked and
listened. I did, too. And I've got to admit that vocal quality wasn't the
real show. Evaun projects some kind of nutty, innocent, born-to-be-
raped sexuality up there. Men stood to watch at the rear tables; women
rocked and swayed in their seats, looking a little lascivious themselves.
I poured the rest of the double shot of whiskey down my throat, bit
the ice cube in two and told myself, grow up before you throw up.

E. B. Damnyou Jones was grinning at me. I looked away and set
myself to thinking song patterns. The "Stardust" pattern is thirty-two
bars, divided into two sixteen-bar halves, yes, and "Sit Right Down"
is one of those, yes sir. Whereas the "Bye Bye Blackbird" pattern is
divided into quarters, featuring two identical eights, a variation called
the release or bridge, and returns to the beginning melody for the final
eight, as also exemplified by "Sweet Lorraine." Something was happening as Evaun reached the bridge for her reprise chorus. The Doctor
was hanging ornaments instead of leading her, and she was slipping
into something mechanical, too much on the beat, singsong, dead, and
the sexuality stopped working when the song did, but Lord, he picked
her up again, the swing was back, and as the dancers Lindyed and the
others started clapping even before it finished, suddenly the whole, mad
bunch of us was hollering with her:

> *Air mayal speshuldee livv—err—reeyeeyee-ai—ee.*

Me too. Jesus, next thing you know I'd be letting them put a funny hat
on me, and hell, she could have done just that, sitting down beside me,
close, shoulder against my arm, body heat, and I wanted to kiss her,

but instead I made myself count down, from twenty-five to not-yet-seventeen.

Mizzourin/**GOOFUS**

The set was over. Here came E. B. Jones.

"You like her song?"

"Everybody loved it."

"Even if she is my sister. Hey Mike, tell what you done to Marvin Merrill . . ."

"You told it already," Evaun said, looked around to make sure, I suppose, that no one in authority was looking, filched the glass of beer E.B.'d just poured himself, and drank off half of it.

"Merrill?"

"That's our ugly uncle, got the music store." It made her, briefly, pensive.

"Hell of a player." This was Doctor Wanderbaum, who had finished chatting with Johnny Billiard and sat down with us now, a cup of coffee in front of him. Seeing him up close, I realized he wore a hairpiece. "You know Marvin, I take it. And if I know Marvin, he probably took it."

"Not very well," I said.

"Shop steward of the union here. Make that shoplifter? Do I hear a second? You're a musician?"

"They swapped horns," E.B. said. "Mike got Marvin's cornet."

Doctor Wanderbaum seemed to find this unremarkable, for he said: "Some feel that Marvin should be voted out as steward, since he is also the sole booker of musicians and often the employer. Sells us reeds, music, instruments, rents us dress clothes. In my view . . ." He took a sip of coffee, made a face as if he were about to spit it out, and then with a look of infinite courage, swallowed. ". . . he is the perfect union rep. He knows the sort of crooks he has to deal with."

"He puts hisself in all the bands that come," E.B. said. "Like Woody Herman last month."

"It's a union regulation," Doctor Wanderbaum said. "It's right there in the contract Marvin negotiated with himself. All touring bands have to use one or two competent local players. Well, is there someone else around in brass who could read Woody Herman's charts? Can Woody Herman read them? Did you know he offered Marvin a regular job? Any time Marvin wants to join them, he's to send a telegram collect."

"Did he?" I thought Evaun looked hopeful.

"I don't know about the telegram, but Marvin's sure to collect."

E. B. Jones said: "He never told us."

The Doctor smiled. There are tufts of gray hair that stick out of his ears, and a shirky little smile that plays under his flat nose. His teeth are very large, incongruous, younger looking than the rest of the face.

While the character analysis of Marvin Merrill was going on, Johnny Billiard was out at one of the tables, where a drunk young customer seemed pretty much asleep, accompanied by a wide-awake, sulky young sober lady—a big brunette with heavy, bare shoulders, a wide mouth and tits like punching bags. Johnny Billiard was treating the sulks by showing her how his wire brushes for the drums went peekaboo into their rubber sleeves; and, from the way he was moving a full highball glass into her hand, maybe he was going to take care of the sobriety soon.

The Doctor was speaking to me: "Did you bring your horn, Mike? Sit in. The worse you are, the better this crowd will like it."

"Thanks, I left it back."

"Shoo, baby," Evaun Barlow said, leaning in, brushing her lips across my cheek and bringing her hand up in front of my face. "What you call this?" And the wretched little pickpocket was holding up the extra flugelhorn mouthpiece which I'd been carrying for luck.

I sputtered and E.B. broke up, laughing and snorting. "She kin do it, caint she do it? Right into the old pocket, never felt a thing, didya?" Picked up the beer pitcher and drank from the edge, spilling beer down his neck and laughing harder.

"Sign of the serious student," Doctor Wanderbaum said. He took the mouthpiece from Evaun and looked it over. "Some may whistle, some may hum." He picked up an empty beer glass, cupped the mouthpiece in his hand, and blew on it into the glass, accurately and with quite a pleasant resonance, the first few bars of "I'm Gonna Sit Right Down." He tossed my mouthpiece back to me. "When I write myself that letter, I must remember to enclose a check," he said, stood, bowed, and strode off to the men's room.

Evaun Barlow looked me in the eye and said: "Can you play at all? Don't lie."

"No." I said. She kissed my ear. "Hey, leave that ear alone. I'm going to learn. Do you think the Doctor would give me lessons?" What was I saying? I was the guy who couldn't wait to wave goodbye to Faraday.

"Teaches me, but not the one for you." Evaun looked at her twin brother. He was beginning to look a little smashed, but he seemed to understand her question, and he nodded. "Uncle Ugly Marvin the best in Carolina," Evaun said.

"Thanks. If I decide to try him, I'll say you recommended him."

"Don't you never." Spookily serious, she seized my arm. "Don't never tell that man I said one word about him."

"Nor me." E.B. was just as urgent. "Mike you got to keep it quiet what we say."

"Okay," I said. "Okay." Smiled my damnedest and patted hands. For reasons I'd have found too metaphysical to explain, these twins could count on me. Send for me anytime and here I'd come, airmail special deliveree.

Mizzourin/THE DIPSY DOODLE

When Doctor Wanderbaum came back from the restroom, Johnny Billiard was still at the table with the heavy-shouldered, sullen brunette, whose date had now passed out cold. Johnny was sitting with them, as a matter of fact, and had his right hand up under her skirt in a friendly sort of way.

I sensed the Doctor didn't approve this style of friendship, but maybe it's hindsense. It wasn't until midnight, when he seemed to be sauce-for-the-gandering, that I saw Doctor Wanderbaum as jealous and a lover. He's been traveling with Johnny Billiard since long before the war began, playing here and there. They've stayed on in Faraday a long time for them, I'm told, because bar business here is bustling since the fort became a discharge center. But other titillations first. Forty minutes yet to go till midnite.

The Doctor said: "If no one else needs to shake the dew off his lily— or hers? Should we say rosy?—we might play. Music, that is." He sounded, unless it's hindhearing, quite fretful. Johnny Billiard had the sullen girl on her feet, was whispering in her ear and moving her toward us. "Lily and rosy games on your own time, please."

"That the only way you can tell the difference between me and E.B.," Evaun asked sweetly. "Shoulda seen us when we was little, Doctor. Mamma used to dress us up the same?" She was getting wicked, squeezing my wrist. "You'da had to turn me right upside down."

"She wouldna kicked you if you had, neither," said E. B. Jones. And the next thing they did was eerily twinlike. They said, at exactly the same moment, exactly the same words with the same wistful inflection. "Mamma old now, Mike. Never knew our dad."

Johnny arrived just then and presented his friend to me with a heavy wink. "This is Lizabeth. She'd like a dance with you, buddy."

"Mike," I said. "Mike Mizzourin. Shall we?" I got up. Evaun pinched my buttock hard. Or E.B. did. They both looked away when I turned my head, then at one another and rolled their eyes.

I didn't mind pitching batting practice, though I'd have been less eager if I'd understood about Doctor Wanderbaum. I was much more aware of Evaun watching with some sort of mixture of amusement and concern, as the set started and I moved in against Lizabeth, whose family name she said was "Haas." That was her whole share of the conversation.

I can't say I tried very hard to keep the chatter going, either, not when I realized that for Lizabeth there was only one dance step; tune and tempo made no difference (they were playing "Rocking Chair"). Her step was Rhombo's rhumbo—I liked it, too, I do confess—the snatchover crotchlock. She saw no reason to let me hold her hand out and away; under my armpit was the place to put one, and around my neck the other, while both of mine belonged low around the waist. In this posture we moved together and inserted legs, fitted pudenda, and had one preliminary twitch for adjustment. Then we were off and rubbing. Do as the Rhombons do.

No one paid a bit of heed except Evaun, and since she was not quite seventeen, I meant for her to get a grapefruit in the eyeful. Let her pick on someone her own age. I gave in to sensuality and danced through the whole four-number set (we half-timed "Runnin' Wild," like everybody else did except the jitterbugs), with a mightily erect lily throbbing against a pulsing rosy, these edifying blossoms separated by, at most, four layers of thin and ever-moister cloth. Lizabeth seemed to address herself to this with no more involvement of personalities than if she'd been at home alone taking care of herself with a doorknob, and perhaps something equivalent held true for me.

During the brief respites between songs, she would draw back and look, first at Johnny Billiard, then over at her sleeping date. Then she'd move up against and around me, as the music started in, and start the hunch. Me too.

I wasn't sure which way to walk her when the set was done, and I had myself rearranged. I looked at Johnny for a signal, and he indicated Lizabeth's date whose head had come up off the table and was waggling or maybe wobbling. So I turned her that way, and she broke off and headed there, gesturing to me not to follow.

I went to the musicians' table. Johnny Billiard said: "Thanks, buddy. Looks like you kept the coffee warm."

Doctor Wanderbaum had gone straight to the men's room this time. Seemed like his kidneys lasted just one set. E.B. was off talking to a man I'd seen behind the bar earlier, and who I'd learned was Tommy Rhombo.

"Glad to oblige," I said.

"Some other night, it's gonna be your turn."

"Take it away, Cobber," I told him. Sure, Lizabeth could get my percolator bubbling, too, but it was still souls I wanted to rub, even with another double whiskey going down, a little stardusting for mine, an old howl at some new moon—and I looked around to see if someone wonderful might have come slipping in by herself to join the party.

"There's lotsa empty cars out there," Johnny mused.

"You the biggest damn fool ever," Evaun said. "First thing, they don't call her Lizabeth no more. They call her Pony. Pony Haas, cause even little boys can ride her."

"Well, that's all right," Johnny said. "I just want once around the fairground."

"You listen, too, you Mike." She caught me a crisp little punch on the upper arm. It hurt. "Pony got two brothers. Call 'em Horse and Mule. Horse Haas a bully, Mule a cop, and there is trouble for anyone them boys catch fooling with Lizabeth, 'cept that drunk over there she's with and gonna marry. Palmer Ingree. The Haas boys aim to see that wedding."

"Well Palmer Whatsisname won't do anyone much anything to-night," Johnny said.

"Third thing, you can find yourself something just a little bit tighter and sweeter, now you know you can."

"Making me an offer, Evaun?" He grinned, and I felt a random impulse to beat his ears in for it.

But young Mrs. Evaun Barlow needed no help from the likes of Mike. "When I want peanuts, I'll take 'em salted," she said. "Fella told me Pony's quite a mare." She made about as lowdown a gesture as I've ever seen, spreading her hands in front of his face, thumb tips down and touching, index fingers touching and up, outlining a space like a cross-section of a good, big pear. "Guess it ain't no bigger than this."

Johnny grimaced and pulled his face away, and Evaun hit my arm again, twice.

*Mizzourin/*DOWN HOME RAG

What the double-knuckling did, with some double-whiskey help, while the trio was playing music and I sat with young Mrs. Evaun Barlow, was loose the tie-down on my tattling tongue. Ah, did it flap and flutter in the breeze of her regard. Like a high school dolt on a high school date, I minnesang the moron song of Mike, knowing myself a knothead, as hard to stop talking as to stop drinking.

If she was almost seventeen, how much younger was I all of a whiskey-sudden?

It started this way.

"Ain't you got to go home and see yore folks, Mike?"

"They're not together. My father went back in the navy when the depression came. He was hardly ever home after I started school."

"All ready for the war, wasn't he?"

"He's a CPO now. On permanent station at Pearl Harbor."

"Hawaii? Oh, that's where I want to go."

"As the guys said in the army, 'If Hawaii's paradise, Pittsburgh must be heaven.' Dad's welcome to it."

"Don't yore mom want to be there?"

"The farther they are apart, the better they get along," I said. "Mom was the town librarian where my brothers and I grew up. As well as ran the farm."

"Librarian here's a mighty sweet lady, Mrs. Miller."

"My mother's more a mighty tough lady," I said. Then I was talking about Mom raising the three of us, putting us through the chores and farmwork, getting us to school winter mornings. Often we'd all four walk two miles, when the Model A wouldn't start or there was no money for gas. I talked about shelving books after school for twenty cents an hour. It was heavy work. We didn't have those little rolling tables. I hauled the books in boxes and by armloads, and everybody used the library in the depression, scattering books around like peanut hulls. Reading was free and the building was heated by the city.

Already I was well on my way to telling her what I've told just two other people, Little Balfour the medic because I felt like it, and Captain Frankel because he had to make reports to my parole officer. At least he didn't delegate it to the first sergeant, so it never got around the company, but I would guess it's also why I never got promoted. Acting Squad Leader Mike, true and forever Pfc.

"Books were my babysitters," I said, "not that I ever paid attention to who wrote them. I figured given time I could read them all. Then I was given time, but it was in a different library."

"Hey, where'd do you your time, Mike?" It was Johnny Billiard overhearing, going by the table, scooping up and drinking off a glass of beer on his way back to comfort Pony Haas whose fiancé had returned to snoreland. "State or federal?"

"Bad-boy time, Johnny," I said. I hadn't expected to be picked up. "Nothing much." I didn't ask where he'd done his.

The subject had wet its diapers and needed changing. but after the break and an awful vocal on "You Are My Sunshine" (the people loved it), Evaun sat down with me and said I was to tell her; and I did. I wanted to play it down because I felt phony, falsely colored as one of the dashing desperado boys, if I didn't explain.

"Ned, my big brother, and I could always find some trouble to get into," I said. "When we weren't fighting each other. Pete, my little brother, would tag along and get smeared, too. The bad Mizzourins. You know what it means to hold back hogs?"

"No, I sure don't."

"When the price is rotten, and you're losing money every pig, that's when the livestock buyers want to make you sell. Farmers get together and say they won't. But there's always some poor bastard can't afford another sack of feed. He's gotta cash out and take his loss, and the buyers come around in their trucks looking for those guys. The rest don't want to see that sale made, so maybe there's a partner in the truck seat with a shotgun, even a deputy. Well, you block the roads with junk machinery. You throw down mower blades and staples for the tires. You carry sugar with you for the gas tank in case you can sneak up on one that's parked.

"Then it comes to bricks. The buyer's got around and got his load. He's on his way, and if you don't get out of it, he'll run you down.

"The day they were breaking the holdback, everyone was pelting trucks. There was a mob surging around town, and ammo piles of bricks on the street corners, and of course Ned and Pete and I were in the middle of it when this guy came barreling at us. We stood our ground long enough to heave our bricks at the windshield, and somebody made a hell of a heave. Splintered the damn thing. The driver swerved, and Ned and I each had another brick. And we smashed them into the driver's side window from close up, because he'd tried to run us over. The guy was hurt. He kept going till he reached the courthouse, hit a fire hydrant in front of it, and jumped out there bloody, where the sheriff was trying to get control.

"We ran. We made it home to the farm. It felt like we'd gotten away with something again. Mom had closed the library because the town was so upset. She was upset, too, because the holdback was failing.

"They might break everybody else, but they weren't going to break us. If we couldn't afford to feed the pigs, we weren't going to give them away to the damn buyers, either. We'd shoot 'em first. Other people were doing it. So the three of us went out and drove the pigs into a ditch down to where the end was blocked. Pete and I started shooting them in the head with our .22s, pretty close up."

"Pore pigs," Evaun said.

"It was awful. Ned was on the tractor, using the blade to cover up the dead ones with dirt. The sheriff drove right across the field, with two cars full of armed deputies following. We saw them. Pete and I threw down our little rifles, and held our hands up. They made Ned get down off the tractor and lined us up. Sheriff said the truck driver was hurt, and the truck was wrecked.

" 'Which one of you was downtown?'

"People had told him a Mizzourin boy, and he didn't realize we'd been more than one downtown. Well, Ned was nineteen, but I was still a juvenile. And Pete was only fourteen. So I stepped forward and said, 'It was me, Andy.'

"So that's how it happened Neddy went to Iowa State, and Pete was able to start on scholarship at MIT, and I did seven months at Eldora, the boys' detention school, till my birthday came and they let me out to join the army."

"Didn't yore brothers feel bad?"

"I don't guess Ned will ever forgive me. Once he came to visit at Eldora and he couldn't stop cussing me. I don't guess Pete will ever stop trying to make up for it. I don't know which is worse. Anyway, I had a term and a half of college by correspondence, and the army let me finish the second term at the junior college in town. EJF, PJC, and AUS."

"What's that mean?"

"Eldora Juvenile Facility, Prairie Junior College, Army of the United States. My alma maters, Evaun. Come on, let's have a college drinking song. Chug-a-lug."

It made me feel unexpectedly good to tell her, though she was less wide-eyed about it than you might have thought. I guess a litle detention isn't all that unusual in Mrs. Barlow's set. She took my hand. "They helped you get your education." She was pleased about it. I was touched.

"It wasn't bad at Eldora. I read and worked in the garden. We had teams, football and baseball, the blues and the greens, we played each other."

"There in the North, they have colored too, right in with you?"

"No. They had a separate barracks. They had a jazz band, too, where all we had was a couple of guitar players. I'd save up cigarettes for after supper and go out and lean against the fence, smoking and listening to the colored guys rehearse and play."

"Mike, didn't them men in jail try to do stuff to you?"

"Dammit, we were all boys," I said. "There weren't any men, except guards. I heard one or two of them were queer, but as far as I'm concerned, EJF was no different than an army training camp. Hey, let's shut up about it, want to? Have a drink."

"You want to dance, Mike?" A little contrite.

Hell yes, I wanted to dance, but not to pull her close for a rub. I felt like holding that light frame lightly out away, so that I could look at her and smile and watch her smile and look back at me. We moved in a way that was almost stately for Rhombo's, to the sound of "Someday Sweetheart." Midnight was coming.

"You goin' back to Iowa, Mike?"

"There's an empty house on what used to be my granddad's farm. Good place to work on the cornet. Ned would have to let me stay there, but I doubt I'll go."

"Won't you stay with us a little bit, Mike?"

"Where I really want's New York."

"Where I really, too."

The song finished. The Doctor called her up on stage, and the people counted down as she led us: "Six, five, four, three, two, one: Happy New Year!" She yelled it and jumped down off the bandstand into my arms and kissed me hard and what the hell. I kissed hard back. Johnny Billiard rumbled into the crowd, separated Pony Haas from her stag-

gering fiancé, and kissed her hard. And Doctor Wanderbaum kissed
Binkie Jones. They were back behind the piano, partly out of sight. I
guess he's a pretty kissable kid.

"They don't think anybody seen 'em," Evaun said, pressing against
me, but neither did she. She was facing away from it. Twins.

It was just what it took to make me twenty-five again, and even as I
held her, I was looking around over her shoulder for the posse of eighteen, nineteen, twenty-year old devils who should have been there to
claim her from me. Mike the caretaker.

The trio regrouped and started in on the obligatory "Auld Lang Syne."
The people sang it, and I danced it with Evaun, fantasizing some bour-
geois enchantress just a few years older than my partner, but she'd not
have come to roughhouse Rhombo's.

Evaun the caretaker. As she fitted herself against me, firm and light,
warm cheek to my cheek, just right, I felt the needle on my drunko-
meter stop swinging back and forth from cross to boisterous and settle
neatly down on mellow. I moved my cheek back from Evaun's to smile
at her. No one was going to take her off my hands, or me off hers, so
we could dance and be fond friends, and I could keep her from the
wolves my age and older, of whom there seemed to be several leering
about, and see her safely home when this was over, which went for her
beamish brother, too, unless he truly and sincerely wanted Wanderbaum, and Evaun couldn't have pinched me harder if she'd been able
to read my patronizing mind. Ouch. On the tender part of the waist,
under the goddamn ribs, and when I jumped away she drew me back,
smiling, and whispered, "Adam an' Eve an' Pinch Me went for a walk."
She had my attention, head to toe.

During this dance, Palmer Ingree, the fiancé, got sick and was hauled
out of the place by friends, on instructions from Tommy Rhombo. The
proprietor tried to make Pony go along too. She stolidly ignored him.
A few minutes later, at the end of the auld lang set, she did leave,
Johnny Billiard having gone out the door to the parking lot thirty seconds ahead of her.

Twenty minutes later a squinchy-faced, fair sized southern cop, with
hands so big it looked like he was wearing baseball gloves, came and
got Doctor Wanderbaum to go with him to the hospital, where Cowboy Johnny Billiard was lying unconscious in what sounded like a mas-
sive state of disrepair.

Mizzourin/I HAD THE CRAZIEST DREAM

Doctor Wanderbaum panicked. It was partly professional panic, I suppose, since it was a pretty sure thing that some of Johnny's moving parts were damaged. But I knew by now that there was romantic panic, too, as the Doctor fumbled to lock up the piano, gave E. B. Binkie Jones a frantic look, and left us.

"Happen before," E.B. said. "Different places, Doctor told me. And they'd gotta leave, only before Johnny not get hurt."

"Before, Horse Haas not waitin' in the parking lot with 'is tire iron," Evaun said. "Doctor better talk sweet."

"What about the cop?" I asked. "The deputy with the big mitts. Is that Mule Haas?"

E.B. nodded, and both halves of a drunken, crotchlocked couple fell across our table, scrambled, disentangled and demanded music.

This was heard and applauded by some other revelers nearby, all grinning good-naturedly about it except for the one who cursed and said he aimed to whip Tommy Rhombo's ass to a bloody froth if the evening's cover charge didn't keep featuring live music. It sounded like he had a preference for the former.

Evaun said: "We can do one."

E.B. said, slurring but happy, "Give'm a good night set, dance'm off to bed, you bet."

And Evaun, peremptorily: "Play drums, Mike."

I stood up with them, but said, "I don't even know how to hold the sticks."

"Brushes," Evaun said. "Come on. You in the band now."

So I went with them onto the stand, picked up the wire brushes, settled onto Johnny Billiard's seat, and as E. B. Jones began a guitar chorus of "Melancholy Baby," I contributed the following sound:

One-swish-two my melancholy baby/ Swish and swish and don't be blue

I don't know if I was anywhere near the beat, but no one out there doing the Rhombo knew either.

Evaun sang it. It's a tune they've worked on, brother and sister, and either I was so mellow that I heard through rose-colored earphones, or she sang it beautifully, tenderly, with, still, that helpless, childlike sexuality that was her very own cloud and silver lining. *Wait until the sun shines through. . . .*

People danced. They actually did, in spite of the way I played. E.B. started "Blue Room" fast and nice. I offered the brushes to Evaun. She smiled and shook me off. I grinned and I played, getting into it. She grinned, paused, counted, grabbed my brushes away and handed me sticks, at which suddenly E.B. stopped, pointed to me and yelled "Mike," slapping the back of his guitar to lead me in. So I slammed the rim and slammed the skin, pedaled the bass, and some idiot cheered out there, and E.B. picked it up again. Jesus. And Tommy Rhombo was there in front, winking at me, clapping, and E.B. took it on back.

We finished. Evaun stood to the mike, and I went back to brushes while she sang "Honeysuckle Rose." What she did when her vocal was done was ripple up to me with an empty beer glass that said *Schlitz* on the side. Then she did take the brushes, slid into the chair I'd just stood up from, and it was only as I watched her take over swishing brushes across the drumhead, looking up at me, humming a little scat chorus that chased fours with E. B. Jones' guitar, that I realized she didn't mean for me to step down and fill that glass with beer.

(Charles: Next page garbled. I'll send on as soon as I can decipher. Uncle John.)

(Dear Charles: The next page is not garbled. It was hidden. I found it while he was out. I typed a copy, unsealed envelope, and here it is. Aunt Christie. I don't know what he's doing. Crazy old man. Love.)

What is unbelievable is that I did it, reached into my pocket for the mouthpiece, straddled a chair between Evaun and E.B., held the beer glass as I'd seen Doctor Wanderbaum hold it, rested the bottom of it on the chair back, and began to honk and squeal "Honeysuckle Rose."

Now I will not say that it was melody, nor even that a sound came out each time I tried to blow a note. But what sounds did were soft, they were in rhythm, getting audible. It was probably more like someone blowing a conch shell or a jug than like any other horn the world has ever known before.

Most likely no one heard except Evaun, E.B. and me, and the two of them were smiling most happily.

It was the nicest I have ever felt in my life. Making some kind of music together. Me and my chums, guitar and drums . . .

Just before the end, though, Evaun leaned over and said in my ear, "Mike, don't look now."

So I finished my last few, strange bars, let E.B. end it, and then looked over at our table. Mule Haas had sat down there, and with him my dear friend Gatch.

"Uh. Ooof. Hello. Fff."
"What?"
"I said, 'Hello.' Wait. Glasses. Oo. Hey! I'm awake now. Is it Roxie?"
"Shh! Dear, he's counterfeiting."
"Darlene? Counterfeiting? Deke?"
"Charles! This is Christie. Christie Johnson."
"Yes. Oh. Yes, Mrs. Johnson. Hi."
"I woke you up again, but you thought it was Roxie. Or Darlene. Would that have been better? Such sweet names. Roxie's the one you wanted it to be, isn't she? Because you said her first."
"Hi, Mrs. Johnson. Christie."
"I'm so sorry it's only me."
"I'm glad to hear from you. I was going to write to thank you for sending the hidden page."
"He makes you call him Uncle John, but Darlene's the one in the office. I remember. Is she pretty? Would you like to call me Aunt Christine? It's not very modern."
"Sure, if you like. I don't know any other aunts."
"I'd like to be one, such a troubling reason that I called."
"What is it, Aunt Christie."
"That does sound nice. It's John. Do you remember? When I didn't want you to write to him at first, but at first I was wrong and it seemed to help him, but now. And I can't stop him."
"Do you mean the editing he did? He just changed the order of things a little. He told me about it. It's all right."
"No."
"Excuse me?"
"It's not all right. It's not just editing. He has an old typewriter, Charles, and you'll have to be so very careful."
"An old typewriter."
"When he left the paper. He took his typewriter. It was, oh, a sentimental matter. And so very old now, and he can't replace the worn old platen any more, the keys, the paint is quite worn off. He keeps it up the best he can, and sometimes uses it."
"I see. Well. That's, uh, touching."
"You don't understand, do you? And it's my fault, too. It's the same

kind as all the other typewriters were on the paper. The same kind of type."

"Wait. Just a minute, I—"

"The same as Mike used."

"Yes."

"Your father used. John wrote on the typewriter this afternoon. I know the sound of it."

"You think he's written a counterfeit page?"

"I know he has."

"Why?"

"To change Evaun and Mike and what you think of them."

"Thank you for telling me, Aunt Christie. Thank you for sending the true page before the false one came."

"Oh, Charles."

"Did you know Evaun?"

"Sometimes I think of the little soiled angels down in hell and feel so sad for them, but then I think, no, an angel can do anything and never be defiled, but I'm running on and in a minute I'll sound as crazy as John, won't I?"

"Did . . . Uncle John know Evaun?"

"Oh, I've been in such a race. You'll see. Will you phone me when John's next letter comes, with the page he wrote? You see, he means it to be the very last thing you'll see of Mike's, but what I've done. He drove off to Capsicum with his page and his letter, and as soon as he was gone, because I have a key to the studio he doesn't know about. I jumped in my car with all the following pages that he'd left out on his desk, the rest are in the safe and I don't have any way of opening it. Not yet. I sped like lightning to Durango, which is the other way, but I knew I'd have time because John is such a poky driver, and I can Xerox too, because the post office. But he goes to his lawyer's office in Capsicum to Xerox and save money, and I knew he'd visit with Jerry, that's the lawyer who's divorced and so he works nights every night, and John sits with him, and they have drinks. You see?"

"I think so. You took some pages to Durango, copied them there, and sent them to me."

"Well. Mrs. Harper."

"Mrs. Harper?"

"My cleaning woman. So reliable, and such a dear. The mailing desk at the post office was closed, but the Xerox machine is in the lobby. So I copied and left them with Mrs. Harper all addressed and everything, and gave her money for the postage, and hurried back through the night and put the pages where he left them, and here I am."

"Thank you, Aunt Christie, very much. May I ask you something?"

"Oh, yes please."

"Do you know if Evaun Barlow's still alive?"

"Such a pretty name."

"Yes. It is."

"But I think Roxie's pretty, too, isn't she the one you like?"

"You did know her."

"No, but of course I'd love to meet her if I ever get to Washington. Now here comes John's car. Wouldn't that be fun?"

"Aunt Christie?"

"Good night, Charles. Good night, dear. Call me, won't you?"

> *c/o American Express*
> *Rome, Italy*
> *March 10, 1980*

Hon. Deke Esterzee
Neph. Charles Mizzourin
Dear Shitheads:

Tough luck. My airplane didn't crash. Here I am, making arrangements to travel the Arab world. Just phoned in my impressions of Rome. Want to know more about it, see the D.M. *Register, your favorite rag. Just happened I was a block away when some commie terrorists shot a lunkhead socialist cabinet pinko in the kneecap. Heard the shot and ran there in time to see the wop cops gun down one of the reds. They were spraying bullets like city farts opening day of deer season, and got them a bystander. Kind of a Guinea Mama type. You could put her in a movie. You know, fat? She wasn't hurt too bad, and I got photographed with my arm around her, blood on my shirt, "giving first aid." Ha, ha. It's going to be your favorite Page One wirefoto, just about the time you get this letter, won't it? Take good care of my office, boys, and remember: when you move out and I move in, I don't want you to leave any lacy little pink curtains on the "men's" room windows, okay?*

> *Yours truly,*
> *Ned Mizzourin*

"Hello?"

"Charlbo. What you doing?"

"Getting ready to cook supper."

"I got the letter here, Charlie. Your Uncle Ned's a friendly fella, ain't he?"

"Did the *Register* come?"

"Hand-carried. Stuart sent it with an airline girl."

"Picture in it?"

"Yeah. Neddy missed guessing by a few pages, though. It's on five."

"I suppose that's something."

"Story starts page one, though. 'CALDER PLAIN MAN AT SCENE OF TERRORIST ATTACK. Edward "Ned" Mizzourin Aids Victim, Vows to Work Against World Violence. Picture and other related stories on Page Five.' "

"Other stories?"

"Two more. One's a sidebar on Italian terrorists. Other's a phone interview with your charming uncle. Says seein' terrorism at first hand makes him want to study it and understand it. Says he's mostly overseas to find his brother, hopes to rescue him, but even if he don't, he'll gain some humble, bumble knowledge that could maybe help a sore and troubled old world, yessir."

"That's my uncle."

"Clickity-click. The wounded grandma and the Eagle Scout. Nice picture. Clear enough for a brochure. Want to hear the rest?"

"There more?"

"Flansburg's column on the op-ed page. He's picked up Republican talk that Ned Mizzourin might make a strong, conservative candidate, tune with the times, so hell: Flansburg called Neddie, too, for a comment. Neddie says he's not gonna humble, bumble think about any such thing, not whilst he's tryin' to solve the mystery of his little brother's disappearance. Next stop Libya."

"Maybe you should go over, Deke. You're the only one that's gotten anywhere with Petrolat."

"I been talking with this airline girl Stuart sent about what it'd cost. She's been traveling over there. Even with free tickets, she still went through five-years' savings in a month or two. Let's have a staff meetin' first thing tomorrow, Charlie. Tell everybody what's going on, and see who's got ideas."

"Okay."

"Who you cooking supper for besides yourself?"

"Matter of fact, I have a lady coming."

"That right? Matter of fact, I have a dinner date myself."

"Darlene?"

"No, Charliedoll. The airline girl."

File on my father (and other matters). Notes:

On with the green-sofa story, kiddo?
Well, the setting changes, but we're moving in the same direction. I seem
to be in love with our Ms. Talley. I love her voice. I love the understated
way she handles herself. It's pretty clear she's got some feeling for me, even
so. I have to fight against getting (Phone)

"Hello?"

"Hello. Jack Deming from the *Des Moines Register* calling for Mr.
Charles Mizzourin?"

"You've got him."

"We've learned that you're Ned's nephew, Mr. Mizzourin. Is that
correct?"

"Yes it is."

"You're also an aide to Deke Esterzee, right?"

"That's right."

"Well, how do you feel about your uncle's heroics?"

"Is that what you really want to know?"

"I tried to call Deke. I can't reach him."

"He'll be at the office tomorrow."

"How do you think your uncle might stack up against Deke in the
fall election?"

"Do you realize it's nearly eleven o'clock here?"

"Hell, you political guys keep late hours, don't you?"

"Not this one, Mr. Deming. If you'll excuse me, I'm going to say
good night."

"Okay, Charlie, okay."

. . . possessive. It was a lovely evening, till I blew it. She was wearing
dark blue silk with (Phone. I think I'll tear its tonsils out.)

"Hello?"

"Charlie, is Deke with you?"

"No, Darlene."

"Know where he is?"

"No, I don't."

"A reporter's trying to get him."

"I know. He got me instead."

"How could he? Your phone was off the hook."

"I'll leave it on now, in case Deke calls."

"I'm going to try some restaurants. Hey, Charlie?"

"Yes?"

"Do you like to hear a beautiful woman say 'shit'?"

"Not especially."

"Shit."

"I didn't mind too much."

"Sweet man."

(Notes:) I had lamb chops to cook, and a bottle of California Columbard. Roxie brought wine, too. French, and it probably can't be as good as I thought it was. The label says *Sancerre*.

"So you'll believe in my sancerrity, you mutt," she said when she gave it to me. "Is that too dreadful a pun?"

I thought it was the most scintillating pun I ever heard in my life. I helped her off with her coat. The blue polka-dot gown is a shirtwaist affair, one of the classic lines, simple and young. I thought it was pretty scintillating too. It set off the blue of her eyes, and the tailoring was the right contrast for the windblown, curly hair.

Her perfume was something simple and wholesome; it made me dizzy. When she brushed her lips across my cheek it made me dizzier.

She went tripping off around the apartment and cried out: "But you haven't changed a thing, you lazy man. Not so much as moved a chair."

I was reminded that she'd known "the chap who just moved out," and knew, from the way I had to bite back the impulse to ask about him, how far gone I was.

It's Roxie's voice, and the things she says that shake me up, as much as anything.

You're repeating yourself.

Listen to this: while I was getting supper, she sat in the kitchen watching me, with her shoes off, and picked up the morning *Post*.

"See here, Charles," she said. "If I'm not to help cook, I shall read the paper to you. Would you care to hear 'News in Brief from Major League Spring Training Camps'?"

"Yes, please," I said. Actually, I'd been about to ask her about her life in England, and why she left, but Roxanne forestalled it.

She'd read a little and then summarized: "That will do for Atlanta. The writer presumes that this Mr. Aaron will create oodles more roundtrippers this year, Charles. Do you agree?"

Even when she talks nonsense, the voice raises hairs on my arms.

We ate and finished the Sancerre. I talked about Uncle Ned. I had a little wood fire going in the fireplace. It felt nice on this damp March evening, and we sat in front of it, close together.

Roxie had her pumps off again, and I was holding her and admiring the smallness of her foot, the toes showing through nylon, when she murmured: "Oh, no. I'm not going to expose my dear little feet for some great brute in hobnails to smash," and she slipped out of my arms, knelt down, untied my shoes and took them off. She was giggling about it in a throaty way, taking off my socks, tickling my ankles. Then she slid the right trouser leg up, massaging and tickling the calf, until she was able to say, "Oh, dear. Such a surprise. A perfectly normal kneecap."

"That's where the commie shot the pinko," I said.

"I haven't my gun." She kissed it, pressed her cheek against it, nibbled away at the hamstring, and ran her hand up the other trouser leg. I felt relaxed and aroused at the same time, if that's possible, my hand caressing the tousled hair, when my doorbell rang.

I got my trouser legs pulled down and straight, took a swift, fond kiss, and went to the door. It was skinny, mugging Angela, the bane of my evenings.

"Sorry to bother, luv," she said. "I must have a word with Roxie, you see. Roxanne!" Angela was in fur. Roxie came along behind me, and I stepped aside.

"Yes, Angie?"

"You're to ring up Suesue. She's been trying to get through on Charles' line for ever so long. Phone off hook time, is it? Sorry, then. Ta-ta."

"You're off?"

"Yes, then. I have a chap waiting." Angela said, and went.

"Oh, Charles," Roxie said, as the door closed. "Can you pretend you didn't get the message? No, that's a dumb question."

She smiled and squeezed my upper arm. "It may amount to nothing," she said, and went to the bedroom to use the phone. I rinsed the damn dishes for something to do. The dishes were done by the time Roxie arrived in the kitchen and said: "Do forgive me, Charles."

"You're leaving?"

"I'm afraid so."

"Going to tell me why?"

"Suesue has a problem."

"I'll go with you."

"It's a female problem. She is in change of life, you know."

"No. I don't know. Why can't she take a drink and a pill and go to bed?"

"But that's just it. She's not at home. She's at a party she wishes to leave. But not with the gentleman who took her."

"Senator Hibben?"

"Charles."

"Old Whip and Cream."

"I hardly think it's he. Most likely it's her air force general, if you must know. I didn't ask, and I must go instantly."

"General?"

"I forget his name. They're bridge partners."

"How did you know where to call Suesue, Roxie?"

"Beg pardon?"

"If she's not home, how did you know where to call? I didn't hear Angela give you a number."

"Are you being beastly suspicious? Frankly, Charles, I knew because I was meant to go to the same bloody party, and preferred coming here to you."

"Okay, Roxie. I'll get your coat."

"Now that will do, my boy."

I turned away, feeling cheated and stupid, and felt her arms come up and around me from behind. She kissed the back of my neck and said, "I'll go to bed with you this instant for five minutes, my darling. Will it help?"

I turned and smiled and hugged. "I'm almost dumb enough to say yes. But no. I'm not quite."

"But there, you see. I am." She pressed up close. "But thank you, dearest Charles."

I called a cab for her, and we did a lot of smiling and aching till it came.

Last Deadline Ranch

Charlie, my boy. It will be best to stop after this, I think. The child does not mean or wish to walk into the master bedroom on a summer evening, where, the flowered pink comforter pulled aside, sheets sliding off the maple bed, striped ticking of the mattress like the bedding's underclothes, the parents grunt and tumble in what looks like desperate combat. Tears of turmoil fill the young eyes. He feels betrayed in ways he cannot name. It will be time hereafter to draw the curtains on your father. You will know him now, I wot, the good, the bad. Join me in saying RIP, UJMJ.

(Notes:) Here follows Johnson's forgery. I like to think I would have guessed.

Mizzourin/I HAD THE CRAZIEST DREAM

What is unbelievable is that I did it, reached into my pocket for the mouthpiece, sat down between Evaun and E.B., straddling a chair, holding the beer glass as I'd seen the demented Wanderbaum hold it, began to honk and squeal "Honeysuckle Rose," a song the recollection of whose suggestive lyrics no doubt helped to ignite me.

It was the randiest I ever felt in my life. Both twins looked equally delicious, but it was Evaun who put her soft little hand trustingly in mine, orbed me with her stunning lavenders, and said: "Honey hon. I know how you boys suffered in the war, ain't you? What can I do to make it up now?"

Drawing the child close, and ignoring the evident apprehension of E. B. Binkie Jones on her behalf, no matter that he had shown himself a decadent, I formed a plan.

The latest double whiskey had, it seems, dissolved my scruples. I wanted flesh now! Clean, fresh, yielding, young meat! I lusted, as I had in times gone by for Harriet! For Penny! For Maureen!

"Don't you look so evil at her, sir," Binkie said, and I showed the effete little wretch a clenched fist, behind Evaun's back. This was no hulking bully of a brother, waiting with tire iron in the parking lot, but someone I could smash with pleasure if he hindered me. I goaded him by letting him see me start to caress a soft young breast, pressing and turning it, until the nipple was showing through the fabric of the gown.

A quick little piece of copper and brass would quench my searing inner fire, meseemed, and so I whispered to her, tongue in ear the while: "I've an old friend at the hotel, just a minute away. Let's go say Happy New Year to him."

Immediately she rose, but said uncertainly, "Did you want for Binkie to come, too?"

"Oh, please, may I?" the boy said, his coral lips aflutter. I rather itched to fatten them.

"You'd better stay and play with your guitar," I said scowling, in case he still dreamed of taking away my prize. "We'll be back for you." I hurried her away, then, putting my Eisenhower jacket around her tremulous shoulders, and my bulging trousers in her twin brother's line of sight. And was the dear lad truly concerned for his sister, or mayhap jealous of her?

Cosmo Selkirk was, as I'd hoped, asleep away from his desk when I used the lobby key to enter. The hotel lounge was deserted, though there was much sound of firm, young revelry upstairs, in the direction of which I urged my firm, young friend, saying I needed a sweater from my room.

Arriving there, I could hear music from nearby. We entered 300G. I closed the door, checked to make sure the spring lock was working, and said: "Music."

" 'Stardust.' "

"Now we shall dance." With this I held her to me, fitting my leg between hers and lifting much of her weight onto my thigh. A step, a half-turn, and we were at the nearer of the two beds. I tightened my embrace, and with my thrusting leg propelled her back and down.

"Don't hurt me," she pleaded, but I was now beside myself with passion. "I'm a virgin."

"Behave," I said, and, lightening my weight upon her but not enough to free her limbs, reached to her ankles for the skirt, and raised it to the navel, exposing long pink limbs and flimsy panties so thin they darkened at the little crotch. Holding her motionless with one strong arm around her waist, I unpanted my rigid flower and greenhouse, at the sight of which she squeaked.

"Behave," I said again, finding the word delicious in the circumstance, and tugged down the waistband of the panties to expose her Southern Carolina, lightly haired and barely cleft. Working her panties down now to her knees and lower, I moved a second leg between her two against which she tried in vain to close herself away. Hands on her hips, reaching one underneath to seize myself and guide, I thrust until I felt the yielding, and pushed in firmly. Meseems she turned a twisting bundle of consent at that, rising to meet me and enfold, and just in time. Hydraulic pressure built almost to the point of pain, held, released, and flooded into her. We were both throbbing from the effort.

Control was everything. "Thank you, my pet," I said, slowly releasing myself and rolling off. "Tidy yourself. We must hurry back."

Acknowledging me her master, the child rose, recovering her panties from the floor, looking at me with huge, worshiping eyes.

It was on our return to Rhombo's, Evaun clinging docile and still trembling a bit to my arm, that suddenly she said: "Don't look now." But I did look, over at our table.

Mule Haas had sat down there, and with him my dear friend Gatch.

Last Deadline Ranch
My dear Charles: Two notes to this lamentable account, which I hope you have read more charitably than I—though I am not insensitive to the pressures of sexual deprivation. 1. Mrs. Evaun Barlow's claim to virginity makes her a little liar who well deserved what she got, unless we choose to consider that her nuptials with the soldier Barlow produced, in fact, un marriage blanc. *2. The*

officers were at Rhombo's to arrest your father for his theft of government prop-
erty, of course. The rest of the manuscript recounts his return to prison and was
written there. I do not think you will want to see it. I hardly need add that we
did not know of his criminal record when we hired him for the newspaper.

                                                                    UJMJ

Dear Uncle John:
The pages you sent about my father and Evaun going to the hotel seem strange
to me. They seem out of character for him and for her as well, and there are
things about the style which disturb me. For example, up to now he has always
used his coinage "Eisenweasel" in place of the name "Eisenhower." The rhythms
are wrong, and some of the archaisms out of place.

I recall your note explaining that you were delaying this material because it
seemed "garbled." This suggests that perhaps, back at the newspaper, some
colleague and confidant wrote the material, garbling it in haste, on my father's
typewriter, and slipped it into the Fake Book journal as a prank.

The information you've asked for about Suesue is not really in hand, except
as a couple of rough guesses which should be refined. Houses like the two she
owns side by side in this neighborhood sell for $150,000 to $200,000 these
days. She probably bought them for quite a bit less, though the conversion into
apartments may have been costly. Aggregate rents may be $45,000 to $50,000
a year, since she probably charges most tenants about twice what I pay ($400).
She owns other conversions, I don't know where or how many—two or three,
I think—as well as her own home, which I described to you. Her net worth
may be as much as a million dollars, though she may also have debts that I
don't know about. Her income, from rentals, is probably $70,000 to $100,000.
Again, there may be other income, as well as other obligations. She seems to
be a shrewd real estate investor, anyway, and may have been guided by influ-
ential friends, of whom Senator Hibben is not the only one.

Even if my father's journal does continue from prison—and I recall your
saying that you are reading not far ahead of what you send me each time, so it
may not turn out so—I want very much to see the rest. My guess is that the
prank continued, and that you will be able to discard further spurious pages. I
hope the next you send me will be genuine.

                                                                    Charlie

"Collect call for Charles Mizzourin from Scott Helmreich. Will you
accept?"
   "Scott Helmreich? Sure."
   "Hello, Knucks."

"Why collect, Scott?"

"Don't want it on my bill here. They pad outrageously. I'll reimburse."

"What bill? Where are you?"

"I'm in the bide-a-wee, drying out."

"You're not coming tomorrow?"

"No, Knucks. That pup won't wag."

"Is something really wrong with you, Scott?"

"Just oversaturation."

"Same bide-a-wee you've visited before, I suppose."

"Awful place. At cocktail hour, it's one martini and all the ice water you can drink. And then a shot, and chow down if you can keep it down. God, they're cheerful about it."

"What made you decide to go in now?"

"It wasn't I. Your baby blue mother."

"What happened?"

"I was pruning apple trees."

"Well. It's that time of year."

"Only the apple trees were in a neighbor's yard, and I didn't know the neighbor. Who phoned the constables."

"They could have come out and asked who you were."

"In the freezing rain at eleven P.M., wearing pajamas and working by flashlight on a Chinese elm? Charlie, your mother will be there anyway. United, Flight 61, Dulles at 12:05."

"I'll meet it."

"Watch your scalp. She's on the war path against males."

"She does get that way. Is it because of what my father did?"

"You've never asked me about that before. Yes, partly."

"It didn't seem fair to ask you, and I won't push you now. I've started doing a little pushing, though. I may go after mother."

"I'll tell you this. I think she ought to open up, for her own sake as much as yours. I've told her so."

File on my father. Notes:

There was a dogfight today at the fashionable Coq d'Or Restaurant between Livia "Borzoi" (Scalinger) Helmreich and Charlie "Terrier" Mizzourin.

I'm just back in the office from it, and still growling.

Neither Mother nor I was in a very affectionate mood when we faced off across the lunch table. Her plane was early, my meeting ran late; she'd had to wait, at which she's never been very good. She was also still revved up about having had to put Scott away in his bide-a-wee yesterday, and not having him to escort her. Men are no damn good. And that certainly goes for her late-to-the-airport son Charles, the notorious hippie, lefty and all-round ingrate.

"Aren't you paid enough to buy clothes?" was the first thing she said after the routine hug and kiss. "That jacket's a disgrace."

I still had a head of steam up from the staff meeting, which was one of those that goes round and round because nobody has a good idea, so they fight on equal terms for their bad ones. The contention was about whether Deke should go abroad during Easter recess to take a hand in the search and try to offset some of Ned's publicity. Joannie and Bob wouldn't give up, and at the end Deke said one of those things that renews my faith in him.

"It's hard to tell much difference, most of the time, 'tween what's good politics and common sense. The other times, I'll still take common sense. I'm talking to people here at Petrolat everyday. What else is it you think I could do in Ay-rabland for Pete, the country, the House, or my damn district?"

Even after that Bob kept fighting for an Easter recess trip, insisting there'd be nothing wrong in paying six or seven thousand dollars for it out of campaign funds that haven't been raised yet. Finally Deke had to tell us what he'd wanted to leave out of the discussion.

"There's one more pretty heavy vote against you, Bob."

"Who's that?"

"The President. He pretty much asked me not to do it yesterday."

Seems Deke had five minutes alone with Carter and asked if there was anything a Congressman could do to help in the Middle East. Carter said no, he didn't see any way to coordinate that kind of thing with everything else they're trying. His own campaign came second to getting the hostages out of Iran alive, and he sure hoped others would see it that way, too.

So I was fifteen minutes late at the airport, and Mother didn't like my jacket.

"I like it fine," I said. "It's comfortable, it's camel's hair—who was it taught me that half of looking well is feeling that you do?"

"Brown-eyed people shouldn't wear tan," said my brown-eyed model mother, who frequently wears tan and looks stunning in it. "Anyway, the jacket's too tight, Charles. You're gaining weight."

That's ultimate cattiness in her former profession; actually, I doubt if I'm a pound different from last time she saw me.

What about your mother, Charlie? How's she look?

Still like a member of her profession, Dad. Thin and dramatic. The pale skin and black hair still shine, but I think she's emaciated. She lives to refute the legend that all Italian women get fat. Dieting is such a lifelong habit, I think a Snickers bar would make her terminally ill. At the peak of her career, she told me once, she lived pretty much on yeast cakes. She'd eat a couple in the taxi cab, going from one photographer's studio to the next. Food is the enemy. She hates to cook as well as eat it, so she and Scott go out to dinner every night. Scott eats and drinks, while mother nurses a Campari and soda and plays with her salad; no dressing.

People her age still find the face familiar, though they may not be able to recall the name. She likes to remember the time when she was on the covers of three national magazines in the same month, and has a photograph to prove it—Livia Scaliger, windblown, on a New York street, looking at the magazine rack of an outdoor newsstand. Three different Livias are looking back at her, one from the old *Life,* one from *Cosmopolitan,* and one from a magazine they used to have named *Colliers.*

One of my favorite rainy-day things to do when I was a little kid was get mother to take down her portfolios. I'd make up a magazine, and then go through hundreds of pictures, deciding which one to use on my next cover.

After each of the girls was born, there'd be a crash program to lose any weight put on during pregnancy, which was when she started looking bony. She still does, but people stare at her.

They stared when we went into the Coq d'Or today. She was wearing black, as usual, and no jewelry except the emerald lavaliere around her neck. She looked like someone famous, though you couldn't quite say who.

She ordered filet of sole, broiled, no sauce. We talked family for a while. She scolded me about my job with Deke, and whatever else came to mind.

Then I took a deep one, and said: "I've been corresponding with someone you used to know. John McRae Johnson."

"John Johnson?" She was startled. "I see."

"I'm learning quite a bit from him, about my father."

"I suggest you stop right there."

"I kind of like Mike Mizzourin, Mother."

"Would you do something very nice for me?" She took a sip of water, and put the glass down, but her eyes never left mine. "Whatever you've learned, would you keep it to yourself, please?"

"I hoped we might be able to talk about it at last."

"You're totally insensitive then."

"You're not willing?"

"Willing? One more word about it and I shall leave this restaurant and get a cab to the airport. I mean that."

"What do you want to do? Tell me more about Pauline's sorority and Lillian's first semester grades?"

"Do you take no interest in your sisters?"

"I saw them just before Christmas. Didn't they tell you?"

"No."

"I rode down on my bike one weekend."

"Yes. They did tell me."

"Why'd you say no, then?"

"Oh, shut up, Charles. Johnny Johnson hated Mike Mizzourin."

"Why?"

"Because he was a dirty, selfish cheat and nearly ruined John's life, along with others'. Now shut up about it."

"How?"

"I suppose you hear from Christine, too." Very bitterly. "Taking advantage of her madness and soft-heartedness. But I'm astonished John would write to you. He must be mad, too."

"I think they're both quite lonely."

"And you don't hesitate to exploit it, do you?"

"You may as well know this. What Johnson sends are pages that my father wrote."

"The Fake Book? Oh, God, how unfair."

"Johnson's doling it out. It's in exchange for some information that he wants."

"What information?" She was alarmed.

"About a woman here in Washington."

"Oh. But you're reading about me, aren't you? How sneaky."

"There's been nothing about you. It's all in North Carolina.

"Yes, I'm sure. Dear old Carolina. That book is mine, Charles. I'm the widow. I won't have my privacy invaded. The Fake Book's mine."

"And I'm the son."

"I want John Johnson's address."

"Why?"

"Charles, I'll sue if I have to. That's poison. It's not for just anyone to see. God, I never dreamed it still existed."

"I'm not 'just anyone.' I'm his son."

"You're not going to help me, are you?"

"I'd hate to see what Mike Mizzourin wrote destroyed."

"But they can read it all they want. John and Christie, can't they? It's too late."

"What is there to conceal? Wouldn't you rather tell me yourself?"

"Yes." She pressed her palms down on the tabletop and gave me a most intense look out of those enormous, dark eyes. "If you'll promise not to read when it gets to me. Charles, it's poison."

"You read it?"

"No. Never. Well, a little bit, by accident. Poison."

Neither one of us was thinking about lunch any longer. The waiter took the plates away.

"Mother, if you're really willing to talk about it now, let's drive to my apartment." We had the car she's rented to drive herself to Charlottesville, which gave me another idea. "Or shall I drive you down to see the girls, and we can talk on the way?"

She never stopped shaking her head. "No. It's too complicated. And serious. You're going to read what Mike wrote anyway, whatever I say. I want to write my side, too. Only I'll tell the truth."

"There's nothing I'd rather read."

"You have to give me time. You have to tell John not to send any parts about me, until I've had time."

"All right. Or if he does, I won't read them before I've heard from you."

"Oh, no. You'll do exactly as you please. The only promise I want from you is that you'll just be fair. Do you happen to know the meaning of the word? Just be fair enough to read both sides before you make up that keen, trained mind of yours, Charles."

"All right."

"Thanks for the happiest, most wonderful lunch I ever had in my life."

She insisted on paying half the check, and drove off tight-lipped without waving.

"Hello?"

"I say, Charles."

"Darlene?"

"My British accent didn't fool you."

"Where is everybody? I just got back from lunch and no one's here."

"Deke and I are in the subcommittee room. I called to say you've got a special delivery from your friend Johnson. It says 'very confidential,' so I put it in the top right-hand drawer."

"Thanks. Okay, got it."

"What kind of dear old fruitypie is Mr. Johnson, anyway?"

"Just another guy who got in trouble with his greenhouse, far as I can tell."

Last Deadline Ranch

Charlot, chirurgeon, what is your fee for a meaculpectomy? Perhaps these pages of correction? Id est . . . but oh, for God's sake, boy. Surely you knew that you were not the target of my little hoax? You were to be disabused instantly (and yes, I did abuse you, and am sorry for it). But now all will be well, for not only am I sending true materials, but I can report the culprit caught and chastened. In spite of your pretending to have seen through the spurious entry by examining the text, it was clear that Christine must have intervened. No sooner did your letter questioning the authenticity of the document arrive than I confronted her with it, and out came the whole sordid tale of her spying and interfering between us. She will spy no more, I have made amply sure of that. Discipline, Charles, is the key to marital concord. Read on.

Mizzourin **THANKS FOR THE MEMORY**

Mule and Gatch were watching us. I put the mouthpiece in my pocket and stood up. E.B. stood and set his guitar on the chair. Evaun got up between us, took E.B.'s elbow in one hand and mine in the other. We moved together across the bandstand that way and stopped, looking down at the law.

There was a pause. The people on the floor and at the tables were hushed and listening.

Finally Evaun nodded at them and said: " 'lo, Mule."

" 'lo, 'vaun."

Gatch said, "Hello, honey," and Evaun behaved as if she hadn't heard.

"Who's your friend?" Mule asked.

"Mike?"

"The squeaker."

"Mike. How's Johnny, Mule?"

"Your drummerboy? He'll live. Long enough to get run out of town, anyhow."

"You gonna let Horse get by with it again?"

"Who said something about Horse?"

"Who needs to? Doctor Wanderbaum not gonna let this go by, Mule. Doctor's got friends here."

"Like who?"

"Tommy." The proprietor, who'd been hovering, stepped back. "Uncle Marvin."

Mule looked up at us thoughtfully. "Stayin' on the right side of your uncle these days are you, Evaun?" I felt her flinch. "Which side is that? Or should I ast Binkie?" He nodded. "I aim to catch who done yo' drummerboy."

Evaun rallied. "Well just go straight on home to yore house and catch him."

"Horse been working the whole evenin' at the army depot, unloadin' flatcars," Mule said. "Gatch seen him over there."

Gatch seemed a little surprised. His turn to rally. "That's exactly right. That's where he was, working for his country on a holiday night. I spoke with Corporal Anspacher, in charge of the civilian detail. He says Horse is one hell of a strong worker."

"And you're one hell of a strong witness, Gatch," I said.

"Come on down here to the table," Mule Haas said. "Wanna talk with you."

"I can talk standing."

"No. Come on." E.B. detached his elbow from Evaun, smiling, skipped down off the bandstand and took a chair. " 'mon, Mike. Let's us have a beer with the fellas."

With that Evaun gave my arm a little shove. "Yeah, Mike. Like E.B. said."

"You better not let me see you drinkin' no beer, Binkie," Mule said. "Not unless you growed up four years all at once."

E.B. settled into a chair at the end of the table, smiling pleasantly. Evaun nudged again, and I left the bandstand with her. We both took seats, me at the end across from E.B., Evaun on my right by Mule. Gatch was across the table from her.

"What's on your mind, Sheriff?" I poured a glass of beer from the pitcher and offered it to him.

"On duty," Mule said. "You want it, Gatch?"

I thought of remarking that Gatch was supposed to be on duty, too, upstairs at the hotel. It wasn't time for that yet. I pushed the glass across the table to him. Gatch pushed it back. I picked it up and drank a long swallow.

Mule said, "Tryin' to find out who messed up this Johnny boy."

Gatch nodded. "Me too. Don't know if military's involved."

"Very upsettin' in our nice town, on a holiday."

"Especially to the drummerboy," I said.

"Look, Mike." Mule paused. "They was a niggah hangin' round the parking lot tonight. Was they? Dressed up niggah?"

"Was they?"

"Said you was talkin' to a niggah."

"Who said? Gatch, I'll bet."

"Never mind who for now."

"It must have been Gatch," I said. "Because he gets around so much. Army depots. Hotels. Parking lots. The perfect witness."

"Was you talkin' to a niggah?"

"There was a colored guy out there listening to the music," I said. "Yeah, we talked."

"Maybe the music didn't suit him," Mule said and smiled, trying to be charming. "You think he mighta wanted to stop somebody playing it?"

"He left before eleven."

"Coulda come back?"

I shrugged.

"You know him?"

"No."

"Say his name?"

"No."

"Describe him for me, please, suh. You know, big or little, dark or light?"

"Dark," I said. "It was dark out there. Ask Gatch."

"You got somethin' agin Gatch?"

"I just admire him," I said. "Because he's such a strong witness. Did you know he's a real ace, too?"

"He's your po-lice, soldier."

"I'm no goddamn soldier," I said.

"All right, all right. Lookee. This niggah had two fingers missing from his right hand, didn't he?"

"No," I said.

"How do you know, if it was so damn dark you couldn't see him?"

"Because I shook hands with him," I said.

"Done what?"

"You having trouble hearing me?"

"Why didn't you shine his shoes for him while you was at it?"

"He didn't ask me to," I said. "He had some Okinawa mud on them. Want to show me yours?"

"I got bad knees."

"Good for you."

"Now come on, Mike. Let's help each other. Now what Gatch did tell, they was a two-finger niggah discharged same day you was. Seems like he stole some pretty valuable kind of horn, maybe."

"Think it's the same one?"

"It could be."

"How the hell could he play the horn with all those fingers missing?"

"Never hear of left-handed?"

"There's a trumpet player with one arm even," Gatch put in, infuriatingly. It wasn't the kind of thing he was supposed to know. "Wingy Manone."

"You don't remember this niggah from yore discharge detachment?"
Mule said.

It was time. "All I remember is, he told me where he hid the box."

"What box, Mike?"

"The box Gatch stood on when he kissed the elephant's ass," I said,
delivering the world's oldest piece of grammar school smartass, and
getting some weight on my feet to move. I was too slow. Gatch swept
up the pitcher and threw beer in my face before I could duck. I bel-
lowed and threw what beer was left in my glass back in his, and here
came Tommy Rhombo with his big, long head and peewee baseball
bat to disconnect the circuit.

"Hold it, men," Tommy yelled, and Mule, rising up, pointed a finger at me and held it steady.

"You can't be as stupid as all that," Mule said.

"I can try." I wiped my face off with my sleeve.

"Better try a lot harder next time," wet Gatch said, and wet Mike
grinned.

The two cops turned to leave. I smiled at E.B. and Evaun. Then
Tommy Rhombo threw us out.

"You kids, git, and take yore friend," he said.

"Aw, Tommy."

"You underage, E.B. Her too, I ain't really sposed to have you
working here, and not her carrying liquor to the tables, neither."

"Come on, Binkie," Evaun said, but E.B. liked to tease.

"Don't you want more music even?"

"I'll give 'em free jukebox."

"We ain't got paid yet." E.B. held out one hand and spanked it with
the other. It was something he might have learned from Doctor Wanderbaum.

"I'll settle with the Doctor."

"We gotta wait for 'm then."

"You want for Mule to come and haul you home to Marvin's in his
po-lice car? Or sent Horse lookin' for this soldier?"

"Not goin' to Marvin's," Evaun said. "Not tonight, but come on,
Binkie. Let's go someplace fun."

"Give us some whiskey, Tommy," E.B. said, who was by now far
from needing it.

"Well." Tommy considered this negotiating point and nodded. "Don't
want to spoil yore good time, neither."

He went off to the front bar, and we three climbed back onto the bandstand to unplug mikes and put them, with the drum set and guitar, back in the big rear storeroom.

"You live with your Uncle Marvin?" I asked Evaun.

"Yessir. How come you lied to Mule?"

"What makes you think I lied?"

"Come on, now. Lookee here." E.B. was back at the table, gleeful. There was a gift-wrapped box with a Christmas ribbon on it standing on the table, and E.B. said he bet it was Old Crow. "Mah favorite."

Even a callous old scut who lied to cops blinked slightly at the notion of a delicate sixteen-year-old having made his whiskey choice already, and a long-faced bar owner knowing what it was.

I offered Evaun my jacket, but she pulled on a sweater over her bare shoulder blades. It was a navy-blue boy's sweater, with a big F sewn on it.

"From when I used to go to high school," she said.

Remembering my first impression of her, I asked: "Were you a cheerleader?"

It brought a small look of pain to her face. "Aw, Mike," she said. "No more than you was, after what you done."

"Let's git outdoors and have a drink," E.B. said, flourishing the Christmas box, and he was right. It was Old Crow.

Mizzourin/**EXACTLY LIKE YOU**

We tapped it in the parking lot. E.B. drank, Evaun wet her lips, and I had a slug and began feeling exceptionally paternal and affectionate toward my big-eyed waifs.

"Hey, where we goin'?" asked the Old Crow man.

"Could go to Jane Evers, but it's just kids," his sister said.

"We can go to the hotel," I said. "There'll be soldier parties there all night."

"Let's us never go to bed," E.B. yelled, and Evaun tightened up on my arm and started skipping.

"Come on, Mike, you pokeyslow."

"Beat you there," I said, and I would have if the little cheats hadn't ganged up, both grabbing me. "Now I got him," Evaun said, locking her arms around me from behind and turning out to be quite strong. "Scoot, Binkie."

It gave him all the start he needed to beat me to the lobby door. I unlocked it, and we went in through the half-lit lobby, picking up the melody of "Lili Marlene," which came floating down the stairs, and singing the words to the chairs and sofas we went by. On the second-floor landing, we stopped for another pull off Old Jug Crow. It sounded pretty boisterous up and down the hall.

"Private parties," I said, and smiled.

"I'll git us into any one of those," Evaun said. "Or Binkie will."

"Shoulda brought my guitar," E.B. said, to which he added: *glug*.

On the third floor it was a little quieter. The lights were dim and blue. We could hear an argument in one room, and laughter with radio music in another.

As we reached my door, Hazel came along the corridor. She was still in her greenish-yellow waitress uniform, which looked pale in the blue light, and her face was tired.

"My, my." Hazel stopped, pushed back her hair and looked at Evaun.

"Hello, Hazel," Evaun said.

And I said: "Keeping busy?" It came out meaner than I meant it to. I guess it bothered me that my young friends should have easy acquaintance with the Lizabeth Pony Haas's and the Hazel Whores in town. But it's not a large town. Everybody must know everybody else, his age or hers, as in Calder Plain, back there, back then. Used to be. There's a little aristocracy, a lot of riffraff, and all kinds of slidearound middle. You can slide out the lower end into the raff pretty easily in Usetabe. If the Pearls hadn't japped Bomb Harbor when they did, I'd have come out of Eldora a certified kid bum, I suppose, and not giving a damn would have made it worse.

When Hazel had got by, I opened the door, showed my fellow, un-certified kid bums in, and said: "We can leave our things. Then we'll slip around and knock on some doors."

"I'm gonna leave my shoes," Evaun said, kicking them off, and then pulling the letter-sweater up and over her head and tossing it on the right-hand bed. E.B. whooped, and tossed himself on the bed beside it. There was a water tumbler wrapped in tissue paper on a little table between the beds. He reached for it, fought the tissue paper off, giggling, and filled the damn thing halfway up with bourbon.

"Here come yore happy new year," he said.

"Binkie Jones!" Evaun wasn't protesting. There was amazement in her voice, and even some delight. "You never took a drink like that afore in yore life."

By the time she said it, most of the whiskey was gone, and E.B. had a silly, baby grin on his face. "Oh, my," he said, or something like it.

His sister took the glass out of his hand, and turned toward me with it.

"You want the rest, Mike?"

"Have some."

She looked into the glass, smiling and shaking her head. "You got any Coke?"

"Sorry."

"Oh, well." She stood flat-footed and spraddle-toed in her stocking feet; her ashen hair had come loose when she took the sweater off. "Here's to livin', then." She drank a swallow, coughed, and held the glass out to me. "No more dyin'."

I went over to her, took the glass, and raised it: "No more dyin'."

"My turn now?" The fuzzy voice of Binkie from the bed. I asked Evaun with my eyebrows, and she said *oh, why not?* with her left shoulder, so I gave him back the glass. He was pretty well reclined and not able to manage holding anything. Evaun took the glass away again and put it on the night table.

"You can't even find your mouth now," she said, humorous and tender. "Try down under yore nose, please?" And she sat beside him, straightening his head out on the pillow, humming "Lily Marlene," and then murmuring, singsong:

> *Underneath yo' nose, boy/ Up above yo' chin/*
> *Here you'll find a pretty mouth/*
> *Fer putting' whiskey in . . .*

She dipped her finger in the glass and put it in his mouth. "See?"

Then she loosened his belt. Seeing that she meant to undress him, I went off into the bathroom. Down the hall they'd turned the music up on the radio.

Something odd was going on when I came out. Evaun had got E.B. stripped down all the way, not stopping at the underwear. He was trying to sit up, quite naked, the bedclothes kicked away, and she was cajoling.

"Lie in the bed, now. I'll get you back yo' drink, honeyboy."

He grinned woozily and let himself be nudged back down onto the pillow. She looked at him, unaware that I was back in the room. She reached down and very lightly, very briefly, squeezed his honeyboy pud. It was a pinkish honeyboy, half-erect, of reasonable size, and the hair around it was light and fine.

"Think it's pretty cute, doncha?" There was not much sex, though, in her sexy voice, no sharp feeling of incestuous intention or response on either side. It was as if she had touched herself, and if anyone responded it was me, a little thrilled, a little shocked. Evaun turned to get the glass, saw me, and yelled, "You, Mike. Who the hell you think yore lookin' at?" It was an interesting question under the circumstances.

Quickly, then, she pulled the sheet and covers over her naked brother, who was muttering a happy mutter. "All right," she said to me. "You can come in." As if I hadn't already. There was some delicacy in that.

She got E.B.'s whiskey again, smiled down at him, tried to put the glass in a hand that couldn't grasp it and returned it to the table. "You'd think he might pass out."

"Is he all right?"

"Oh, sure." She got up, came toward me and stopped.

I said, low-voiced, "Can we leave him and go look for a party?"

"Ain't I party enough for you?" She held out her arms. "Dance with me, Mike?"

Then we danced, to faint sounds. It may have been Guy Lombardo. It may have been "The Very Thought of You." It may not have mattered. She was, I thought, a very sleepy schoolgirl, doing a pretty good job of giving me the same sensations a grown woman might, moving and pressing up against me. I felt unbearably fond of her and much too interested. As the faint music paused, I danced her over to the bedside where her twin lay, more or less asleep now, kissed her forehead and let her loose.

"You puttin' me to bed like I done him?"

"Not everything you did."

"Oh, shut up." She gave me a push, and I let it move me back.

"You goin' off and find a party?" She didn't say it with a pout. Rather, her tone seemed to ask for my presence, maybe my protection. So I smiled.

"No, Evaun. I'm going off to the other bed and go to sleep."

"You got any pajamas?"

"We didn't use them in the army."

"I can sleep in my dress."

She sat on the bed, rolled her stockings off, swung her legs up, and pulled the sheet and blanket over her raised knees. E.B. stirred beside her and said something unintelligible.

"You shut up, too," she said, and smiled at him, and I asked if she'd like to use the bathroom before I took a shower.

"You go ahead," she said. "Mike?" She reached for my hand and held it for a minute.

"Yes?"

"Leave me a little kinda light on? I hate sleepin' in the dark."

"Okay."

I went into the hall and snitched a blue lightbulb for the lamp on the table between the beds. When I got back with it, she was nestled in the bedding, turned toward Binkie, and her eyes were closed. I changed the bulb. They couldn't have looked younger or more beautiful.

*Mizzourin/*MY BLUE HEAVEN

As I watched a moment longer, Evaun drifted closer to her passed-out twin, put an arm over him and cuddled close. I felt the pinch absurd of jealousy, as if some childish game of bodies might just start as soon as I should leave the room again. And suppose it did, Mike Mizzourin, between these unearthly Appalachian samelings? Some game of stimulation and gratification learned in the cradle, practiced and refined?

I went into the bathroom, taking incestuous images with me—the shoulder straps slid off, the bodice of the dress pushed down, the skirt up under the covers, E.B. already naked, familiar fingers and familiar hands—these flamed around enough to heat and bother me a good bit in the shower. Had to turn the sonofabitch dead cold to get myself decalcified. Then I felt kind of good, laughed at myself, went into the room and tingling into bed in army shorts, with a nice smooth swallow of E.B.'s Old Crow to plump my pillow, pushing away the feeling that there was yet another thing to do. To do.

My young wards were sleeping close in the blue light, touching but not twined—but if they had been, I confess the devil might have found perverse work for an idle hand. But no: I floated off, up and over in the calm blue dark. I had some duty, couldn't quite think what it was, let myself off, as I remembered playing music. Something like music, anyway, away, way.

I don't know how much later I began to have an idiotically persuasive and erotic dream. I was standing inside a closet with the door open. In the doorway a ladder rose in front of me. Facing me, up two rungs on the ladder, with a helpless little frown, was my high-school classmate Penny Davis, whom I hadn't thought of once in five years, whom I barely knew at all. Penny, in the dream, was short with frizzy hair and a dumb face, wearing a red sweater and a khaki skirt. Behind Penny, grinning and waiting, stood a plump, good-hearted, moon-faced young fellow I'd known quite casually, not in high school but the army, a hospital orderly named Steve.

As soon as Penny raised her right foot to the next rung of the ladder, the rules of the situation provided, Steve was required to step forward and start feeling her up, whether she wished him to or not. Penny had no say in the matter. So she raised and planted the foot, Steve moved in, and I watched his left hand come around and hold her steady by the left breast, through the sweater, stopping her from climbing farther, up or down, while right hand raised her short skirt from behind, disappeared under the elastic and into the crotch of her underclothes, where it bulged and thrust vigorously under the fabric.

Poor Penny was required by the rules of the dream, which we all three understood had been laid down by final authority, to submit to this work with both arms raised and holding to the rung above her head. Her expression was resigned; sometimes her lips pursed, her head moved forward, and she looked at me; and the amazing and exciting third rule was that it was to be my turn in a moment, whether Steve liked it or not. Or Penny. Rules were rules.

I am cherry so far as wet dreams go, even stupid ones like that, a genuine, old-world demivierge of dreamland. Nocturnally, I just don't emit. I wake, as the climax seems about to gather, and a dreary, letdown, waking-up it is.

But now, as the moment came and I half-woke from my unworthy and, for some reason, heart-ripping position, facing Penny on her ladder, there was inexplicably no letdown at all, no chill, no emptiness. Steve, Penny and the ladder melted into smooth skin on my cheek around which, finding it to be a thigh, I closed my arm. There were soft arms around my own thighs, too, and at my throbbing soldierboy moist warmth and gentle suction, making enormous love.

I ran my hand over nude buttocks to a naked back, between the shoulder blades to silky hair, opened my eyes and dimly saw a small breast, pressed flat and outward from my lowest ribs.

Tenderly, I turned and gathered in the lovely succubus. Her lips came past my ear, and as she moved against and under me, right-side up, and took my rod and cast her hips to pull it up inside, she whispered: "Thought you never would wake up."

So we were fit together after all, Evaun and I, and a firmer, seemlier, warmer joint was never made before by God the Carpenter. For a moment, it was nothing but a tightening of flesh around my own, but then an eagerness spread out inside her, and I was all awake, happy and intent and thrilled. Just before my mind melted into my loins I stopped, and lifted up my cheek to see her face.

"Come on, honey Mike," she said. "Yore sweet girl's in her safe time," and she pulled me down, all fluid and friction, and there was filling and bursting of the organ like I've never felt before. She pressed up, tightened up and trembled, and we rose to the bottom of the deep blue moon.

Mizzourin/**BLUE MOON**

> *You knew just what I was there for/ You heard me whisper*
> *a prayer for/ Someone I really could care for.*

What a thing I learned from Evaun Barlow in the night. Clutching her, I went all dreamy soup, as my bones cooked on, thinking something like:

> *Blue Moon/ This is the meaning of my stupid life.*

That was a little vague, and I refined it. Blue Moon, the act of love is altogether different from the speech of love. The act goes into places speech can't reach, with consequences words can't have, becoming a communication words can't make.

Or maybe, Blue Moon, sir, it's the opposite. Maybe it makes the words literal and accurate. For making love is nothing like fornication, after all, but exactly what the words do say: creating love. Love, having been made, exists, even for kid bums, whether or not that was what either of us had in mind.

> *I heard somebody whisper "Please adore me"*

Yes, I did. Though the actual words were more like, "Golly, Mike. Look over, now. We didn't wake up Binkie, did we?"

Frankly, I'd forgot there was a Binkie. Then she reached down and learned something that made her giggle and said: "Guess I am yore sweet girl, ain't I?"

Guess she was, till somewhere around three o'clock on New Year's morning; guess she was.

It was at three that we woke up again, and Evaun said my sweet girl better wake up next time in the other bed. But it was hard for me to let her leave, and we sat up a few minutes, side by side, my arm around her slim back, hers around my neck, chatting, drowsy and fond, about the evening.

She was saying: "Like the way you give it back to Muley Haas about the nigra . . . threw that beer on Gatch . . . ain't Gatch a sorry thing . . ."

"Wait," I said.

"Can't, Honeymike." She started to push up.

"I mean, something . . ." I knew exactly what I meant, but stopped myself from saying what had finally emerged into the front of my slow mind. I got up, helped Evaun to her feet. She got the wrinkled evening dress back on and trailed it to the other bed. I softshoed after her, to the side away from E.B., helped her into bed, and held her hand until she went to sleep, smiling.

I slipped my hand away, went around to the table and poured myself a fair drink, cursing myself mildly. I can't say I was eager to be off.

Then Honeymike put on his honeyclothes, and over them Evaun's navy-blue letter-sweater, turned inside out; and a knit cap for invisibility. I got Cosmo Selkirk's blackjack and put it in my honeypocket for company. The back of my mind had known, since shortly after midnight, that I must go, sooner or later, out through the dark morning streets of Faraday like this.

Mizzourin/IN THE STILL OF THE NIGHT

There are no border posts in Faraday between Redneck City and Niggertown. You know you've crossed the line when the streetlights end. You know you've reached Jocasta's when you see the bundles.

The bundles are men passed out along he housewall. There were four of them this New Year's morning.

Jocasta's is a frame house, the only two-story building in the city-state of Niggertown, the only house with lights at four A.M. These included a fifteen-watter just above the door, by which I could study the hand-painted top panel. *JOCASTA'S CASTLE* it said, in scroll, with yellow sun, blue sky and battlements of red, bright and alone in the dark.

Standing outside I could hear odd music, and that was the only sound in town. The music was mostly a flow of energy, very rhythmic, solo piano blues, with a thin, staccato treble and a full, hard, bass.

I stood there in the yard listening, trying to figure out what was discrepant, and another sound developed north of me, a motor. I looked, and two blocks away, coming fast, were slits to let out just a bit of headlight, a blacked-out military vehicle. I dove, and now there were five bundles.

I pulled the knit cap over my forehead, pulled the heavy, navy-blue sweater down over my belly and rump, and made fists inside the sleeves to hide my hands. I poked my legs along between the next bundle and the wall, far enough to hide my khakis. I threw an arm across my face, peered out under it, and saw what I expected, an MP jeep. It's the MPs who check the brothels of the world, wherever our brave fighting men are stationed, not the local cops—and, in addition, Gatch had had that operation he and I discussed: he'd been deputized.

The motor went off. Two men with flashlights jumped out. Inside, the piano went silent.

"Jesus, drunked-out spades," a voice said, and a flashlight played along the inert line of us.

"Any military?" This one was Gatch's voice.

"Bunch of eightballs, asleep in the deep."

"Check the boots, ding dong."

The light had reached the end of our row. I stuck my feet firmly under my neighbor bundle and practiced not breathing. The two light beams came back, more slowly and together. I thought one hesitated on me, but I can't be sure. There was a muffled, slamming sound inside, and the Gatch voice said, "Come on."

"We oughta roll these out," said Ding Dong.

"For Christ's sake, come on." The flashlights swung up, boots went humping up the wooden steps, the door was tried, then pounded.

"Military police," one shouted, and the other, "Hey, Jocasta. Open up."

After a moment, I heard the door open, and a woman's voice said, "We closed up, Gatch. Sure had a party. Whew."

"Someone run out the back door just now?"

"You heard my chair fall over?"

"Any military in there?" It was Ding Dong this time.

"No, suh, officer."

"Let us in. Come on Jocasta, unhook the chain," Gatch said.

"I got customers sleeping over with Susan and Milla. You gonna disturb them, gotta have a warrant, like before."

"How about you let us in. Bring the shoes out of the bedrooms and show them to us in the hall?" Gatch said. "Like before."

"Come on, then, gentlemen. I'm awful tired."

"I'll watch outside," Ding Dong said. "For sure there's someone in the yard."

I heard the door close behind Gatch. Then I was aware of Ding Dong going to work, doing pockets. There was a bulge in one of mine. It was the blackjack. I hitched a little bit, got it out, in my hand and under me. Ding Dong was moving up the row. As soon as he got by me, I was going to rear up, crease the bastard and run.

"Shit, Jocasta." Ding Dong was whining to himself. "You keepin' these men's wallets for 'em, aren't you." A hand patted my hip, squeezed the flesh under my empty pocket, reached around under me to try the other hip where all it felt was keys. "Shit."

He straightened up. He pushed at me with his toe and sighed. There was a little tattoo on the house siding around the corner, and Ding Dong's light went wildly around; he yelled "Who's there?"; he took a step. Then he stopped, and I guessed that he didn't want to go around to the dark side of the house by himself, even with a light and a gun for leverage. He muttered something and went stamping up the steps and in the door, hurrying.

A soft voice in the night said, "Little Mike."

I jumped up and tried to see.

"Come 'round the corner."

I ran that way and was grabbed by a pair of hands from a dark body, still against the south wall.

"Be still."

"Scholay?"

"Come on now, and hold your nose." He was guiding me away from the house, toward the back fence.

"How'd you know it was me?" I whispered.

"Knew I'd only got four stacked out there. Then I saw a white hand move."

"Where we going?" We were trotting on tiptoe.

"Behind the outhouse, till they're gone." He chuckled. "Jocasta's indoor plumbing is for girls only." We reached the small, odorous, whitewashed building, and went into a patch of shoulder-high weeds between it and the wooden fence. "Girls, white boys and me."

"You?"

"I'm helping out and playing a little bad music."

"That was you playing blues?"

"Gopeters' eight-finger blues," he said. "Awful. Shhh."

The back door of the house flew open, and one of the MPs came out fast behind his flashlight.

"No one here, Gatch," he yelled.

Apparently Gatch had made a coordinated sortie out the front door. He came chugging around now, and lights bobbed everywhere for a minute or so. They kept avoiding the outhouse, and I could almost see Scholay's grin. Then one light went off, and Gatch said, "Come on, Jimmy," and Ding Dong Jimmy said, "Let's go."

They got in their jeep and moved out.

"The smell's not so bad," I said.

"I put a ton of lime in yesterday."

"Let's hold still a minute. That jeep can turn and come back."

"You are a military man," Scholay said. "Me too. I was thinking the same."

We waited and the jeep did drift back by, coasting to a stop silently with its headlights off. The flashlights swept the yard again and went away.

We left our place and reached the back stoop. Scholay knocked on the door.

"Jocasta's got some strategy, too," he said, while we waited. "The shoes. Keeps an old pair of civilian shoes in every room of this place. Knows Gatch is going to let her bring them out to show—he's razor-shy 'bout going in himself."

The image of someone slicing Gatch in the dark gave me pause. Puzzled pause. Then, though we heard Jocasta coming to the door, I said to Scholay, "Wait a minute," and trotted back toward the outhouse.

"You can use the one inside," he called, but I kept going, opened the little wooden door, and went in. I took the blackjack out of my pocket again and dropped it down the hole. I'd come close to bashing an MP with it. MPs had guns and clubs, and my body was full of fragile bones, but in truth that was not my reason for disarmament. In truth, I realized, I didn't want to hurt anyone with anything, not ever again.

"Hey, Scholay," I said, getting back to the stoop, going into the house after him, following Jocasta. "I think the war's over."

Mizzourin/SUNRISE SERENADE

Scholay stood at the piano, looking at the keyboard. "What I do is play crossover sometimes," he said. "Octaves are all right, not when you're floating tenths." He pantomimed with the thumb and little finger of his right hand, from which the first two fingers are gone. "Used to think when I got done drumming, I might play some of this."

Jocasta was still watching us. She is a very thin, majestically ugly, middle-aged woman, more Indian-than negro-looking.

She said, "You boys want beer or whiskey?" And left us for a moment in her living room, which features a well-used sofa against every wall, heavy drapes and no carpet on the floor.

"There was dancing," Scholay said.

"Those MPs were probably looking for you."

"Seemed like. What for? I'm civilian."

"Doing a favor for the civil cops. The MPs check here all the time."

"They got to. It's off-limits."

"They can look around for military. Happen to see a three-finger civilian, grab him for the sheriff."

He looked at his hand. "What's the sheriff want with this?"

"The bass player from the trio got beat up bad out in the parking lot. Hospital bad. Man with the tire-iron was the deputy's brother. Seems Johnny was out to play a little rhythm on the boy's sister. I don't think they meant to hurt him that bad."

"And there was a nigger seen hanging around the parking lot earlier," Scholay said. "Some crazy, wildass, don't-know-his-place kind of combat nigger. That's the worst kind . . . why would they think of me for it, Mike? They need to put it on somebody, but how come I got lucky?"

"My fault," I said.

"You never told my name?"

"I didn't tell them anything. I stole a horn."

"Knew you had something that day we got discharged. Thought it might be a gun."

"They know who got discharged that morning. One was colored, with some fingers gone. Gatch pulls him in on suspicion, takes him to the sheriff's office."

"Oh, yeah," Scholay said. " 'Horn's nothing, nigger. You damn near killed a white man, didn't you?' "

"Scholay, they'll find out about their horn in the morning," I said. "I'd have told them tonight, if I hadn't been so dumb and happy I didn't realize what they had in mind."

Scholay smiled. "I was pretty happy, too," he said.

"Can you stay hid till I block their play?"

"Get out of here." It wasn't Scholay speaking. It was Jocasta, standing in the living room doorway, fully dressed in a rather smart, gabardine suit, wearing riding boots, some sort of black bowler hat, and pigskin gloves. She had keys in one hand. "You, Scholay, get your luggage and your ass in the trunk of the Buick, hear? Quick, boy."

I didn't especially want to know where she meant to go in the Buick. "Good night, then," I said. "I'll clear things up in the morning."

"Don't you clear nothing but your throat, Mike," Jocasta said. "Unless you dumber than you look. They don't need no horn no more for what they aim to do. Move, Scholay, move. Want to spend New Year's with my sister in Virginia, listen to that Rose Bowl on the radio."

Scholay moved off, stopped, and grinned at me: "Who you picking to win, Mike?"

"Who's playing?" I asked.

"Damned if I know."

"Cal," Jocasta said. "Gonna win it, too, because they're Golden Bears. Now come on, niggers, move."

Us niggers moved. I went back down the stoop and headed for the streetlights, lighter than air. I floated through pearly vapors. A rosy-fingered breeze goosed me skyward, gandered me over toward the Grand Commerce Hotel, past shuttered shops, past the first shining milk truck of 1946, in through the lobby using Cosmo's key, on past the shutdown desk, and up the easy stairs to 300G.

I could sleep now. Opened up quietly. Don't wake the kid-bum sleepers. Looked at my own bed first. Remembered tenderly the way she'd left it. Glanced at the other double, covers heaped. And looked again. In it was E. B. "Binkie" Jones, alone. Snoring a satisfied pink snore.

There was nothing of his sister but her shoes. They were still in the middle of the floor. I checked the bathroom. I even listened jealously at silent doors down the hall. She seemed to have left the hotel barefoot, and without her sweater, which I still had on. I didn't understand.

I let E.B. sleep a litle longer, while I sat and thought. Here's how far I got: *Evaun. Rhymes with fawn, and gone in the dawn.*

File on my father. Notes:

I've had the strangest feeling all day long, as I went here and there, doing this and that, of something looming up that requires me to take action. It's weirdly parallel to my father's "Still of the Night" feeling about Scholay, something in the back of my mind that I've got to move forward.

"(Shit) . . . Hello?"

"Oooh, diddums make parenthetical remark?"

"Don't be a four-foot Kewpie doll, Darlene. Please."

"Know where I am?"

"Aren't you supposed to be with Deke, opening the subcommittee hearing?"

"It's delayed. I'm across the street, with Chet."

"Am I supposed to know who Chet is? Oh, Chester Brinnegar?"

"He's the subcommittee investigator you hired, sweets."

"Yes. I know."

"We ran out of other things to do, so Chet's been making phone calls for you."

"Isn't that nice."

"Not very. Interesting, though."

"Darlene, I'm trying to figure something out . . ."

"Remember, you were having lunch with Suesue? And Deke asked you to leave her number with me, in case we had to call?"

"Where the hell is Deke by the way?"

"He's caucusing."

"What about Suesue's phone number?"

"Deke's always caucusing these days, isn't he? Do you think he should see someone about it?"

"Come on."

"Lovesickle, I've been around Congress a long time. And that number sounded just a little bit familiar. So, the other day I checked my old phone file, and oh my goodness. Gosh."

"Gee."

"Whilakers."

"Whiz."

"You win. Suesue's was the number I used to give out when my former Congressman had sporty gents in town."

"How sporty?"

"Maybe a nice evening with cards and booze and girls."

(Pause)

"Charlie?"

"Yep."

"Shall I put Chester on?"

"What for?"

"He's my snoopydoll."

"All right."

"He knows people to call and questions to ask."

"I don't . . . All right. Yes. Put Chester on."

"Hi, Charlie."

"You've been getting information about Mrs. Landau?"

"Very superficial. Preliminary raw notes. Hearsay. Nothing veri-fied."

"Okay, Chester."

"Nothing for attribution, if you were going to ask about my sources."

"I wasn't."

"These are things I can nail down, if your boss approves. I mean, we've got the stuff for his hearings. There'll be more as it goes on, but right now I've got time."

"Congratulations."

"I said, I'm working for you people, and I've got time."

"Yes. You did say that."

"I'm a guy that doesn't like to sit around when I'm being paid."

"Why don't you tell me what you've got?"

"I'll read, okay? 'Suesue Landau. Real name Suzanne. Age forty-nine. Came to D.C. from New York, early Eisenhower. Protector was John McRae Johnson—' "

"You can skip some of that."

"I'll summarize, okay? Receptionist, Pentagon, 1954. Look, Johnson leaves town, 1957. Landau did all right—dinners, presents, weekends—but things really started going her way when she picked up a navy captain. I'll hold the name for now. Captain happened to be the guy who signed R&D contracts—"

"Research and Development?"

"Right. Big defense was good to Suesue. Nobody can prove right now, or wants to, that she got kickbacks, but it wasn't too long before she had capital to go into the market. She was a wonder at picking the right defense stocks, too. When her captain went back to Mrs. Captain and the little sailors, Suesue sold out and started putting it in real estate.

It seems she knew some people, especially Representative Hibben on the D.C. Committee, which decides where civic improvement money's going to be spent. It helps if you're buying real estate.

"She's got something else going. Cards. She plays good bridge for big money."

"Darlene said something about card parties."

"Well, but that's not bridge. Blackjack. She runs a party house, you might call it, with a blackjack game."

"Every night?"

"Two or three nights a week. Sometimes private, if someone wants to set it up. Sometimes kind of discreetly public—I got a bunch of names of patrons. I'll hold for now on the names, but a lot of military, diplomats, lawyers, lobbyists. Free booze, so she doesn't need a license. No gambling equipment except chips. She's careful. Game's honest, probably, but the house cut's high. Get the picture?"

"Darlene also said girls."

"Well, guys don't exactly take their wives to Suesue's."

"Thank you, Chester."

"I'm not saying there's anything illegal going on except the gambling, and her protection's A-1 on that. Her partner Otis Hibben takes care of that. Anyway this stuff's on the hoof, you know? Raw? You want confirmed facts and figures, I can go to work. Darlene's nodding." (IS IT OKAY WITH DEKE?) "She says yes. So I check Landau out the right way. Don't worry. I'm thorough."

"I don't know, Chester. Maybe I'd rather ask her myself."

"There's no expense."

"Thank you, anyway."

"Hard lines for you, huh? Here's Darlene."

"Hello, Big Money. Boy, what a sexy thing to call a man."

"Hello."

"Hey, you unhappy with us?"

"No."

"Just unhappy."

"Darlene, tell me something."

"All right."

"There's a bunch of daffodils on my desk. Did you put them here?"

"Well, I *put* them there, in the blue little vase."

"I thought maybe Joannie did. We had words this morning."

"Joannie's been out. She could have sent them."

"I like daffodils."

"They came by messenger."

"No note?"

"It isn't there?"

"No."

"I might have forgot to . . . I can tell you what it said."

"Will you please?"

" 'Spring's here, and I hope you've got rocks in your head.' "

"That doesn't sound like Joannie."

"R-O-X. Rox. Phone call to make?"

"Thank you, Darlene. Thank Chester for me."

"See the new note from your uncle?"

"There's a copy here in front of me."

"What do you think?"

"I'll try to start thinking again when I get my head turned back to where the nose points forward."

"All right. Chet's going to buy me a drink. Jealous?"

"Have a nice evening."

File on my father. Notes:

Yes, I've got a phone call to make, but not to Roxanne Talley. It's suddenly quite clear what the action is I need to take, slow as I was to realize it, and I think I'd better tape the call.

"Johnson here."

"Mr. Johnson, this is Charles Mizzourin."

"Charlie, my boy. How good of you to call your Uncle Johnny. Got the real story from me, didn't you, and no harm done?"

"I'm calling about your note."

"Good. Was it clear enough?"

"You speak of disciplining Mrs. Johnson."

"Right enough. That one's taken care of. No more of her damn prying. I padlocked my studio. Padlocked her car in the garage. Wearing both keys around my neck. Had her private phone line disconnected, too. Okay?"

"Anything else?"

"If you don't think I've been severe enough, Charlie, I've got another padlock."

"No."

"I can put it on the closet where she keeps her shoes, and she won't be able to leave the house at all."

"Mr. Johns . . . Uncle John."

"Like that one do you? Thought you would."

"Aunt Christie was trying to help me."

"Help you do what? Look like a priceless fool?"

"I feel very badly that you and she are having trouble over me."

"I just told you. I've got her fixed."

"Look. Sir. I'd like you to return Mrs. Johnson's car and phone."

"Return 'em? To whom?"

"I think you understand. And I'd like to speak to her."

"See here, Mizzourin. You trying to meddle in my internal affairs?"

"My part of the deal concerns Suesue Landau. There's new information. I can have it professionally investigated and verified."

"Why the hell can't you investigate it yourself?"

"What?"

"For God's sake, Mike. This is a newspaper, not a play school."

"Uncle John!"

"Huh?"

"This is Charlie."

"Yes. Yes, I know. Well, I've got plenty more pages for you. You do your job, I'll do mine."

"No. That's not the deal."

"Don't want 'em, sonny?"

"I want Mrs. Johnson to have her car and telephone."

"You what? Car?"

"Yes."

"Christine wrecked her car."

"Is that true?"

"Just a minute. Just a minute, dammit. What are we talking about? If you can't tell me in a sentence, you're not on a story. You're on a fishing trip."

"I'm . . . I'm on a story."

"This paper doesn't pay for fishing trips, Mizzourin."

"No, I'm sure it doesn't."

"What's this about Landau? Give me a headline."

(YES, OF COURSE I'M ALL RIGHT, DAMMIT.)

"Is Aunt Christie there?"

(OUT OF THE ROOM, YOU. I'M HAVING A BUSINESS CONVERSATION. WITH . . . CHARLIE. CHARLIE.)

"Yes, my boy. I've got things organized here. Just . . . right. Now, you gave me a good start. Otis Hibben, former Representative, Senator, now lobbyist. Called the lawyer I used to have in Washington. He had one of his bright young men ask some questions. Maybe he's a brighter young man than you are, Charlie. Landau's a tramp. This Hibben moved her in about six months after I left town."

"Yes. I could add to that."

"What? Let's see how good your stuff is."

"There was a man between you and Hibben. A navy captain. I can get his name, I suppose, if it matters."

"How about this? Hibben's a well-known flagellant and flagellator. Disgusting man."

"I've heard that rumor."

"Say he likes 'em two at a time. Harder the one spanks him, harder he whacks on the other." (Laughter) "Three in a row with him in the middle. That your idea of a party?"

"No."

"How come you don't report these things? I haven't heard diddly from you about Landau."

"Because it's unconfirmed. Because Hibben and Landau haven't lived together for twenty years. What I can have investigated is whether there's still a business relationship.

"Hold on. Let me get a pencil."

"Why does all this matter? Uncle John?"

"Why?"

"Do Suesue's liaisons matter all that much to you?"

"Not liaisons. Money, you young idiot. Money."

"Are you still sending Suesue money?"

"Who are you investigating, anyhow?"

"She doesn't need money. I'm sure of that."

"Listen, Charlie. I never gave her money. I loaned it to her. Listen, now. I've got receipts. From 1955, total $2,300. That was for clothes, and a trip she took, and a little car so we didn't ride around in public in mine. And 1956, $2,500. She had a horse trainer crazy about her and talked me into backing her for a big bet. We were going to split the winnings. It was all set."

"What happened?"

"Damn jockey rode into another horse and got disqualified. Biggest loan was $3,200 in 1957. Down payment on a condo. I'd been paying her rent, and this looked like a real deal. Only when she sold the condo, she never paid me back. Next year, I left town, but I sent her two checks, total $500. No, it was money orders. Then in 1961—Charlie, I was such a fool. I thought she was still my woman."

"She's quite a woman."

"I went back to Washington, just to see her. Couldn't wait. She was doing well. She took me out to dinner, spent a hundred dollars on it. I walked into this fancy place called Jason's with her, wearing a Stetson hat, with that handsome woman on my arm. The headwaiter was dancing around us like Nijinsky. We got snuggled up in a dark leather booth, and when the check came she just blew the waiter a kiss. She had a charge account at Jason's. And a hired limousine, waiting outside to drive us around town. All the lights, monuments, sweet talk and a refrigerator in the car for ice, and my kind of bourbon. It was a good time. Don't be nosy. Except, I'd been hoping I could start collecting from her, and I wound up lending her another $1,500 instead. I can't even remember what the investment was supposed to be. Tell me I'm a fool."

"I guess we've all been fooled."

"I've got receipts here for $12,000. Six percent was the interest in those days. Not compounding, it still comes to $27,900. I send a statement every year in January. In February, she sends back a valentine. Charlie, tell her I'll settle it for $25,000."

"I could probably tell her that."

"Anything you can get over $20,000, you can keep."

"Thanks. But isn't it a lawyer's job?"

"They won't try. Statute of Limitations, for one thing, and these receipts aren't witnessed, either. They don't say anything about a re-payment date. Not like demand notes. Maybe you better get that investigation."

"I think I'd rather just ask her about it, first."

"Do it for me. Start the ball rolling."

"All right. Now may I speak with Aunt Christine?"

"Come on, boy. Play fair."

"It's not a game."

"You want fifty pages?"

"That's not the deal."

"You don't care where little Evaun went New Year's morning?" (Laughter) "Not to church, you can bet on that."

"You set me up for that, didn't you? It's still not the deal."

(CHRISTIE. CHRISTINE, COME IN HERE.)

"Please give her the key, and then I'd like to speak with her."

"Merde, Mizzourin." (GET IN HERE. COME ON. HERE'S YOUR GODDAMN GARAGE KEY. YOU'VE GOT YOUR CAR BACK.)

"May I speak with her, please."

"Merciful minced *merde* on a meatball." (I'LL GET YOUR PHONE BACK TOMORROW. STOP HOLDING YOUR CROTCH. SOMEONE WANTS TO TALK TO YOU.)

"Hello?"

"Hello, Charles."

"Is he all right?"

"Yes. I think so."

"How about yourself?"

"I have my keys. Thank you, Charles."

"You were right. I shouldn't have started the correspondence."

"It's going to be all right, I'm sure, isn't it? He's gone out of the room now. I hope it's, but it probably is. To get a drink."

"For a moment or two he seemed to think I was Mike."

"He did? What did he say?"

"Nothing I could make sense of. Something about—"

"Oh. Oh, Charles. I'll go to him."

"Aunt Christie . . ."

"Thank you, dear. Goodbye."

Dear Tutti-Fruttis:

That's you in Italian. Now that I've got that language learned, I've got a new one, Libyan. Got here this morning. Pete was working out of the Petrolat office here, and in it is a dish named Cherry, and guess who's going to show the old farmer how to eat couscous tonight?

Breakfast at this hotel I got to talk to some ex-Vietnam ex-Yanks. Now they work for Khadafy. They're black (as all us candidates say these days) mercenaries. Some white ones here, too. Don't believe a word they told me, but it's a wild story and the dumb Register won't know the difference. See page one, I hope. Cherry had a nice idea for an illustration: she went shopping with me for a pith helmet. Then I took it to a local tattoo artist, and he did a nice big full-color ink of the De Kalb seed corn logo on the front. You know that one? Had it on some stationery, because I'm a dealer. Big handsome yellow ear of corn, with a pair of red and green wings, ready to soar through the sky. Might borrow that when I get home for my bumper stickers and yard signs. It would say MIZZOURIN, not De Kalb, right?

Anyway, I got a photog from the company to take pix (as us journalists say) of me and my logo helmet standing in front of a mosque with some of the mercenary boys, arm-in-arm and grinning big—that is, they're grinning. I'm scowling, to show I don't trust them. How about that, suckers? Haven't got a whole lot of blacks in our district, but I'll take every vote I can get. Fact, I might just take them all. Easier to count that way.

Pan-Am crew staying the night here, flying to Chi in the morning, and one of the stews will take my pix to Chi and split the fifty bucks with her room-mate, who flies Chi–Des Moines, and hand-carry to the paper with my mer-cenary story about how I hope to persuade the homesick boys to give it up and be Americans again.

Don't bother writing me one of your nice little perfumy letters back, on the lavender stationery, because I doubt I'll be here long enough to get it. And don't get your earrings caught in the hair dryer, either.

Hon. Ned, Iowa Eighth

"Charlie Mizzourin here."

"Bo, what you doin' at the office after five?"

"Looking at daffodils."

"Better not let Uncle Ned catch you. Hey, tried you first at home. Got a big idea."

"About Ned?"

"Screw Ned and his friend Cherry, too. Crosswise. No. Remember I was telling you about my basketball star in the pros?"

"Tad somebody."

"Schwartzendruber. Had him the last year I coached high school. Seventy-two."

"Year of the Deke-McGovern landslide."

"Yeah, I lost bigger even than he did. Second time I ran, too. But we sure won the basketball, thanks to the way this kid could shoot outside. Tad. Kind of a Gail Goodrich. We went to the state tourna-ment, smallest school there, and won it."

"Think that had anything to do with why you got elected in seventy-four?"

"You're edgy tonight, aren't you? It had everything in the world to do with it, bo."

"Your man Tad played for Notre Dame, and then broke in with the Sonics, didn't he?"

"Right. Now get ready. Tad's been traded to New York."

"The Nets? Hey, no, Deke."

"Makes his first start tonight. Charliebo, he's put aside two box-seat tickets for me. How about you and me meet at the six-thirty shuttle plane and go see that game?"

"Yes."

"Did you say yes?"

"I did."

"I don't have to twist any wrist?"

"Nope."

"Threaten to dock your pay?"

"I'd just as soon be away from home tonight. Who are we playing?"

"Philadelphia."

"Dr. J. and Moses. Yes. Let's go."

"We'll be late getting back."

"Later the better."

"Daffodil problems?"

"Don't we all?"

"That why you're hidin' in the office?"

"Place to sit."

"Look. Get something to eat. I'm going to pick up a deli sandwich and have it on the plane. With two Bloody Mary's."

"I'll join you."

"Six-thirty shuttle."

"That gives me an hour."

"You down tonight, ain't you, bo?"

"I'll get up."

"Don't just sit there with your yellow flowers, brooding."

"How good is Chester Brinnegar, Deke?"

"He's a pro. You hired him yourself, you oughta know."

"Yep. See you at the shuttle."

"Deke Esterzee's office."

"Hello, Darlene."

"Boy, are you ever not home."

"I'm in New York still. Deke and I came up Friday night."

"I know. So how come this time you're the one who made a long weekend out of it instead of him?"

"You'll have to ask Deke."

"I don't think I'm strong enough to hear the answer this morning."

"Tell him I'm getting the ten o'clock shuttle back, okay?"

"You tell him, Charlie. It'll do you both good." (CHARLIE ON TWO)

"Hey, bo. Where in hell did you split to?"

"Friday after the game? You were the split man, Deke. I stayed at the bar with Tad and the trainer. Lot later than we should have. Tad put me up."

"Big night out. Yeah."

"First of a set of three. You have a good time?"

"Yeah."

"What's the matter, Deke?"

"Tell me all about your big weekend in the Apple."

"You really want to hear it?"

"Yeah."

"Saturday I got hold of some guys I used to race bikes with. We did some crazy stuff. Got rather drunk. Sunday we took a long ride, came in tired, drank some more and I decided to sleep over again last night."

"You did, bo?"

"That's right, Deke."

"Once there were twelve little marines in Korea, took a long walk. They got tired and decided to sleep over, instead of walking back to company position. In the morning there were roughly one and a half million Chinese sitting there looking at them, talking over different recipes for balls foo yung."

"You told me that."

"I wanta tell it again. They took these twelve marines to the nice Chinese doctors, and eleven of them got pretty good food and interesting treatment, all except the youngest and dumbest. The Chinese doctors tested him. Know what they said?"

"Yes, Deke."

"No brain-tickee, no brain-washee."

"You were eighteen."

"Charlie, get your ass down here."

"Something's happened?"

"Nice new letter from Uncle Ned. This one you've gotta read."

"I'll be there."

                                                    c/o American Express
                                                    Istanbul, Turkey
                                                    March 24, 1980

Deke & Charlie
House Office Building (Temporary)

Dear Penis-Enviers:
Ms. Cherry Nelson of Petrolat, who was sent along here to Turkey with me
as a chaperone, is gone for the day, and I've been busy. Here's for starters: The
good old pinko, arty-farty Register *knows a good man when it hears one on*
the overseas telephone. I wish my pain-in-the-ass little brother Mike was alive
to read this. I'm a goddamn foreign correspondent. Please send trench coat to fit
over bib overalls. I'm doing TV stuff here for use back home. Be on local for
sure, which is best for my purpose when I get back, but probably national, too.

Before I tell you more about that, just wanted you to know that from now
on, anything I do for the newspaper doesn't just get printed—I get paid, too.
With a regular little picture of me every time. Isn't that how us big-time po-
liticos get name recognition?

Here's how it happened, suckers. You remember I was telling about how I
ran into some 'Nam vets back in Libya the other day? They work for Khadafy,
training antiguerrilla tactics. Well, when I got back to the hotel, after my dinner
date with the lovely Miss Cherry of Petrolat, I picked up with three of the
black guys at the bar. They wrote these names they use: Mtongha, Cetshwayo,
and Mgidlana. Two are from Detroit, and one from Lawrence, Mass.

"Those your Black Moslem names?" I ask them, being a dumb farmer.

"Moslem? Those are Zulu names," Mtongha (Michael Harris) says. He's
the one from Lawrence, and he says it in a whisper, since Libya's a big Moslem
country. Sure, it was the white man came to Africa to buy slaves, they told me,
but it was the Arabs who caught the Africans and sold them. Black Africa's
going to stomp the camel shit out of Mohammed's boys, soon as they take care
of whitey together. "That will be the second wave of vengeance," Mgidlana
(Pete Pomfret) said.

Then they tell me that they're Nuzulus, and I say: "What the hell's that?"

So they grin and push each other, and talk a lot of silly stuff, and I say:
"Any of you Zulus arm wrestle?"

Cetshwayo's a big sonofabitch, and bets me a round of drinks, so we arm
wrestle, and I take him down in about ten minutes. Not bad for a sixty-four-
year-old country boy. Anyway, they liked that.

They wanted to know what I was doing, and I said the damned Moslems grabbed my brother, somewhere out here, and I'd come to find him. They liked that, too. They tell me about the camp where they stay, fifty or sixty mercenaries from all over the world, about twenty of them in this Nuzulu outfit.

"We got a basketball team, we box. We want to start competing and get some publicity," Mtongha says. They have this idea that they could start a movement, like the Black Moslems, if people knew about them back home. "Zulus are proud warriors, with a strong code of honor."

"Not just anyone can get in," Cetshwayo says. "We've got a warrior's initiation, like in the old days." Seems there still are quite a few real Zulus down in South Africa, but my friends haven't got much use for them because they've got their own deal with the South African government instead of joining the other blacks down there. Out at their camp my guys have lion skins they put on, and they practice fighting with assguys (probably spelled wrong), which are spears, like the old-time Zulus did. That's the initiation: you fight some other guy until your spear is bloodied, and you've been wounded, too. All three had scars to show me.

"I hope you're not telling me anything you don't want in the newspapers," I remind them, but as I said, they want publicity. "If that's the case, I'd like to see some of this assguy fighting," and they say they'll set it up for the next day and if I want to buy a half-hour tape for it, they'll let me film it with their TV camera that they got to make tapes of boxing. Naturally, I thought about how a tape like that is something I could show on television, with a little commentary by your favorite anchorman.

After that Mtongha, who is one strong little guy, took me on arm wrestling, had my wrist on the table in no time, and us boys went off to see the town. We picked up with some of the white 'Nam vets, hit a few bars, and got in a whorehouse fight with some Libyan marines. It was fun for a while (the Libyans know kick-fighting, like they do in France, and I got knocked for a loop by one of them, not expecting a foot in my face, but after that I was up and held my own until we see that there are too damn many of them and the cops are coming, so we run.)

Well, hell, that was a big enough night, and by the way, I forgot to tell you that I know a little more about Pete which is why I'm here in Turkey. (But that's not saying Pete's in Turkey, and I can't tell you what I found out. Anyhow, hold on. The best part's coming.)

Next morning, we ride a pickup truck out to the mercenary camp. They show me how to use their TV camera, and Cetshwayo and Mgidlana put on their lion skins and stage this assguy fight ("Don't do the blood part," I say, but damned if they don't keep it going until each one has pricked the other.) Anyway, all the other guys in camp come to watch the show and cheer, except

*for one I notice who looks bored and disgusted and walks away after a minute,
a little white jerk with a broad-brim hat, a beard and shiny black eyes.*

"Who's that?" I ask Mtongha.

"He's a royal pain," Mtongha says. "Got this eviler-than-thou attitude."

*When the match is over, and we're done milling around, Mtongha tells his
friends: "Sidney came for a minute, but he didn't stay."*

*"Sidney can take a long walk in the desert and stay lost," Mgidlana says.
"Ouch." That's because they just put some antiseptic on his new wound.*

"Who in hell's Sidney?" I ask.

*"Thinks he's big-time stuff," Cetshwayo says. "We're all supposed to kiss
his feet or something, because he's wanted in France and Italy as well as Japan."*

*"He likes to call himself 'the world's most wanted man.' Tell you where I
want him." Mdiglana holds up his assguy. "Right on the end of this."*

*"The big international hit man. All he ever did for sure was take a shot at
the premier of Japan and miss," Cetshwayo says. "I don't know how they got
him out of there."*

*"He must have been in something in Italy," Mtongha says. "I heard Sidney
could get extradited if they knew where he was."*

*"Nobody here's going to rat on him," Cetshwayo says. "But that doesn't
mean we like the kind of crap he does. We're fighting men, not assassins."*

"What's he doing here?"

*"He teaches marksmanship. He's really a good rifle shot. Somebody bumped
his arm there in Japan."*

*And I'm hiding a smile as best I can while they talk, because the world's
going to know where Sidney is real soon. I've got him on my tape. CBS News
guys here in Turkey have got it already, and me filmed talking about it, and
Sidney. The tape I shot isn't what they call "broadcast quality," but they're
flying it to New York for electronic enhancement, and if Sidney shows up good,
watch for him (and me) at 5:30 Central Standard Time, whoo boy.*

*And guess what? State Department's fixing it up for me to fly down to
Beirut to parley with Babyfat, excuse me, Arafat. I don't think he's going to
be able to tell me much about Pete, but I can ask him about seeing the Ayatollah, which he just did, and how the hostages are and all that shit, for my next
story. And he might be able to tell me who to see about Pete, and there might
be a photo of me and Airyfart kind of facing off, like I'm telling him to mend
his dirty terrorist ways just a little bit. That would be for U.S. consumption;
papers here would just see us talking serious, like concerned buddies.*

*Keep those committee hearings going on whether the government's got the
right to raise prices on the Kotex machines in the national park restrooms, and*

maybe even the women's movement will start seeing you're a real couple of sisters.

Next Rep. Ned (R)

"Charlie, it's Deke on one."

"Hi, Deke."

"Hey, bo. You all recovered?"

"Sure. You're at Petrolat?"

"Starting to feel like they oughta give me my own desk and telephone over here."

"What's going on?"

"Well, you might say baited breath."

"I might say it, but I wouldn't know what I was talking about."

"All comes down to electronic enhancement, don't it?"

"Probably."

"Well, if what comes up from the film lab isn't any more than Ned talking about spears and lion skins an' some fuzzy film, CBS might use it for filler, or maybe use it daytime for the regional affiliates' news. Ned'll get a little play, and Petrolat will be a little pissed. But if the film's good and the Sidney part comes out clear, it'll be national, Ned'll be a sensation, and Petrolat will be tear-ass."

"Is Sidney really the world's most wanted?"

"Chester can tell you more about that. If it's who Chester thinks it is, the Japanese are going to be pretty excited, but let's get back to Petrolat. They're a mite displeased with us."

"Because we sent them Ned?"

"They seem to think we owe them one."

"What do they want?"

"They're not real sure, but I've got'm listening to the idea that maybe we could do something or other helpful over there."

"Great. You may be going after all?"

"Not me, Charlie. Someone that's not flamboyant, doesn't want publicity. Someone that's interested in Pete, and not himself."

"No, Deke."

"Yes, Charlie."

"Ned would arm wrestle me right into the Bosphorus."

"Ned's got too public. He can't be anything but gracious."

"Is Petrolat really interested?"

"Like I said, they're listening. They're talking to their overseas people. My gut says that if I tell'm I'm sending you, they'll cooperate."

"How do we pay for this, Deke? If we do it."

"Not sure, bo. That's not today's problem, but hell, I've raised money before."

"You really want me to go."

"Yeah. You want to?"

"Do I get to think about it?"

"How 'bout overnight? Hey, you wanta watch the news at my place later?"

"Sounds like the start of another party. No, I'd better think tonight."

"Okay, bo. I won't disturb you."

"Hello?"

"I say, Charlie."

"Roxanne?"

"No, it's Angela actually. I say, did you watch the news just now on the telly?"

"I don't have a telly."

"Have you someone in your family called Ned? Ned Mizzourin?"

"He's my uncle."

"Your proper uncle is he? Nice-looking old bloke. Chesty, with a smile like yours when you do smile. Most bizarre film of him. Explaining, while some American blacks were sticking one another with spears, and this international criminal looked on, I think it was. Does that make sense?"

"As much sense as anything."

"A shame you missed it all. Perhaps your Congressman can arrange a viewing for you?"

"Perhaps. If he hasn't already stuck himself on an assguy."

"What? Look here, Charlie. Roxie is feeling quite neglected by you. Is there some reason?"

"I hope there's no reason, Angela."

"Stupid moodiness, perhaps?"

"Let's say so."

"Very well. If you promise not to be a mutt, I should like to put her on."

"Did she ask you to call?"

"That being a question that concerns her, I shall let her answer, if you care to inquire further. Here, Roxie. Here's your mutt. God knows what you want with him."

"Hello, darling."

"Thank you for the daffodils. It was rude of me not to answer."

"Would you like to give me a drink?"

"Well. Sure. Come on over."

"Are you a bit reluctant then?"

"No. I'm not."

"I daresay there's other chaps I could ring who'd fancy buying a pretty bird like me a drink."

"Sure there are. Please come over."

"I am unusually pretty, you know."

"Yes."

"And rather adorable would you say?"

"Yes. You are."

"It's not as if we all have uncles who can run around with spears, in lion skins, right on the telly, or whatever it was Angie saw."

"You didn't see it?"

"I was in the bath, darling, making myself look ever so clean and smell ever so sweet. Angie said the criminal looked like Charles Manson."

"I'll get the Scotch out that you gave me."

"It'll be a minute. I'm not altogether dressed, luv. In fact," (ANGIE DON'T. BEAST.) "The beast has snapped a Polaroid of me at the telephone, with nothing on at all." (ANGIE, DO LET'S SEE. OH, GOLLY.)

(SHALL YOU TAKE IT TO CHARLES?)

(OH DEAR GOD, NO. SHALL I ASK HIM?) "Charlie?"

"Hello."

"Do you want to see the Polaroid?"

"It may be too much for me."

"Well, then. You must build a fire on the hearth, and set my Scotch out ready on your little table in front of it. And I'll consider. But you've only just time."

"I'll get busy."

"And none of your bloody American ice."

File on my father (and other matters.) Notes:
>   *Story of the green sofa, part three?*
>   It deserves a new title.
>   *Get on with it. More horny stuff?*
>   Bad stuff, in a way. I'm not eager to start on this.
>   *Take your time, guilty-locks.*

You know, it looks like Christine Johnson's made off with quite a few more pages? There's a fat package here from her, in the evening mail. I haven't opened it yet.

Don't care to read about your old man anymore?

Well, I thought I'd try thinking through Deke's little proposal first. And have the new pages to read when things slow down.

Feeling exhilarated?

Just confused.

Interesting little Polaroid shot you've got there.

Dammit. She arrived so hyper, it was as if she were dancing on a tight-rope made from her own nerves strung out.

My plan, if I had a plan, was to be nice. I wanted to tell her that I didn't think I could handle caring for her, without hurting any pride, without giving any reasons.

She knocked, I opened the door, and she fired off just one word.

"Well?" She was standing with both hands behind her back, thrusting a no-bra bosom at me from underneath a thin, red dress. She wasn't wearing any coat or wrap. She'd run, I guess, the twenty yards from her house to mine, through the cold.

"Come in."

"Are you quite sure?"

"Come on, Roxie."

"Do you know what I should like most in the world to do?"

"No."

"Kick you," she said, and she did, rather sharply, in the left shin.

I made myself smile and wait a beat, and then said, "Ouch." She already had me playing back to her.

Then she came in, hands still behind her back, turning so that I couldn't see what was in them. I closed the door, and she danced off backward, away from me. My indicated step in the minuet was the mock lunge, and I wish I could say I didn't make it. I did. It was almost involuntary.

"No." She evaded the lunge. I was programmed to stop and grin. I stopped and grinned. "I want to tell you why I kicked you. And shall again, perhaps. It felt ever so nice." Now she did the mock lunge, stopped, tossed head and shoulders: "Charles, Charles. Do you know I practically stayed in all week-end, waiting for you to call?"

"I was in New York."

"So I learned, from your Mr. Esterzee."

"You called Deke?"

"Well, actually Angie did it for me. He said you'd surely be back Sunday morning, and I was ass enough to try to phone you then myself."

That voice.

"I wanted to fix your breakfast, and then spend a cozy morning, all rolled up in newspapers. But you didn't come back. 'Let's go have a drink on M Street,' Angie said, and I refused. Certain you'd get back and call. So Angie bet you wouldn't. Wicked creature. Bet me a pair of pantyhose, and do you know what? It was my last pair without ladders, and she took them, too. Did you ever hear such greed? That's why I've nothing on under this dress whatsoever tonight."

"Roxie, it's time for a drink," I said, and she moved in front of the fire and brought her right hand forward. She'd been hiding a small bottle of Grand Marnier.

"I felt like something sweet."

I couldn't stop my asinine self. "You're something sweet, Roxie."

The left hand came around from behind her back now, and she covered what it held with the right, sat down on the sofa, and put the two hands with whatever was between them—the Polaroid shot, of course—in her lap.

I opened the Grand Marnier, poured some in her glass and Scotch in mine.

"Since you didn't come along last night, either, I got quite drunk."

I didn't want to hear with whom, so why did I say: "By yourself?"

"Oh, no. With Angie, and some chaps who called. They wanted to take us out, but even quite late in the evening, I was still . . . you've been trifling with me, haven't you?"

"No." It was time for me to start declaring myself.

"I'd not have thought it of you."

"I haven't been trifling."

"And was I on your mind in New York? Did you never think of calling me from there? Sit here, Charlie."

I sat beside her, and I actually took in some breath with which to start saying what I had to say. But as I did, she reached to the table, first for my drink, then for hers, held up her glass for me to touch with mine—and handed me the photograph.

"Drink to it, Charlie. It's yours, you know."

I looked at it. It's a touching picture, really, of Roxie at the telephone, taken from one side and a little bit behind. It would be rather pretty, except that Angela's camera was a little tilted, and the glare of the flash leaches away the color.

If it had been professional and provocative, perhaps I could have made a light remark and handed it back. But because it was amateur and awkward, and offered with an altogether vulnerable and girlish confidence in what its effect must be, I played my part again.

"That's a lovely woman at the telephone." We clinked glasses and drank.

"I know," she said, and almost casually flipped her glass into the fire. In the flare of Grand Marnier, we embraced.

"Cad," she breathed into my ear after a moment. "Bastard. Aren't you even going to let me take my shoes off?"

She was squirming against me, and I against her, feeling totally inflamed, and even a little mean. *What the hell?* I was thinking. *Why in God's name not?* As the dress came off in my hands, and she went for my buttons, kissing each part of my chest as she exposed it, I ripped away at my ugly pants.

I realized, as we coupled at last, how very slight she is, and at the climax had the feeling that I was whipping her back and forth like something impaled.

Look out. Making love means creating love.

I know.

4/18/80 Conference Transcript. Confidential.

Copies: Congressman Esterzee, Charles Mizzourin, Chester Brinnegar. File. (Transcribed: D. Rhodes.)

Rep. Esterzee: Sit down, Charlie.

Mr. Mizzourin: Why so sober? Ned's being on TV can't hurt us all that much.

Esterzee: Better listen to what Chester's got.

Mr. Brinnegar: Istanbul's sharing reports with us because a constituent's involved.

Mizzourin: You mean Pete.

Esterzee: He means listen.

Brinnegar: "4/18/80. Istanbul, confidential, urgent. Edward 'Ned' Mizzourin departed 4/16/80, following TV taping. Exact time of departure unknown. Used Hertz rental car, Volvo sedan, blue, license 2Z-4871, rental contract number TURK 1980-33-801. Crossed Syrian border approximately 4:15 P.M., in violation of rental contract. Destination declared as Beirut, Lebanon. Detained Aleppo police two hours. Released and proceeded."

Mizzourin: He got to Beirut? That's a relief.

Esterzee: Just listen.

Brinnegar: "Rental car abandoned Beirut, Hotel Nouvelle Marseilles parking facility, 4/17/80." That is, he parked it last night, they found it this morning. "Luggage and personal effects still in room 1919, Hotel Nouvelle Marseilles. Room bill guaranteed by Cred Card AX 26 dash 417 dash 8444. Expires 9/27/80."

Esterzee: Gettin' all them good numbers are you, Charlie?

Mizzourin: Can we cut it shorter? Do I have another uncle missing?

Esterzee: Let Chester read his notes and numbers, bo. So you'll know everything we know.

Brinnegar: Shall I resume?

Esterzee: No, just keep on readin'.

Brinnegar: "U.S. observer confirmation lacking. Concierge told inter-
rogator believes subject left hotel in company of two, probably Syrian, possibly PLO, agents. Information account, \$20 U.S. Nothing
further. File continuation requested."

Mizzourin: PLO. He said he was going to try to see Arafat.

Esterzee: 'member a little trick called Cherry?

Mizzourin: Ned took her out to dinner in Libya, where she helped him.
Then Petrolat sent her to Istanbul with him.

Esterzee: Chester's friends are talking with the oil company boys. Over
there, they ain't quite so close-mouthed as the home-office types we
been seein'.

Mizzourin: We're talking about Cherry.

Esterzee: Chester?

Brinnegar: Yes, sir. "Cherry Nelson, born Racine, Wisconsin, 12/24/54."

Esterzee: Just missed being a Christmas baby, didn't she? Make sure
you give us all those numbers, Chester. Fascinating.

Brinnegar: Well, to summarize, Cherry Nelson has worked for Petrolat
four and a half years and is doing well with the company. Edward
Mizzourin was mistaken in thinking her just a secretary.

Mizzourin: She was in charge of Ned?

Brinnegar: "Unconfirmed possibility that Edward 'Ned' Mizzourin is
authorized by company to negotiate ransom for Peter 'Pete' Mizzourin, now believed held somewhere in Syria."

Mizzourin: Hey.

Esterzee: Don't jump so fast, Charbo. Ned took off without telling
Cherry.

Brinnegar: He evaded her.

Esterzee: No. He took off without telling her. Charlie, how long will
it take you to get your racing bike crated up? Hell of a big road race
or something going on in Turkey later this week, Charlie. Seems
Miss Cherry Nelson wants to see you ride in it.

Mizzourin: Huh?

Esterzee: Chester's got entry forms coming for you in the diplomatic
pouch.

Mizzourin: What good would a cover be? The name Mizzourin's pretty
transparent.

Brinnegar: Miss Nelson suggested you use your middle name. Travel as
Charles Scaliger on the passenger list, so as not to attract media notice.

Mizzourin: I thought Miss Nelson wasn't cooperating.

Esterzee: It's us cooperatin' with her now, and don't tell the State Department.

Mizzourin: But why the race?

Esterzee: You can ask when you see her.

Mizzourin: Okay. I can get a crate.

Esterzee: How soon?

Mizzourin: Tomorrow morning, I think.

Esterzee: Good. Your plane's tomorrow evening, eight o'clock.

Mizzourin: Not tomorrow, dammit.

Brinnegar: Eight P.M. Departing Dulles International, Pan American Flight 67.

"Hulloo?"

"Roxy?"

"Hulloo, darling."

"I'm glad it's not Angela for once."

"Can you actually not tell the difference?"

"You sound pretty much alike."

"Do not. Angela whinnies like a horse."

"Okay. You're right, and I'm going to Turkey."

"Tell me I sound an absolute turtle dove. You're what?"

"Going to Turkey."

"Whenever must you do that?"

"Tomorrow night. The plane's at eight."

"That's utter nonsense. You're taking me to dinner tomorrow at seven-thirty."

"Can we make it tonight?"

"Oh, love."

"Okay?"

"I'm doubly spoken for tonight, I fear. I'm just now getting dressed to go."

"After dinner?"

"No, darling. I'll be very late. I'm sorry."

"No way to cut it short?"

"Not this I can't. But Turkey. Is it Istanbul?"

"Yep."

"For how long?"

"As long as it takes."

"I've such a romantic idea."

"Me too."

"Not for tonight, love. It can't be helped at all, I'm so sorry. But you know, we'd have spent so much money going to dinner. Such a chump, aren't you, to want to do it? When we could have had a quiet nibble on one another at home. And I've—"

"Roxie . . ."

"Well, what I want you to do, and actually it will cost much less, and be so nice. Will you call me from Istanbul when you get in?"

"Rox—"

"Angela will be quite beside herself if I have a call from Istanbul. I shall let her answer first, and perhaps the operator will berate Angela in Turkish. I'll be sitting waiting, in my blue silk wrapper, so that you can picture me."

"Roxie, where are you going tonight?"

"Oh, quite a tiresome party, dear. I do wish I could chuck it, but it simply can't be done." (Pause) "Charlie, are you there?"

"Yes."

"Now don't be a nosy darling Parker. It's quite all right, really, a regular thing for which I'm counted on, and rather like business. Shall you phone me in the morning, then? Not too early, and maybe we could have coffee, if you're not too busy running the government. Do say you'll do the Istanbul call, in any event. And I'm aching to see you."

"Yes."

"Oh, lovely."

"You'll hear from me soon."

"Ta-ta, love."

"451-6518."

"Chester? This is Charlie Mizzourin."

"Hi, Charlie."

"Is this blackjack night at Suesue Landau's?"

"Yes, it is."

"Thanks, Chester."

> "Hi, hi, hi. It's Suesue speaking, and I'm sorry I'm not at the telephone right now. I'm having a nice evening, and hope you are, too. Do leave your . . ."

" 'lo?"

"Deke. It's Charlie."

"Whoof. This time of night?"

"Sorry about the hour."

"Goddamn; you sober?"

"I'm in jail."

"Yeah. Boy, some guys'll do anything to get out of going to Turkey."

"Can you bail me out? This is my one phone call. You're supposed to be my lawyer."

"Happens I am one, or did you forget?"

"I remembered."

"GI-bill lawyer. I forget it half the time myself. They holdin' this call to three minutes?"

"I don't think so. The guys who brought me in were tender about it. And the one who booked me is over there smiling and shaking his head. They're all black guys."

"What you do? Kill some honkeys? All right, bo. Lemme talk to your desk guy first a minute."

(SERGEANT PRESTON. 12TH PRECINCT.)

(YES, SIR.)

(THEY ANSWERED A CALL TO PICK HIM UP ON THE STREET.)

(PATROLMEN SAID IT WAS TWO BIG MEN IN EVENING SUITS. CUBANS, AND ONE MAD DRESSED-UP LADY.)

(FRANKLY, WE'VE BEEN WANTING TO RAID THE PLACE. NOT ALLOWED.)

(ADMINISTRATIVE RESTRAINT.)

(TALK AS LONG AS YOU WANT, CONGRESSMAN. HERE, CHARLIE.)

"Okay, Deke?"

"Okay, bo. I got the tape on, and I want to hear it. Maybe we can do something better than bail, if the guys you killed ain't too important."

"I'm charged with attempted assault. That's the worst. We've also got forcible entry, trespass, obscene language, public nuisance, and drunk. Which I wasn't."

"Start where it started. Where you went. I gotta pretty good idea. Why you went there, what you did. Dumbass."

"It starts with a girl, Deke. Her name's Roxanne."

"Roxanne Talley. Late of England. I know all about her."

"How come?"

"Come on. You the one in jail, not me."

"We had a dinner date for tomorrow. I called to say I was leaving, could we make it tonight? She said 'no.' "

"Exactly two million other women in Washington, son. Every one of them hungry."

"I met Roxanne through Suesue Landau."

"Do tell."

"What don't you know? Suesue runs a blackjack party Tuesday, Thursday, Friday. I figured that's where Roxanne had to be, but I didn't like thinking so. I couldn't go off to Turkey, half in love and half disgusted. So when I left the office, I went home and packed.

"About nine o'clock, I put on a dark suit, white shirt and tie. Blue and gold Brooks Brothers tie my stepfather sent me. About nine-thirty, I called a cab. It got me to Suesue's house just before ten.

"I stood on the curb across the street and watched people going in. Men. Some in dinner jackets. No women.

"They'd ring the bell, wait, and ring again. The curtains were drawn, but when the door opened I'd see lights and hear music. Next car that came, a couple of guys got out, and I strolled over and went up the steps behind them. One pushed the bell twice. They looked at me and must have decided I was another guest. Guy rang again, once, and I said, 'Is this Fred Eckleman's party?'

" 'No, not at all,' the man said. I thanked him and turned back down about the time the door opened.

"I waited a couple more minutes, went back up, and gave the signal.

"A big guy in tails came and said, 'Good evening, sir?' and held the door open. When I was inside, he said, 'Name, please?'

" 'I'm a friend of Suesue's.'

" 'May I have your name?'

" 'Tell her it's Charlie Mizzourin.'

"The big guy went upstairs to the living room. I didn't wait for him to announce me. I went up after him. Upstairs in the floor-through living room, it was a damn movie set. There were three or four couples dancing on the left, and a bar and buffet. Soft lights. On the right were pools of bright light, four of them, and under each one a card table, with a guy in tails dealing blackjack. Otis Hibben sort of supervising. I'd been hoping Roxanne would be a dealer. Nope.

"I saw her roommate Angela, first, leaning over some guy from behind, arms around his neck while he played. Roxie was with a player, too. A dinner jacket guy. She was sitting on his lap. I went that way, and the dealer had just finished dealing a round of cards. The dinner jacket guy said something and squeezed her breast, and she laughed. Things got a little blurred, but the bastard must have squeezed hard because I heard Roxie give a shriek.

"And just then Suesue loomed up in front of me, with the doorman behind her, saying 'Charlie. Charlie, dear.' She had a bottle of champagne in her hand; she'd been filling glasses at the tables with it, till she veered off at me, and I grabbed it away, and pushed past her, toward Roxie. I yelled, 'Let her go.' I knew who the guy was. This Peruvian. Roxie jumped up and he laughed and grabbed her around the hips.

"The doorman got me by the jacket. Suesue was coming up on the other side, and I went berserk getting loose. I had the bottle up, and I was charging at the card table, when another guy stood up and pushed me. Then Suesue caught me and was holding on—she's pretty strong—and was saying something. Roxie got in front of me and was scolding at me, too. 'Charles. No.' And right then this fucking Peruvian turns back to his hand of cards—it was a frozen moment—and I heard him say to the dealer in a bored, smug way, 'Hit me.'

"Boy, did it give me strength. I broke loose, and yeah, I could have hit him, I could have smashed his head with the champagne bottle. But I didn't. I saw Roxie crying and heard Suesue screaming, and everybody in the room was looking. I felt a wave of disgust and dropped the bottle on the floor and turned around to leave."

"Good for you, bo."

"Yep. I guess so. Except about fifteen people grabbed me then and wrestled me around. The doorman and Hibben got me, and one of the dealers punched me a couple. Angela was screaming in my face, and Suesue too. I lost track of Roxie. The guys got me down the stairs, with Suesue following, and at the bottom she slapped me and said, 'After all I've done for you, you little shit. You're like your shit father, headstrong, butt-in,' and she socked me again. Then she told the doorman, 'Take him out on the street.'

"There was another guy to help, and a third, and she says to someone else, 'Call the cops. Tell them it's a private party and this little shit tried to crash and attacked one of the guests.'

"So they took me outside. And the cops came. And here I am."

"Okay, bo. I got it. California?"

"What?"

"The champagne."

"Jesus, Deke. All right. It was Dom Perignon."

"Vintage? What year?"

"You know, I didn't really study the label."

"Chester's going to be damn disappointed in you, bo."

"What the hell does Chester have to do with it?"

"He's been takin' quite an interest in Suesue. Me too. I think I better go see her, fore I come get you out."

"What for?"

"See if she really wants you gas-chambered, or maybe settle for a country stomping. I think these charges gonna get dropped."

"You and Chester. You've been seeing Suesue."

"Won't say we haven't."

"Is that where the money's coming from, for me to go to Turkey?"

"You pretty sharp for this time of night."

"If you're shaking that woman down, the trip's off."

"Charliebo. You listen to me, and you learn. Suesue put up six grand, but it's no shakedown. Her idea, as a matter of fact. She wants you out of the country."

"Why?"

"Your little Roxanne's valuable to Suesue. The girl was sposed to get you going, bo. Manage you. What she wasn't sposed to do was fall for you herself."

"Sure."

"Seems like you overdid the charm, old prince."

"Tell Suesue she's got no worries on that score. None at all. Tell her I'll be glad to take as much grand tour at her expense as she's willing to pay for. Just get me out of here, Deke, and get me on that plane tomorrow."

"Okay, bo."

"Seventy-two."

"I'll tell Chester. He'll be proud."

File on my father. Notes:

Oh what a beautiful morning, with too much to do. Hey, Dad?

Hey, bird.

Did I throw my blackjack down the outhouse hole?

Not in the pure, classic sense, but maybe you're learning.

Roxanne in a black, waltz-length dress with a ruffle all around the hem; Angela in silver, Suesue in gold.

Charlie in waltz-length black and blue.

I guess I've got what Johnson wants to know now, anyway, though I don't know how much good it's going to do him.

Who cares?

Christine seems to have sent a real bundle of pages. Maybe now I can get it all.

Good luck.

Write Johnson.

Pick up crate.

Take nap.

Fly.

Charles:
You are being an utter schoolboy ass. Refusing to speak to me on the phone, and not answering my knock just now on your precious door. Except to say in your litle schoolboy voice, "I'm sorry, Roxie, I don't want to talk." Pure childishness. It hardly deserves the effort I am making to write this note to put under your stupid door. Read it, damn you. And have the goodness to think about it as you fly off to Turkey. If you weren't going, I should jolly well wait and let you come round to me, or stew, whichever you might bloody prefer. I suppose this much is my fault: there is no reason why I shouldn't have explained that Angela and I work for Suesue as hostesses at her card parties, and on other occasions as well. This is all we do. If a guest chances to get familiar, as does happen, please realize that we find it distasteful, but we laugh about it. There is no other way to take it, and nothing else we can do to survive. We don't have green cards. We are not permitted to work at regular jobs, though I believe I might do very well at one. I'm a most loyal person, I'm fun to be with, and I take the greatest pains in taking care of those I love. You are not to go off bitterly, hating me and not understanding. You must understand. It's a harsh, hilarious, FUNNY, AWFUL world, Charles. I long for your help to survive in it, not your anger which I promise quite simply I have never done and shall never do anything to deserve. I shan't expect you to phone, shall be out in any case from now on until after you have flown away. But please keep this, read it over, think it over, and know that quite a

large piece of my foolish heart shall fly away with you. Won't you come back from there, my dear, and melt me with your treacherous Mizzourin smile once more?

Love,
Roxanne

Washington, D.C.
April 19, 1980

Mr. John McRae Johnson
Last Deadline Ranch
Capsicum, Colo., 81666

Dear Uncle John:

This will have to be very brief. I'm packing to fly to Turkey this evening, on a mission for my Congressman, but one which concerns me quite directly, too. It has to do with my uncles, Ned and Pete, but I won't try to explain it just now.

I do want you to know that there is quite an accurate and up-to-date file of information on Suesue Landau now. Though I would not do so without also making it available to her, I can authorize that a copy be sent to you if you wish.

I must tell you frankly, though, that I am not the man to organize and evaluate the information for you, because I can't be objective about Suesue. We are no longer friends. You can learn what there is to know directly from a man named Chester Brinnegar. He is a competent, professional investigator who works for my Congressman's subcommittee.

On my own authority, I will say this much: Suesue may have been involved in the past in some fairly steamy stuff, but now she lives a relatively respectable life. I say "relatively" because her source of income, and it is considerable, is illegal, but not one which sophisticated people find morally repulsive. She is hostess and proprietor of regular, private gambling parties at which a lot of money seems to change hands and from which she takes, probably, no more than the normal house percentage. There are some shadow areas connected with the operation which Chester is very likely continuing to investigate, but I'm not sure I want to know what he learns.

From your standpoint, what has been confirmed is probably enough for you to attempt recovery of the money you loaned her years ago, basing your appeal simply on the knowledge that she is affluent, rather than on any sort of threat of exposure. This is Deke's advice, as well as my own.

I believe that Suesue still feels genuine affection for you, and some gratitude as well. It might appeal to her to repay a sentimental debt, or part of it, if the appeal made were to her generosity and good nature. She might even welcome your admiration for her success, if you should feel some.

How long my trip will take I don't know. I'll be in touch when I return. Meanwhile, if you want to talk or write to Chester, you can reach him through Darlene in our Congressional office.

Fondly,
Charlie

"Hello?"

"It's Christine Johnson, Charles."

"Aunt Christie. How odd. I've just come back from mailing a letter to Uncle John."

"He's gone."

"Gone out?"

"He left, Charles. Oh, like other times. John has disappeared. Don't you remember?"

"No. I did hear of one once. How long has he been gone?"

"This is the fourth day, Charles. The fourth. Has he tried to reach you?"

"I don't think so. Not that I know of. Would he?"

"A really long part, by registered airmail. Did you? But he found the post office receipt in my purse. And poor Mrs. Harper, my house-keeper, you remember? Who mailed them for me."

"Has something happened to Mrs. Harper?"

"Furious. He could tell the weight of the package from the receipt. Livid. So many pages, did you get them? And called up Mrs. Harper and said he was sending musclemen to beat her up, especially Luigi."

"Luigi?"

"He said Luigi was a specialist in granny-bashing, beating up nosy old women."

"There isn't a Luigi, is there?"

"Oh, dear. Not for years. I think he was in Circulation on the paper when they had those fights, wasn't he?"

"Aunt Christie. I got the package. Thank you. I haven't opened it. Would it help if I returned it?"

"Oh no. Please read it, dear. I don't know how far it goes."

"You didn't read it first?"

"Oh no. I never do."

"If Uncle John does call today, I'll let you know."

"And tomorrow?"

"I'll be gone tomorrow. I have to go to Turkey. It's funny. I was so pleased to have all the manuscript to read on the plane."

"Charles. John took the rest. Grabbed it, and his things, and went running out to his car and away. Away."

"I'm sorry. If he tries to get me at the office, I'll have them ask where he is and get word to you."

"So moody."

"But he always comes back to you, doesn't he?"

"Yes. He'll be in some motel or cabin, and so drunk, I think. And rant and rave and growl. And then be sick. And they'll find him. I've told the police to look. He's so fond of you, and has it all."

"Yes."

"Except what I sent."

"Thank you."

"He said he'd burn it, but that was just to make me cry. Like calling Mrs. Harper."

"I'm sure it will be all right, Aunt Christie. Thank you. Wish me *bon voyage*. There's a car waiting for me now."

"Oh, yes."

"Please call Deke Esterzee if there's anything to be done here."

"Oh, yes."

"Goodbye."

"Goodbye, dear."

(Notes on a boarding pass:)

PAN AMERICAN AIRLINES.   PAN AMERICAN AIRLINES
THIS IS YOUR BOARDING PASS.
Flt. # 67F. *From:* Dulles. *To:* Casablanca, Rome, Istanbul.
FIRST CLASS
Seat Assignment: 14C, nonsmoking.
First-class Charlie. Thanks for the champagne ride, Suesue. I'm going to enjoy it.
Charles Scaliger? Mother would love it. She might not love my having seventy-five new pages here on my lap.
Evaun. Rhymes with faun, and gone in the dawn.
Let's be on our way, Pops.
Pops? Up yours, too, Baby Bird.

"CAPTAIN PETERSON HAS TURNED ON THE NO SMOK-
ING SIGN."

*Mizzourin/*THE WORLD IS WAITING FOR THE SUNRISE

I woke Bink Jones at 5:45 A.M. on New Year's morning. He looked
at me and put it simply: "Marv come."

"Who?"

"Marvin come for her. Merrill."

"Musical Marvin," I said.

"He keeps her at his house sometimes. Sometimes me."

"What does 'keeps' mean, E.B.?"

"Well, now, he's Mamma's brother, Mike."

"I know that."

"Well, now, he's a bachelor man. Needs someone to do for him."

"Do what?"

"Well, cleaning, Mike. And cooking."

"Sure."

"Well, housekeeping."

"You said that."

"Mike, what Marvin did was find yore name from Tommy Rhombo.
Then he come here and found that Hazel waitress sleeping on a sofa,
all tuckered out, in the lobby, and Hazel told him which yore room
was."

"What did Marvin say?"

"Not much at all. Just stood there outside the door whistling 'Beale
Street Blues,' and we was both awake like . . . Hey, Mike?"

"Hey, E.B."

"I know she was in yore bed. Knowed she would be, too."

"I like your sister a lot. I'm sorry she's so young."

"We ain't never been young, soldier."

I let that one go. I asked: "Did Marvin raise you?"

"Might say he helped. Owns Mamma's house, gives her allowance.
She not too strong in the mind, Mike. He gave us our whippings. If he
knowed she was with you, he'd whip Evaun right now."

"Would he like it?"

"Still whips me, can he catch me out. But look, I got my job in the
store from him. He books the trio, me and 'vaun git paid."

It was all so reasonable, I didn't want to hear any more. "I'm going
out again," I said. "I'm going to take a walk."

"Don't you want to take a drink?" E.B. was eyeing his bottle. "Maybe sleep a little more?" He took a belt of whiskey and held a glass out to me. "Marv's all right. Kind to us."

"Yeah," I said. "He whips you, and makes you throw up."

"Ain't simple."

"Does he make Evaun throw up?"

"She can handle him better than me."

"Take it easy," I said, moving toward the door.

"Mike?"

"Yeah. What?"

"He'd make a player out of you, quicker than anybody."

"He'd make a raving idiot out of me."

"Mike?"

I looked at him.

"You goin' back to Ohio?"

"Iowa."

"You goin' there?"

"No. What's the matter, E.B.?"

"Nothin'."

"You scared to have me leave?"

"Don't want to be here alone when he comes back for Evaun's shoes."

"Get dressed and take them to her."

"You want I should go, Mike?" He looked crushed.

"No," I said. "Relax. I'm going for a short walk. I'll keep the hotel in sight, in case he arrives. If he doesn't, I'll bring you some coffee."

That uncrushed him fine. "Extra cream, and three sugars," said E. B. Jones.

Mizzourin/**GOODY GOODY**

The hotel coffee shop was open when I went by, but there wasn't much business, only Cosmo Selkirk having breakfast. I didn't stop to visit.

Out on the street it was half-cold and all quiet. I was wearing Evaun's high-school letter-sweater again with F for Faraday turned inside. I wondered who the boy had been that gave it to her. It was a pretty youthful item for a girl whose twin said they'd never been young.

I walked past dark Rhombo's to the corner, turned right along the square past the iron-shuttered music store, and right again past the locked-up courthouse. Entertainment, commerce and justice weren't doing much business yet at 6:15, but neither was I. I was just walking and changing colors.

Rosy Mike was rasping away on a mouthpiece, rattling a drum, with a couple of musical zanies for an audience of drunks. Red Mike was the color of flame thrown into a cave, with his ears splitting from the whine of an air full of mortar rounds and ricochets. Pink Mike, turning blue, and green, and yellow, was some kind of damn rainbow of tenderness, conjecture, irritation and concern over some kind of damn infanta of the boondocks.

I stopped, and looked up at a statue of a World War I doughboy in front of the courthouse. "Hi, Doughboy," I said. "I think I just fell off the roof."

I went around the square about six times, slowly. The seventh time I went fast. A green and artful Dodge sedan was pulling in and parking in front of the hotel. A door opened, and Marvin Merrill got out the driver's side. Then Doctor Wanderbaum got out the other.

I wasn't far behind them when I reached the lobby.

I needn't have hurried. They weren't on their way upstairs to bully E. B. Jones. Not yet. They were turning into the coffee shop, and then finding a table to sit down at. I looked around for Cosmo, but apparently he'd done eating and gone off to bed. There was only one other customer in there, a big, hungover-looking man in a brown sweater, with a forkful of grits, trying to look a fried egg in the eye.

A waitress, nothing like the Hazel model but a gray-haired one with pale freckles, was pouring coffee for Marvin and the Doctor. Marvin saw me, looking through the doorway from the lobby. He turned his body my way, and the lenses of his glasses spread the darkness of his pupils from rim to rim. He raised his arm in a slow arc, motioning to me to come in. I couldn't think of any reason not to, but I kept the brown-sweater hangover guy in view as I moved, in case he was one of Marvin's troops.

"Good morning, drummer," Marvin said, with his eery smile. "Have some nice good coffee with us here, right now."

"Happy New Ear," said Doctor Wanderbaum. "As the lady said to Van Gogh, in another connection. Or rather disconnection."

"You sit." Suddenly Marvin was holding a five-dollar bill out toward me. "Take this, now. Want to thank you for staying with the trio, want to pay you, Tommy Rhombo says you're just as natural as a limestone spring." He put the bill down at the place he'd indicated for me to sit at. "Hey, Ruth," he called. "Coffee for my drummer here."

"I didn't do ten cents' worth of drumming," I said. "But coffee sounds good." I sat, but I didn't pick up the bill.

The Doctor did. "No pay, no play," he said, and tucked the money in my shirt pocket. "First rule of the professional musician. There may be a second rule, but I forget what it is."

"I was terrible," I said. "I didn't even know how to hold the sticks."

"The way we heard," Marvin said. "Took you ten seconds to learn. Ten more, you had 'em dancing on the tables, yes you did."

"How's Johnny Billiard?" I asked, before things got any weirder. What were they conning me about?

"They broke his stupid collarbone," the Doctor said. "Which is considerably smarter than his head bone. Which is a genius compared to the organ inside it. The world's only brain bone."

"Want you to play with Doctor Wanderbaum now, while pore Johnny mends," Marvin said. "Can't pay but ten a night, two nights a week, that's Friday, Saturday, say, could you do it for us now, did you have to go away someplace? We countin' on you, Mike."

I started to object that there must be a dozen people in town who could play drums, but I stopped myself, gave them my best smile instead and let it come forth.

"As for holding the sticks," the Doctor said. "It's difficult to grasp. Grasp one in your right hand, and the other firmly between your teeth. This provides nourishment and music at the same time. No, seriously, my boy, and who said I wanted a serious boy? I happen to hold my doctorate in musicology. I'll undertake to teach you reading and theory, as well as rehearse you in percussion rudiments until you twitch like a spastic."

While he was twitching like a spastic for me, Marvin began to outline the plan, and a dilly of a plan it is.

There is money to be made, under the GI Bill of Rights, by starting a school in which veterans can be trained. Their's will be called the Carolina School of Popular Music. Doctor Wanderbaum will be president, Marvin one of the instructors. For each of us veterans they can sign up as students, the Veterans' Administration will pay tuition, buy books and even instruments. The VA will also pay each student twenty dollars a week for room and board. In addition to our music lessons, we'll receive on-the-job training.

I was crass enough to ask about the Doctor's PhD.

"Trumbauer College of Art and Music, class of 1924," he said.

"Did it burn down in 1925?"

"1926, and ceased to function, all records having been destroyed. But Marvin's friend at the Veterans' Administration has been kind enough to take my word for it."

"Nobody's gonna get rich, Mike," Marvin said. "And we'll work hard for the money, too, and anyway, what d'you care, now, what you want is learn to play, now, ain't it? What other music school could you get into, wanta hear the best part? Gonna have some other students, Mister Mike."

"That's the best part?"

"Soon as you can blow a little horn, it's goodbye sticks. You'll have a combo, train you up a reed man and a fine trombone. There's good times comin', we can book some little bands. Our first one, I see you, I gotta high school boy he's purty good piano and 4-F, only the Doctor'd play with you to start, and Johnny an' E.B. Soon as we can add some front line, and a singer, we could go to work, and see, we substitute the new ones when they good enough, pull Johnny and the Doctor back to break in more, you'll play in Pindar, Winston-Salem and Columbia, Chapel Hill, wherever there's a college, the Carolina bands, I got connections in the jukebox business, bookin' comes from that, come on now, say it, Mike, you've only gotta fill a little form?"

"I filled it for him," said Doctor Wanderbaum, producing a set of applications from the VA. "Of course there'll be some others, but to start, why all you have to do is start."

By now that was probably what I wanted to do, so I took the papers and the pen, put them aside and said to Marvin: "Where's Evaun?"

During the pause, I wondered if that grin Doctor Wanderbaum was swallowing tasted pretty good.

Marvin saw my raise and bumped it. "Evaun, she's down to home at my house, sleepin' pretty sleep of bliss and innocence, let it be, you know? A funny thing? That Muley Haas boy depitty you seen last night? The MPs got him lookin' for a certain army horn."

I played it for a bluff. Nothing would make him give the flugel up. "Do you see Evaun working with this combo, Marv?"

"Doctor and me, we got another vocalist we training."

"You said we'd use E.B. Would you split Evaun and her brother up?"

"Well, hell, why don't we all jus' work together?" Marvin said, and pushed the papers at me.

Well, hell. I signed.

One more player was going to take a chair in our game, sandbag all of us to take the pot.

This new boy was E. B. Jones, who laid down a hand of Gypsy cards I don't know how to read.

Marvin, the Doctor and I went up to my room to fetch Evaun's shoes and take E.B. his syrupy coffee.

The kid was up and dressed, and the little snoop had been into my closet and found Cosmo's gift, my Snakespeare, *Bitus Andpanicus.* From what he told me later, Binkie scared himself transparent when he opened it.

Doctor Wanderbaum was the first victim. He actually asked to see the beautiful book, but E.B. and I put him off, talking captured trophy from the library of an old Buddhist monastery until Marvin went to the bathroom, which is something Marvin does a lot. Then we wandered the Doctor's baum pretty good, hoping the yell he gave was so hoarse and low-pitched as to pass for something else, as heard through a bathroom door.

Marvin came out. The Doctor was handing the refastened volume back to E.B., who wiped it, polishing the leather with the corner of a bedsheet, and asked me: "This is the only thing you brought home from Japan, Mike?"

"Only thing." I took a step toward the closet, stopped, and said to Marvin: "Did you want to see it?"

"Lemme."

"Be careful with it," E.B. said, as I handed it over to Marvin.

"Sure." Marvin took it, held it, turned it around a couple of times, and then stared at the spine. He smiled his pale smile and offered it back to me. "Go ahead," he said. "Let's see you make the snake jump out."

I shrugged, and would have put the thing away if I hadn't seen E. B. wink. "Okay, Marvin," I said, undoing the clasp and holding against the spring inside. "You can see the snake."

Marvin smirked. Doctor Wanderbaum quizzicked. I let the lid flip up. The snake jumped, and E.B. screamed, a shrill, terrifying, soprano shriek of fear.

"Don't, oh God, Mike, no-oooo." It was horrible. He trembled, and fell, screaming, clutching his arm, against Doctor Wanderbaum, who grabbed him. It made me jump back, even though I'd been expecting something, and it half-destroyed Marvin Merrill. E.B. screamed again.

Marvin let out a huge, involuntary, gulping noise, went paler, and staggered a step to where he could grasp the footboard of the bed, staring at Binkie Jones.

Binkie's chuckle started small. He pushed away from Doctor Wanderbaum. He pointed at Marvin.

"Oh, lookee there at him," he said, and the chuckle grew into a laugh, the laugh into a guffaw so hard it shook his body as he hooted, "Oh, my God, Uncle Marvin," and by then E.B. was laughing so hard he had to let himself fall to the floor, where he rolled around, holding his rib cage with one hand and hitting his ass with the other.

The Doctor laughed more covertly. I couldn't do much else but stare. Marvin made it to the bed and sat recovering for a time, and then, as E.B. sat up, gasping and grinning, Marvin said, choking it out: "Don't never do that. Never." Then he added quite humbly: "Please, boy."

Mizzourin/ON BLUEBERRY HILL

I will skip now, to January 2, 1946. I am in Marvin Merrill's office, having had an excruciating first lesson on the cornet and signed up for about a hundred bucks worth of method books and practice equipment for percussion and brass. These were authorized by President Wanderbaum, and will be billed to the Veterans' Administration by the purveyor, Merrill Music Mart, the purchase order to be okayed by Marvin's man at the VA.

That buck made, Marvin turned stoutly to the next, as if it weren't all enough to wear a fella out. "Mike, now you kin take a room right there with my sister Margaret, that's the twins' mamma, now that'd be just right. Have E.B. there to practice with too, you would, and Margaret, she'll give you country cookin', yes, good, look after yore clothes, won't hardly charge nothin', no she won't."

"The music college dorm?"

"No, now what do you say, let's think, let's talk, don't be in a hurry, but you know—"

"I'll find a place," I said.

It wasn't long afterward that I heard Binkie, for the first time, sounding very much like his uncle. I was trying to drum. It was noon in the back room at Rhombo's, and Doctor Wanderbaum had been running us through some songs. We took a break. Evaun was there. The Doctor went up to the front bar to talk to Tommy Rhombo about something. Binkie's notion went like this.

"Mike, you kin bunk in with a friend of our'n, Skinny, the barber.

Got a big ol' farm house on the edge of town, right there, away all day and most evenin's he plays cards? Talks like sixty, never tells a thing, not Skinny . . ."

"Mike'd rather be alone," Evaun said, and smiled. It was the first time I'd heard the twins even slightly at odds.

"Well that's what I say. Skinny, when's he ever to home?"

"Why can't Mike use the captain's cabin at the old CCC camp?"

"Aw."

"You still got the key Dave gave you?"

Dave, a forester, lived at the camp after the CCC closed down, and was E.B.'s scoutmaster. And friend. And is gone now.

"It's agin the law."

"Who's gonna know?"

"Mike'd be lonesome out there."

"Maybe not all the time." She smiled again and looked at me. "Lot of the time, you would. But it's so pretty there."

"Where is this place?" I asked, and they explained: twelve miles by road, seven by footpath over the mountain, nothing at all near it—a shut down CCC camp, with only the captain's cabin and one tool shed left standing. I wanted to practice unheard. I wanted to come and go without words. I wanted a place where I might see Evaun sometimes. That's all I wanted.

I said it sounded perfect. E.B. said, giving in, that he'd get the car and drive me out with my stuff. Evaun said she didn't think she dast come along, not today, and took me by the hand, saying to Binkie: "Play us a chord when he's comin'." Binkie moved his chair so that he could see farther up into the barroom; Evaun led me back into the storeroom, where we keep our stuff. The storeroom's big and dark and kisses good, but C-sharp seventh can push two bodies apart very fast. Did I mention what I wanted?

My colleagues left after that. I finished putting the instruments away, locked the storeroom, and waited for E.B. and the car.

There's paved road out of town for a couple of miles, to a place called Mineral Springs, a closed-down resort. Then the road turns gravel and goes on out past some farms and hamlets, but to reach the former CCC camp you turn west onto dirt, through pretty, piny hills, along a pretty, piny creek.

Creek's on the left, going west. On the right, you come to a break in the trees and can see the foundations where the barracks and the mess hall and latrines stood, in three parallel rows. Behind them, hidden now by rhododendron bushes, is an empty tool shed.

Along the road, unused except by moonshiners in these days when deerhunters and trout fishermen can't get gas, is a set of signs, one by each foundation: U.S. GOVERNMENT PROPERTY, FOREST SERVICE, DEPARTMENT OF THE INTERIOR, KEEP OUT. What once were streets snake up the hill into the mountain laurel and Virginia creeper.

The captain's cabin is across the creek. There is a nice footbridge to it, though the bridge is barricaded and has its own KEEP OUT sign. The cabin does, too, and is padlocked, or was until E.B. unlocked it. The window shutters were nailed up, until I found a hammer. It's a square, tight log cabin: a living room with a fieldstone fireplace, two bedrooms each with a little stove, and a kitchen with a big stove. There's a bathroom, with a pump that works and a water heater that doesn't.

"Forest service keeps it for emergency shelter," E.B. explained. "Why they keep the power on. On'y Fo'stah Dave, he bypassed the meter, so the use don't show."

District Forester Dave had lived here until halfway through the war, when it was suggested to him by friends of Marvin Merrill's that it might agree with Dave's health to get married and move to Pindar. But sometimes marriage would pall, it seems, and District Dave would travel back miles, starting before dawn, for a schoolday tryst at the cabin with the truant reason for his expulsion from it, his old premarried love— Binkie Jones.

E.B. wasn't eager to begin telling me this, nor did I press him, but once started it came out fast and unpunctuated: ". . . now Fo'stah Dave the scoutmaster Uncle Marvin sure did think I oughta woodcraft an' outdoors and birds now othah boys say I was twelve . . ."

By the time of the Forest Master's wedding, Uncle Marvin was keeping his garçon fatal indoors and housecrafting. But a few months later there began unalibi'd truancies from junior high, and mean suspicions. A second message was delivered to the recent bridegroom by Marvin's business associates in Pindar. Since which, pore Dave had stayed out of Faraday and the camp and cabin like they were full of pisen gas, leaving lavender eyes the keys.

You can't beat the rent here: secrecy. And an hour's walk through pretty piny Friday mornings to my weekend work, an hour back through high-bush huckleberry Sunday afternoons.

"Trail over the mountain starts right here ahind yore cabin," E.B. said, and showed it to me. "Got little signs to point the turns. I useta run the downhill part when I'd come out to meet with Dave." Saying that seemed finally to embarrass him, not telling what he'd done but confessing his emotions, and he drove away quickly.

I watched the car leave, put my food away in the kitchen, and began devising a routine.

This was the greatest of possible pleasures for a piece of programmed monkey poop, subjected for four years to routines devised by noncommissioned piles of baboon doodoo.

1. Every morning of my life, now, I sleep until I wake. 2. Every evening of my life I go to bed when I feel like lying down. 3. Between that stop and start of time, I work, on cornet and on drums, cut wood, read, write, eat, drink, and only sometimes wish for company. 4. I do these things in the order of impulse, for the duration of wish. 5. I am careful not to plan, out here. But in town, Friday morning to Sunday afternoon, every minute's planned, so much so that Evaun and I haven't been alone since New Year's morning. We brush fingertips, press feet together under tables, and make love with our eyes.

Mizzourin/THE HUCKLE BUCK

I woke eager and early Friday, day before yesterday, packed the cornet and my weekend stuff into the musette bag, and was out on the trail over the mountain by sunrise. It was pretty cold, and the birds were so loud it was almost noisy; crows and jays, woodpeckers, grouse drumming. I wondered where I might stay Fridays and Saturdays, the two nights I'd have to be in town.

I got to the hotel in time to have breakfast with Cosmo and get some good news.

"Daryl says that trunk room's all yours, Friday-Sattiday. Got th'alarm hooked up alreaduh." Daryl is the manager. I moved a rollaway, lamp, chair and table into the litle room with no windows where they used to keep people's trunks, and tore out a couple of shelves. The alarm is a bell connected to Cosmo's desk. Sometimes there's early morning trouble on the weekends. I'm to sleep in my clothes.

Arranging the room didn't take long. At ten o'clock, I went to the music store for my second cornet lesson. I can play for about twenty minutes now, before I start feeling like someone has me by the lip with a nutcracker. I can produce sounds in several pitches, but the sounds are squawks and the pitches lurch. Crows and jays.

"First thing ever' day," Marvin said. "Play a dozen middle Cs. Start him soft, get loud, let off just on one breath. Dozen Gs, same thing. Now lemme hear some."

After we'd done that a while, Marvin wrote me out three scales, with fingering, and marked some exercise in my method book.

Then he said: "Gonna give you one little song to work on, just to keep yore nerve up and yore pecker down. I taught a lot of boys." The thought made him leer. "Be blowing away, playing mechanics, and something else creep in their mind and that ain't what the valve oil's for at all, huh, huh . . ."

I can count on Marvin to come up with something like that about any time I start to halfway like him. But the song he wrote out for me, transposing it from G down to C, is "Ja-Da," which he played for me two weeks ago, and he got me stumbling through it, which was nice for my confidence. I had no idea I could.

Then he undercut me by getting out the famous flugel and playing "Ja-Da" with me as a dumb little duet, at first making us sound piny pretty, and then mocking my awful tones by playing worse ones.

E.B. was sweeping the sidewalk in front of the store when I left.

"Lemme see yore cornet here a minute please?" he said. I handed him the case. He opened it, took out the horn, held it up, tried the valves, and put it back again with a note tucked underneath.

I read the note in the trunk room. It was from Evaun. *Can't see you till tonight. Oh Mike. Hurry up sundown.*

I spent the whole afternoon in Roseland, which is what Tommy Rhombo likes us to call his back room. The first couple of hours I was with the Doctor. We had a theory lesson based on the "Ja-Da" chords, which was pretty interesting. We took a break, and then worked on drums. For now, I'm only to use brushes when we play for the public, but the Doctor is getting me comfortable with the sticks, and with Johnny's rather elaborate drum set. Woodpeckers, grouse.

After lessons, I set up Rhombo's Roseland for the evening, the part of my on-the-job training for which Tommy pays an extra $6 a week. I arranged chairs and tables, spread wax, checked the gelatins in the floodlights, washed a couple of windows and changed some of the records on the jukebox, which plays when the trio takes breaks. Napkin dispensers, salt shakers, ashtrays, nevermind.

When I got done, I went into the kitchen, where Morgan the cook made me a steak sandwich and asked could we play "I Can't Get Started" tonight, because he's going to have someone pretty nice helping him and they can hear the music if the doors are open.

There was still some time. I went over to the Piggly-Wiggly and bought bacon, beans, and butter and some other things to carry back out here to the cabin. I bought a bottle of sherry to drink during the week—I'd rather have beer, but it's too much to carry. I was back at Roseland with the lights dim and the jukebox playing, hoping Evaun would come early, by eight-fifteen. The trio doesn't start till nine, which was exactly the time Marvin dropped the twins off.

It was a quiet night. I concentrated hard when we played, and Evaun and I held hands under the table on the breaks. She was wearing an ankle-length navy-blue skirt and a white sweater with fake pearls and sequins sewed around the collar. When she sang, I wondered how in hell one could put some feeling into swishing a wire brush over the head of a snare drum, and whistled, without sound, the phrases I might some day play behind her on cornet.

We looked at each other a lot. By the end of the evening, we couldn't stand it any longer, and the moment Doctor Wanderbaum left we ran to the hotel and the trunk room, leaving E.B. waiting in the lobby to walk her home. But, of course, her safe time was over, and I hadn't thought to go to the drugstore earlier.

She dared stay only ten minutes or so, because Marvin would be waiting up. So Evaun and I talked and clutched and accommodated.

Saturday I cleaned Roseland in the morning and set it up again in the afternoon. In between I spent more time with the Doctor. The VA requires twelve hours a week, and counting the time with Marvin, too, I come pretty close to doing that many.

The high point of Saturday, though, was getting to the drugstore. I got back into uniform to do it, to make myself anonymous; it's a small town.

The low point of Saturday was eleven-thirty at night, when the trio takes a long break. Marvin showed up. He had a purchase order with him for a cocktail drum and a Turkish cymbal, which he wanted Doctor Wanderbaum to certify as needed, and me to countersign. Then he sat and listened to us through the last set. Part of the time he appeared to be talking business with Tommy. Anyway, he was there to take Evaun off home, and E.B. said probably Tommy squealed about the night before, so I don't guess I'll discuss with Mr. Rhombo the following conversation which took place while Doctor Wanderbaum and E. B. Jones were trading fours on "Blue Moon."

"Mike, can you hear me?" She was looking straight out over the dance floor, standing just behind me.

"Yep." I didn't look at her, either.

"Wednesday. Maybe I'll get the car. Should I?"

"Oh, God, of course."

"Don't even tell Bink."

"Okay," I said, but I don't really understand why not.

Mizzourin/YOU AND THE NIGHT AND THE MUSIC

It's Thursday, and a mawkish man am I.

My freedom routine worked fine Monday and Tuesday. My lip is stronger. I can play octaves now. It hurts, but I can play the sonsofbitches, and all three of Marvin's scales—C, F and D. And once, three notes higher, which is the open G. Marvin said I'd be struck by lightning if I tried, so of course I tried. But I didn't make it Monday, Tuesday or Wednesday morning, either.

For drum practice, I have brushes and sticks, a pad, and a foot-pedal device clamped to a small garbage can. I also have a small, tin-speakered radio on which I can get music to practice to. In the morning it's country, squeaky fiddles and nasal singing to a banjo beat, to which I play with a heavy bass drum and plenty of stick to drown it out. When I practice in the afternoon, I can get the Pindar colored station, which plays blue and raucous. In the evening the armed forces network from Faraday plays swing, old jazz sometimes, and sometimes a new jazz which I find quite awful, but is recognizably related to what Scholay Gopeters found interesting in Doctor Wanderbaum's piano.

Sometimes I try to play cornet along with something on the radio, but it's only a honking, zonking travesty of playing. Tuesday night I sounded almost good, before I got lost halfway through a chorus of "High Society."

I read. I haven't a library card yet, but I have scrounged up a lovely assortment of books. I won't do the whole card index, but A's for *Alice Adams* by Booth Tarkington, M is *Marcus Aurelius,* and Z's *Zenda, The Prisoner of.* I talk to myself, sometimes, a friendly chat over a glass of sherry.

Wednesday it was hard to keep my mind on any kind of practice.

Yesterday I must have cut and carried in a dozen loads of wood until I felt exhausted. Then I did three more, and used up most of one in the big kitchen stove heating water to take a bath. I put on clean clothes. I was ready for her, wasn't I?

Not quite. The hors d'oeuvres were not prepared, and already four in the afternoon. I cut up some bread in little squares, put butter and cheese on them, and lined them up on a cookie sheet, ready for the oven. Built up the stove fire, too, so the oven would be hot. Changed my shirt. Changed it back again. Then it was five-thirty and getting dark, and I put the bread and cheese out for the raccoons.

On Wednesdays, folks, Marvin Merrill goes by truck to the Rhombo cattle farm, with Horse Haas. Marvin, along with his other skills, is a meat cutter. Horse handles the carcasses, which Tommy's brother has butchered, skinned and hung. Marvin cuts a week's illegal beef for the tavern. He cuts some for himself, and some for private customers. He and Horse run it in after dark. This means that not only is the Big Uncle absent from home, his green car is present and unused. It had been, so I figured out, Evaun's plan to make use of the situation. Something must have gone wrong. It was about all I could do to keep myself from starting in on the trail over the mountain then and there.

I didn't. I drank some sherry, which made me feel sad. I took a walk and watched the stars come out. I kept on the road, so that if headlights happened back behind me, I could show the stars some speed.

I turned back, and as I got back near the footbridge, I stopped and yelled, "Goddammit Pete, come out of the woods and get some goddamn supper." I don't know why it was my little brother I suddenly wanted to entertain, except that he and I have always felt good with one another, and never had to talk about why.

Back in the cabin, I put the sherry away and tried to think of anything to eat I wouldn't gag on. I decided to try the larks' tongues, flambé, but couldn't find the flam, so I read *Tarzan and the Lost Tribe* all the way through. Tarzan found the tribe, with some help from large animals. There was a lion who was really very helpful. Tarzan and the lion felt good with one another, and never had to talk about why.

Just after midnight, I went out on my front stoop with the cornet, warmed up with a D-scale, and tried to hurl an open G into the night, like a shriek. I think I got it, but my ear said it was flat. I got undressed and drank a coffee cup full of sherry, hoping it would make me sleepy, and it did. Clunk. But I was awake again and fretting, when I wasn't mawking, at five A.M.

Mizzourin/**MY DARLING**

My darling. I was coming to see you Wednesday in Marvin's car. This is
the note she left with Cosmo for me, so I'd know as soon as I arrived
in town on Friday. *Only the car hit a tree when I was backing up, because I
didn't understand how you steer when you go back. Binkie always has to drive,
so I never yet learnt right. I got the bumper caught, and the fender bended, and
the neighbor saw and called Muley Haas. (Nosy.) And Muley come and got
the car loose and took the keys away from me because I've got no license.
Marvin don't want me driving, and he licked Binkie any time he let me try,
but oh, Mike, when am I going to hold you in my real arms and not just
dreaming? I love you. Evaun Barlow.*

I love you, Evaun Barlow, you dope.

Friday's lesson started with Marvin listening to the stuff he'd assigned and criticizing my tone: "What'd I tell you about that damn little
pink tongue now? You keep him flat, now play me yore D scale and
legato . . . You call that legato, drummerboy?" "You know there's
gotta be a B flat in that dominant seventh, doncha know that? Woncha
play it right now, just to please a pore sick man that's begging you for
one little nice B flat?"

Surprise time was coming: "Wouldja lemme hear yore 'Ja-Da' one
time please, the way I wrote it special for you, please?"

The way he'd written it, in C, the highest note was going to be an
A. What I'd done was study "Ja-Da" in the Fake Book, where the key
is F, which means that trumpet has to play in G. Five tones higher. I
grinned at Marvin, and I played it that way, too, going up to E clearer
and better than I had the day before in practice. Went through the first
eight bars without an error. Got caught in the middle, playing C natural where there's supposed to be a sharp. but I kept going, corrected
on the repetition, and finished fairly strong.

Marvin was looking at me in something like amazement. "Good God
Almigh," he said. "Maybe you gonna play some brass one of these
times, after all."

"Thanks."

"That was all right. You want to rest, or should we do it together?"
We did it together, with Marvin playing decorations on the flugel. It
was fun. Then he piled it on me: "You got it in C and G. Now you get
home, you write it in D and F and B flat, and learn it in ever one, and
I don't ever want to hear you miss the accidental again, doncha understand that's cause the chord's diminished?"

No, I hadn't understood that, and when I asked him why so many keys, he said you always had to be ready to place a song for a vocalist. Then he gave me my surprise.

"Like, you gonna have a different vocalist tonight, you listen how Binkie and Doctor Wanderbaum accommodate her."

"Evaun's not singing?"

"Hazel. You know Hazel? Works waitress at the hotel."

"Is Evaun all right?"

"Just fine, even if she wrecked my car. You hear about that? Took it into her head she was gonna practice driving, but I can't stay mad. We going to Pindar, soon as Binkie gets here to mind the store."

"Is she singing in Pindar?"

Marvin winked. "Song of sixpence maybe," he said. "I'm taking her over to buy clothes is what. Maybe have a good dinner tonight, do some business tomorrow. Come back Sunday late."

Wanting to hide my disappointment, wanting to catch him offguard, I asked abruptly: "What was Barlow like? Evaun's soldier husband."

As if he were ignoring out of kindness something that didn't make sense, Marvin said: "Well, you see on Wednesdays I go out to the country, and that means Binkie got to be in the store here by himself so what she done was go on over to her mamma's and in Binkie's room he keeps the spare key to the car, and well, you see, she wrecked it once before and he took the blame."

I couldn't let it go. "Barlow must have been quite a guy."

Marvin picked up the flugelhorn and blew the spit out of it. Then, in staccato to emphasize each note, he began playing "My Heart Belongs to Daddy." My question and I were dismissed.

Muley Haas and his brother Horse stopped by at Rhombo's that afternoon while I was setting up Roseland, and I remembered that they'd come by last Friday, too. This time, probably because there were quite a few customers in the bar, Tommy brought them back to where I was working and invited me to step outside. About half an hour later, Gatch and a partner—I suppose it was Ding Dong—paid a similar visit. I went into the storeroom to get some balloons to blow up and hang.

When I came out, Tommy was still sitting there, his mournful-dog face glummer than usual.

"Cost of doing business go up?" I asked.

He nodded. "Cause it's a new year, they all want more." He sighed. "Muley lets us run past closing time. Gatch keeps the place on-limits."

I smiled. "Imagine the state troopers will be here soon."

It made him laugh. He got up and put a hand on my shoulder. "You be careful, won't you?" he said.

I guessed he was talking about Evaun, but I didn't want to ask.

Hazel came in about nine-thirty that night, when the Coffee Shoppe closed. She was wearing a peach-colored evening dress, cut low in front, and the Doctor called for "Paper Doll."

Hazel smiled at me like an old friend, pinched Binkie on the cheek, kissed Doctor Wanderbaum's bald spot, and picked up the mike. I clenched my teeth, ready for harsh sounds, and was absolutely wrong. Hazel has a pleasant, husky voice, sweet and steady, though I'm not sure she'd be audible without an amplifier. Wholesome-looking, too. All-American Hazel. She did "Sunny Side of the Street" next and sounded really happy.

"You." She sat down next to me at the break, pouted and tossed her hair. "Never said you was a drummer."

"Can't you tell I'm not?"

"Shoo."

"I liked your songs."

"Sure you did. Bet you tickled to see me here, too."

E.B., sitting on her other side, said: "Mike knew you was coming." Put his shameless cheek on her shameless shoulder. "Listen, we always glad to play with you-oo. Specially me."

She shoved him. "Stop trying to make up to me, Binkie, you sorry thing."

So he kissed the shoulder, and she grabbed his cheeks between her hands, gave him a shake, and turned back to me.

"When we gonna have a date?" she asked.

"I guess I'm not a dating man."

"Well, pardon my French," she said indignantly, and stood up. There was a swaying soldier in the middle distance looking at her. Hazel smiled and took a step that way. Then she paused and said to E.B.: "You tell Mike about the time the band come from New York, with a girl piano player?" And she went to dance to jukebox music with the soldier.

I was enjoying my beer and looking forward to the next set. I'd begun to have a little confidence in my drumming and was finding it fun to play. "A girl piano player, E.B.?"

"The john," he muttered, and pushed off. It made me curious.

"What did happen?" I asked, when he came back.

"Wasn't nothing," E.B. said.

Hazel, finished with her dance, came up behind me. The Doctor arrived at the other side of the table with a cup of coffee.

"You ask him?" Hazel said.

I shook my head, smiling. I didn't want to hear about E.B.'s antics with a girl piano player from New York with the Doctor listening. "His secret's safe tonight."

Hazel leaned over. Hazel whispered in my right ear. "Not him. Evaun."

I moved my ear away. "Okay."

"You understand what I'm telling you?" She pulled me up and walked me away from E.B., who was sitting with his head in his hands.

"Yes, Hazel. I understand."

"How 'bout Muley? That okay with you, too?"

"What about him?"

"All last year yore sweetheart rode that patrol car with him, 'bout every evening." Flounced. "What about Skinny, from the barber shop? How you think she gets her hair done?"

"I don't like the song you're singing now," I said.

"Don't you get high and mighty with me."

"No. No, I won't. Let's go make some music."

Mizzourin/OH, WHAT A BEAUTIFUL MORNING

Dr. Wanderbaum was at his most garrulous Saturday afternoon prattling about Bix and Tram, Hoagy, Chicago jazz, touring with Goldkette and Whiteman. Johnny Billiard has his cast off, and though the arm's still in a sling, he should be able to play bass with us again next week. The Doctor's pretty excited about it. So am I. We did a lot of work with the sticks; he wants me to be able to solo, because it charges up a crowd so, and had written me out some patterns to practice. We did more chord progressions. Then he wanted to hear how I was coming along on cornet, so I tried "Ja-Da" with him. ("I shan't laugh up my sleeve. It tickles the armpit. But never mind, for one who has only been at it two weeks, you are coming along. Two weeks? And still coming? Don't you ever run dry? Never mind, I said. That's what Jellyroll said, too, but when he said it, they put it to music and Jelly got royalties . . .")

He seems to know words and music to any song I name, a one-man, living Fake Book. He sang "Sister Kate" for me, croaking it out, and I was moved. This aging, talented man sitting in the half-dark of Rhombo's Roseland, on an empty Saturday afternoon, in an out of the way town, celebrating his wayward lover's recovery from injury with a song he must have learned in Chicago, playing then with people whose names are known . . .

My mother wanted to know last night/Why all the boys treated Katie so right . . .

Saturday evening, for a while, Johnny did sit in. The left wrist moves, the right arm's okay, and he's more of a drummer with a hand and a half than I am with two. He is also bored, and eager for next weekend when we'll play as a quartet for the first time. He showed me some things about the drums that helped, and seemed to be enjoying it until Muley Haas came in, just after intermission. They did some pretty grim staring.

When the deputy left, Johnny said: "I know who that cocksucker is. I know who gave me a New Year's Eve present, too."

Then he left, to go back to the apartment he and the Doctor share and lie down.

Hazel came late and did one short set. Doctor Wanderbaum said she'd have to work at least an hour to get any pay, and Hazel laughed at him and wiggled her butt.

When we finished playing, the Doctor and Binky left with an artillery captain named Garris, who'd been sitting with us part of the evening. They were all going over to join Johnny. Party night, with Marvin away. I locked up the instruments and went over to the hotel, feeling truly blue and lonesome.

"Matter, Mike?" Cosmo asked, when I let myself in. He was at the desk, reading the weekly paper. "Someone's cows get in yer corn?"

"Does it show?"

"Like they went and cut yer lobster traps."

"Thinking about moving on," I said.

"Leav-up y' lessons 'n job?"

"No, not really. Hell, no," I said. "When you going to come hear us play?"

"Whenevah you're ready with the horn. Gonna play me 'Happy Birthday' on it?"

"When's that?"

"Valentine's Day, I was born. You got one month."

"I'll be ready," I promised.

There aren't any windows in the trunk room, no clock, no watch. When I wake up there, I've got no idea of the time. When I woke up this morning, Sunday, took a shower down the hall, got dressed and went out to the coffee shop, it wasn't even seven A.M. yet, though I'd been up until after two. I ordered a breakfast of scrambled echs and sawdust links, which I couldn't eat. The coffee seemed to have been processed in the bladder of a dog.

I was at Rhombo's before eight to start my clean-up. The bar doesn't open until noon on Sundays, and I had the place to myself, which was fine.

Then, as I stepped into Roseland from the parking lot entrance, I saw that the storeroom door was ajar, and knew damn well that I'd locked it when I put the instruments away. Roseland was dead quiet. I stopped and stared, holding the door to the outside open behind me to keep my own noise down. I thought of slipping back out quietly and phoning Tommy Rhombo, or even the Haas patrol. Then I heard a slight sound of movement in the storeroom. I dropped my voice as low as I could and yelled tough: "Come out of there. Right now."

Evaun appeared in the storeroom doorway. She looked startled, even scared, and said with a tear in her voice: "Mike. You mad?" She was wearing a little tan seersucker dress and her eyes were huge with lavender.

"Oh, God," I said. "Oh no. Evaun." My heartbeat went crazy. I saw her start to smile. I took a running start, like a kid heading for the ice, hit the wax of the dance floor and slid to her, arms open and grinning like a mandrill.

She came tripping across the bandstand to meet me, jumped off it at me, and I caught her, shouting, knowing we'd go down, and falling on my hip so that her ninety-nine pounds landed on top. We rolled once, yelling and laughing, and then she was astride me, hitting with both fists and saying, "Bastard, jerk, nogood dumbass . . ." and I figured first things first, went for her panties and spilled her out of them. We danced horizontally. I hunched her across the floor. She tasted like Pepsodent and felt like hot velvet inside. How we pumped, how we laughed, how we squeezed, and laughing, erupted together, our bodies shuddering in unison as I turned her up on top again. Panting now, subsiding, holding on, and I said, "I'll dumbass you, girl."

And she said, "You just did. Come on, I made a bed."

We gathered up our clothes and went back into the storeroom. I'd got a big splinter in my ass, and Evaun knelt to pull it out with her teeth, which started us laughing again.

She'd made a pile of tarps, bar coats and aprons in one corner, and we disappeared into it for ten loving minutes. Then we clung, all naked, and then we talked a little.

"Bet if you'd had yore gun you'da shot me."

"How'd you get in here?"

"Took Marvin's key ring from his trousers."

"He told me you wouldn't be back till tonight."

" 'bout two this morning, in the tourist cabins in Pindar. When I was little, he'd take jus' one for the both of us, and people thought he was my daddy. But now he takes two cabins, 'fraid they'll jus' see a man with an underage girl. Well, I knocked and woke him up. Said I was scared and wanted to come home. And I was, too. Scared I'd die if I didn't see you. Scared like that all the time now."

"Me too," I said. "Me too."

When they'd got here at 4:30, she had seen to Marvin's having a couple of drinks and a Seconal, and left the house a little after six.

"Bet I woke up that same minute," I said.

"Course you did."

She supposed now that she'd better go get ready to cook Sunday breakfast for her uncle. Wished she were cooking it for me.

"Or me for you. What shall I fix?"

"You, Mike. You," she said and Marvin's eggs got to spend another twenty minutes in their shells.

Finally, she did get up and slip away. I finished my cleanup, got my stuff together, and walked on out here, eager to write it down, and having done so, I shall eat a hundred pounds of country ham, five pecks of home-fried spuds, bushel of lettuce; and grab a century of sleep.

. . . BE ON THE GROUND IN CASABLANCA FOR AN HOUR AND FIFTEEN MINUTES. THOSE PASSENGERS WISHING TO STROLL ABOUT THE TERMINAL, PLEASE GET A RE-BOARDING PASS FROM YOUR CABIN ATTENDANT.

"Congressman Esterzee's office."

"Darlene, it's Charlie."

"You're not in Turkey yet!"

"No, I'm in Casablanca."

"Want Deke?"

"Wanted to talk to you a minute first."

"Business, pain or pleasure?"

"You know the main reason? You seemed pretty down when we said goodbye. Are things okay?"

"Did you really worry about that?"

"Yup."

"You're a sweet man. What's the other reason?"

"I wanted you to know that John McRae Johnson's disappeared. His wife seemed to think he might try to reach me. If he does, see if you can find out if he's all right."

"That's two of us you're worried about. Who else? How about Chester? Want me to see if his hernia's okay these days?"

"Take care, Darlene. May I say hello to Deke?"

"Deke? It's Rudolph Valentino calling from the Casbah."

"Hello, Sheik."

"Hi. Anything new I need to know before I get to Turkey?"

"Just watch your ass. Petrolat and State aren't together on this at all. You decide which one is right for you and play it their way. How's your flight?"

"Like crossing the ocean on a Greyhound bus."

"What's happening with your dad?"

"Staying out of trouble so far."

"Charlie, when you get to Istanbul there's a guy named Marshall you'll meet. He's the one Chester's been in touch with."

"Does that mean I should work with him?"

"What did I just get finished saying? No, I only wanted you to know his name."

"Okay. Thanks, Deke. Reboarding time."

"Take care."

"I will."

"Keep an eye on things in Carolina."

"I wish I could."

Mizzourin/**THE JAZZ-ME BLUES**

I was washing dishes and thinking drums. I heard a motor and went to the living-room window. The blind was drawn; I looked out through the crack between it and the frame. There was an army jeep out there. It stopped.

In it were Binkie Jones, his guitar, his amplifier and his sister. I ran out and across the footbridge, vaulted the barrier and yelled "Hooray," grabbed ninety-nine pounds of something soft and swung it around and around. It squealed. Its brother said, "Help me with the speaker, durn it, Mike."

We put the hardware across the barrier, got into the jeep and drove it up the old company street, between the overgrown foundations, to where we could turn past the tool shed into a firebreak and have the vehicle hidden from the road. Binkie had borrowed the jeep from Garris, the army artillery captain who'd gone off partying with him and the Doctor and Johnny a week ago Saturday.

"Well, wow," I said, as we started back. "Captain Garris has a carpool jeep checked out, and he let you take it?"

We were walking back down the former street, up to our ankles in myrtle and duff, my arm around Evaun's waist, and Binkie grinning like an acrobat just off the high wire.

"Well," he said. "Well, sure."

"Careless love," I said. "Or is that carless love? Hey, I made a Wanderbaum."

"Cap'n is getting his hair cut," Binkie explained.

"Hairless love." I was feeling pretty giddy.

"Cap'n don't like the barbers at the fort."

"Surly bunch," I agreed. "Rude. Arrogant."

"Well, he kind of give me the key. To move the jeep and park it for him. So I just thought I'd go on and do a few things, long as I had it."

"Perfectly reasonable," I said. "Why, a good haircut might take three or four hours."

"Ain't love grand?" Evaun said, snuggling.

"Better enjoy the jeep today," I said to E.B. "You may not see it again for a while."

"Don't be too sure," Evaun said, and I looked at her twin and was struck all over again by his plain, dumb beauty, more disturbing than hers because males aren't supposed to look that way.

So here he was, to play guitar and help me with my music, and bringing Evaun. I don't know why I had suddenly to remember Hazel, remember tension between the twins when the barber was mentioned before, go slightly rigid, and say: "Is that the one you call Skinny?"

Evaun didn't stiffen. She and E.B. went into a wonderful brother-sister obfuscation act, which must have been their first line of mutual defense since childhood.

"Don't you see, Mike? It's the law."

"Oh, sure. Anyone can see that."

" 'Tis, too."

"She's right. Why they put it right through the legislature."

"The beauticians."

"Mean, too."

"Sure," I said. "They're as bad as the barbers at the fort. What in the hell are we talking about?"

Patiently, as to a child: "Says you can't do barbering and hairdressing in the same shop."

"Ain't that unfair?"

"Well, I hadn't much considered doing either one," I said.

"Ol' Skinny kin cut and set a girl's hair better than any one of them women at the beauty parlor, I don't care what you say."

"Only, he's got to sneak and do mine after hours."

"That's just not right," said E. B. Jones, boy moralist, and as for M. Mizzourin, boy jealousist, two of them was more than I could handle, and I let it go for then. They weren't going to let me spoil what they were doing for me, no matter how big a jerk I was.

Evaun insisted on housecleaning and finishing the dishes, while Binkie and I worked on some tunes: "When the Saints Go Marching In," because it's easiest of all. "September in the Rain" to do one that puts the cornet in F, and "Where or When" to do another. For sharp keys, we had "Ja-Da" in G, and "Birth of the Blues" in D, though the release in that is a little high for me. It was fun playing together.

"You all over that horn today," the little fake said when my lip reached limp noodle. "It's yore morning, but now I'm goin' fishing." And damned if he didn't have a fishing rod and a can of garden worms down by the bridge, and damned if he didn't go whistling off along the creek, and damned if he didn't somewhat resemble a sixteen-year-old boy.

As for the sixteen-year-old girl, when we were back in the cabin, and I said, "Want to tell me about the barber?" she shook her head and stepped back away from me.

"I think you better settle me first."

It was our first test of wills. I felt numb and a little angry. Then I realized how completely askew I was in the situation, how right she was, and she smiled and moved back toward me, trustful, and we settled one another.

"Now let's be dressed and hold each other in the sun," she said. It was time to talk, and she did, though not about Skinny the barber very much. Two years before, when she was fourteen, the man had been after her, even wanted to marry her.

"I was surprised by that. Thought I was damaged goods, but Skinny didn't care, and I was grateful and I let him. Once. That's all. It wasn't much, and we friends now. Mike, I've never been no virgin. Can you understand that?"

"I guess I better be able to, if Skinny could," I said. "Marvin?"

"He don't bother tryin' to get me anymore," she said. "But he can't stand for me to run loose, neither. When we was little, he plain owned me and Binkie. He had his hands on us and his fingers in us fore I can remember. Guess I was eight when he started trying to get hisself inside me. He'd call me in his room in a special tone of voice I got to recognize, and I thought I'd got to go. Then he'd take my panties down and set me straddle on his lap to face him, and he'd try. Does this bother you too much?"

"No," I said, surprised to find it didn't. "It makes me want to cry for you, and smash Marvin." I hugged her very tight. We were on a cushion, our backs against the front wall, outside the cabin. The creek rippled, the sun sparkled, a little breeze danced. She told what she had to tell as unaffectedly as if she'd been reviewing it silently in her own thoughts, but I thought saying the words aloud to me, into the fine day, was right, that what was nasty became cleansed, and thinned out, and went away into the clear air.

"When I was ten, he finally could. I ain't even going to say it hurt much. Mostly, it was just a big relief that I wouldn't have his stuff all over between my legs when he got done. Mike, when I was thirteen and started getting my period, it were hell on Binkie. But then Marvin got this doctor in Pindar to fit me a diaphragm, told the man I was wild. And I guess I was.

"Marvin chased me a whole lot then. Sometimes I'll have to say he caught me. Didn't make me feel much like the other girls at school, did it? Skinny. He taught me there was other men in the world might like me. So I looked around, and there was one was guaranteed to scare Marvin off."

"Muley Haas."

"Did someone tell you that?"

"Sure. But it doesn't matter. Marvin was scared of Muley?"

"Marvin was scared of jail. Muley's the law. What there is of it around here. Marvin was just that worried I might tell, he gave me presents like he never did when he was chasing me, and I never once played up to him again, like Binkie does sometimes. I got shed of Muley when I married Billy, and after Billy left, well, Marvin, he made a deal. He'd take care of me and Bink, and stop pestering, long as I'd stay in and be good. Mostly he does. Mostly I do.''

She relaxed then, leaning her head back against my shoulder, clasping the hand that came around in both of hers, and holding it against her bosom.

"Mike?"

I pressed the light, lithe, eager body a little tighter and said, "Hush. Lie still."

"I'm still lyin'," said Evaun, and there was a breathy laugh, muffled against my neck, which told me the little joke was highly intentional. "Pore you. Here I was, having my fun and a little trouble, and you 'uz out there, sick of living." I never told her that. "Wasn't you, Mike? Lettin' them stinky Japs shoot rifle bullets at you, hoping you'd get killed? Please be glad that yore alive now, Mike."

"I'm as glad as a man can be," I said. "Tell about Barlow?"

"You won't get mad and jealous?"

I kissed her right ear and her left ear, squeezed both breasts together under her light sweater, rubbed her jeans, over the stomach, and put my hand between her legs till she wiggled. "That's how jealous and mad I'll get," I said.

"Billy Barlow was a handsome man. Blond and wavy hair, a private, wild like me. Stationed here to get his basic. I never even could tell Binkie how we started off. Can I tell you? He 'uz just eighteen. From Denver."

"Your first boy."

"Sometimes, I pretend he really was the first of all."

"I'll pretend it with you."

"First weekend pass that Billy had, he come out of the fort, and I was standing there, by the patrol car. Waiting on Muley to come out from some store that called him.

"Billy saw me, and he stopped and said, 'That's sure an ugly kinda car fur such a pretty girl.'

"So I said, 'Maybe I need it to protect me.'

" 'Who from?'

" 'Maybe from ugly soldiers?'

" 'Is there one of those around?'

" 'Take a look in the car mirror.'

" 'You gonna give me a chance?'

" 'To do what?'

" 'Take a walk with me. Just once around the block.'

" 'Just once? You promise?'

" 'Course I do.'

" 'You better get me out of here quick,' I said. 'Fore somebody comes back.'

"We started off, but then when we got to the alley, I took his hand and we didn't stop running till we got to Mamma's house. She was out, and Binkie was staying at Marvin's, and Mike, we just kissed then and had fun. I cooked him hot dogs, and we danced to the radio. But then the second pass he had, we run right off to Raleigh on the bus and got married secret. So then I had to tell, Binkie and Mamma first, I was so proud. And wanting Billy with me, too. Seventeen weeks is basic training. He had fourteen left, but never got to finish them. It might be Marvin got this corporal—I don't know—to pick a fist fight with my Billy. Billy was hotheaded. After the fight he run AWOL, come back to get me, and got caught, and sent up to some prison. And after, maybe overseas? I never knew. We had us seven weekends, man and wife."

"You don't know what happened to him?"

"Never heard. He never put me on his army records. I was going to try to visit Billy at the prison, but Marvin, well, Marvin got me thinking I was bad for Billy, caused that fightin'. Made him wild. It's not so, but you know how Marvin can spin a person's head. Always could me. Seems he kin always get me to do what he wants, if he tries hard enough."

Yes, I knew how Marvin could get a person spinning, remembering an hour of one-way dickering over a flugelhorn.

"I'd just wish I could of got notified if something happened. Or where he went. Don't spose I'll ever know."

"Maybe he'll be back, now that the war's over."

"If he was comin', he'd be back by now, or let me know."

"You miss him, don't you?"

"Not now, Mike. But before you came, I yearned my heart. Not like I do for you, though, after just a day apart. Here's what I want to tell you, though. All right?"

"All right."

"After that with Marvin, wouldn't you think I'd not like bein' with a man? Billy showed me. It ain't what you do. It's how you feel about the one you do it with. Billy Barlow 'uz a damn jackrabbit, jump on, jump off, but I still—I don't know how to say it. Made me ready for you, Mike."

"Nothing ever happened to make me ready for you," I said. I had a pretty meager history to recite. She hardly listened.

"I ain't been no saint," she said.

"I didn't ask for one."

"But I'll be yours."

We dozed in the sun till there was a splashing and a hoot, and up the bank came E. B. Jones with two fat trout. He cleaned the fish, and left them with me, for lunch.

Mizzourin/DON'T BE THAT WAY

Friday morning, back in town once more, I found Marvin the Molester with ants in his pants, bees in his bonnet, and one good-sized bat in his belfry.

I guess his bat looked like me, or is it a ghastly butterfly, a frightful moth, he can't pin down? There's fear and suspicion now, but nothing he knows for sure, and in his misery I know he weighs the wan satisfaction of incomplete possession against the damage of revelation of what this town suspects full well. Evaun never came right out and told Muley about her uncle.

Oddly enough, I have no wish to use it against Marvin. Better it be forgot, and meanwhile I find him no more, no less repulsive and fascinating than before. I guess I'd pretty much assumed the story Evaun told me Thursday in the sun.

I shan't be long in Faraday, three months perhaps. Then Evaun will be seventeen, I'll have a little band experience, and I hope we will be on our way. I do not mean to leave her here. Come, spring, oh, Carolina, let your creature go.

The early part of the job Friday night was pretty much routine, except that nothing is routine when I'm with Evaun. As always, we sat together holding hands under the table between sets, and I glowered at the guys who talked to her. She'll never turn one off who comes by for conversation. With her or Binkie. He's got a following, too.

"Mike, come on. We like to meet folks."

"Guys." But I grinned.

"Just talk."

"Flirt." Grinned again.

"Well, I like to flirt."

"I know." Third grin. Pat a warm hand. Grin four. Take your base.

About ten-thirty Johnny showed up. He is still using the sling, but just for resting. The arm works again. He lifted it out, and I got his bass from the storeroom. He played a couple of sets with us, and what a difference it makes, that beat that boxes you in to set you free.

It is Evaun's time of month, and so we didn't try for the trunk room.

Saturday morning, as I finished putting Roseland back in shape, in came a procession: Doctor W., Binkie J., Johnny B., and Johnny's drum student, who played snare in his high-school band, and is learning dance work. They set up briskly to rehearse, as I finished spreading wax, and the Doctor called out: "Michael. Set down the mop. Raise up your horn."

I hadn't realized I was to be part of it. I washed my hands, quickly, and got the horn from the storeroom.

"Sit," said the Doctor. "Call a tune."

And E.B. said, " 'Saints,' Mike."

So I said, " 'Saints,' " and "Saints" we played. I didn't need the music, and I played quite well until the end, when I tried to add a two-bar lick Binkie had taught me and messed up.

"It's bad enough," the Doctor yelled, "someone let the cat in, without you stepping on his tail." But then he led me through the lick, playing with one finger in the treble, a dozen times until I had it.

And we did "Ja-Da," of course, and "Birth of the Blues," quite elaborately, and "Where or When," which is my best, slow and simple enough so that I can think about tone and phrasing.

Evaun B. arrived, and I got to rest while they worked with her on "Sweet Georgia Brown," which she sings with neat, suggestive mockery, and which I can't play yet because it's in A for trumpet and full of neat, suggestive accidentals.

That night saw the premiere appearance of The New Doctor Wanderbaum Trio, with Evaun Barlow, vocalist, and Guest Artist Mike Mizzourin on cornet. I won't try to describe it. It was good, it was bad. I remember drifting smoothly from box to box in "Where or When," knowing that my tone was really nice, happy and relaxed, and when we got to the release—*Some things that happen for the first time/ Seem to be happening again*—I realized partway through that the Doctor had the other instruments on soft stop-time, that I was playing whole phrases alone, in round, pure notes, seeing the people on the dance floor move to them. I loved it. The last eight, which just goes swelling up the F scale, with everyone increasing, holding back, teasing toward crescendo: I think it was music. Ed, the new drummer, who's a nice, gangly guy, was swishing brushes and looking happy enough to pass out, and the Doctor signaled for another chorus, signaled Evaun to stand up for a vocal, signaled a Pfc named Sam to sit in with a clarinet. I know it was music.

Then on "Birth of the Blues," I picked up a repeat at the wrong place and made an awful jumble of it, which E.B. and the Doctor had to play us out of. But at the end of the song, when we do a little four-bar thing to take it out, I was with them again, and Johnny Billiard said in a low voice to me, as we put down our instruments, "Start good, end good, Mike. It doesn't matter how damn much you fuck up in the middle." Then he said, "Shit, look who's here."

It was Muley again, just like last week, and just like last week the two stared at one another.

"Got a stupid brother, cop?" Johnny said, but he said it to me, in the same low voice. "Big, stupid brother, don't you?"

I had one song left to play. "Saints." Cosmo Selkirk was there to hear me play it. Cosmo has the day shift at the desk now. He's had it for a week. He drank a whiskey with us at the musicians' table. Evaun and I fussed over him.

When we got up to play, an MP had come in, checking the crowd the way they do, but it wasn't Gatch. It was a fat, blond corporal. I assume it was Gatch's partner, whom I couldn't see the night they were together, and who Gatch calls Ding Dong. He walked out in the middle of the tune. Ah, Ding Dong.

*Mizzourin/*TWO SLEEPY PEOPLE

I never spent a night in bed with anyone before, except, I suppose, Ned or Pete when we were baby boys.

Last night, just as I finished writing my reproach to Ding Dong, headlights appeared on the road, and damned if Binkie didn't have poor Garris' jeep again. Only this time, Garris was in it, drunk, so drunk that Binkie swore there was no way the captain could have known how they got here in the dark.

I don't know why I wrote "poor Garris." He's kind of a mean bastard. They'd run over a cat on the way out, and while they stayed, which wasn't long, the captain would wake up every couple of minutes and laugh and say, "Kitty, kitty, kitty."

With me they left Evaun, her nightie, her Pepsodent and a dozen chocolate-chip cookies that she'd baked; I've never been so close to anyone before. Marvin had been called off to Pindar, to play rippling rhythm with Shep Fields.

Evaun and I cooked together, ate together, listened together to music on the radio. She wanted me to read something to her, and I did, read her about how I stole the horn. And then we slept together, but didn't sleep very much. It's a little bed. I opened the door of the woodstove and watched her sleep by firelight. And wake, and smile, and sleep again.

In the morning she unpacked and cooked some homemade sausage and country eggs, with deep, deep yellow yolks. God they were good. She loves to eat, and so do I.

She had brought boots. I walked with her, over the mountain, to the border of my piny, pretty forest. We could see town from there. I watched her walk off toward it, watched as long as I could see her, and started feeling lonely before she was out of earshot.

Mizzourin/WANG WANG BLUES

I have an uninvited guest this Sunday night, passed out in my uninvited-guest room, hot damn. But I finally know what went on last night in Faraday, holy shit; but let's start with Friday.

The weekend was already warmed up. Skinny's Barber Shop was robbed by daylight Friday noon while the proprietor was out to lunch. There was an unrelated fist fight at the city council meeting in the morning, and Tommy Rhombo's brother's car caught fire. There are those who say someone torched it, which is a pretty drastic thing to do to someone these days, with cars so hard to get. (My guest snores.)

When I wasn't busy with student, musician or janitorial duties, I was organizing things for Cosmo's seventy-first birthday party, which will be next week. Tommy's renting Roseland to me for an hour or so, for just ten bucks; the trio's agreed to play, Marvin will join us, and Doctor Wanderbaum has come through with something special. I asked him if he could remember a song called "My Sweetheart's the Man in the Moon," and he could indeed, words and all. He's written it out, including a vocal for Evaun and a flugelhorn descant for Marvin. The song turns out to be a pretty little waltz, and when we do it for Cosmo, the old scamp's going to melt into a puddle of seventy-one-year-old

molasses. I have a list of his friends and got most of them invited—
Evaun is going to do the rest.

This brings us to Saturday night, hot time in the old town. Johnny
was back full time, no sling. I alternated with him on the drums, blew
some adequate cornet, and just before intermission we were up to five,
with clarinet Sam sitting in on "Birth of the Blues," and Captain Garris, who knows his way around a drum set, joining us as well. I remember now feeling that Garris wasn't there just for the pleasure of
playing, that there was some kind of current running between him and
Johnny and E.B., but I forgot about it as intermission started because
Evaun took hold of my wrist until it started boiling, and whispered:
"You better take me over to that hotel of yourn right now."

While I waited for her to put her sweater on, Johnny was sitting with
Captain Garris, and both were watching Doctor Wanderbaum go off
across the floor. As soon as he was out of sight, the two got up and
left.

"Something going on?" I asked E.B., not caring much.

"No," E.B. said. "Lemme finish your whiskey." Which he did. Then
he added: "I don't know. You don't wanna know."

"What's the matter?"

"They might be ready. Now, go on."

Evaun signaled to me from the door. We all but carried one another,
running down the street together to the side entrance of the Grand
Commerce Hotel, at which once they unloaded drays with luggage for
the trunk room. We spent no time whatsoever unloading luggage, or
discussing artillery captains and bass players. We detonated one another. It builds up that much.

We are getting indiscreet. We walked back to Rhombo's leaning together, my arm around her shoulders, hers around my waist.

E.B. was sitting where he had been when we left. The Doctor was
across from him. Captain Garris had returned and was sitting by E.B.
Johnny was missing. There didn't seem to be much conversation going
on.

Before Evaun and I could sit, Gatch and Ding Dong followed us in
and came up to the table.

"Captain Garris."

"Hello, Gatch."

"Enjoying an evening around town, sir?"

"Yes, thank you."

"Is that your jeep in the parking lot?"

"I wish it were. No. It's the jeep assigned to me, though."

"The engine's quite warm. Have you just come in?"

"No, I've been here a little while. How long, Binkie?"

" 'Bout twenny, thirty minutes, Cap'n. Since just before intermission, and sitting right here since."

To this, suddenly and explosively, Doctor Wanderbaum cried: "Yes. Yes, exactly."

Gatch looked at me and Evaun, and said, "So you've all been right here, visiting?"

I smiled and said, "Not me, Gatch."

Evaun said, "Nor me, either."

And Ding Dong played the last lick: "Yeah. We just seen you."

"Gosh," I said. "What sharp eyes."

"Where's the other guy?" Gatch asked. "The cowboy?"

"He's still a little weak," the Doctor said. "Went home to rest."

"Where's that?"

"Any place you're not, Gatch," I said, "is home to most of us."

"Button it," Gatch said. "You're not in it this time, buddy boy. Or are you?"

"In what?"

He ignored me. "Captain Garris, we'd like to ask you some questions, please."

"Hadn't you better get an officer for that?"

Just then Muley and Marvin came in, got the two MPs into conference for a moment. Then Muley came over and demanded that Garris go with them, and they all five left.

We played out the job without Johnny. Binkie dummied up. The Doctor was incredibly silent.

"What's going on?" Evaun asked me when we were finished.

"I wonder."

"I'll make Binkie tell me, walking home."

"Okay. I've got to stay and pick up."

"Shall I come here in the morning if I can?"

"I hope you can."

She didn't make it this Sunday morning, though. The streets of Faraday were spooky quiet, and no one showed up while I was cleaning Roseland to tell me why. I went over to the Jones' house. Mrs. Jones said E.B.'d been called to his Uncle Marvin's.

Back at the hotel Cosmo said he hadn't heard anything but that Marvin and Doctor Wanderbaum, who generally have Sunday morning breakfast together in the cafe, hadn't been in.

It occurred to me to walk over to Jocasta's Castle. Jocasta was in, along with several of her girls. She remembered me, and had heard from Scholay in New York.

"Sent money he didn't owe, but anyhow he's well and working," she said. " 'Cept he don't much like his job. Playing music he can't like for some black man he can't like much either." She sighed and said something amazing and sad. "What do it matter if the slaves be free, when the free are slaves, Little Mike?"

But no, she knew about the barber shop robbery, the city council fight and the car burning, but not of anything that might have happened in the middle of Saturday night.

I walked back past the music store, thinking Binkie might have it open Sunday afternoon, but it was closed. Marvin's school bus, which he's bought for the band to travel in and keeps parked out back, was gone for some reason. I went over to Rhombo's and tried calling Marvin's house. Evaun answered the phone, and I said, "Hi. It's Mike."

She said, "Well, Mr. Merrill can't come to the phone right now, but I'll be glad to take a message."

I said, "The message is that damn fool Mike Mizzourin's head over heels in love."

And she said, "Mmmmm, too."

"Is there trouble?"

"Well, Well, maybe not if you're going out of town."

"All right," I said. "I guess I understand."

So I loaded up my backpack and walked.

My trail comes down the mountain behind the cabin, right to the back door. I was whistling "Deep Henderson," coming around the last turn, having decided something like this: that if there was trouble in Faraday, it was nice to be able to walk away from it.

I stopped whistling right there. There was someone sitting on my rear stoop. I moved behind a pine tree to look and make sure before I let him see me. I was right. It was the missing man, Cowboy Johnny Billiard. My guest.

"Got anything to eat, Mike?" was the first thing he said when he saw me.

"Sure. Come in." I opened the door, showed him into the kitchen and gave him some bread and peanut butter.

"Got anything to drink?"

"Just sherry," I said, and put the bottle out, realizing now that Evaun had been trying to tell me I'd better get out here. "Help yourself."

He drank some sherry, made a face, and went after the peanut butter with his finger. I put a couple of hamburgers in the skillet.

Johnny took another slug of sherry, looked at me, nodded, and said: "We got him, Mike. That fucking Horse. We got him good."

"Yeah? You and Captain Garris?"

"I won't say who helped."

"What did you do?"

"Give him an injun belly-ride. Oh, shit. Can I drink more of your wine? I feel better."

"What's an injun belly-ride?"

"I shouldn't of done it, Mike. Not now, when Doc's got everything going so nice, money coming in. I've always been that way."

"What way?"

"Get an impulse, and I can't control it. Piss right in the pie every time. Hey, that Garris is some wild faggot, isn't he?"

"I wouldn't know, myself."

"Look, we been scouting Horse the last few nights. Any time Garris came with the jeep, we'd go watch Horse get off work, about eleven, at the base depot where he unloads. Have the jeep a little bit hid, and watch Horse come out and turn down the alley to walk home. We weren't looking to do it last night, just scout again, but hey. I never told you I was a roper, did I?"

"Yes, you did."

"Been a rodeo team roper. I was good enough to be in the circus, too."

I decided I'd have a little of the sherry before he finished the bottle.

"Hey, drink up, Mike. I roped the fucker." It excited him, and he got up and jumped around a little, talking. "We watched him in the alley, and I was on one knee, on the jeep seat, standing, with my loop going slow around, along the side. Captain starts the jeep then, and suddenly he says, 'Want to do it, John? Come on.' 'Right now?' 'Hell, yes.' 'Drive it,' I said.

"So that wildass, he turned into the alley after Horse and beeped the horn. When Horse turned his head, Garris cut on the spotlight, right in his eyes. Jacklighted the bastard, and yelled 'Do it,' and I dropped a loop on Horse and took a dally on the seat back, and let the rope slide down around his ankles. Blam. Captain hit the brake, backed up a peg, and Hoss was sliding." Johnny began to laugh. "Backed a big U-turn in front of the fort, 'bout five miles an hour, hey? And into the alley, backing up, Horse fighting to keep his head off the ground and bumping, thumping. Didn't we ride him? Feet first, yelling and twisting, bounce on those cobbles, one side, then the other. God, we laughed, I'll bet you we came close to skinning him. How 'bout it, Mike?"

"Bet you came close to skinning him," I said.

"Oh, we did it right. Five miles an hour, shouldn't of broken anything, but bruise? That fucker's going to be just one big skinless bruise."

"Johnny. How'd you get out here?"

He was still laughing. "Took fucking Marvin's school bus," he said. "Hot-wired it, and out I came. Binkie drew a map."

"Where's the bus now?"

"Up in the firebreak, out of sight. Don't worry."

"Get it the hell out of here," I said. "Drive it back to Mineral Springs, you can leave it there behind the buildings. Someone will spot it. Figure joyriders."

"How am I going to get back here?"

"Walk."

"Mike, if I get caught . . . "

"They'll beat you half to death," I said. "All right. I'll do the bus."

Mizzourin/**STUMBLING**

In a way, I didn't mind, though I was tired. But I wanted either me or him out of there for a while. I needed to learn to stand the thought of somebody, Horse or anybody, being dragged. It was pretty awful.

I walked up to the firebreak thinking how the horn would sound, the light come into your eyes and something, you wouldn't know it was a rope, slide over you and grab your ankles, jerk you off your feet, and start to pull you backward. It must be a rope, and you'd try to get your hands down to it, try to keep your head from bumping, howl at the unknown roper through the dark and pain and fright.

I reached the bus, got in, connected the ignition, started up and turned around. By the headlights, I could see that Johnny had apparently opened up the tool house, though I couldn't imagine why. The door was swinging in the wind.

Well, Horse busted Johnny up. Johnny busted Horse up. The weasel in civvies. When I reached the pavement, I drove a litle way past Mineral Springs with the headlights out. There was plenty of moonlight. I turned around without letting the wheels get off the pavement. Then I drove into the cluster of buildings from the south, so that the tire marks going in over dirt will be coming from the direction of town. I dumped the bus behind the pavilion, where high school kids come to neck. White, silent, empty buildings in the moonlight. My shadow walking through them. I left and skirted the edge of the woods, along farm fields, to where my trail starts.

Mizzourin/WHEN IT'S SLEEPY TIME DOWN SOUTH

I was in the trunk room, waiting for Evaun to come back, and everything had been corny and perfect. We were, it's true, one guest short, Captain Garris. He was restricted to quarters, but they didn't have anything on him beyond his having bribed people at the motor pool to sign the jeep out to him when it wasn't authorized.

I'd gone over to Roseland about seven-thirty, and Tommy was so much in the spirit of the evening that he left his dinner crowd to help me set up, carrying stuff in and out of the storeroom.

At nine, with Binkie and the Doctor ready, the guests were all on hand. We had the postmaster and his wife, several guys from the permanent cadre at the base whom Cosmo likes, Daryl Clarke the hotel manager, and Nora, the big lady cashier from the Coffee Shoppe, with her husband in a wheelchair. There were Hazel, toward whom Cosmo feels like an indulgent but reproachful father, and another waitress named Betty, escorted by the soldiery, as well as Henrietta, the housekeeper, Tansy who owns the diner, and Cosmo's pinochle cronies, Fred and Thomas, both retired.

Evaun and I went over to the hotel to walk Cosmo over, and found him looking quite elegant in dinner jacket, spats and cane and wearing the army good conduct ribbon I once gave him.

As we walked him in, of course, everybody cut loose with "Happy Birthday," and Henrietta the housekeeper hugged Cosmo and waltzed him to his table. We had a litle pile of presents there, cigars and a necktie, handkerchiefs. Evaun and Binkie gave him a magnifying glass to read with. I gave him an illustrated biography of his hero, Teddy Roosevelt, so he'd have something to use the glass on besides the newspaper; it was a copy the librarian agreed to sell me, since it was due for discard. And Henrietta gave him a wool cardigan that she'd knit herself.

As he opened the presents, in came Tommy Rhombo, with champagne and pretzels on the house. There was clapping and whooping and music and chatter, and one of the permanent cadre guys made a pretty fair comic speech based on inventions in which Cosmo's being presumed overage for the sport duped many husbands and took ladies by surprise. To this, Doctor Wanderbaum played silent-movie piano in the background, and I can report that Henrietta, who's about fifty, blushed.

At ten Marvin arrived with the flugelhorn and joined Binkie and the Doctor on the bandstand. Evaun and I got up from the table where we were sitting with Cosmo, Henrietta and Hazel. Evaun took the mike and I the brushes, and we did our production number, sweet and glorious.

> *My sweetheart's the man in the moon*
> *I'm going to marry him soon*
> *'Twould fill me with bliss*
> *Just to give him one kiss*
> *But I know that a dozen I never would miss.*
> *I'll go up in a great big balloon*
> *And see my sweetheart in the moon*
> *Then behind some dark cloud*
> *Where no one is allowed*
> *I'll make love to the man in the moon.*

Marvin's descant, over Evaun's reprise of the chorus, was moondust, crumbling and glowing. Cosmo's face also was moondust, crumbling and glowing, with pleasure and pain, love and longing.

Evaun went to him and held out her hands. He stood up and they waltzed through the next chorus. When it was time to start a new one, she stopped him, held both his hands again, and sang:

> *Last night when the stars brightly shone*
> *He told me through love's telephone*
> *That when we were wed*
> *He'd go early to bed*
> *And never go out with the boys, so he said.*

Fred and Thomas, the cronies, whooped and clapped on that one, and Evaun turned her partner over to Henrietta and came back on the bandstand to finish.

Then it was Binkie's turn to make moondust, and he did, soft and the closest I've heard him play to country. Piny, pretty country. I was watching and listening to him when, rather abruptly, Evaun left the bandstand, ran out to the dancers and, with Henrietta, helped Cosmo back to the table. I got to them as they were lowering our birthday boy, chuckling, wheezing, sobbing, into his chair. He couldn't breathe very well for a minute, but he never stopped smiling, and the first thing he said when he recovered was to everybody there:

"I can't cry for laughing. Thank you all."

I signaled the Doctor, went back to my brushes, and Evaun knelt and sang a last chorus to him, there at the table.

It was enough. It was all the party anybody needed, and all the party Cosmo Selkirk could take. He was shaken but smiling when Evaun, Henrietta and I helped him into the new cardigan and walked him back to the hotel. Henrietta carried the dinner jacket. I was holding up a good part of his weight, but it's not much weight, and he was humming the song of the evening all the way.

The ladies waited outside the door of his little room behind the desk, and the new night clerk, who's called Butch, helped me take Cosmo's shoes and pants off, and the sweater which my old friend clutched like a stuffed animal toy when we eased him onto his cot and eased the covers over him.

"Thank you, Butch," he said dreamily, drifting off toward sleep. "Thank you, Mike."

"Happy birthday, sir," I said, and for some reason saluted, just as Cosmo once saluted me.

We went out. Tommy had offered to put things away and tidy up in the storeroom, and Evaun said she'd go back to Roseland to help him. I'd have gone too, but Evaun winked and nodded in the direction of the trunk room. She shrugged, too, meaning she didn't know. After an hour I decided she must have been required to ride home with Marvin.

At midnight I felt wide awake, and worried enough that restless Johnny could do something stupid so that I took my horn and started walking out. It was a mild, bright February midnight.

When I got to the top of the mountain, I stopped, sat on a rock, got out the cornet, and made a little moondust of my own on that sweet, old, silly little waltz.

Mizzourin/I MAY BE WRONG (2/18/46)

New York City, New York
Washington's Birthday

What do it matter if the slaves be free, when the free are slaves?

I have had a meal, and found a room, and before I engage this city must put what happened down in Carolina into writing, to dim the scenes and still the voices in my head.

I see myself, first, waiting in the trunk room, deciding then to walk back to the CCC camp from the Grand Commerce Hotel. And so I did. And stopped and played on the mountain top. And so everything went according to plan. Oh, yes it did.

Every light in the cabin seemed to be on as I came down the trail back there in Carolina. I remember feeling relief that Johnny hadn't scooted off to town, then irritation at all the light he was showing. And then I felt stupid. Something must be going on.

So instead of going straight to the back door, I walked around to the front of the cabin, staying out of the light from the windows, though there was plenty of moonlight for anyone to see me by. There was plenty of moonlight for me to see by, too, and what I saw was Marvin's schoolbus, parked down on the road, across the creek at the end of the footbridge.

Who knew that I'd left it parked behind the pavilion at Mineral Springs? Binkie Jones knew that.

I heard the front door of the cabin open, spun around, and saw Evaun running toward me.

"Oh, Mike," she said, coming into my arms and letting me hold her for a moment. "They said for me to tell you."

"Tell me what? What's happened?" I squeezed her. She pressed her head against my shoulder. I stroked her hair, expecting maybe tears, but she startled me by laughing, pulling her head away and tossing ashy hair back so that it rippled and gleamed. "I don't care," she cried. "I don't care. I'm with you."

"And I'm with you," I said and hugged her again. "Now tell me."

"All right." Hand in hand, we went down onto the footbridge. Was it really just three days ago that we stood side by side at the rail in the moonlight, watching the sparkle of the creek?

When she left me at the hotel and went back to Roseland, Evaun said, two odd things were going on. Marvin was still playing, along with Binkie and the Doctor, which was odd because Marvin never plays for free. He'd been willing to do one song, as his birthday present to Cosmo, and he'd planned to leave right afterward.

Instead, there he was, calling songs and playing, and that was keeping people there, and bringing more in from the bar. The other odd thing was that Tommy Rhombo refused to let her start collecting ashtrays and glasses to be washed and put away in the storeroom. Tommy told her to relax and enjoy the music, and even asked if she didn't want to go get Mike to come back. For some reason, Marvin and Tommy were keeping the party going.

Puzzled, Evaun stepped out into the parking lot to clear her head. As she stood there, Hazel came along, walking and cuddling with Gatch's partner, whose name is not Ding Dong, curiously enough, but Jimmy. They asked about the music.

Hazel said, "Is that the jukebox? We want to dance."

"No," Evaun said. "Trio's still playing."

Hazel said to Jimmy, "I thought you said your sarge went to the piano player's place?"

"Yeah, but I didn't say old Wanderbug was there, did I?" He gave Hazel a push.

Evaun knew better than to ask questions. She said a little of this and a little of that and walked back inside with them. As soon as she could, Evaun got Binkie aside and said it looked like Gatch and maybe Muley were searching Doctor Wanderbaum's apartment.

Binkie guessed they'd got Captain Garris to talk; then he said, "Marvin called 'Small Hotel.' Ask him can you sing it?"

While she sang "Small Hotel," with Marvin playing behind the vocal, Binkie slid onto the piano bench and told Doctor Wanderbaum the news. Doctor Wanderbaum looked shook up.

As soon as "Small Hotel" was over, the Doctor called nervously for "Lull in my Life," another of Evaun's vocal numbers. Marvin wanted to play up-tempo, and they agreed on "Blue Skies"; when Evaun finished singing that one, Marvin and the Doctor each took a long solo of the new-sounding music. While they were playing, Binkie slipped off.

The tune ended. Marvin looked around and asked her, "Where's our guitar?"

"Think he had too much champagne," Evaun said, and Marvin laughed and told the Doctor to play "Lullaby," or that's what Evaun thought he said. It didn't sound like any lullaby she'd ever heard. It was almost funny to her from then on, if she hadn't felt the tension, because Doctor Wanderbaum was playing things to keep Marvin there, and

Marvin things to hold the Doctor. That kept on until Tommy came in from the bar and nodded to Marvin, at which Doctor Wanderbaum rose up, hollered "Men's room" and ran. He looked really scared.

As he scooted, he signaled Evaun, and she knew he meant he'd keep going, past the men's room, through the bar and out onto the street. She got on out there and he was still running. She ran after him, across the square and around behind the courthouse. There was Marvin's schoolbus, engine running, lights out, Binkie at the wheel. Evaun and the Doctor got in.

They hightailed out toward Mineral Springs, but as soon as they were out of town, Evaun told Binkie to stop the bus. Things didn't add up.

"You're right, Sis," Binkie said, slowing down.

"Keep driving," said the Doctor. "Faster, boy."

"Not till you say what we're running for," Evaun said. "You know those cops wouldn't find Johnny at your place."

"They must have found something else," the Doctor said. "God's sake, boy, move this thing."

"Found what?"

"Tell us what we're getting into."

"Johnny's lasso. I told him to burn it, but he wouldn't. Hid it with some clothes. There's dry blood on that rope. Can't we go? Are you forgetting, Mike's been sheltering Johnny?"

Binkie looked at Evaun. They nodded at one another. Johnny didn't mean much to them, but they'd never rat on Mike.

"That Binkie really cranked her up, then," Evaun said. "Oh, Mike. Everyone's looking for that cowboy of yours now. Muley. Gatch. Marvin. Tommy. And they'll have men from Pindar soon."

That was the story. I took time to kiss the storyteller. Then I said, "Hard to play cornet with your thumbs busted." I squeezed her hand and smiled. "Why the hell am I so glad to see you?"

"Cause I'm yore sweet girl," she said. "That's why."

"Come to think of it, you are," I agreed, and hugged her. "Any plans?"

"The Doctor says they're taking the schoolbus. Says Binkie and I can walk back, and lie we was abducted or something. But Mike, that still leaves you."

"Nobody knows I'm here. Or that Johnny's been staying here."

"They're bound to figure it all out." She squeezed my arm, and for some reason whispered the next thing to me. "Mike, let's us go, too. With Doctor and Johnny? Least to where we can get a bus or a train."

"You're on, country girl," I yelled. "Hey. That's just what I've been wanting to hear." I had about eighty-five bucks saved up. "Binkie too?"

"You know if I go he'll go. Oh, come on. Git packed. We made Doctor and Johnny wait until you got here, but they're wetting their pants." We turned up the slope. "Where will we go, Mike?

"New York," I said. "City girl. New York." And I picked her up from behind and carried her up to the door on my shoulder. "Hey, slats, let's go." I hugged her buttocks, pressed her stomach against my face. She chattered at the top of my head, hanging onto my ears.

"Mike, get you a job, and lessons? Binkie can play good enough to work. Could I get lessons? Hey now, I'll work too."

"We're going to try, we'll try." I pointed west, up the gravel road, away from Faraday. "Slim, that road goes straight to Tennessee."

"Ain't never been to Tennessee," she sang, and we burst through the door, right in on a scared-looking pair of tramp musicians and a thoughtful-looking twin.

"Mike said it," Evaun cried. "We're all going to Tennessee," and faces brightened.

It didn't take long to pack. Within an hour, we had the bus loaded. We took my food, and things to cook in and eat on, took the blankets. We had no idea how far Tennessee might be, or what towns we might come to first. We even put the empty cans and bottles in the bus and swept up, getting rid of signs the cabin had been lived in.

"Nobody knew you were here?" the Doctor asked. "Well, I suppose you knew you were here . . . " He was recovering himself.

"Unless it was Captain Garris," I said. "He came once, drunk."

"No," said Binkie. "I asted him next day. He couldn't remember it at all."

We turned off the cabin lights and locked the locks.

"Want me to drive?" Johnny asked.

"I'll drive first," I said. The lead man wanted to take charge, and off we started in the moonlight.

In the right-hand seat in front, all wrapped in blankets, Evaun and Binkie sat together and were asleep in a couple of minutes. The Doctor sat behind me, monologuing. I didn't bother to listen. Johnny sat way back. Maybe he felt safer back there. There were some pretty mean people after Johnny Billiard. After a while, the Doctor shut up and moved back, too. They were on the bench seat across the back. They hadn't been together for a while.

I drove along, not fast but steadily, for twenty minutes, I suppose, enjoying the bright night and the quietness, before I saw the man, tied to a tree which had been cut down to block the road.

The high beam picked up the man's eyes, as they do any other animal's. He was tied around the waist, with his arms pulled back over the tree trunk and his legs pulled up underneath it. He couldn't move much, but he was rolling his head back and forth, making all the movement he could, I think, so I'd be sure to see him. It was Captain Garris.

There wasn't room to turn away, and I don't know that I would have. I braked the bus down gently, stopped, told my passengers to stay put, and got out.

Muley, Gatch and Marvin Merrill stepped into the light. There was a stranger with them. Muley had a revolver. Gatch had a carbine.

"That's him," said the stranger.

"Who are you?" I asked.

"This is our forester, Dave McLane," Marvin said, "who was good enough, yes he was, public spirit is what you expect, and drove to town to tell us when it looked like you were taking away, did you do it, Mike? Oh, Mike. His young friend . . . "

"Binkie," the forester said. "Is Binkie all right?"

"Just fine," I said. "You've been sleeping in the tool shed?"

Muley Haas put an end to this somewhat disorderly conversation. "Want to get your hands up?" Muley said. "Jimmy's got you covered." He holstered his own gun, smiling rather pleasantly, and frisked me. I glanced over to the side of the road, and there the erstwhile Ding Dong stood, with a riot gun at port arms. "Who's in that bus, Mike?"

There wasn't any reason to stall. "Everyone you're looking for," I said. My eyes were used to the light, now, and I saw that Muley's patrol car was parked off one side of the road, and Marvin's green Dodge off the other, both facing back toward Faraday in case I'd tried to back and turn the bus.

Muley hauled out his piece again and took a step toward the bus.

"Everybody out," he called. Gatch was untying Garris, talking softly to him, calling him a little cocksucker, having a good time, alternately goosing him and hitting him on the head.

Evaun came out first, stepping down in an oddly upright posture, with her right shoulder back out of line. After her came Doctor Wanderbaum, holding the right arm behind her in a hammerlock and with something in his other hand pressed into her back.

"I have a gun," the Doctor announced. "A gun? It isn't loaded, is it? If it isn't, let's go out and get loaded. Hello, Deputy Haas. Hello, Marvin."

"Turn her loose," Marvin said.

"No, no. I'm holding her for you. Johnny has the other little runaway."

Out came Binkie then. This time Johnny Billiard had the hammerlock.

"Binkie," Forester Dave said. "Binkie boy."

"God now. Don't lets anyone get hurt," said Marvin.

"No one's being rough here," Muley said, and I saw Captain Garris' eyes roll on that one. Gatch had brought him to the edge of the group, holding him up almost off the ground by the waistband of his trousers. Garris was sobbing.

"Guns and car keys," Doctor Wanderbaum said. "Just toss them out, please. Right in front of John." He gave a little jerk on Evaun's arm, and she squeaked.

I said, "You sonofabitch. Don't do that again."

And Marvin said, "Now hold on, Mike, that's right, now here's my keys, right here . . . " And tossed his key ring over.

"Sheriff?" Muley tossed his keys over, too, and then his pistol.

"Sergeant?"

Gatch complied, and erstwhile Dong, following directions, went over to Marvin's Dodge, opened both front doors, and tossed his riot gun and sidearm onto the front seat. Now that Johnny had a real gun, Muley's, we could see that what the Doctor held was nothing but a pair of pliers with one handle in his hand and the other extended. For some reason he kept it in Evaun's back, though, as he moved away toward one side of the car, and Johnny maneuvered Binkie until he'd got to the open door by the driver's seat. Then he told Binkie to kneel down, gave him a push, got in the car and started the motor. Doctor Wanderbaum pushed Evaun away, got in right-hand seat. The car doors slammed closed together, Johnny revved the motor and they were on their way in a swirl.

Gatch yelled, "Come on," turned and jumped over the tree, and I saw that his jeep was back at one end, hitched to the tree by a log chain they'd used to drag it around. There was a crosscut saw in the back seat, too. With a fair amount of swearing, he had to drag the tree again before they could turn the jeep and head our way. Then the other two lawmen jumped in with him, and the three tore off after the green Dodge which was already out of sight. The crosscut fell out with a clatter as they left.

"Binkie," Marvin said. "Evaun."

"Aw," said E. B. Binkie Jones.

"I'm going with Mike," Evaun said. "Marvin, I'm going with Mike. Don't make no difference what you say."

"Mike's not going anyplace but jail," Marvin said. "That where you're going with him?"

"You want me to say who's going to jail and what for?" Evaun asked. "Right here, with Forester Dave and Captain Garris listening?"

Binkie grinned at that. "We going to New York with Mike," he said. "Uncle Marvin, ride us to the bus?"

"Evaun, I got to talk to you," Marvin said. "I surely do."

"Go on and talk."

"Private. It's important. It sure is, isn't it now . . . "

"No."

"Honey, there's something's happened you don't know about."

"Here come the lies."

"Just step off here, just over here and let me tell you just one thing . . . " He was backing away, beckoning.

"Better be, you'll let us get our clothes and leave." She took two steps.

"No."

I started after her, but not before Marvin could whisper something, quick and earnest, that made her jerk away from him, crying out, outraged, "That's a damn lie, Marvin, and you know it is."

"Honey, it's true, you know I wouldn't, now the thing is—"

Evaun had run to Captain Garris. "He says the old man died."

"Yes," Garris said, none too steadily. He had found Forester Dave's shoulder to lean on. I thought they deserved each other. "Yes. I think so."

"Cosmo?" I asked.

"They were saying so in the car," Captain Garris said.

"Oh, Mike." She came to me. "Oh, Mike."

I put my arms around her and said to Marvin, over her head: "Cosmo is dead?"

"That's what I told, and here these gentlemen, now Butch, the night clerk said it, Mr. Selkirk he was dying likely whilst you put him in his bed, the pore old man, maybe was breathing his last breath on this earth." Marvin, the crooner. "It comes to all men, Mike, let her come to me."

I unhugged Evaun and took her hand. We took a step toward Marvin, and I said, "If you're right, he went out with a smile on his face."

Evaun was crying quietly.

"Let her come to me."

"Marvin, I don't think you understand. I love this girl. She seems to love me. Her husband's gone . . . "

"Now love is what I need to talk to her about," Marvin said getting into high slur. "Now that's the very thing itself, and what I got to tell makes a whole lot of difference to you both, now let her come."

Idiot that I was, I let go Evaun's hand, and she walked after Marvin, twenty yards down the road, as if he had her radio-controlled.

Binkie must, I guess, have stepped into the woods to relieve himself, because the next thing I knew he was at my shoulder, saying urgently, "Mike. What's happening?"

I pointed down at Marvin, talking to Evaun. She was standing close in front of him with her head bowed. "Cosmo Selkirk died," I said. "Right after the party. Evaun's taking it pretty hard, and I think Marvin's trying to comfort—"

Binkie Jones hit me on the arm as hard as he could. "You better break that up," he said. "You go, make him stop that talking." And he hit me again. It wasn't a bad punch for a slim guy. "Don't you know better?"

As he said it, I heard Evaun's sobbing grow louder, saw her move closer to Marvin, saw his arm go around her heaving shoulders, and I went, with Binkie right behind me.

"That's enough," I yelled, running. "Let her go." I stopped.

Evaun turned in Marvin's arms, but she shrank away from me. "Mike, Mike. I kilt that old man, singin' that song. It was too much for his old heart to bear, too much memory, too strong . . . "

"Stop it," I said.

"It filled up his heart too full with song and bursted it. I did that."

"Is this the crap that you've been telling her?" I was about to go for Marvin's wrists and force his arms away from her, but he moved first, releasing her to Binkie but keeping a hand on her shoulder. "This child has got the magic power is true, you know, to use for good or evil, now you know she does, and can she help herself to keep from using it? Don't you see? Now think one time . . . "

"Stop the goddamn nonsense, Marvin," I said.

"Don't cuss, Mike," Evaun said. Now she touched me on the hand. "Mike? We've gotta respect the dead. Mike, I'm never goin' to sing again."

She let Binkie lead her away then, up and onto the bus. He showed me the palm of his hand covertly, moving it downward. Then Marvin and I stood there debating, getting stupider and stupider, Marvin saying weirder and weirder stuff, me alternating between satire and anger.

"All right," I said. "Let's ride back. She'll see it differently in the morning."

"You sure you want to be there in the morning?" Marvin asked. "Why, shoo, you know old Muley's gonna have to keep you in the jail, it's public duty and he took his oath, don't matter now how much you friends with Muley, gotta serve his oath, don't he, that's right, charged with bus stealing, yes you are, course I guess you meant to give it back, but then there's kidnap, trespass on the govmint, hidin' fugitives, and aiding and abetting, started out you stole a horn, Gatch might come there to the jail to question you, Muley'd sure have to let him see you, Mike, now you ask Captain Garris here—"

"Shut up, Marvin," I said.

"But shoot, you put your head on in the bus and ask Evaun, does she want you riding with us now to Faraday, you ask . . . " He was actually pushing me toward the open door of the vehicle at this point; it made me want to pull back the other way, but I didn't. I jumped forward and up, inside the bus instead, and closed the door in his face and Dave's. I had some idea of getting back behind the wheel, now that the tree was gone from across the road, and driving past them and away, and a stupid idea it was.

Binkie, huddled in the half-dark with Evaun, whose face was pressed against her brother's chest, had more sense. "Go, Mike," he whispered. "Go on now, to New York. You go and let us follow soon's we can."

"I'd better stay and play this out." I went close. Evaun still wouldn't look at me.

"Here's too much trouble now. You stay, you'll make it worse. You go, we be there soon, I swear. Be there by Fourth of July."

"Evaun?"

She wouldn't answer, but she did look quickly at me before she hid her face again.

"She'll see it different in a little time," Binkie said. Marvin and Dave had started pounding on the bus door, Dave with a log. He meant to break the glass. "Now hurry, Mike, we'll be there, Mike. New York!"

This time I thought Evaun nodded, but I can't be sure.

"I'll send an address," I said, grabbing my things. "Okay, and money to you, at your mother's."

I snatched the door open, pushing Dave and Marvin back, and jumped out past them. Dave almost got me with his log. I wheeled toward them and dropped my things, ready to fight. But now Garris had Dave's log, and Marvin was urging both the others on to the bus. The door closed. The lights went on.

I watched the bus start up and make its turn back east. I picked up my musette bag, duffel and cornet and started walking west, too tired to go far. Spent a long night in the woods, cold and wondering, each time I woke, hoping and doubting.

In the morning I walked on, until I came to a paved road, intersecting my gravel one. I turned north and waited for a ride. It was a long, cool time before the traffic started and a car stopped.

While I waited, sitting on my duffel bag, I didn't think I felt like playing my horn. I had been practicing five and six hours a day and thought I'd take a day off now. After a time, I got the cornet out, though, just to look at it. And then I checked to make sure that the valves still went up and down. I made sure the mouthpiece still went in and out. Figured I ought to clear the spit, so as not to put it away with wet insides. And then I played "Don't Be That Way" for a while, and played it pretty well, but she was only sixteen, and had a life to live in Faraday.

"HEY! THIS IS CAPTAIN PETERSON, AND I MEAN EXCLA-MATION POINT, WHAT A DAY, WHAT A DAY!

"THOSE IN THE LEFT-HAND SEATS, NOW, YOU CAN SEE GIBRALTAR! KNOW HOW GIBRALTAR GOT ITS NAME?

"NAMED FOR THE GREAT POET OF LEBANON, KHALIL GIBRAN, AND IT MEANS 'ALTAR OF GIBRAN,' YES SIR!

"PRO'BLY MOST OF YOU HAVE READ HIS BEAUTIFUL POEM BOOK, 'THE PROPHET,' BUT JUST NOW YOUR CABIN ATTENDANT, CINDY ELLIS, GAVE THE BOOK TO ME AND SAID HOW GIBRALTAR GOT ITS NAME.

"AND I HOPE IT'S OKAY FOR AN OLD JUMBO-JET JOCKEY

TO SHARE THIS BEAUTIFUL, SWEET MOMENT WITH YOU,
'CAUSE WHEN CINDY HANDED ME THE BOOK, SHE SAID
SHE'D STAND WITH ME AT THE ALTAR OF GIBRAN.
"SAY SOMETHING, CINDY HONEY."
"THIS IS THE HAPPIEST DAY OF MY LIFE."

April, '80 Istanbul. Notes:

1. I expected Embassy to meet me. Instead, it was Cherry Nelson, the young woman exec from Petrolat who came here with Uncle Ned. She's tall with short blond hair, well-turned out, and businesslike. She didn't hesitate to approach several of the guys getting off the plane before me, asking each, I guess, if he were Charles Mizzourin, in a crisp, amused voice, with a cool smile on her face to show there were no soft feelings.

    About the time I was admitting I was me, I heard "Charles Scaliger" being paged; apparently she intercepted me. She gave me to understand by her manner, so brisk it was easy to forget she's quite pretty, that we'd not talk about anything in a public place.

    Once the Turkish driver had the company car going, she closed the glass panel between the front and back seats, handed me a typed sheet and said: "Here's your schedule. We generally start people with a rest day, for jet lag, but there may not be much time. How do you feel?"

    "Fine," I said. The first item on the list she gave me was, *1300, Lunch, C. Nelson, Office.* The next was *1430–1600, Tune-up and conditioning, Velodrome.* "Am I Mizzourin or Scaliger?"

    "You're entered in the bicycle race as Scaliger, because the list is public."

    "Okay."

    "We have a Spanish mechanic putting your machine together. He's been on a number of racing teams. All right?"

    "When's the race?"

    She frowned and slewed her hazel eyes forward at the driver, even though the sound was blocked off. I'm supposed to know all about the race, of course. "The Spanish are damn good," I said. "Though mine's a Swedish bike."

    She smiled at my having said something right, nodded, and asked if I were very hungry. "If not, I'll have us driven around past some of the sights."

    "I'd like that. I know enough about this city to be curious to see some things."

    "Of course. You did nineteenth century Russian. When poor old blundering Turkey was the sick man of Europe."

    "Are you a historian?"

    "Yes. Once I got severely shot down in seminar for saying that Europe

versus Russia with Turkey in the middle had more to do with economics
than with religion and empire. I did Middle East."

"Where?"

"Petrolat hired me right out of Bloomington, as soon as I finished my
M.A."

"Hey, Cherry," I said. "How did Gibraltar get its name?"

"I have no idea," Cherry said.

2. It wasn't until we were sitting at her desk across from one another, eating
pieces of shaslik tucked into flat bread with cucumber and yogurt sauce, that
Cherry started filling me in, beginning with the road race.

"We've sponsored your entry in the fifth qualifying heat. That gives you
a couple of days."

"I'm riding for Petrolat? Why, Cherry?"

"There's a plan. When you need to know, I'll tell you."

"Tell me now."

"No. When you meet embassy and news people, the less you know the
better."

"Why not share it with the embassy?"

"What are you here for, Charles?"

"Information. And to see if there's anything I can do."

"Well, then. We know quite a lot more than the embassy does. And we
may use you. They wouldn't."

"They know you've got me in the race?"

"Yes. It's something you're doing here to pass the time while waiting for
news, as far as they're concerned."

"Are you sharing with the CIA?"

"Absolutely not. The Carter administration's only thought these days is
the hostages in Iran. We're not going to let one of our people become a chip
in that game."

"Are you going to share the information with me, Cherry? Or do I get
the slanted version, guaranteed to manipulate?"

"You don't trust my company?"

"Some reason why I should?"

"Have they been dishonest with you?"

"In Washington? No. Just totally evasive."

"And the State Department?"

"Dithering."

"The CIA?"

"Redundant and elaborate."

"Petrolat is a very large company. It's got more money in its bank ac-
counts than a lot of countries have in their treasuries."

"Hooray."

"It controls several million acres of land. But we're multinational, not a separate country. We may have our own diplomacy and intelligence and alliances. Some of our contracts are as difficult to negotiate as treaties. But we're still a business. We get things done."

"Without an army, navy or an air force."

"Don't be silly."

"No. I won't. How many men could you put in the field with light arms?"

She smiled, shrugged, and made me respect her. We grinned at one another. We were friends, sort of.

"The company's got a foundation, too. To help us support culture and so on in host countries."

"Sporting events?"

"Yes. It's the foundation that's sponsoring you in the race."

"Do they think I'm a real contestant?"

"They don't know anything and don't need to. I doubt you'll even meet any of them."

"Will I meet the embassy people and the CIA?"

"I doubt we can avoid it."

"Should we want to?"

"All right. When your Uncle Pete was kidnapped—"

"Kidnapped?"

"Yes."

"I was told he was arrested."

"That was deliberate. Kidnapping's a big story, arrest is a small one. The quieter we keep something like this, the safer for our people all around the world. And the quicker we move, the better, of course. Getting State in is not the way to speed things up."

"Cherry, where the hell is Pete? And where's Uncle Ned?"

"Do you want a fast answer to that?"

"No. Sorry. I'd like to hear the whole thing."

"There's a group in Syria, something that translates, more or less, the Young Men of the Mountain. They're a Nusairi splinter group, if that means anything to you."

"Nothing."

"The Nusairi are a sect of Moslems. Somewhat apocalyptic. The Young Men are much more so."

"Violent?"

"They don't disbelieve in it. We maintain a rest and recreation house for company employees in Baalbek. Your uncle Pete—I don't know him, by the way—apparently wanted to see the Roman ruins, which are lovely. When there aren't guns going off."

"There aren't now?"

"No. We hear there may be soon. Anyway, the Young Men took your uncle Pete in Baalbek, in broad daylight. They took him as he got out of a company car, at the gate of the Temple of Apollo, and drove off on the Damascus road. Then they probably went northwest, to the Ansariyan Mountains. That was all we knew for a time. Then they wanted a quarter-million dollars for ransom. We were willing to pay."

"Insured?"

"You may suspect my company, but it's loyal to its people."

"Has to be, doesn't it? Or the people would go work for someone else."

"I hope you'll see us differently when I get through."

"All right. I hope so, too."

"We were ready to negotiate the ransom demand, and meet it if we had to. Or so I understand. I don't mean to sound like someone who's in on that kind of decision making. But the Young Men also wanted us to negotiate some sort of recognition for them from the Syrians."

"They got it. The Syrians offered to take custody, but not to release Pete without the Young Men's consent. Pete was transferred to a Syrian jail. The Syrians didn't want to antagonize the Young Men, and they did want to do what they could for us. So far, so good, and no publicity. The money agreement was reached. The Young Men wanted to take payment on the Syrian side. We decided that with the Syrians eager to get rid of Pete, they'd see to it that the Young Men kept their part of the bargain. Now the only question was who to send in with the financial certificates to make the trade. We didn't like the idea of its being another Petrolat employee. If things went wrong, they'd have two of our people. There was talk of letting the CIA provide a person, but we don't want our company connected with the CIA in the minds of the Syrians."

"And then along came Uncle Ned," I said.

"He seemed perfect. Fearless. Not stupid but pigheaded, which is much the same—what he didn't choose to understand was just what we didn't want understood. He was unconnected with us and unconnected with the government. Just a farmer, come to get his brother safely out."

"And totally averse to publicity," I said.

She came fairly close to shuddering. "I almost lost my job over that awful TV mess he staged. The world's most wanted man. Oh, God. By the time we realized he was a grandstander, running for Congress, it was too late. He'd been told too much. I was sent over here from Libya with him for one purpose, to keep reminding him that things had to be kept quiet until Pete came out, and the first thing he did was call CBS about his film. He and I had a big shouting match. I said I was going to recommend that we cancel Ned, and let the CIA do it after all. I'm not sure I meant it. I was trying to make him behave. But the next morning he was gone, and the financial certificates were with him. He'd decided to do it on his own."

"He was stopped in Aleppo. They let him go."

"Yes. We heard that. By the time he got to Beirut, the Syrians had decided he was our courier, just as he said he was, so they had him met and taken over into Syria. It wasn't what I was supposed to arrange, but I said, look, he's where we want him to be, doing what we were going to send him to do. Let's tell the Syrians he's okay."

"You were protecting him."

"And myself. But he's a hell of a man. I'm infuriated by him, but I'm sympathetic and entertained, too. I'm even attracted, Charles. If he were a little younger . . . "

"I'm sure he sees it that way, too."

She laughed. Then, abruptly, she stopped, looked very serious, and said, "But I'm afraid that's not all. I hate telling you the rest. We have friends in Syria. There are pipelines through the country that are just as important to us as they are to them. Common interests. Our best friend is in Interior and has been a help—I'm telling you this first, because I don't want you to think things are hopeless. Interior has been mediating between Ned and the Young Men."

"Mediating? Weren't the negotiations all done?"

"Well . . . "

"It's something new?"

She nodded, and I realized that she'd put off getting to this as long as she could.

"What's happened?"

"You said you wanted to hear the whole thing."

"I did."

"Then be good enough to let me tell it in my own way."

"Something went wrong, didn't it?"

"If I need someone to bark at me, I'll get a dog."

"Do you still expect me to keep the embassy out of this?"

"Shut up, Charles, and listen. The business between Ned and the Young Men was quite simple to start with. It was all done yesterday afternoon. Apparently there was some shouting and table pounding on both sides, with the Syrians from Interior being soothing. But they kept reminding the Young Men that Ned was a farmer, which means 'peasant' to them, and they're students and were being patronizing to the peasant. Meanwhile Ned was calling them the Charlie Brown and Lucy terrorist group and stuff like that, which must have been wild in translation. I gather there were tones of voice on both sides that undercut the translator's trying to keep things tactful."

"I hope I don't see what we're headed for."

"In the evening there was supposed to be a friendly dinner, handshakes all around, plans finalized for reuniting the brothers in the morning, notifying the ambassador. The Syrians wanted to be considerate hosts. They don't officially serve liquor, but they had a covert bottle for Ned. There came a point when the hosts were out of the room, caucusing about some matter, and Ned was alone with two of the Young Men. A dispute started. By the time the yelling was loud enough for our particular friend to hear it and run back, Ned had the leader of the Young Men on his back, knee on his chest. He was fighting off a second Young Man with one hand, and with the other he was pouring Chivas over the leader's clenched lips, trying to make him drink and calling him a pansy."

"Oh my God," I said.

"The Syrians barely got Ned out of there and over to the jail with Pete, for his own protection."

"And now they're both in jail."

"Yes. Our Syrian friend, who sent the news, is working around the clock on it. He says most of his colleagues in Interior want both your uncles out of there as fast as possible, but the minister's not so sure. He has to listen to the Young Men, too, and try to keep peace with them. And they're outraged."

"Isn't this when the embassy could help?"

"No, Charles, no. Please don't be stupid."

"Oh? All right, Cherry. I'll try to curb the tendency."

"Do you want to hear this?"

"In your own tactful phrase, please don't be stupid."

She got up and walked around the room, mad, poured herself more coffee, and decided, I guess, that calming down was the way to handle me.

"Once it's government to government," she said, "that's the end of anything quick and quiet."

"Okay. What's happening right now?"

"The situation's being debated on every level of the Syrian government, right up to the top. Our friend thinks reason's going to win. If it does, we may be putting you in motion very fast."

"Me?"

"Isn't that why you're here?"

"It's the first I've heard of it," I said. "But I guess it must be."

3. There was a man from the embassy watching me work out this afternoon at the Velodrome. Cherry had told me he'd be there. He took me off afterward to meet Marshall, the guy Deke and Chester have been in touch with out here. Presumably, Marshall is CIA, but of course we don't say so.

Marshall had pretty much the same stuff to tell me that I'd heard from Chester in Washington, yesterday. Yesterday? Good God, I'm sleepy, and I'm going to shorten this up. Marshall and the embassy man (I can't recall his name) wanted to know what Cherry'd told me. I said I'd be seeing Cherry in the morning. They seem to think I must be their boy, since my introduction is Congressional. They didn't press me very hard.

Marshall said: "Petrolat's got some smart dudes, Charlie boy. Drink up. Watch out for them. I've been out here long enough to know my way across the street, and it seems like there's always a guy from Petrolat directing traffic."

"Been out here how long?" I asked.

"Six years, in the tire business." He didn't wink with his eye. He put the wink in his voice.

"You can count on him, Charlie boy," the embassy guy said. "Marsh knows the Mediterranean like a private fish pond. He's caught some big ones, too."

"Really? How'd Gibraltar get its name, Marsh?" I asked.

"When the Moors took Spain, they called it Rock of Allah," Marshall said. "What we've got now is a corrupt Moroccan leftover." This time he did an actual wink, a left-eye job. "Befouling the sirocco."

4. Here it is, before I go to sleep. On the way past the hotel drawing room, I borrowed Volume XI, FRA to GIB, of an eleventh edition Britannica. Leatherbound, India paper; beautiful. I remembered Shakespeare, *Bitus And-panicus.*

There was a Berber named Tarik Ben Zaid, who in the eighth century whipped the Christian army in a big, three-day battle in Andalusia. To keep his communications with Africa protected, he ordered a strong castle built on the peninsular rock which sticks out off the tip of southern Spain. The Romans had called the rock Mons Calpe. To the Greeks, it was one of the Pillars of Hercules.

Tarik Ben Zaid's fortress took thirty-one years to build. When it was done, they renamed the peninsular rock "Mount Tarik." Mountain in Arabic is Jebel. Jebel Tarik—Gibraltar.

" 'lo?"

"Charles. You Turkish dog."

"Darl . . . Roxie?"

"You were to call me, you know. Did you start to say *Darling?*"

"God. I was so sound asleep."

"If you were going to say *Darling,* I'll forgive you."

"It's dawn here."

"Oh, love. Will you watch the sun rise over the Blue Mosque, then, while you talk to me?"

"You shouldn't have called."

"Yes, well, I see. Now say something sweet, please, so that Angela will stop gloating."

"I'd like to go back to sleep now."

"Oh, I see. Is it because I'm a bit of a whore?"

"I don't much want to talk about it."

"Ah. Do let's be tart to the tart, then."

"I'm sorry."

"You can jolly well bugger yourself with your bicycle seat, Charles."

"I'm sorry."

"Ta-ta, then."

"Sorry . . . Roxie? Roxie? . . . Shit."

5. Cherry picked me up after breakfast in a Fiat two-seater that she's rented, which is a lot more fun than the company car. She was worried about what I might have told Marshall, whom she dislikes. I said I didn't much care for him, either.

"Is that why you're going along with us, Charles?"

"Just call me Charlie boy," I said. "No. My reason's so trivial, only my father would have understood it."

"Try me."

"How did Gibraltar get its name?"

"I told you. I don't know."

"That's why I'm going along with you."

She pulled the car over to the curb, stopped it, and pulled down her sunglasses to look at me. I looked back at her and smiled. Cherry Nelson smiled, and looked suddenly very pretty. "I have good news."

Since I have to meet the ambassador for lunch in forty-five minutes, I'll summarize: I will be coming out of Syria with my uncles Pete and Ned tomorrow, if nothing goes wrong with the following plan, designed to mislead the press, the embassy and our friend Marshall.

In tomorrow's qualifying run, in which I'm in the final heat as Charles Scaliger, we're supposed to do 50 kilometers in a very hilly stretch close and parallel to the Syrian border. At 17.4 km., the Petrolat car will be parked, and Cherry and a couple of other people will be standing beside it, watching us go by. She'll wave to me with her handkerchief if everything is all set. If she doesn't wave, I keep riding. If she does, I turn off on a steep, downhill road, at 20.9 km. I may be going as fast as fifty miles an hour when I cross the border. The gate will be up, and the Turkish guards will be looking away. I'll leave the bike at the Syrian customs shed, where I'm to be met by a Syrian party and taken by car to a town called K'abnajeeb six miles off.

Pete and Ned are to be moved to K'abnajeeb tonight. When I arrive there tomorrow, I'm to identify them (as if I knew them well), and sign various release papers. The Syrians will take the three of us back to the border, I'll recover the bike, we'll reenter Turkey on foot, and the Petrolat car will be waiting.

"Will you do it, Charles?" she asked.

"Sure," I said, with a false and jaunty smile. My stomach has been wrapped down around my pelvis ever since.

She took me on to the morning workout at the Velodrome and stayed to
watch. Quite a few of my competitors were there today. I did laps and
looked at their leg muscles. Their legs look like something that would bend
a nail if you tried to drive one in. None are English-speaking, so they ignored me except for an Italian who called out "Hello, Joe" every time he
passed me. He passed me a lot. Cherry said no one would notice when I
peel off at 14.9 km. because they'll be so intent. No, Cherry. They'll be too
far out in front.

6. The ambassador is a correct, distressed man. We didn't discuss my business
in Turkey at lunch. He knows Deke slightly. We talked election politics.
He's sure Bush will be nominated, and that Carter can beat him.

The ambassador had met Ned, and tried to stop the TV broadcast.

When Marshall, the supposed tire magnate, joined us after lunch, the ambassador became less genial and asked if there were anything I'd learned
from Petrolat that he should know.

"It's not Ambassador Orden asking that question, Charlie," Marshall said.
"It's your country."

"Thanks for explaining it, Marsh," I said.

"A U.S. ambassador is the United States here. You are in United States
territory in his residence. He does not represent your President. He embod-
ies your President. Charlie, if you were in the Oval Office, and President
Carter asked you what Ambassador Orden just asked, what would you say?"

"Sir, thank you for lunch." I stood up. "Deke will appreciate your enter-
taining me."

"Sit down," Marshall said. "What's your hurry?"

"I'm due back at the Velodrome for an equipment check."

"Charlie, you've never competed at this level before."

"No. I'm here because my uncle disappeared from here. As long as I'm
waiting, it'll be interesting to try riding with these guys."

"And Petrolat was nice enough to fix it up so you could."

"They're taking care of me well."

"Your heat is at eleven tomorrow morning?"

"Yes."

"Good luck, Charlie boy," Marshall said.

"I admire the amateur spirit," said the ambassador. "I used to shoot some
trap against professionals . . . "

"I'm not that fond of amateurs in my work," Marshall said.

"Frankly, I'd be scared silly to try anything like your work," I told him.

"Can we count on that?"

They can sure count on me being scared.

7. Rereading that this morning, I wonder how much being scared had to do
with my eve-of-battle act last night?

Cherry is staying at an apartment, borrowed from some Petrolat employee who's on home leave. Cherry suggested that we eat supper there; she wants me out of sight as much as possible.

"You sure you want to cook?" I asked. "I can hide out in my hotel room and have supper sent up."

"You can help me with the cooking."

"Your place it is, then."

It was about four-thirty, after the afternoon workout, when she let me off. I came up here to the room, had a shower, a shot and a cool, dark beer, put on fresh socks and went sound asleep under my bath towel.

She got back to her place and found the company car waiting to take her to a hurry-up conference. Tried to phone me. I must have been in the shower and didn't hear the ring. She left a message at the desk, which I never got. She was an hour and a half late getting back here. I slept blissfully through every lovely minute of it.

When the phone rang again, Cherry was in the lobby and I was thirstier than I was hungry. I drank another cool, dark one, standing nude at the telephone, and listened to her say she wished I'd gone ahead and eaten without her.

I said, "I slept. It was delicious. How about you?"

She laughed. "Not a wink. But I didn't get to the market, either. What are we going to do about supper?"

It was in her voice; it was in my image of her in the Fiat, lowering her sunglasses and smiling; maybe Roxie's call to me at sunrise made it swarm and buzz in the steamy air of Istanbul yesterday; sting of the hornybee. (Who's been influencing my prose style?) Anyway, I thought of unconfining that jiggly bosom from its executive clothes and my groin flipped.

"Get on the elevator and press the little button that says 'five,' " I suggested. "And I'll order supper."

"Oh, how I'd love it," she said. "And stretch out with my shoes off, and a nice drink. Mmmmmm. Charles, the bell captain here is your friend Marshall's man."

"Then let's go to your place, and have a drink and talk it over."

"You're on, racer," she said, with only a touch of girlish hesitation.

Once, in Florida, I saw an alligator chase a poodle. The way I went after Cherry when we got to her place was just as intent and half as graceful, but the poodle still had all its curls in place and seemed to be enjoying the romp half an hour later, when she pushed me away and said: "We're definitely going to eat something now."

"Rats," I said. "I thought there wasn't anything."

"We're going to eat eggs."

I followed her to the kitchen and watched her get out one of those flat pans with four aluminum cups nested in it that the British use to steam eggs.

She buttered the cups, broke the eggs, and started them. She gave me a bottle of Glenlivet to sip on, murmuring, "You Mizzourins."

She made toast. When she handed it to me on a little plate with two dear little eggs, I made one bite of each of them.

She made her eggs last a little longer, washed her mouth with Scotch, and made me tell her how Gibraltar got its name.

"I knew you'd look it up," she said.

"Did you, too?"

"Of course."

I never realized the tactical disadvantage a woman is at sitting in an armchair with a man swarming at her from one side and above. I hope Cherry put herself in that physical situation on purpose, where it's awkward for her to use her hands for fending, and her legs just won't stay together. Finally, when it was skirts up and pants away, she did start pushing at my shoulders with enough determination so that I sat back, with what was probably a fairly offensive grin on my face. There was heavy breathing on both sides.

"You Mizzourins." She said it again. Her breasts were out, and her skirt up around her waist, but she wasn't making repairs.

"I hope this doesn't mean I have to eat another egg," I said.

Her smile went crooked, and I lunged again and lifted her out of the chair, gave her a long kiss standing, and a short walk to the bedroom, but it's not clear which was the alligator, which the poodle, after that.

Afterward, we lay close for a while. She didn't feel like getting up to drive me back to the hotel and said we shouldn't risk my going out and getting in the wrong taxicab.

"I'm sure your friend Marshall's got the news of where you are this evening. He could have a cab out there to try to pick you off."

"Do you mind his knowing if I spend the night?"

"I can't really bring a clear head to that question," Cherry said, settled herself against me, and said it for the third time but in a different voice: "You Mizzourins."

She seemed to want to be asked, so I did. "Was Ned a problem?"

"At least he believes it when a girl says no. Not that he won't come at you like a bull again tomorrow."

"Did you like that?"

"No. Yes. Shut up, dear."

"Do I look like Ned at all?"

"Yes. But you're young and scrawny. You have the same amazing smile, but yours hasn't got mean yet." She chuckled. "You'll see tomorrow. Anyway, Ned must have something. He's the oldest man I've ever kissed, by twenty years. Listen." She sat up. "You know what it's like for a woman out here? First, about all you know are company guys. You can party with them all, or pick one out and let him put his name tag on you. The third alternative's to stand off and ache by yourself, just for someone to hold you sometimes. You uncle's a sexy old bastard, Charlie. I was waiting for him to come back out before I decided what to do about it, though. Well," she said. "I've decided, haven't I, racer?"

There was something a little malicious in the way she said it, and something a little malicious in the pleasure I felt about it, too. I don't guess this is going to help my uncle and me make friends exactly.

Now I have killed the right amount of time writing this morning, and the hour has come: helmet, gloves, cleated shoes, black chamois-padded shorts, water bottle, Bollé sunglasses, folded spare tire, banana for the jersey pocket—and what a jersey Cherry's had made for me. It's purple and gold, with Petrolat embroidered in red on the back and *Charlie* on the chest.

7. I am in Syria, waiting in the customs shed. I have been waiting more than an hour for a car to come. The customs men are friendly and have given me pen and paper with which to write these notes, since I can't read their Arabic newspapers or magazines.

I keep telling myself that the Syrians won't let this thing go wrong. Nobody wants to welsh on Petrolat. There's too much money involved. I also tell myself that there was so much dumb luck involved in my getting this far that it isn't going to run out now.

I didn't see Cherry this morning before the race. A pickup truck came to the hotel for me. We went to the Velodrome for Ignacio, the mechanic, and loaded the bike. Ignacio believes that I'm a serious and qualified contender and kept saying that we would show them all. He loves the sport of cycling, and I hated deceiving him.

Marshall and his embassy friend were waiting to watch the start. It was a sunny morning, but there was a crosswind out of the south. It was an uphill start, riding east into the damnedest climb I'd ever seen, one hairpin turn after another, up a small mountain.

There were a hundred of us trying to qualify, twenty to a heat, and I was in the third of four rows in the last heat for the start.

For a couple of kilometers, I was pleased with myself, working hard and steadily, passing and being passed the way you do. I even went by my Italian acquaintance, who called out "Good morning, Joe" and quite nonchalantly passed me back, waving.

Then, as the pack began to string out, a rider in green silk passed me, pulled in front, and slacked off. As I followed him, I read the lettering on his jersey: *Pneumatique Internationale*. Tires. Sponsored by a tire company—wait. And I could hear Marshall saying, with a vocal wink: *Six years in the tire business.*

There was an easy way to find out if this rider in green was Marshall's man. I sped up a little and pulled even with him. He sped up to get in front again. I slowed down. So did the rider in the green silk shirt, doing what you never do: looking back to keep track of me. So it was going to be a race between him and me. I looked at his legs. They didn't look as if they'd bend nails any more than mine would.

I had less than ten miles to find out how tough Marshall's rider was. I hoped he couldn't ride with me, but if he could we were either going to turn off together, and cross the border together, or I was going to have to decide to scrub it for today. I didn't like either choice. I pulled over left, shifted gears, and sprinted by him, getting forty yards on him before he started after me. "Orders, Mizzourin," he yelled. "Turn back." I sprinted harder.

We were passing people, riding in this idiotic way, and it was agony. I registered the Italian rider calling out amazed "Hey, Joe?" as we went by him.

We were almost in front of the pack when the tire man made his move. I heard it coming, heard his breathing just behind me, knew he was trying to ride into me. I swerved just before his front wheel took me from behind, and in the swerve and braking, down I went. He plunged by, overcorrecting, and went down, too. Riders were going by us who had seen what he tried to do, and were yelling at him for it. I was pretty well scraped from the left hip on down, as I got myself and my bike up and remounted. He was dong the same, but I got going again first.

"Let's race," I called out as I went by, went into an enormous gear and moved up toward the next hairpin. The pack was by us now; I could feel my teeth clench. I could taste the air that sucked through them. My legs were screaming. I thought about my uncles, and I don't know whether what came to me then was a second wind, a third wind, or Mike Mizzourin entering his son Charlie's body to help. I can only say that it seemed to me that Ned and Pete were my own brothers and that the pain went out of my legs.

That's what was in my mind when I went by Cherry and the Petrolat car. I saw her wave the white handkerchief, and I, too, did what you never do, glanced back and saw I had the tire man by a turn and a half and was still gaining on him. When I came to the gravel road at kilo 20.9 and made my turn, I'd got beyond his line of sight. Then it was downhill, steep, and the gravel was loose, and I fought to lose speed to avoid another spill.

When I was sure I wasn't followed, I stopped, slapped my feet out of the toeclips and straps, swung off, and walked the bike a little way until my body stopped heaving. There was less gravel as I went downhill. The surface was hardpan dirt. When I could see the raised gates at the border station, I got back on, strapped my feet back in the pedals, and rode. I wanted to go by the Turkish guards and enter Syria like a real racer, and I did.

Asphalt commenced near the gate itself, and when I went through it I was pumping hard in high. Here on the Syrian side, two young soldiers flagged me down, took charge of the bike, led me into this shed, and let me use the contents of their first-aid kit to treat my scrape. And now I'm waiting.

8. It's over. I am back in Istanbul. There is time to finish this record.

After I'd been in the customs shed two hours, a Russian-made limousine drove slowly up to the door. There were two Syrian officers in uniform and two men in suits, as well as a driver. They had me sit in front with the driver, who kept his revolver drawn, while an officer looked through my papers, nodded, and handed them to one of the civilians.

"Charles Mizzourin?" He spoke to me through the window of the car. He had a heavy accent.

I smiled. I didn't see why a little civility wouldn't be appropriate. This was supposedly a happy occasion. So I said, "Yes. Good afternoon." And offered a hand to shake.

The civilian took my hand, but he held more than shook it, looked at the others, and one of the officers said, "We do not speak English," in perfect English. Then he got in front beside me and the other three got in back. They didn't seem hostile or surly, just silent.

We drove along slowly, the three in back not even talking among themselves. We came to a village of stucco houses with wooden doors. We stopped at one, a little larger than the others, which had Arabic writing on a sign beside the door. There were a couple of policemen in front of it, another, smaller limousine parked nearby, and a Russian-built jeep with two more soldiers.

We stopped, and everyone got out. There was some low-key, rather nervous-sounding, Arabic conversation. Then the officer who didn't speak English said, "Come inside, please. Watch your step. It's a little bit dark." I followed him into the building, into a stone-walled room full of shadow. A man was sitting, waiting, on the edge of the desk, which was the only piece of furniture. He stood up when we came in. The clothes he was wearing didn't fit. His eyes were sad and brown, and somehow he looked as I expected him to. But there was no one else in the room except for one more soldier, this one with a drawn gun, standing in the interior doorway.

"Uncle Ned," I said.

"No. I'm Pete." We rushed into one another's arms and hugged. Pete was crying a little, snuffling. "Charlie," he said. "Ned didn't make it. Neddie's dead."

I kept hugging him until his sobs stopped and he was able to step away. "What's happened, Uncle?" I asked. "Can you come with me? Are they letting you go?"

"Yeah," he said, and hugged me again. "Some kind of beer I'm buying you, aren't I? Let's go, Charlie. Let's get the hell out of this country."

There was a cheap valise on the floor without much in it. A civilian said something, and the soldier from the doorway put away his submachine gun and picked up the bag. Pete was holding tight to my arm. In the daylight he looked pale, a strong, brown-eyed man, shorter and burlier than me, who'd begun to waste away.

They let us sit in back together, some of them getting in the other car. The officer who didn't speak English sat in front, listening, but we ignored it.

"Ned was out of his head when they brought him to jail," Pete said. "And he got worse and worse. He kept trying to bribe people, which might have worked if he'd had the right cash, but his only money was Turkish. What he wanted was alcohol, he was really deprived, but they laughed at his promises. I'd been getting pretty good treatment; much better than when I was held up in the hills, but they got rough when Ned came. He kept yelling that he had diplomatic immunity, they couldn't hold him. He'd throw the food when they brought it. They'd take him to the office and try to calm him down but he'd be madder than ever when he came back. Part of the time he'd be mad at me, and part of the time pleading with me to use my Arabic, get him a drink, get him a bath, threaten a guard. Finally, he bought a knife from another prisoner, a half-wit, with his Turkish money. There was a guard who'd been giving us a hard time. Ned was out in the corridor, being taken to the office again, when this guard cuffed him and Ned pulled the knife. Ned was old and tough. The guard was young and tough. It was a hell of a fight, Charlie. Neither one of them seemed to be a damn bit afraid. I could never understand that. I yelled and yelled for help. No one came. The knife changed hands a couple of times. They stabbed each other, beat on each other, strangled, banged heads against steel bars. And finally, the young guard had the better and must have stuck Ned twenty times, and Ned fighting and bellowing till the last gasp, never cried his pain till men came running, grabbed the guard and carried Ned away."

I put my arm around Uncle Pete. "Rest now," I said. We rode back into Turkey that way without saying much more. But just as we got to the border, he raised his head, smiled a shaky smile, and said: "You look like him, Charlie."

"Like my father?"

"Like Ned, when he was young. Well, Mike, too. A little taller like Ned, and a lot thinner, like Mike."

The Petrolat car, with Cherry and a couple of guys who knew Pete, was waiting in the other side when we walked across the border together. The Syrian officials wanted to shake hands, and there wasn't any reason not to. But Uncle Pete didn't seem to notice them. His head was down, and his eyes were full of tears.

"Hello?"

"Welcome goddamn home, bo."

"Hi, Deke."

"I got debriefing stuff from State all over my desk. Damn, I'm sorry about Ned."

"He was a violent man."

"It's a loss, after all, and a lot of flack about it. You did good, Charlie. Your name is Utter Pig Shit at State, so you must have done good."

"I've got to go over there in a few minutes. I guess they want to whack on me some."

"They'll be nicer than you think. Whatever happened day before yesterday, today they want to look good. How's Pete?"

"He's staying here at the apartment. He's out now, walking in the snow. He says walking feels good."

"Anything we can do for him?"

"Could Darlene make travel arrangements?"

"I'll have her call Pete."

"He wants to get out to Calder Plain as soon as he can to see Ned's family."

"I phoned them. Did you know Jimmy Carter phoned them?"

"Did he? That's pretty nice, Deke, I'm glad. Did a cable come from Cherry Nelson?"

"Yeah, bo. Says she got the furlough from Petrolat. She's in the air right now, flying toward us."

"Do I have a flight to meet?"

"Cable says not. Company gets her first."

"I suppose."

"Disappointed?"

"Sure. Anything else?"

"Ton of mail and phone messages. A lot of crank stuff. I'll send it all. Be there when you get back from State. Hey, this Roxie called three times. Read about you in the papers."

"I'll write her a note."

"They call it 'The Great Bicycle Escape.' "

"They don't get things very straight, do they?"

"Don't want to talk to Roxie, bo?"

"Seems better not."

"How about media? You got interview requests a mile long. Pete, too."

"How about this? The State Department won't let me talk, and Pete's not well enough."

"You're something, Charlie. Guy like me would give year's pay. Another one might figure he had something to sell. But I don't think you ought to go mysterious. They'll really hound you if you do. Pick one, get it over, and say no to the others."

"Which one shall I pick?"

"Well, let's see. You got State this afternoon. You got your mail to read, and calls to answer. Why don't you do the Cavendish news interview tonight, ten-thirty. Late night, live. Others will pick it up for tomorrow's papers and news shows and you'll be done."

"Pete, too?"

"He won't have to say much. Hey, do I get to meet Pete, fore he goes home?"

"Sure. Come have a drink after work."

"CC and Seven. Lots of ice. Hey Charlie?"

"Yes?"

"Feel like you're getting to know your dad, now, meeting Pete?"

"We talked some on the plane. Pete would sleep a while and then wake up and talk some more. Way of handling pain, I guess. Reminiscing. I was glad if it helped, but I felt distant from it. Fond of Pete but only half-listening to the boyhood tales."

"Ghosts gettin' put to rest."

"The last of the wild Mizzourin boys. Ned was the wildest. Mike was the one people thought had the most stuff. Pete seems to have been the one that everybody liked. That's all I really needed to know about their growing up. New York's still a mystery, and how it ended for my father. That'll lay the ghosts. But Pete and Ned went to Dad and Mother's wedding. I never knew that. Pete heard Dad play the trumpet there. He says Mother was the most beautiful woman he ever saw."

"Model of the Year, one year. What's her married name now again?"

"Helmreich. Mrs. Scott Helmreich."

"That's what I thought. You got a big fat letter from Mrs. Helmreich, coming with the messenger. And one from Colorado."

"Johnson's reappeared?"

"I don't know. The letter's from Mrs. Johnson."

"Hope the old man's all right."

"See you at booze time, bo."

"Take care, Deke."

Dear Roxie:

Thank you for your concern for me and my uncle. Deke told me you'd called several times. The newspapers seem to have made it much more dramatic than it really was, though it was more than exciting enough for me. The State Department and Intelligence people joined in distorting what really happened, so that it would sound like some sort of American success. It wasn't really. It was quirkish, and sad, and uncontrolled by anyone, although the Syrians did their best. That's the way history goes, I guess. I hope you'll understand that I want to keep my life low-key for a while now. I don't mean to resume old connections, and have no reason to suppose you'll want to hear from me any-way, beyond this note. I'll be leaving this apartment as soon as I can find another. I love it here, but I realized that in taking it I became beholden to Suesue. I'm sure she regrets what she has done for me, and I'm sorry. On balance, she was more than kind, and so were you, very much more. I hope that Suesue, Angela, and especially you, bear me no hard feelings.

Sincerely,
Charlie

Last Deadline Ranch
Capsicum, Colorado
April 20, 1980.

Dear Charles:

John is still missing, and I'm very, very worried. Please call me if you are back from Turkey, but of course you must be if you are reading this, aren't you? Of course, I want to know if you are all right, and your dear, real uncles whom I hope you have met by now, so very brave of you to go there. But as I said, now you're back, and I got the locksmith to open John's study for me, with police authorization, the missing persons bureau, they were so nice about it in case of clues. There weren't any clues, though, but a few more scraps of your father's journal, well, not scraps really but three more of his wonderful little essays. I remember all those songs, and now you'll find out how he met your lovely mother, which is a happy ending to the story for you, although of course the real ending was so tragic. I don't know if there was any more that John destroyed or took away.

Love,
Aunt Christine

"Hello?"
"Aunt Christie. It's Charles."

"Oh, Charles. Oh my dear. I've read all about and I'm so sorry about your uncle Ned, but he was a hero, wasn't he? Risking his life to save his brother. Have you heard from John?"

"No. Have you?"

"No, Charles."

"Do you have some reason to think he might get in touch with me?"

"Just woman's intuition. Well, he did say often that he ought to go to Washington, didn't he?"

"I've been away, of course. Are you all right?"

"Mrs. Harper is staying with me. My cleaning woman, such a dear. Oh, Charles, have you read the one called 'My Reverie'?"

"No, not yet."

"It's about your mother."

"Yes, you said. I have a letter from my mother that she promised me she'd write."

"About Mike?"

"I think so."

"Oh, dear. Have you read it?"

"No, not yet."

"I hope it won't make you unhappy."

"It was very long ago, Aunt Christie."

"Do read what I sent first."

"To put off unhappiness?"

"They were sweet days . . . " (ALL RIGHT, MRS. HARPER) "She wants me to rest."

"I'll be on television tonight. The Cavendish Show."

"Oh, I'll watch Charles. I'll watch, and if John calls, even if he says not to tell me?"

"I hardly think he will, but yes. Of course."

Mizzourin/**OH BY JINGO**

No word from Evaun, but Fourth of July's still six weeks off. And there was a Carolina reunion of another kind today.

I was walking on Tenth Avenue in the soft May sun, carrying the cornet on my way to practice time, when I heard sweet and awful around the corner on Fifty-eighth. It was piano, drums and alto. The sax lead was stiff and loud, overenunciated, and almost comically self-assured. The song was "Margie."

I thought for a wild moment, something about the chords, that the piano might be Doctor Wanderbaum, fallen low, but when I turned the corner, I saw that the musicians were three negroes in the back of a pickup truck. They were parked at the curb, playing energetically, two musicians, really, and the plumber on alto, drawing a small crowd of tenement women and kids.

They finished "Margie" and the alto, a short, gray-headed, shabbily dapper man with a goatee, jumped down on the pavement, hauled out a box of wind-up toy dogs, and started three or four of them doing circles on the sidewalk. *Two buckers each, and three for five, now here's a pet that don't make wet . . .* I was in no hurry. The practice rooms are open all day. I drew nigher to the toy tycoon, admiring his auctioneering and the way hands were reaching for his doggies, when I heard a sharp little blast on the drums, looked up and it was Scholay.

The toycoon looked up too, startled, and Scholay sang out, "That's no cop, Tyner. That's Little Mike."

Tyner laughed and went back to his unlicensed work, and I leapt into the truck bed for a rough embrace. I swear we didn't say a word for seven minutes, just hugged and laughed like longlost, till Scholay said at longlast: "What's in that case? What is that? You got salami sandwiches in there?"

The pianist, who plays a spinet roped to the back of the cab, is young and light skinned, with reddish hair. "Can this Mike eat that kinda sandwich any?" he asked.

"Damn if I know," Scholay told him. "Last time I saw Mike he was throwing a blackjack down the hole in the outhouse of a whorehouse. You play, Mike?"

"Learning," I said. "Taking lessons, little way up Tenth, and go there every day to practice. What's with you?"

"Shit me easy," Scholay said. "You can't play ace on trey, now can you?"

"Play your ass off, buddy," I said.

Scholay poked me with a drumstick, grinning. "Lotta suckers carrying those cases, got their dirty socks and maryjane inside."

I grinned back and opened up to show cornet. "What's this?"

"Lotta cases got horns, dust in the tubes, cobwebs, little spiders running 'round inside."

"Margie-dust in this one, bastard," said I, hauled out, slipped in a double-cap mouthpiece for street sound, hoped they'd let me get away with buzzing the song in C, and took off, medium bounce. My ears were working. I survived okay, and felt confident enough to get a little fancy with some passing notes off the beat in the second half of the chorus. Old Tyner and his customers listened and clapped time; we even had a solo jitterbug, but Scholay stopped us after a second "Margie" chorus with a series of rimshots, out of tempo, grinning even harder and saying, "Hold it, hold it now."

"Whatsa matter?" Old Tyner peered around and down the street.

"Nobody coming," Scholay said. "Just gotta talk."

"Make more noise, sell more toys," Tyner said, but Scholay ignored him, looking at the pianist instead.

"Knock me your sound and well-thought-out opinion, Mister Red," he said.

The pianist shrugged but he didn't seem unhappy. "Lowest I *ever* hear a cat play 'Margie,' " he said. "Wanta do it now in F? That's G for horn?"

"Play something else," I said. "Something simple for a cold lip."

" 'Blue Moon,' " Scholay said.

"Horn in F," said Red. I knew that, but I nodded thanks. "Blue Moon" is my warm-up tune, easy as twinkle-twink and nothing higher than a D.

Scholay started to give us a beat, but Tyner was loading up and made us hold it back. I seemed to have joined his command. "Next block, boys," he said, including me as if I was on the payroll, pushing his box of doggies onto the bed, casing his alto, raising the tailgate and then going around to the driver's seat.

Red was looking at me. "Your Mike's a rough horn, Scholay," he said. "But he's got drive."

It was pretty nice, riding and playing with them in the sun. Tyner didn't make a move toward getting out his sax again. We'd turn into a tenement block, and if there was life, people sitting on the steps, Tyner'd signal us by slowing down and we'd start to play.

Scholay told me that they worked for Tyner Fridays and Saturdays. It's the only paid job they have right now, and not what you'd call really making any music. But a friend of theirs named Sutton's got a loft on the Lower East Side. Saturday evenings when they get done, Tyner drives them to the loft, and they carry Red's spinet up three flights of stairs.

"We got a rehearsal band," Scholay said. "No pay, no thanks, long hours every night and get chewed by the blackest man alive. He's fine bass, though. Wanta try out?"

Mizzourin/I'VE GOT THE WORLD ON A STRING

Sutton's fine bass indeed, and very black. Aldo's tenor, white and thirty-one. Jim is some kind of Filipino genius kid with a strange guitar. It's electric with no sound box, and Jim's complicated and surprising solos come directly from the amplifier. Scholay and Red are thrilled by him, and even Sutton forgets to sneer sometimes.

Since I don't solo, Sutton doesn't get to criticize me for ideas, but he hears and groans at every mechanical error, and snarls about it afterward ("What do you think this is, boy, music lessons? Gonna pay me?") It's terrific, actually. I hardly ever make mechanical errors anymore. Sutton can get pretty mean about my tone, too, but we have a real difference going there—I like a big, open sound, and he prefers it clipped and terse. ("Bring your cornet next time. Leave the moose call home.") When we met last night said he had booked us later for a party in a Greenwich Avenue studio.

"I may die of shame," said Sutton, giving us the address. "You got time to go home and change your ugly clothes. Let's look like something even if we can't play like nothing."

I loved playing at the party, except for the marijuana which people seemed to feel obliged to offer us. I tried it. It made me cough and lose enough coordination so that I sat out a set. Sutton was sympathetic. He neither smokes nor drinks. I'd only taken two drags, and I doubt I'll ever take a third. No head for it. When I got my fingers back, I got a bottle of very cold beer and made it last so long it was warm before I finished it. When I play, music's the only high I can take.

There was dancing at the party, real dancing, not the Carolina crotchlock, nice to watch. When the solos started, after a chorus or two, I'd rest my lip, watch, sip the beer, and wait for Red's signal to come back in. It was pretty close to total bliss—don't tell the shop steward—and nothing like playing with the trio at Rhombo's. I wish Evaun could hear; she'd be proud.

July Fourth has come and gone. No word from Carolina. I did send some cash. I miss Evaun. I even miss her impossible brother.

There was a college boy from Princeton at the party who seemed to know some music, and he's offered us a date at his club at the university next weekend.

At intermission, Scholay and I were talking.

"You sure seem to like playing a job," he said.

"Love it. My lip feels like a hundred pushups, but I love it."

"I was watching you. You like to make the people move."

"Could you tell?"

"You were playing and watching their feet and smiling through your horn."

"I wouldn't care for playing on a stage, or concert hall."

"Want you to come hear Monk at the Blue Note tomorrow," Scholay said. "And Dizzy at Birdland. That's a stage."

"No practice?" I didn't want to miss any.

"Day off after a job, redhot. Get you off your records and hear some men live."

Mizzourin/MY REVERIE

It has been a hot summer in New York, and I haven't written for six weeks. Aldo's brother, who's a longshoreman, got us on as substitutes. In August there was steady work. Some regulars would just decide to beat the heat by staying home; others went on vacation. Now that it's cooling off, I don't get on the docks so often. It's just as well. I was getting exhausted, working days, rehearsing nights. Weekends we played jobs pretty often. The band has caught on a little.

I can't say I'm rich, but I no longer fear the VA money running out, and actually have stopped drawing it except to pay for lessons. I didn't get to the lessons too often during the summer, either.

Sutton and I are always first to get there for rehearsal. While we wait, he works me over like a missionary, trying to convert me to progressive. He sits at the piano, playing sequences and changes with the chords altered and expanded. I can play his weird chords in arpeggios with him, but when I try to use them in a solo, I just plain get lost. And don't like what I hear. It gets me too far off the melody.

"Forget about solo," Sutton says. "You'll never make it."

"I liked the way I sounded on 'September in the Rain' last night," I said, looking for praise.

"Hotel music," he said. "Sure, you can take an old Bunk and Bixie kind of solo, sound okay where people got no ears."

"I was only away four years, Sutton," I said. "You telling me my songs are out already?"

"Your songs, your music and your moose call, too," Sutton said. "You want to work a year from now, better get up your reading. Better play your *Arban*. Better learn to play the charts. Work for you's going to be studio, that's all. Not jazz. Trumpet's going out. Not cool enough for jazz."

"Gillespie," I said, of course. "Ferguson. Brown. Terry."

"Listen to the MJQ. Listen to that boy Sonny when he comes."

"He doesn't know the songs."

"Doesn't play songs. Plays music. Songs is all you *can* play."

"I love the songs, Sutton," I said.

"Pander. Go ahead."

Scholay and Red arrived, and I said quick to Sutton: "Understand we're pandering down at Princeton again Friday."

Scholay agrees with Sutton, though he's nice about it. "You want to make a living in music now, gotta go to music school, not just lessons and have fun. You wanta play jazz, Little Mike, you gotta open up your head a little, not just your heart."

They're serious, they're studious. Sutton went through Juilliard and still takes composition. Scholay's learning to read, which used to be unheard of for a drummer. Red doesn't study, but he's a zealot for modern jazz, has fine technique and a marvelous memory; he plays cocktail piano in a Harlem lounge now, three nights a week.

As for me: I'm wrong. To want to play good-time music and pretty ballads and make the people move isn't it anymore. But music school sounds like drudgery, written music is dull, my kind of jazz is over, and I've met a girl.

That, Scholay says, is the real trouble.

"Going to square off and get a job, aren't you baby?"

"I've signed up at the employment place."

"Not for music, did you?"

Newspaper work, I told Scholay. I used to do high-school sports at home, before the war. It was on my army job classification sheet, and when the war ended, they moved me into Regimental HQ Company to put out the mimeographed daily until discharge time. It was easy. I can't say the same for Livia Scaliger.

"Can you play 'Deep Purple'?"

It was at a Princeton Club party, she was beautiful, and the guys were laughing at me, the man without a woman.

"Mind if we do 'Deep Purple'?" I said to Sutton.

"Oh, please, please," Scholay said.

"Be so nice," said Red. "And tender."

The beautiful girl had moved back onto the dance floor and was waiting in her partner's pudgy arms. Absurd-looking youth, wasn't he?

"Play it for me," said Aldo, hand on his heart. Sutton consented, playing an unnecessarily soulful F-major arpeggio with his bow.

Red let me off, playing a medium-speed intro which kept me from getting so mushy on the horn I'd have had to hide my head afterward. Still I admit to more vibrato on the lead than I usually permit myself. Aldo took his usual kind of nice, conventional solo, and then Jim one of his slightly amazing things, double time and pretty, at the end of which Red would normally have had a chorus. Instead, he yelled "Horn," took a couple of lead notes and stopped. Everybody stopped. I guess I'd felt it coming, been aware of them trying not to grin, but I didn't have it thought out.

I had to stand. I blew a kind of four-bar cascade of G, D-diminished, G-minor. I even added the ninth and the eleventh to the G-minor, the way Sutton kept wanting me to, and as a cry to Sutton for a little help. He responded, giving me a bass line, nicely retarded, and I soared. I played an absolutely straight, pure chorus of the melody, keeping the vibrato out this time, trying to do not so much a Berrigan as a Coleman Hawkins, caressing the song instead of changing it. The guys were in again behind me when I finished, soft and hovering, like they were hatching me. Aldo signaled that he wanted another solo, and did me the honor of playing in the same style and tempo. We did a swell ensemble, picking up the beat enough to swing, and you know where the beautiful girl was then?

Neither do I. Ladies room, probably.

Her name is Livia Scaliger. I said that already. She's a model. She was back later asking for "Besame Mucho." Aldo said he'd like to bass her mucho, and I wondered how well he could play tenor with a fat lip. I didn't say it, of course. I grinned myself some kind of a face. Got her phone number, too. Am about to make a call. Good luck, Little Mike.

"Hello?"

"Charles, see here. This is Angela Hibben, and if you ring off I swear I shall have you thrashed."

"Angela *Hibben?*"

"Otis and I have been married, as you might well know if you had the courtesy to stay in touch with your friends."

"Mrs. Monterrey Jack."

"That will be quite enough of that. Stop laughing."

"Angela Yogurt Otis. Sorry. I can't help it."

"Stop it."

"Okay. So you're not living next door any longer?"

"Certainly not, nor is Roxanne, as you might have noticed if you weren't totally blind."

"Well. Where is Roxanne?"

"I shouldn't dream of telling you. Very well, she's staying with Suesue, of course."

"Why of course?"

"Because it's a very quiet place just now. You know that you managed to get Suesue's card game closed down."

"No. I didn't know."

"Oh, she and Otis will get it started off again in time. Meanwhile, you've made more than your share of trouble, haven't you? Don't you feel it's time you started setting things right?"

"It's been nice hearing from you, Angela. Please congratulate Senator Hibben for me."

"Charles, are you going to phone Roxanne and talk it out with her?"

"No, Angela. I've written Roxie a note."

"But why not phone her?"

"I expect to have a friend here, after my uncle leaves."

"A friend of what sort? One of your bloody bitches?"

"I wouldn't call her that. Her name is Cherry Nelson. She's on furlough from Petrolat. She helped me a great deal in Turkey."

"Are you so very fond of this, er, lady executive then?"

"Quite, Angela, as they say in your language."

"Please, won't you at least see Roxanne and let her know? It will be most unkind if I have to tell her."

"There's nothing to tell, really."

"Oh, just bloody business friends, it it? Is that what I'm to tell Roxanne?"

"Tell her I'm happy. Tell her I hope she'll be. I really do. I care about Roxanne."

"Bugger yourself."

"I'm sorry."

"Bugger your Iron Maiden, too."

"Ouch."

"You worm."

"Goodbye, Angela."

Dear Aunt Christie:

Just a note, to explain the enclosure. It's a copy of the long letter from my mother, which I've just now read. You and Mr. Johnson are mentioned in its later pages, but with affection, not in a damaging way.

Fondly,
Charles.

LIVIA SCALIGER HELMREICH

My dear son Charles:

This is my fourth beginning of this letter which I promised. I do not write easily as some people do, and never did, but I don't lie as some people do, either. This will be the truth, whatever your father's "fake book" may say. Nobody has the right to hurt the one he loves, as he did to me, and also what happened was his fault.

I met Michael Mizzourin at a Colony Club football weekend dance at Princeton University on a Friday night in September, 1946. I was attending Barnard College and working with great success as a fashion model at Bonwit Teller, after school. My parents were easily able to send me to college, but I enjoyed earning my own clothes and spending money. At Bonwit's we did many fashion shows and were able to buy beautiful clothing at a very good discount. My friend (roommate) Phoebe and I were very popular in New York, and at the best colleges such as Princeton and Yale. We did not like the kind of boys who went to Harvard as they were smart alecky and wore "horn rims" and "white bucks."

My most serious date was Scott Helmreich, who is now your stepfather who I am married to. He was then in Princeton studying economics and business training, and was ever-faithful to me. I will never forget him. That is, I couldn't exactly forget him, as we are married, but I will always remember him.

I was dancing with Scott Helmreich, whose friends were always very jealous of him because of me, and we were having a very lovely time as usual as I was wearing a Schiaparelli dress of scarlet silk net over a matching taffeta sheath. The band was supposed to be quite special, according to the boy who hired it and who knew a great deal about popular music and bands. Scott Helmreich and I did not like the way this band played some of the fast numbers, because they made it hard to "jitterbug," which we both enjoyed doing and was quite harmless fun and exercise, unlike the "disco" dancing of today. I told Scott I thought the strange way they sometimes played was because the band had several negroes in it, and a very strange-looking dark boy on guitar, but on some numbers the fast music was very good, and it was always very good on slow songs.

The one who was supposed to know about music said that the white boy who played trumpet (it was really a cornet) was the leader (but it was really Sutton, the bass player). So I went up and asked the trumpet player for a request, which I don't remember what it was. Probably "Deep Purple," as that was my favorite. I'm afraid that the white trumpeter (your father to be!) played it so beautifully that I felt like dancing very close to Scott, and went outside with Scott in the moonlight before the song was over.

Later I asked for a Latin song because I could tell that this white trumpet player (cornet) would do anything I said, and Scott and I were the leading dancers at the club and were in demand to lead the conga line, if you know what that is. I was very confident of my beauty in days of yore, so when I went to thank the trumpet (cornet) player (Mike Mizzourin), it was during the intermission. It was something like this because I admit I enjoyed the harmless fun of flirting in days of yore also. Scott Helmreich was in a crap game.

"Do you always play so beautifully, as you did on my request?"

"Always. I can't control myself."

"I thought it was specially for me."

"Ask for another one. I'll put your name on it."

"Livia. What's yours?"

"Mike."

"I'd love to get you something from the bar, Mike."

What he said was so odd, it made me notice him differently. "The last time a lady bought me a drink, I lost three months of my life."

"Will you take a chance on me?"

"Probably."

"My date will be glad to buy it."

"Pudgy Peter?"

"His name is Scott. He wants to thank you for the song. Do you know Eric?"

"No."

"But he's the one that hired you. He says you're an exciting young trumpeter, and that this band is going places."

"Home to bed, lovely lady. Make it a beer. Heineken, if your date's a real spender."

"That depends on how he's doing in the crap game."

Just before the dance ended, I asked Mike for "Day by Day," and he said, "Any day, any night, lovely Livia."

I was very bold and sort of whispered, "But if you play it for me, you mustn't ever play it when I'm not there."

"Except in solitude. It'll be your song."

So I made a little kissing face, which was something that used to drive men wild.

"You have to sign it for me to make it yours," he said, and that's the first time I ever saw the "fake book," which he got out and opened to "Day by Day," on page 14.

I sort of giggled, and signed my name, and put a little row of x's under it. He pointed to the x's and said:

"I can't make out that phone number."

"Do you think I should give you my phone number?"

"Signature's not valid without it."

So I crossed out the x's and wrote in my phone number, and then I put one x back, and Mike said:

"Shall we get Pudgy Pete to witness it?"

This made me cross, and I said, "His name's Scott Helmreich, and we're practically engaged," and I walked off, but he played "Day by Day" for me anyway, and I have to admit it was beautiful. But later he said the negroes teased him about it. I also have to admit that it didn't make me feel like dancing closer to Scott as before, because this time I wanted to listen carefully to the tune.

Mike called the very next morning, as I knew he would. It was Saturday and I had made Scott drive me home to my little apartment in New York in midtown, although he had reserved a room for me at the Nassau Inn. But you see, I was going to have to be at work at Bonwit's that day at one P.M. for a luncheon fashion show, and I explained to Scott that I would have to wash my hair and get ready in the morning (and Phoebe, too, my roommate). It was definitely not because of expecting Mike to call.

In fact, I remember that my hair was all full of shampoo when Mike did call at eleven A.M. He wanted me to go and hear some music with him that night on 54th Street, because he said there was no rehearsal that night because of playing at the Colony Club in Princeton the night before.

"I've been thinking of you," I said.

"I have about you, too. Goes without saying, doesn't it, since I'm on the tweeter?" Everyone started calling telephones "tweeters" later that year, but Mike was the first I ever heard say it.

"I mean, I've been thinking it wouldn't be fair of me to go out with you. Because of Scott."

"Fair to him or fair to me?"

"Both of you."

"I've been taking care of myself for years, Livia. I'll bet Scott's a big boy now, too."

"He's a Phi Bete."

So this dumb Mike starts singing, "Okay, wow. How's it go? He's a Phi Bete, And a great date, And he's never late, Make a first-rate mate . . . "

I couldn't help laughing, but I said I had to hang up, he could call again sometime if he wanted, I had this fashion show luncheon at the store. Bonwit Teller.

Well, I was never so mad in my whole life as over what Mike did. There was a model agency woman at the luncheon, scouting for photographic models, which was the career I wished to choose so I wanted to make my best impression. I was standing with Mrs. Stallings, the Bonwit haute couture buyer, who was hostess for the luncheon, helping her to receive the guests and hoping to meet the model agency woman, when Mike Mizzourin stepped into the end of the line of people we were greeting with his negro friend from the band, Scholay Gopeters, the drummer. He was Mike's best friend. They looked very strange. Mike was wearing the purple pants of a zoot suit that must have belonged to Scholay, and Scholay was wearing a gray flannel suit that I learned later Mike had bought at Brooks Brothers to go job hunting in. Scholay had on a white shirt, and button-down collar and tie, and this ridiculous opera hat in his hand they had borrowed from a dancer, and a cane. Mike had the zoot pants, and a cummerbund, and some kind of Russian-looking blouse, and a little dinky black jacket that didn't close, and short black boots, and a fez. Red, with a tassel!

When it was their turn to introduce themselves, Mike bowed this silly bow to Mrs. Stallings, clicked his heels, and said in the dumbest French accent: "Eet ees me who call you oop. I am secretaire for Prince Gopete. Here ees Prince."

And Scholay bowed and kissed Mrs. Stallings' hand. She was thrilled.

"Oh, Livia," she said. "The Prince is from Mozambique."

I was trying so hard not to laugh. And I was furious, too.

"If he see nice dress, ees one problem I don' explique before," Mike said. "Must buy for all wifes, so as not to make ze jealousy. Fourteen dress, must all be same but different size, ees possible?"

Scholay was bowing and nodding and clicking his heels, and asking, "Unnerstand Inglees?" about Mike, and Mike said, "All right, boss. She unnerstand. Fine lady."

Mrs. Stallings was quite flustered and said it would be terribly expensive, the dresses we were modeling were all originals and cost several hundred dollars each.

Mike said, "Prince pretty rich you bet," and pretended to translate the conversation in some outlandish way, like "Zumba wallah wooky," and Scholay got out a checkbook and waved it around, only I could see it said First National

Bank of Harlem, but Mrs. Stallings didn't notice. So she said I must show them to a special table that was all set up, and I scolded them all the way and asked them please please please to leave. They stayed through the whole show! They were having a fine time, eating salmon mousse and potato puffs and taking notes on the dresses. Watching them made me so hungry, and of course, when I'd go by Mike would ask me to pause, and then say things to try to make me laugh, like, "Hey, Mees. Prince Gopete want to know why you so skinny. Been sick?" With this great big grin. And then when I went by again, he said, oh, it was so embarrassing: "Prince say you come Mozambique, we fry you up fat locusts. Gain plenty pound."

Do you know Mrs. Stallings had the general manager of the whole store come down to meet "Prince Gopete"? It nearly broke up my friendship with my best friend (roommate) Phoebe, because she thought it was all so funny, and I was absolutely outraged. I called Mike Mizzourin that very same afternoon and told him not to dare ever try to speak to me again. Do you know what he did? He said all right, he wouldn't speak but wait just a minute, and then he started playing "Day by Day" on his trumpet (cornet) right over the telephone.

Phoebe was right there with me, and she kept saying "What is it? What's he saying?" and finally grabbed the telephone, and listened and gave it back to me with this awful wink. You know, if it hadn't been for Phoebe doing that, I probably never would have seen Mike Mizzourin again? Because while he was still playing, Phoebe handed back the phone and said: "A little too much for you to handle, isn't he, Livia?"

And so I went out with Mike that night to hear the music just to show Phoebe she was wrong.

"¶*"*

What happened next was what is called "a whirlwind courtship." I admit I was "swept off my feet." Mike Mizzourin was too, and here is why.

I was five feet eight inches, which was quite tall even for a model in days of yore (taller than Mike), although there are now many girls six feet tall in my profession. I had mysterious black eyes and lovely black hair, and kept myself very slim because you always photograph ten pounds heavier than your real weight. I had what we called a "high-fashion figure," not large in the bosom but well-defined, and a really smart, small waist and hips, so that I looked totally elegant in whatsoever clothing. I was just beginning to be in demand with the fashion photographers, and also a leading model for hands because my hands were considered the best in New York. One week I made $215 for hand pictures alone! Not bad for a college girl! But my best feature was my skin which God gave me, and is pale and glowing without any blemishes of any kind. It was (and still is) like that all over my body, so that I was also in *demand for swimsuit and negligee work, but nothing suggestive. I was very busy, although it was not until after I was married that I became "Model of the Year of 1948." I have to tell you about something before the marriage which may embarrass you (it certainly does me!), which is that I was untouched by any man until I was married. I admit that like any other healthy being, I had desires, but was able to keep them under control with Scott Helmreich (and many others!).*

I also admit that it was more difficult to keep them under control with Mike Mizzourin because of some kind of chemistry we had, which he felt, too, but he helped me, unlike any other man. Sometimes I would daydream that he was being quite forceful in causing me to "surrender the fort," and when we were together would tell him hints of my difficulty of resisting him, if he would choose to be very firm to me. There was a "dirty" song then, and I fell so low as to sing it to him sometimes when we were alone and which went: "Violate me in violet time in the vilest way you know" (I'm blushing!). But he would sing back from a pretty old song called "Peg O' My Heart," of which he had given me a beautiful jazz record by a trombone player named Miff Mole: "Since I heard your lilting laughter, It's your Irish heart I'm after . . . " (I don't think "Miff" was his real name.)

Even on our first date, when we went up and down 54th Street, in and out of bars, listening to the music, he was declaring his interest in me. I remember in Jimmy Ryan's there was a negro trumpeter named Roy Eldridge who Mike called "Little Jazz," and who played this song named "Cherry," and when it was done the band took a break. I knew Mike didn't have very much money so I wanted to buy him a beer and myself club soda with a twist, which is what we had been drinking, and he said: "No. You bought me a beer at Princeton."

I said, "That was Scott Helmreich."

"Big Scott. He's not really your cup of tea, is he?"

"!"

Well. I was just going to see Mike that once to show Phoebe I could do as I liked, but then when he was telling me goodnight (Our first kiss! Forgive me, Charles. It is so long since I let myself remember these things. Now the dam is broken. Sometimes I want to stop writing and cry a little, but not unhappy crying. And then I want to remember it all, and write it all. For the first time I am not bitter in remembering the days of my love, but want to write it all.) Anyway, Mike said: "I'm working on the docks tomorrow, Livia. In the evening we have rehearsal. Would you like to come and hear the band rehearse? I'll pick you up."

Well, I did like him but had firmly decided the kindest thing would be not to see him again, but it seemed wrong to tell him so right after our first kiss, and it would be easier for him to understand after working as a longshoreman all day and then practicing with the negroes in a warehouse, that it wouldn't be suitable for us to be serious. Oh I admit I was very attracted by his dark hair and ruddy cheeks and flashing white smile, but above all the way he had so much life! Energy! He made me vibrate! I thought, well, I was still very young, and before I settled down with Scott Helmreich, there wouldn't be any harm in a light romance with someone so different from the boys I grew up with in Bronxville. (Mike was a little like one of them, though, who was a high school baseball player from the "wrong side of the tracks." I used to see this boy on the sly, and secretly even had "late dates" with him, but I was a foolish girl in high school and thought I could do anything I wanted, but as I said before, even on the late dates I never went all the way, and the boy was killed in the War.)

Against my better judgment, I went to the rehearsal with Mike, and supper afterwards way up in Harlem. I will tell you a secret: I didn't really like the music they were playing very well. I hadn't either the night before on 54th Street. Except when Roy Eldridge (Little Jazz) played "Cherry." . . .

"Hello?"

"Hello, darling."

"Cherry. The damnedest coincidence. It's terrific."

"What is?"

"I just read your name, in a letter from my mother. It mentioned a song called 'Cherry,' the phone rang, and it's you."

"It must mean we have your mother's approval. How are you?"

"Swamped, but fine, now that you're here. You?"

"Swamped, but I love being here. Oh God, I have one appointment after another, and then they want to helicopter me to Newport News tonight."

"What for?"

"More debriefing. There's so much thunder about Ned's killing."

"I know. I heard about it at State."

"Was it bad?"

"I got through. I've got to do the Cavendish Show tonight. Then I'll be clear."

"What's a Cavendish Show?"

"He does live interviews with people in the news."

"I'll watch in Newport News."

"When do we see each other in the flesh?"

"Tomorrow lunch? Can I come there for flesh?"

"You sure they'll let you?"

"I'll break heads if they don't. I'm having my luggage sent there, darling. You'll be home to receive it?"

"Yep. Right here reading and taking care of Uncle Pete. He'll be gone tomorrow, by the way."

"Making room for me."

"Yes, come to think of it."

. . . (Little Jazz) played "Cherry."

After the rehearsal and supper, Mike took me home. Phoebe and I lived in a very small apartment in the East 50s, just the two bedrooms, and the living room between and kitchenette. I asked Mike if he would like to come in (of course he would!). We had to sit in my bedroom, because there was nowhere comfortable to sit in the kitchen. This was the reason I had never had Scott Helmreich come in, except for coffee and when Phoebe was home. I felt asking a man into my bedroom would be misunderstood by Scott. However, Mike was more of a free spirit, and would understand that nothing suggestive was meant by my invitation.

As you know, since you inherited this weakness, my eyes are not strong and in fact I would always have to limit the time I could spend under lights during photo sessions, so while we were sitting on the bed I explained to Mike about my sensitivity and asked if he minded turning out the light, which he did. That is, he did not mind, but he did turn out the light as requested, but what I want to make clear anyway is that it was an accident and no fault of ours if things got a little "hot and heavy" between us on that very first occasion. After he left pretty abruptly though, and I had a chance to "calm down," I realized that I was very grateful for his self-control. But nevertheless, it seemed to be a little too late for us to stop seeing one another by then.

I phoned Scott at Princeton next day and pointed out that I was going to be very busy at the store, as well as my photographic modeling career starting to pick up just then, and I spent every night that week at the warehouse, with Mike rehearsing, and after, until Thursday when they had a job. It was a negro party in Harlem which I attended, and I remember that when I was trying to decide whether to go I had a ridiculous idea that Mike might be temporarily attracted to some "high yellow" girl at such a party, and silly though I was being, couldn't stay away.

I did go on seeing Scott that fall, now and then, which Mike said was all right (but Mike was not so all right with Scott), and one day when I was hurrying to get ready for an appointment, Scott called up and wanted to come to the city and go out, and I said I was busy.

"The trumpet player?" Scott asked.

"Cornet."

"I talked to Phoebe about it. Your friend doesn't think it's very wise, either."

"Roommate," I said.

"I think you'd better straighten up, Livia," Scott said. "You're flying up-side down."

"Mike has asked me to marry him," I said. This was more or less true.

The exact truth was that I had told Mike I wanted to break off unless he was serious. *The physical strain between us was causing me sleepless nights after he would leave, and the idea of "beauty sleep" is real when you are in the modeling profession, which Mike called "the snooty cutie business." To show he was serious, I said, Mike would have to settle down, choose a regular profession, keep regular hours and have regular friends. He saw that I was right, but I'm afraid he wasn't yet working very hard at job hunting, but Dad (my father) would have taken Mike into business (merchandising and display).*

"Why don't you go off somewhere for a weekend with him, and get it out of your system?" Phoebe thought Mike was funny and attractive but high-strung, and that if I was the cause of his leaving his music, it would bring trouble later. She also thought Scott Helmreich would get quite rich (she was right).

"Is love something you get out of your system over a weekend?"

Phoebe had just had her first complete relationship with a man (Jon Sims from Yale). It hadn't gone on afterwards because the completing part was a disappointment. Phoebe said she had a better time most mornings brushing her teeth. She said, "Frankly, I got more excited when the doctor removed my wart."

"That's just it," I said. "I don't get excited with Scott the way I do with Mike. He's going to give up all that rehearsing and just play sometimes for fun, and jobs on the weekends. Really. He says he isn't good enough to spend his life in music."

"Do you think he'll be so much better at newspaper work?"

"I think he'll be wonderful," I said. Mike was having interviews at the Herald Tribune, *which was a fine newspaper. It was the one Dad (my father) liked to read, because the* Times *was "pinko." It was my dream for Mike that when he had some experience, he could work for* Time *magazine or even* Life!

Anyway, your father did get into that kind of work, first with the Associated Press, and then went to the Herald Tribune. *Well. At the end of his first day there, he was waiting on the street at the employees' entrance to Bonwit's when*

*I came out. He was standing against the wall so I wouldn't see him right away.
I was tired that evening and decided to take a taxi home. I flagged one down
and was getting into it, and realized there was someone just behind me, holding
the door so I couldn't close it, saying, "Just a minute, Miss Scaliger. Two more
questions, please."*

*He tried to say it in a high, squeaky, unnatural voice, but of course I knew
it was Mike and I hugged him so hard. Then he put me into the cab, got in
and closed the door, and said "Village Vanguard" to the driver. His friend Red
was playing piano at the Vanguard.*

*As the cab started, he got out his notebook and a pencil, and I said to stop
being silly, because I wanted him to hug and kiss me, not play being a reporter.
But he said, "No kiss until you answer two questions."*

*But I kissed him anyway, all over the cheek, and snuggled up against him,
because I knew what the first question was going to be.*

"Livia Dunbar Scaliger," he said. "Are you dumb enough to marry me?"

*Oh, I kissed and kissed him, and said, "Oh yes, Mike, yes, Mike," and he
said, "Hey. Let's do it soon. Do you think this cabdriver could marry us?"*

"Is that the other question?" I was so happy.

*"No, Livia Dunbar," he said, putting both arms around me. "The other
thing I need to know is, where was Phoebe's wart?"*

Charles, I am crying now, and will have to stop writing until tomorrow.

*This is tomorrow (if you know what I mean). Next, I want to tell you
about the wedding . . .*

"Hello?"

"Darling . . . "

"Hi, Cherry."

"Am I disturbing you?"

"Of course not. I'm still reading mother's letter."

"I'm so excited. I've asked for reassignment stateside, and I think I'll
get it."

"In the Washington office?"

"That's what I've asked for."

"Wouldn't that be great?"

"It's a dream."

"Want to say hello to Uncle Pete?"

"Do it for me. I've got to run."

"Just as well. He's resting up for the TV thing."

"I know you'll both be splendid. Put in a good word for Petrolat. We're being made to look like villains as far as Ned's death goes."

"Ned was his own villain, poor old guy."

"Aren't we all? Bye darling."

"Bye."

. . . about the wedding. It was June 21, 1947. Mike and I both wanted it sooner, but Dad, my father, asked us to wait. He didn't trust Mike, and thought I might decide to break the engagement, as he said if I wanted a big wedding (as every girl does), he'd pay for it in June but no sooner. And he wanted to be sure that Mike was settled in his new job at the Herald Tribune *(which he wasn't, really, because not too long after the wedding Mike left and went to the* World Telegram *to work for Mr. Johnson.)*

Frankly, there was a difficulty about the negroes, which will sound very old-fashioned, but Dad, my father, was an old-fashioned man. He was quite artistic in his business, which was merchandising and display, where he designed sometimes and was consulted by many outstanding firms. He was also a sportsman, and an excellent sailor, and belonged to a number of clubs in New York, and was then in the prime of life, which was forty-one, although I'm sorry to say that he drank too much, as do many men from Dartmouth. Also, he had been a commander in the navy in the war under "Bull" Halsey, and was on the battleship New Jersey *in the Battle of Leyte Gulf, and invalided out because of damage to his ears from gunfire to return to his business in 1944 (which my grandfather came out of retirement to manage on a "caretaker" basis, while Dad, my father, was on active duty). My father was an outstanding man, but he didn't think it was suitable to have the wedding in Bronxville if Mike's guests were to include the negroes. But Mike said, "Some of my best men are negroes," and he meant Scholay. I got to like Scholay, I really did, but I'd been hoping Mike would have one of his brothers be best man.*

What happened was that Dad, my father, had designing and painting firms who were subcontractors for his business go in and decorate the loft on the Lower East Side where the band rehearsed. This was for the reception, after the cathedral, and was breathtaking, all green and white with lovely lighting and masses of pink and white flowers, as if we were in a tent in a lovely big garden, with the sides rolled up. Phoebe said it made her feel "onstage" (she was maid of honor), and actually she and Scholay looked wonderful together. The people at my wedding were so beautiful, Charles! Most of my bridesmaids were models, and their escorts from advertising and magazines and photographers from the fashion world and men from Princeton and Yale. There were also friends of Mike's he'd made while living and playing in Greenwich Village, and there

*were many negroes beautifully dressed, and newspaper people and musicians—
so many musicians, and they all took turns playing for us, and we were all over
the society pages on Sunday. There were over two hundred people.*

*It was a rosy time in 1947. Everybody was through with the war and young,
and starting magazines and businesses and theaters, and getting educated and
getting married. Oh, it was fine. I don't quite know how to say it. We felt so
strong then, and went to parties, and talked about everything, and ran everywhere, and photographers followed us, and New York was ours!*

*The only people who were not at the wedding were the parents of the groom.
Mike's mother was a librarian (did you know that?) who had gone to Paraguay
to serve her country, and his father was also serving the country, being in the
regular navy and stationed in the Philippines. But the brothers of the groom
were certainly there, and you have to understand that Dad idolized me, and
drank too much and struck up this great friendship with Ned Mizzourin. They
simply found each other.*

*It was after most of the older people from Bronxville and older business
friends and club friends had left, and the musicians were playing madly and
calling for Mike to come up and play with them. So we went up, and he played
with his left arm around me, so that I had to hold up his horn (cornet) for him,
with my head leaned back against his shoulder and laughing. Then Ned came
up and wanted the horn, and was trying to play a high school band marching
song, and the real musicians were laughing and helping him play it, and Dad,
my father, started dancing to it and he had a silver-painted wooden chair for his
partner. Ned got a chair then, and they two were dancing all around with their
chairs. Then they'd sit together, each with his own bottle of champagne, drinking out of it like it was a bottle of beer, and Dad, my father, yelling for Tom
Dewey to be President, and Ned yelling for Senator Robert Taft of Ohio, and
then they'd pretend they were going to fight about it, and had this kind of duel
with the silver chairs until they broke them, and Mike's other brother Pete was
sitting there grinning, the way all the Mizzourins did, but Pete had something
really to grin about because Phoebe was sitting on his lap!*

*It wasn't until the end, and luckily all the society reporters were gone, that
it got so violent. Ned and Dad, my father, took over the microphone, and before
Scholay managed to unplug it, they were saying a lot of wild things about the
war being over and veterans freeloading on the taxpayer, and Dad, my father,
said his daughter was marrying the wrong Mizzourin boy, marrying the biggest
freeloader of them all, the government paying for his music training and newspaper training, and Ned grabbed the microphone and said, "If he wants to be a
plumber next, they'll by God pay for his toilet training." And Mike was going
to go after Ned, but then Scholay got us out of there before any fight really*

started, and I heard that Ned said Dad, my father, couldn't talk about his stupid brother that way, and Pete separated them. Then everybody started smashing up the silver chairs, and the music got louder and louder, and we got away in a friend's car to our beautiful honeymoon at Saratoga Springs. But when we got back, everybody was claiming they had been at the reception, it was a famous party, and sometimes we'd meet someone who'd brought away a leg of a silver chair as a souvenir. Scott Helmreich had one.

We were so much in love. We had so many friends. We went out night after night, all summer, but in the fall we had to think about success, and just go out on weekends. Mike started working for Mr. Johnson, on the World-Telegram, *and was able to feel professional, though he was not well-paid. I earned much more than he did. I was reaching the peak of my modeling career. I was on five magazine covers in 1947!*

I was screen-tested several times, but was really too busy to find time for voice training. I was often recognized, and Mike and I were a much-talked-about young couple. It was wonderful, the first year.

Of course there were little temperamental things we fought about. Mike couldn't sit still. He was always early up and late to bed, working away at something, going to the practice room with his cornet, seeing people, writing things, reading, listening to his records with earphones. I liked it when he'd slow down a little and just love me.

Phoebe's wedding present was to move out of the apartment, which was a big thing in the time of shortages. With her gone, I had two closets, almost enough room for my clothes, but Mike objected because I still had some things neatly folded and on top of the dresser, and some but not all the chairs.

Mike had very few clothes, but he had records, my God, and bought more every payday, and books. Paperbacks. Once he got a hundred-dollar reward for information leading to the arrest of a man in a robbery Mike eyewitnessed when he was writing a series about pawnshops. He didn't want to take it, because of being a newspaperman in the line of work, but Mr. Johnson (Mike was working for the World-Telegram *by then) said he should. He spent every cent of it on books and records, except he did take me out to dinner with some of it. Well, I was mad. We had so many bills. Mike said yes, but they were for French drycleaning and Swedish hairdressing and Italian makeup, so if the United Nations wouldn't pay, then my modeling income ought to. I was generous with my money, but felt Mike should support us. That was a big fight.*

I couldn't understand why Mike was always buying bebop records, since he didn't like bebop, but sometimes when he'd practice with his mute in in the bathroom and a towel stuffed under the door crack, it sounded like bebop. And when we did what he liked best weekends, which was "sit in" with musicians and "jam," he could play pretty much the way the others did, I thought, but he didn't.

"I lose fourteen days a week," he said. "It takes me two years to change as much as the music does in one. But you know what, Weaver?" He often called me that. "Now that I'm an amateur again, I love it all the more."

"You'd better be an amateur about me too, then," I said.

His relations with Mr. Johnson at that time were very strange. John McRae was always critical of anything Mike wrote or did, but he always wanted to be with Mike, too. He and Christine often went out with us, as an older couple and a younger one sometimes do. They were ten years older. We'd see movies together. (John McRae used to fuss about it, but he got free movie tickets through the newspaper reviewer, and sometimes theater tickets if a play wasn't doing too well.) Then, because he'd got the tickets, he'd expect us to pay for drinks and supper after. So often, because we couldn't afford it any other way, we would invite them to our apartment, stopping at the deli for bread and cheese and beer or wine. Sometimes John McRae would buy a bottle of California brandy, but when he did, he didn't really like it if someone else wanted a drink of the brandy. (Except me, for he was soft on me, but I seldom drank anything but seltzer. Mike wasn't a real drinker, either. He could tuck away the deli food, though, and never gain an ounce. How I envied him!) We had some very good times as two couples.

Mike used to say, "You flirted outrageously with poor Johnson."

"I did not."

"Maybe not outrageous this time. Just preposterous."

"What about you and Christine?"

"Think I have eyes for Christine?"

"She does for you."

"Maternal eyes, Weaver. She wants to protect me from a cruel world that might be out there somewhere, making young reporters cynical. She doesn't know what a sugarcoated life I live."

I'd soften up when he said something like that. And I think Christine's softness for Mike was really like he said, but Mr. Johnson's feelings about me weren't at all fatherly. He was a very lustful man but I didn't mind because I knew Mike could trust me, and John McRae could be a lot of fun and even get pretty wild when he had his brandy to drink and forgot to be a skinflint. Once he took us all to a Russian place for caviar, because I said I loved it so. (You should have seen your father gobble it up. It was the first time he'd ever had it.) That night, John McRae drank so much vodka he was stopped for drunk driving. He wouldn't let Christine drive because he thought she was bad at it, but when the police learned who he was, one of them got out of the patrol car and drove the Johnsons home.

There came the time when the little band with Sutton, Red and Scholay and the others broke up. It was sad for Mike. He'd kept on being friends with them, sometimes sitting in, although after Mike left, then Aldo, the other white musician left, and there was a negro saxophone player named Sonny and they didn't have trumpet or cornet, but instead a trombone and another saxophone and no whites. Anyway, it broke up. We went to hear them their last night, last job, with the Johnsons. It was at the Village Vanguard, our special place. They asked Mike to play with them for many numbers, and I'll admit they sounded wonderful together that night.

John McRae Johnson was being quite funny about the music, which made Mike grin these sad grins, because John wasn't sensitive to the way the musicians felt about this being their last time.

Anyway, we four and Scholay were sitting at our table between sets, and John McRae was saying something like: "Whatever happened to Sigmund Romberg? Victor Herbert? How about Jeanette MacDonald and Nelson Eddy? Ever play this new guy, George M. Cohan? Scholay, I'll give you ten bucks for the band to play a Strauss waltz."

"We've been trying three-four blues, believe it or not," Scholay said, and then this funny expression came over his face. He was looking past Mike. He said: "Hello, true beauty."

And I looked, and this thin, very striking young girl was behind Mike, and put her hand on his shoulder, and said, " 'lo, Mike." That was the first time I ever saw Evaun Barlow, and there was the most beautiful, thin boy standing behind her with a guitar case, and that was E. B. Jones.

My first thought as soon as I looked at Evaun Barlow was that she could go right to work in my profession, she had her own strange, orphan beauty that some photographers could make you smile and cry to see. She had a cheap look, too, in the flesh, but the photographers could change that into something like stray-kitten prettiness, or playing or wistful, with the lights and makeup.

Then I saw Mike, my husband's, face. It was like he saw his own ghost.

He took her hand off his shoulder and held it, and reached for the other hand, and sort of pulled her around to look at her. "Rhymes with faun," he said. "And gone in the dawn. Beaver-Weaver, these are my friends from Faraday. Evaun, this is Livia. We're married."

"I heered," she said, and took her hands loose.

Well, I'd heard him talk about the twins a little, but not so I knew all she

might have been to him. Scholay and Mike and John stood up, and the John-
sons were introduced, and Christine couldn't take her eyes off the twins. Some
chairs were moved, and I said "Hello," but Christine said, "Oh, my dears."

And Mike hugged E.B. before he sat down, and E.B. said, "We folksing
now, Mike."

"All that Greensleevey kinda stuff," Evaun said.

"You don't like doing it?"

"It's purty."

Her accent was so thick I always thought she faked it. Scholay said, "When
Jim was sick, Mike, a couple weeks ago, we auditioned some one-night guitars,
and this boy tried out, his sister with him. I knew them right away, but I
haven't seen you to say."

"I can't play with'm at all," E. B. Jones said. "Mike, don't they sure sound
good? Now that's what Doctor Wanderbaum was getting at. I finally heard it
live."

I was watching how Mike said, "You like it?" Evaun couldn't take her eyes
off Mike.

"Learning to. But I can't play it either now."

"Nor me."

"You newspaper reporter now?"

"Learning that, too. From Mr. Johnson. Hey, did you ever hear what happened to the Doctor and Johnny? Sometimes I wake up at night worrying about
those tramps."

"Needn't to, Mike," E.B. said, kind of crowing. "They got clean away."
His face was all lighted up and I suddenly knew his kind of beauty wouldn't
probably photograph after all, or hers. It was like they had light inside them,
and the studio lights would wash it out. "Hey, they done took out in that green
sedan? Time Gatch and Muley had their jeep going, them rascals had a fifteen
minutes lead, way I figured. And now Captain Garris, remember?"

"Sure," Mike said.

"This here's the funny part. Captain Garris said that military jeep, it had
a governor, wouldn't go over fifty mile an hour. So Gatch and Muley couldn't
get nothing but hinder. Doctor and Johnny dumped off that sedan in Pindar and
stoled a Packard car, least it was probably them, and dumped that Packard in
Raleigh, and plain disappeared."

Mike hesitated, and then said: "Well. Did Marvin bring you up here, folk-
singing?"

Evaun shook her head. "Something caught Marvin by the throat, Mike."

"Had an operation for it," E.B. said. "He's got no voice left to talk. Just
kinda whispers. Can't get his breath to play the horn."

"I'm sorry," Mike said. "About the horn." And told the rest of us. "Marvin was my teacher."

"Marvin told our Mamma she'd gotta move in with him now. He's an invalid, needs nursing. Now, he wanted me and Evaun to run the store, you know? But we didn't say yes, didn't say no. Just packed up and come on here."

"I'm surprised you were able to get on the bus."

"Well," Evaun said.

"Marvin did kinda have the ticket seller. Well, he wouldn't have sold us . . . Aw, Mike. You know Evaun could always get old Skinny do anything she said. He took out at night, drove us all the way to Winston-Salem."

Mike nodded and didn't say anything for a moment. Then he said, "You're working?"

"Two blocks down. That Tenth Street coffee house? What I gotta do is play guitar fer anybody wants to sing, every key they is. But mostly now, they wanta hear Evaun."

"I want to hear Evaun," Mike said.

Then Christine Johnson said: "Oh, so do I. So do I."

Charles dear: This is all I can write. I have been crying so much that Scott forbids me to go on, and he's right. He's also very angry at what I said about him earlier, which I didn't mean for him to read. He said: "Livia, get that damn thing out of the house. Send it to Charlie with a great big period. THE END!" I hope you're satisfied to know about your father now.

Love,
Mother

Cavendish Show, 5.2.80. Transcript (edited).

Cavendish: . . . a release and rescue for which the world is grateful, but which left a dead American behind and a number of questions unanswered. Here are two men who can answer them if anyone can: Peter Mizzourin, the Petrolat engineer who suffered three months of captivity. Good evening Peter.

P. Mizzourin: You want me to say something?

Cavendish: I'll have some questions for you after I've introduced your nephew, Charles, who, in this world of electronics and satellites and spy planes, effected his part of the mission on a simple bicycle. Let's start with you, Peter. Your family has been in the news a lot recently, starting with your brother's arrival abroad. How do you feel about it?

P. Mizzourin: Not so good.

Cavendish: How were you treated in the terrorist camp?

P. Mizzourin: No, they had a house. The Young Men. They were okay.

Cavendish: You look like a man who's lost a lot of weight. Was there enough to eat?

P. Mizzourin: The boys didn't have a lot. They shared what they had. They made these grape leaf dolmas, you know? They were good.

Cavendish: And when you were transferred to the Syrian jail?

P. Mizzourin: No more dolmas.

Cavendish: The mystery, of course, is about your brother Edward's death in the Syrian prison. Can we talk about that?

P. Mizzourin: I'd rather not.

Cavendish: I understand. Perhaps I ought to address that question to your nephew. Charlie, can you throw some light on the circumstances of your Uncle Ned's death?

C. Mizzourin: All I know is what Uncle Pete tells me.

Cavendish: And what does he tell you?

C. Mizzourin: Things he just declined to tell you, Mr. Cavendish.

Cavendish: Look here, now. There are rumors you gentlemen may not be aware of. It's rumored that Petrolat, Peter Mizzourin's company, acted independently of the State Department. If efforts had been better coordinated, might not Edward Mizzourin's tragic death have been avoided?

C. Mizzourin: No.

Cavendish: But what about the propriety of a multinational company taking a matter like this into its own hands? Peter, do you feel that your company acted prudently, properly, and in your own best interest, as well as the national interest?

C. Mizzourin: I'll take it, Uncle Pete. Mr. Cavendish, Petrolat acted properly. The State Department acted properly. Neither agency was at fault for what went wrong. I'll say this much: my Uncle Ned may have been at fault, but I wouldn't care to expand on that.

P. Mizzourin: I might have been at fault, too, if that's what you want to know. I guess I was.

C. Mizzourin: Feet of clay, Mr. Cavendish. We've got 'em.

Cavendish: But if Petrolat had been a little more patient, might not Edward Mizzourin be here to celebrate his freedom with us tonight?

P. Mizzourin: I don't see how.

C. Mizzourin: Not from what Pete tells me, anyway.

Cavendish: But if you and your uncle won't tell the rest of us what happened in that grim, cold jail in Syria . . .

P. Mizzourin: Should I tell it, Charlie, and get this over with?

C. Mizzourin: I think we've given him enough.

Cavendish: How so? Why are you protecting your company, Peter?

P. Mizzourin: You think that's what I'm doing?

Cavendish: Why is your uncle protecting his company, Charlie?

C. Mizzourin: He's not. It's a family matter. Those feet of clay, they're all ours.

Cavendish: It is not a family matter, sir. It is a very highly public matter. Just one minute ago your uncle was ready to discuss it. Charles, why are you preventing him? Why?

C. Mizzourin: My uncle is a very tired man. He made that offer only because he'd like to get out of here. So would I.

Cavendish: All right, Charles. You work for Congressman David Esterzee, who, like every other member of the House, is running for reelection. Iowa sources say Ned Mizzourin would have run strongly against Representative Esterzee. How does your congressman feel about his rival's removal from the race?

C. Mizzourin: He feels pretty damn bad about it.

Cavendish: But certainly he will benefit?

C. Mizzourin: Where do you think we are? Chile?

P. Mizzourin: Don't get hot, Charlie. He's all right.

C. Mizzourin: Sure he is. Deep-dish Cavendish.

P. Mizzourin: He's a real thinker.

C. Mizzourin: Hell of a prober, too.

Cavendish: Can we get back to the subject, please?

C. Mizzourin: Sure. Deke Esterzee admired Ned Mizzourin's energy and toughness. Deke's a fighter. He was looking forward to a vigorous campaign.

Cavendish: Let's get back to Petrolat. Peter, how long have you been with the company?

P. Mizzourin: Sixteen years.

Cavendish: The company's been good to you?

P. Mizzourin: I'm still with 'em.

Cavendish: You have no complaints, other than the way they handled your late brother's entrance into Syria?

P. Mizzourin: Did I say that, Charlie?

C. Mizzourin: No, Uncle Pete. You sure didn't say anything like that.

Cavendish: If there's nothing to hide, why can't he answer my question? Is there something to hide, Peter?

P. Mizzourin: No. Just things I'm not about to tell you.

Cavendish: Things you haven't told the authorities? Things you haven't
  even told your company!

P. Mizzourin: What . . . ?

C. Mizzourin: Hold it, Uncle Pete. Are you enjoying this?

P. Mizzourin: Oh, golly, Charlie . . .

Cavendish: Sit down, Charles.

C. Mizzourin: Why? Maybe my ass is tired of sitting down . . .

Cavendish: May I remind you that we're on the air?

C. Mizzourin: No we're not. You're on the air, Ace. Come on, Uncle
  Pete.

P. Mizzourin: Can we go?

C. Mizzourin: Sure we can. Sure we can.

(SHOUTING. CONFUSION. BLACKOUT. COMMERCIAL.)

By messenger.

*Darling: what a hectic morning we had. I'll always remember it as "no lunch
and a peck on the cheek." I'm glad I was able to help with the wretched telephone while you were outside trying to talk to all the reporters. Incidentally,
be careful about going out. At least two of the calls I handled were threats,
probably cranks, but you must be careful. I've just learned that I'm to go back
to Newport News again, so I won't be there with you tonight. I'm not sure
you should stay there either. I did get a chance to look around your rooms. I'm
sorry you feel we must leave them, but in many ways I'd prefer a more modern
apartment in Maryland or Virginia. I called your landlady to give notice. Spoke
to a woman with a British accent who seemed tearful about it, but it can't be all
that hard to find tenants. This is the kind of thing we haven't had a chance to
discuss, but perhaps you'll want to give it a few minutes thought. I believe we
should each buy a car. I'll certainly need one, and I don't think it's safe for you
to bike to work from as far out as Virginia or Maryland. Petrolat can get very
good deals on Datsuns (corporate linkage). Even though I'm to be in Newport
News tonight, the company has got me a room at the Mayflower. Stop for an
hour. (Cocktail hour, 5 P.M. My helicopter's at 6:30.) Use the room tonight
if you want. Love, Cherry.*

"Hello?"

"Hello, Charles. Are you all right, dear?"

"Yes, Mother. I'm fine."

"You were wonderful on television."

"Damn right, kid. This is Scott on the extension. You socked it to 'em."

"All dried out, Scott? It's good to hear from you again."

"I mean you put the silver quarter right in their jukebox, fella, and pushed A29."

"Excuse me?"

"Fried their crumpets and buttered their buns."

"Scott!"

"Yes, Scott. I see what you mean."

"Wish you were here so we could have a pull off the old jug together."

"Scott, while I have you and Mother both . . ."

"Yes, dear?"

"Mother. You broke off the story you were writing. I wish you hadn't."

"I'm sorry, Charles."

"Whoa. Going the wrong way on a one-way street, fella."

"I'd really like to know the rest."

"Running every stop sign in town."

"Please, Charles. I put all that behind me once. I shouldn't have brought it out again."

"Scott. Could you take my side in this?"

"Citizen's arrest, fella. You're out of control."

"I'm sorry, dear."

"All right. Mrs. Johnson phoned, too."

"Christine?"

"I've talked with her a lot this spring. Just now, she sounded quite odd about your letter. I'd sent her a Xerox."

"Oh, Charles. Did you really?"

"Do you mind?"

"No. Not very much."

"I thought the way you spoke of her was nice, but she didn't seem to agree. She kept saying I really musn't trust my mother's memory about herself and John. That it was very long ago, and you were quite confused—"

"That's enough, Charles."

"All right. She's confused, too. Mr. Johnson's missing."

"Missing? John McRae?"

"He disappeared a couple of weeks ago. Just before I went to Tur-

key. He's done it before, so he's probably all right. But he's also probably destroyed whatever was left of Dad's Fake Book writing."

"Good thing, too, Charlie. You open the door of that oven again,
the whole souffle's going to fall."

"Charles . . ."

"You've got to learn to stop putting sweet vermouth in your martini
sometime."

"Charles, I can't. I can't. Oh, talk to Scott."

"Scott?"

"Bet your tweeter's ringing its nuts off, Knucks. We'll let you toast
your marshmallows. Brown outside, runny inside . . ."

"Scott, why is mother still so emotional about something that happened thirty years ago?"

"Well . . ."

"Why, Scott?"

"That question's been a feature of my hangovers for years, Knucks,
like red eyes and a puffy head. I can't say the answer's a great big aspirin
tablet either. The way I read it, Livia married Mike because she loved
the guy, but she was marrying down, wasn't she? Sacrificing. Then
things started happening. Mike got on a year-long roll on his job. He
wrote a series about the waterfront. He knew his stuff, because he'd
worked there, and you learned about the racketeering part, but he made
it colorful and funny, too. Then those interviews with Truman. You
could tell the President liked him. Suddenly he was Johnson's pet and
getting fat assignments. The man had plans for Mike. A column. Low
life, high life, gypsies, kings—people talked about Mike's stuff, and
now Livia wasn't the only celebrity at their house. They were rolling
together, toward something it hadn't crossed her mind to dream about
before. I don't know what the hell the phrase is for it this year—then it
was Café Society, and then the Beautiful People, the Jet Set—film fes-
tivals, Paris openings, the Pope's ring, riverboating up the Blue Nile.
Livia started wanting that, and it was coming her way. And then it
wasn't. She was betrayed. Deserted. A widow with a babe in arms.
Nothing left but life with poor old Scott."

"Good old Scott."

"Thank you, Lucky Knuckles."

"Deke Esterzee's office. Darlene is here to help you."

"Hi, Darlene. You sound cheerful."

"Pure chuckleball, dear, what with handling all your women for you."

"Tell me about it."

"Note by messenger from Roxie. Cherry breezed in and out."

"You approve?"

"Cherry's all right if you like good looks, poise and brains."

"I guess I do. Did Pete get off?"

"Yep."

"May I speak to Deke?"

"Deke, Charlie on one."

"Hey, bo."

"Hey, Deke. I've got to get out of this apartment for twenty-four hours."

"I know. Phone ringing. Ree-porters knocking at the redoubt. Wish it were mine."

"Can I crash at your place tonight?"

"Sure, bo. We'll do some drinking and some talking."

"I'll put a couple of things in the backpack and jump on my bike. See you there at the office."

"Okay. Want to bring Cherry over tonight? Spare room's mighty spare."

"She'll be out of town."

"When do you get to cuddle up?"

"We have an appointment for that. Five-thirty, I think, at the May-flower. I'm waiting for her to call and confirm—then I'll be on my way."

"Hello, just a second. Cherry?"

"No, I haven't been cherry for years. That Charlie Mizzourin?"

"Yes."

"Well, all right. All right."

"Look, sir. I'm just on my way out. But can I help you?"

"If I need help, I'll sure let you know. You need any?"

"Thanks. I'm okay, sir."

"Do you know who this is?"

"No. I don't."

"Scholay Gopeters. Remember meeting in—"

"Scholay!"

"Read about you, watched you, heard you. Mike would have been that proud."

"Thank you, Scholay. I've tried hard to find you."

"And me you. Never guessed you'd land in politics."

"I'm not, really. Just somebody's aide."

"Aid and comfort? How's your mom?"

"She's fine. Scholay."

"Good. That's nice. Tell her I miss the parties she and Mike used to give. Best parties in New York. I'm divorced a couple of times, but that's my fault."

"Where are you calling from?"

"Chicago. I'm in a band that works steady. Nightclub work. Look, you wanted to ask me about your dad that time."

"I still do. Let me call you back?"

"No, sir. If your dad was calling up my boy Kit, you think Little Mike would ever let Kit pay? Would he?"

"Sorry."

"What do you want to know, Charlie?"

"I want to know how Mike Mizzourin died."

"Automobile accident. I think with a lady named Mrs. Johnson driving."

"Christine Johnson?"

"Yes. She might have died, too. I never heard any details."

"Christine Johnson."

"You so surprised?"

"I wonder why I didn't think of it. She's still alive, Scholay."

"That's good, I guess. What else? Do you know anything?"

"You knew Evaun Barlow and Binkie Jones?"

"Sure. I'd seen him once, in Carolina. Unforgettable. Then the twins came to New York. Sang folk around the coffee houses. She was a pretty thing. Pretty singer. A lot of men were crazy for her. She favored Mike."

"Did she die, too?"

"I never heard, never knew. Couldn't find out, or maybe I was too sad to try. I haven't heard her name around in music, not for years. She and her brother made one record. I've got it. Never throw a record away. It's a 78. Want me to send it to you?"

"You bet. Or could you tape it for me?"

"Charlie, I never play it. More a souvenir than a record to me. I'd like real well for you to have it."

"I'd like it, too. Real well. Scholay, according to a letter from my mother, you'd seen Evaun and E.B. in New York before my father met them again, or knew they were there."

"That's right. One day our band had an audition call out for guitar. We had a piano player then called Red, and Red had a gay streak in him. You mind my telling that?"

"A lot of people have that streak."

"There were people coming in and out to audition. Suddenly Red grabs my shoulder and said, 'Look there. One for you and one for me.' It was the twins. I knew exactly who they were. The boy played for us then; not too shabby, either, though we couldn't use him. I took them out for coffee, knowing they'd been good to Mike. I got her one-night singing jobs with dance bands, but folk was what was right for her. She'd sing it straight and high, little jazz intonation in her styling but kept right to the song. And he was perfect with her, too. You'll hear."

"I can't tell you how I'm looking forward to it."

"She wanted to know where Mike was, and I told her Mike was married. She wanted me to find out if Mike wanted to see her, and I meant to do it too. But it was a frantic time in New York, everybody coming, everybody going, a real scene and right away the twins were part of it. I'd seen them here and there, mostly in the gay bars, where E.B. had a lot more fellas than his sister. Fact, if she had any, I didn't know it, not that they weren't after her. But once she and Mike met again, they couldn't stay away from each other. About ten days after, Mike told Livia. He moved out, or she moved him. I don't know. They didn't have one of these things they call an open marriage, or swing, or anything like that. Mike wasn't that way, and I won't say she was. But they were modern. She'd see a man for lunch, business of course, and never try to hide it. It was business just for her to be seen in places, places Mike didn't care that much about and couldn't afford, and what used to piss him mostly was she wouldn't eat the lunch some man had paid for.

" 'Hey, twenty dollars for a glass of water?'

"But about Evaun. Mike stayed with me a while, after he left Livia, and saw the girl most every night. Go where she was working, if she worked. Bring her around to where we were playing when she was off, or to the gay bars where E.B. was having a whirl. He was getting famous, E. B. Jones. Like a big wild beauty around town might have a reputation in some circles, E.B. was known in his, and to be seen with the boy would make a fagman proud, I heard.

"What I heard, Mike's boss, Mr. Johnson, had a cutie of his own he saw two nights a week. Those nights, sometimes your friend Christine might go out along with Mike. She doted on the twins. Sometimes it was like they were her own kids. Other times, if they came in where we were playing, it seemed a little freaky, like she loved them different from a mother, but that was just the feeling I'd get.

"Mike went back to Livia when it turned out she was pregnant with you. She was almost four months gone before she'd admit to herself that it was probably so and get checked up. She hated being pregnant because of what she feared about her figure, and she was hateful to Mike. He said he didn't blame her, and he quit seeing Evaun, but they'd talk on the telephone. In the summer, the twins went out on the resort circuit. In the autumn, you were born. You spent a lot of time with your grandparents in Bronxville and a nurse. Your granddad wasn't well, and wasn't making so much money as before. Mike and Livia needed money, too, because she hadn't worked in a while. They were together in public, but a lot of nights Mike would come up to the loft and stay with me. The twins were back in town.

"He still didn't see Evaun, though. Those were the days when Christine took the twins out, certain nights, and paid the tab. E.B. was more popular than ever. Groups knew they could get bookings if they'd hire and feature him in certain bars, and he worked solo plenty, too. Seemed like she didn't much. Music's a small world. You hear those things.

"Mr. Johnson, on the paper, didn't like the way things were going, heard rumors about his wife, didn't want to give up his other lady, either. Took it out on Mike, riding him all the time, giving him shit assignments. Those last few weeks before it all went crazy, but I never knew just how, Mike was putting in his hours for the paycheck, would have got another job if he could have found it. But he couldn't, couldn't get along with Livia. All he had, really, was his horn. When he wasn't working, or making an appearance with his wife, then all he wanted was to play. Not with the band, even. Sit in the loft, playing and playing by himself."

"Was he good, Scholay?"

"I can't say that. He might have been. He was catching up. I heard him play some wonderful things those last weeks, and I heard him screw up plenty, too. The way you do when you're working by yourself, and trying. But when it was right—no, I'm too prejudiced. But I think it was really right, once or twice."

"I don't guess there's any recording of that, is there, Scholay?"

"Wish I'd done it. He bought himself a flugelhorn, there at the end, and he could make it wail, but he'd stop when he heard me coming in. Listen, Charlie. I've just got a few more minutes, but I'll put my address and phone in with Evaun Barlow's record. I'll send them today with my boy Kit, he flies freight for Emory through Washington. The record ought to get to you today."

"I'd like to meet him."

"Afraid he'll just be stopping to unload, and then on to Atlanta, but he can send it into town with someone."

"Scholay, I don't know how to thank you. When things quiet down, may I come out to Chicago to see you?"

"Like that better than anything. Don't guess it would be safe for you to stay with me, this part of town. This new, dumb world. Out of its damn, dumb mind. But we'll get us a hotel room, you and me, and go out for dinner. Get a bottle and go back and talk."

"As soon as I can, Scholay."

"You'll meet Kit. And Sutton, the bass player. We still work together, and he'll talk about Mike. He never thought too much about Mike's music, but he didn't hear it at the end."

"May I hear you and Sutton play?"

"All you want. And some of the songs Mike liked, too. 'My Old Flame.' 'The Song is You.' You know those tunes?"

"Only by name. I wouldn't recognize them, but I know a lot of names."

"Well, then, we'll play them for you one more time."

"Hello?"

"Hello, darling."

"Hi, Cherry."

"Listen, good news. I'm going to get the reassignment."

"Hey!"

"Isn't that great?"

"Yes."

"Well. What would you say to Seattle? That's where I'm needed. Because of the oil from Alaska."

"Oh. Cherry, I thought we were talking about D.C."

"Seattle's where I'm needed. Soon, too. As soon as my leave is over."

"Two weeks?"

"I thought we might run down to Florida for two weeks. Or the Caribbean. Now wait. I've saved a lot of money from overseas."

"I know you have."

"So the vacation's on me."

"Seattle, Cherry?"

"I've been working it out. You could go to the university, get a TA if you want and finish your PhD."

"I could."

"Or get a real job. Or do high school teaching? Anyway, we have two weeks to rest and plan it out."

"I don't exactly have a vacation coming."

"Deke will understand. If he doesn't, you can always quit, can't you? You must anyway if we're going to Seattle."

"Cherry, it's the wrong time for me to leave Deke. This is election year."

"Of course, but . . . Charles, is Deke so precious to you?"

"I don't love him more than I do you, if that's the question. But you met him this morning. He's quite a guy, isn't he?"

"He has a certain crude charm. He's a very good-looking man. But I think his foreign policy views very questionable."

"You have a long talk?"

"Long enough for him to give me a very thorough looking over."

"I'm sure he did."

"And someone called Darlene?"

"I'm sure she did, too."

"Do you really fit in so well in that office?"

"Seriously?"

"Of course not, darling. But it's not exactly a tight ship, is it? Look, it's all set for the Mayflower. I've ordered champagne. Sorry if I've come at you too fast with too many things."

"We have a lot to talk about."

"Isn't it exciting?"

My dear Charlie:

You shan't be bothered with me anymore, but wanted to say several things. I watched and cried and felt proud of you on the tellee. I thought you made a proper chump out of that Cavendish person, with his insinuation that your trip abroad was some kind of election-year ploy. That's one thing. Another is that some woman, a secretary it sounded, has phoned to say that you are giving up the flat. Suesue is away in Florida with Otis, playing bridge (and leaving Angela behind with me), and so I had to answer your secretary as best I could. It wasn't easy, because I had such dreams of you and me being together in those lovely rooms once, but well, done is done. Suesue, with whom I've had a talk just now, says you are not to be bothered with giving notice and such matters. Suesue saw you on the tellee, too, and like me was proud. This is what she would like you to know: When you and she first met, you see, she was having serious business dificulties with Otis and felt she might have to give him the glove. Therefore, she determined to learn the present circumstance and situation of her old paramour Johnson, the first man in her life, with whom her affair went off and on for so many years. She did not wish to correspond directly, and so, my dear, while Johnson was using you to get word of Suesue, his former lady was finding you equally useful in learning about Johnson. I don't know that she was pleased with what she learned, but has, in any case, got Otis back in hand now, through marrying him off to Angela (not at all what I should have wished for my dearest friend, but A. is far more practical than I, and says the arrangement suits her—particularly, I'm afraid, when her bridegroom is out of town playing bridge). Well, then. The message for you from Suesue is that all is forgiven, but that should you hear from Johnson, and although Suesue can't help being rather dear and sentimental about him, it would be best if you could discourage the old man from trying to get in touch, as I gather he has done. Think kindly of me, Charlie, won't you?

> *Ever,*
> *Roxie*

"Morning. Deke Esterzee speaking."

"Morning, Deke. Answering your own phone today?"

"Darlene's in the john. Bob's late. I'm early. You back at your house?"

"Just walked in, Deke. Thanks for your hospitality."

"Couple of crying drunks, weren't we? Playin' 'I Know My Love' and 'I Know Where I'm Goin' over and over on a scratchy record. And the whiskey comin' out our ears. You take the record with you?"

"Got it here, Deke."

"I want a copy. God, couldn't that little girl sing those songs?"

"Couldn't her brother play? Look, Deke. Reason I called. Something's wrong here."

"At your place?"

"Yes. Looks like the door's been forced. It won't lock properly."

"Anything missing?"

"No."

"It happened yesterday, but I just heard this morning."

"What?"

"Chester was in there working. Bunch of reporters waiting outside thought it was you. They kind of leaned against the door, and it kind of gave way."

"Chester was working on what in here?"

"Puttin' in some bugs. There's been a few threats, Charlie. We want to keep track. Chester's either listening to us or recording us right now."

"Chester, if you're listening, get the hell off the phone. If you're recording, here's a message. Come get the damn bugs out of here. Deke, you might have told me."

"Knew you wouldn't like it."

"Do you know where the bugs are?"

"Phone. Kitchen. Bedroom. Bathroom, probably . . ."

"You heard my message."

"Sorry, bo. I'll get after Chester. You call Cherry yet?"

"No. There's a note here from her."

DARLING: Welcome home. Phone soonest. Action on several matters. Petrolate required yes or no on Seattle. Have said affirmative. Petrolat, Seattle, will arrange job interviews for you. Need your CV soonest. Also: phoned Admissions at U. Wash. Probably no problem for you to resume PhD coursework, if you wish, but transcript required immediately.

Love,
Cherry.

Transcription from Brinnegar listening device:

"Who's there . . . dammit, I hear you in this closet. Who is it?"

"Open the door."

"Is that Chester, for God's sake?"

"Please."

"What'd you do, lock yourself in the damn closet trying to bug the joint?"

"Open it. Open it."

"Are you Chester?"

"Oooh . . ."

"I'm wedging a chair top under this door handle. Don't try to push. It's going to stay there till the cops come."

"Please. It's John Johnson."

"Who?"

"Johnson. Johnson."

"My God, Uncle John? Here, now. Here. Come out."

"Mike."

"Excuse me. Here, take my hand. Now come on, are you hurt? Come on, Uncle John."

"Mike. Thank you boy. It was—"

"It's not Mike, sir. It's Charlie."

". . . just a little joke. I was going to surprise you and locked myself . . . is Livia here?"

"My mother's in Connecticut. Please, come sit down. You look exhausted."

"The light's so bright."

"Come on. Lie down. Right here, and close your eyes."

"I brought the last three pages of your journal, Mike."

"Hold on, now. I want to get a washcloth."

"It's just three pages. Christine got the rest."

"Christine?"

"She pushed me in the study. Grabbed it all and ran to the fireplace. All I could get—"

"Christine tried to burn . . . never mind. Please. Rest. Tell me later."

"All I could get was just three pages from the top. Out of the fire. And then I ran out to the car. Oh, Mike. Looking for Suesue. Do you know where Suesue is?"

"Where is your car, sir?"

"Sleeping in my car. I can't find Suesue. Mike. New York has changed so much."

"We're in Washington, Uncle John. Let me wash your face. Come on . . . That's better . . . I'm going to take your shoes off. Let me put this blanket on you. Here's some water. Easy. Here."

"Ahhh. Thank you, Mike. Do you want a foreign assignment? You and Livia could go abroad. With the baby, and start—"

"Don't try to talk any more just now. Please rest."

"Haylo?"

"That must be Mrs. Harper. This is Charles Mizzourin. Is Mrs. Johnson there?"

"She's outdoors walkin', with the dog."

"Please tell her Mr. Johnson's here. He's safe."

"The dog threw up."

"Did you hear me? Mr. Johnson is with Charles. Mr. Johnson is found."

"I'll tell her when she comes in."

"Now. Are you feeling better, Uncle John?"

"That's not Mike. Mike Mizzourin? Don't play your tricks."

"No. It isn't Mike."

"I can play tricks, too."

"We needn't talk. Thank you for rescuing these pages. The edges are charred. You must have put your hand in the fire to get them."

"I don't want to be disturbed. No calls. Unless it's . . . No calls, Mike."

"Good. Sleep a little more."

Mizzourin/NO NAME JIVE

I am sitting at my desk in the City Room, waiting for Christine. No one else is here, except the nightwire crew across the way. Whoever's supposed to be on City Desk is late, taking advantage of Board Meeting Night, as we call the evenings JMJ spends with his friend Suesue.

Half an hour ago, in the apartment, the phone rang. Livia answered, as she always does. She frowned and puzzled, and finally said, "I can't understand this, Mike. It's something strange."

Yes, it was strange, a voiceless voice. What it was saying, after I could make it out, was, "Soldier, soldier, don't you see? She's gotta come here now, she's gotta come . . ." In a terrible whisper. "Soldier?"

I remembered about his throat: "Marvin?"

It took a while for me to understand that he was calling from Trenton, New Jersey. Then he put E.B. on.

"Mike?" E.B. sounded scared and puny and hurt. "Mike, they doin' me awful rough."

"Who's they?"

"Well, it's Horse, with Marvin. I was playing at Dee Light's. And I was playin' my nice solo on that 'Mad About the Boy.' And clappin' right ahint my head, and looked ahint and there was Marvin grinnin' at me, and all teeth 'cause his face has got so thin like death. He says, 'Nice playin', Binkie,' but you know . . . owww, all right. Quit. Owww . . . wants me to hurry, Mike. He says, but you know there at Dee Light's he had to come down real close, it's more a whisper, says, 'Bet if we turned you upside down, your brownie button be as-miling, too,' he said. We? I looked up there aside him, there was Horse, and Horse said, 'Come on, Binkie. Come outside.' An' I knew he was fixin' to tear up anythin' he had to if'n I din't, but I said, 'No, I'm stayin' here,' and Marvin give a nod to Horse, and Horse picked up this little guy I know named Plim, picked him right up from his chair by the head, Mike. Monkeygripped him. Owww . . . ''

Then that shadow of a voice came back and said, "You bring Evaun, soldier. Bring her here. She ain't got no car, you gotta do it."

"If she wants me to," I said.

I guess the dry, rustling sound that came was Marvin's laugh.

I hung up. Livia said, "Whatever was it, Mike?" She was shivering.

"Binkie Jones," I said. "He's been snatched by his Uncle Marvin."

"Stay out of it, please Mike. Please stay out of it."

"I can't," I said.

"Let those people settle their own affairs for once."

"I'm going to the office, Livia, to try to get a car. If I can't, I'll phone around. I've got to find a car and drive to Trenton."

"You don't have to, Mike. You don't."

"I'm going to take Evaun to Trenton. I wish I thought she wouldn't go, but Binkie's there."

"Please Mike. If you love me, please stay out of it."

"I'm your husband, Livia. You're pregnant. I'll be back."

"If you go now, don't bother to come back."

It wasn't something I could stay and argue over. I got my jacket on, and she tried physically to hold me back, ran down the stairs after me, crying, and out onto the street in her nightgown in the rain, and stood there crying while I went off to the subway. Thought I could get some-one here to check me out a car, but no one's here. Board Meeting Night.

There's a pay phone in the hall where Evaun and E.B. are staying. I called it just now. Someone answered and went to get Evaun. Someone was gone a long time doing that.

When Evaun came to the phone, she didn't know anything but she said, "Mike. Something's wrong, is it Binkie? Mike, I got a feeling." Until she said that, I'd had a small hope that she might want to stay away, and I'd have gone to Trenton by myself to try to intervene.

"I know where he is," I said. "He needs you. Please wait there."

I called Livia to try to reassure her. She invited me to drop dead.

Then I called Christine. She says she doesn't have their car, but she's coming down here by cab right away. I'd better lock this up. Better put this away. Between the pages of the Great Fake Book.

"Haylo?"

"Mrs. Harper, this is Charles Mizzourin."

"She's lyin' down, dear. I gave her the good news."

"Does she want to speak with me?"

"Well, I don't know now. I'll just find out."

(Long pause)

"Charles."

"Hello, Aunt Christie."

"Oh, Charles, thank heaven. Is John all right?"

"I don't know where he's been. No, he's not all right. He's exhausted. He's had a little rest, but his mind doesn't seem strong."

"He went there to see Suesue, didn't he?"

"I don't know. He came to my apartment while I was away overnight. For some reason, he hid himself in the closet. The door locked itself. He may have been frightened. He must have been locked up in the dark by himself sixteen, seventeen hours, and I doubt he'd eaten much before."

"Has he seen Suesue, Charles?"

"She's out of town. He's in no condition to talk with her anyway and I don't think there's anything for them to talk about."

"But I'm sure he went there to see you, so fond, but of course we both . . . "

"Aunt Christie, he doesn't know me. He thinks I'm my father. He thinks he's in New York."

"Oh. Oh, dear, because we both, you see, when he left here."

"He keeps calling me Mike, and asking for Livia."

"He was so fond of Livia."

"I don't know how to help him."

"His mind is back in the time before the accident, isn't that it? And Richard Nixon was a Congressman, did you know they had the same birthday? Those were John's best days."

"Should I know about the accident now, Aunt Christie?"

"Oh, poor John."

"All right. Do you want to come for him?"

"Oh, yes."

"I think he can travel all right, if someone's with him. Shall I fly out there with him to you."

"No, oh no. I'll come. Charles?"

"You're feeling strong enough?"

"Charles, did he tell you? What happened, why he left here?"

"Yes, he did."

"He saved them, didn't he? The last few pages that Mike wrote?"

"Waiting for you, in the City Room."

"It wasn't really my fault, but John has always blamed me."

"Would it be best if I bring him out there to you?"

"It was a terrible night. A terrible thing, it was raining out."

"I know."

"And all the way to Trenton."

"Don't tell me if you'd rather not."

(MRS. HARPER, DEAR, WOULD YOU MIND GOING IN THE OTHER ROOM?)

"You don't have to do this, Aunt Christie."

" . . . was waiting for me at the paper, staring at his typewriter. He got up. 'Christie, can you get a car?'

"I said, 'John has the car. It will be on the street, by Suesue Landau's house.'

"Mike said: 'Can we get the key from John? I'll go in and ask.'

" 'Oh, no. He'd never give it to you. But I have a key.'

" 'Shouldn't I phone and tell him that we're taking it?'

" 'Oh, no. Let's get the car, and get Evaun and Binkie.' "

"He had his instrument case under his desk. He picked it up, with one of his smiles. 'Hate to be parted from it,' he said, and carried it along.

"We took a cab to near where Suesue lived. The streets were very shiny in the rain. Mike paid the cab, and we found the car. I had my ignition key, but we couldn't get it to unlock the door. John had some kind of extra safety lock. But my key opened the trunk, and Mike got out the lug wrench thing and broke the window open with it.

"Then we got in, and I drove, and we went to pick up Evaun at the rooming house. She was waiting in the rain, in front of that rooming house in the Seventies, and I knew the way, forgive me, Charles. I knew the way for I'd been there before."

"Do you want to stop now, Aunt Christie?"

"Waiting in the rain, with her little bag packed, and she got in front between us, and Mike kept his arm around her all the way to Trenton. She squeezed against him, and I felt a little jealous, and we didn't talk very much. Except that now and then Mike would say she didn't have to go back to Carolina, we could turn around, that he'd take care of her. I would have done the same. It would have been fairer, even Evaun said that: 'You got a baby to take care of, Mike.' Then she'd say, 'I cain't leave Binkie with'm to go back alone. I gotta go, too. You know it, don't you?'

"I drove very fast. I was a good driver in those days. When we got to Trenton, Mike said: 'I don't think coming back here was their plan, Evaun. I think they probably meant to get you in New York, too, but Horse hurt someone at Dee Light's. They had to run.'

" 'Needed a place to beat on Binkie,' Evaun said. 'That's what they come here for.'

"Mike had an address, and he got directions to a dirty little hotel in the slums. But there were five or ten police cars all around the hotel, weren't there?"

"Are you sure you want to go on, Aunt Christie?"

"Oh, yes, because John kept it out of the paper, didn't he? and it wasn't such a big story that other papers, oh, forgive me, Charles. Yes, yes. I do want to tell you, please?"

"Of course."

"For I'm the only one that ever knew, not even John. I never told him. Anyone.

"Mike got out and went up to one of the police cars. I could hear because the window beside me was broken out, but not very well. Mike showed his pass and said he was a reporter from New York.

" 'What do you want with this? It's just a faggot rumble.'

" 'Like what?'

" 'Maybe the kid was trying to run off with their dough, the way they do, and the other ones restrained him kind of hard. Who's the ladies with you?'

" 'They're from the paper, too,' Mike said. 'We were down here on another story when this went over the wire, and the editor called me.'

" 'You want to see inside?'

" 'The boy's dead?'

" 'Never seen deader.'

" 'How about the guys that did it?'

" 'Long gone, and God knows where. They called it in themselves, and then they ran. Maybe they thought the ambulance would be in time.'

"Mike said: 'I don't think it's one for us, Sarge. Thanks a lot.'

"He came back to the car. By then I was standing beside it. I'd got out so I could hear better. Evaun was cold, lying down in back, and had Mike's topcoat wrapped around her, shivering. Mike said, 'Let's go, Christie. I'll ride in back with her.'

"Then he was kneeling down in back, with Evaun stretched out on the seat, and right away she said: 'Binkie's kilt, ain't he?' Mike was holding her, and I started driving back to New York.

"We were on old Route One when it happened. Evaun had been crying off and on back there, but suddenly she stopped and said: 'We always been yore bad luck, Mike.'

" 'No, little love. No, little love.'

" 'Git up in front now. I'm done cryin'. Play me somethin' sweet.'

"They argued about it softly, and finally Mike climbed forward over the back of the seat and got out his horn. It was cold from the rain and the broken window. He said, 'What shall I play?'

" 'Play "My Sweetheart's the Man in the Moon." ' "

"He hesitated a long time. Then he said, 'I don't remember it, little love. I don't remember it.'

" 'Play me that "Georgia" then.'

"So I was driving along, quite fast, and Mike started to play. Softly. It was a song I knew, too, and he was playing it, all absorbed, and suddenly it got much colder. The back door was open, and Mike yelled, 'Stop, Christie, stop. She's gone.' I put on the brakes, and the car swerved and skidded, and Mike already had his door open, and when we hit the pole it pitched him out as the car crashed, and I was left unconscious till the state policeman was lifting me away, with my ribs broken and the front all smashed, and Mike gone. Evaun gone. And the horn. I was a little crazy, asking for the horn, but it was gone, too. And they never found it, Charles."

Last Notes:
They never found it, Dad.

Is it true you couldn't remember "My Sweetheart's the Man in the Moon"? If there's someone around who could hum or whistle the tune, who'd fake it for me now?

Know who's running against Deke now, after all? Your brother Pete. At least he's being nice about it, being Pete. Deke's philosophical. 'Republican year comin'. Jemmy gone get the hostages out, it seems like, but he won't beat the movie actor, and I doubt I can beat Pete, either. People get confused. Half a dozen told me already Pete was let out of Iran.'

Deke doesn't want to go back to Iowa to coach or practice law. After one term he might have. After three his only home is here. He's talking to the national committee. He might do Peace Corps, even. As usual, I need to think, and as you said once, that's the hardest thing there is.

Don't hurt your head.

Mr. Johnson is much more lucid, and ready to leave when Mrs. Johnson gets here to morrow. I've bought him some clothes. God knows what the old guy went through in the three weeks that he can't account for. I talked with Suesue, and she came to see him, after all, and left him a couple of hundred dollars. She says her affairs are in a mess, but she has friends. And winks.

Cherry has gone to Seattle, leaving me a brisk note with instructions to phone and follow.

I'm not sure what to do with the pages I have stored up from your Fake Book. I think Christine would like to have them for her fireplace in Colorado, along with all the others.

Let 'em go, bird.

Okay, Mike. Old Dad. And practice pachydermnemonics, which is the art of never forgetting.

And now I think I'll put an old, old record on, and call my girl.

I know my love/ By her way of walkin'
And I know my love/ By her way of talkin'

"Hulloo?"

"Roxie!"

"It's Angela, mutt. She's sunbathing and hasn't a care. So I shall put her on, and she'll bloody well tick you off, I'm sure, for good and all."

And I know my love/ Dressed in . . .

"Charles. I'm weeping, you beast. Great stupid tears running right between my boobs. Nice, really, but small. I shall smile presently . . . "

"Hello, Roxie. So will I."